The Lost Girl

Rosie Goodwin is the bestselling author of more than forty novels. She is the first author in the world to be allowed to follow three of Catherine Cookson's trilogies with her own sequels. Having worked in the social services sector for many years, then fostered a number of children, she is now a full-time novelist. She is one of the top 50 most borrowed authors from UK libraries and has sold over four million copies across her career. Rosie lives in Nuneaton, the setting for many of her books, with her husband and their beloved dogs.

Rosie GOODWIN

The Lost Girl

ZAFFRE

First published in the UK in 2023 by
ZAFFRE
An imprint of The Zaffre Publishing Group
A Bonnier Books UK company
4th Floor, Victoria House, Bloomsbury Square, London, England, WC1B 4DA
Owned by Bonnier Books
Sveavägen 56, Stockholm, Sweden

A CIP catalogue record for this book is
available from the British Library.

ISBN: 978-1-83877-365-6

Also available as an ebook and an audiobook

1 3 5 7 9 10 8 6 4 2

Typeset by IDSUK (Data Connection) Ltd
Printed and bound in Great Britain by Clays Ltd, Elcograf S.p.A.

Zaffre is an imprint of Bonnier Books UK
www.bonnierbooks.co.uk

In loving memory of
Doreen Ellen Ivy Goodwin, 27th October 1943–13th February 2023.

Sleep tight dear cousin, you are missed!

Chapter One

Nottingham, November 1875

'Is there any sign of your dadda, Gabriel?' the woman lying on the bed muttered feverishly.

The young boy beside her mopped her forehead and shook his head sadly. 'Not yet, Mammy, but he's sure to be back soon.'

She sighed. He had been telling her the same thing for weeks. In the meantime, they had been surviving on the scraps of food Gabriel could buy with the little he earned doing any jobs he could find. But now all hope of her husband ever returning was fast fading, and Constance knew that she was too.

The old vardo she lay in had been the only home either Gabriel or his younger sister Esmeralda had ever known, but since Django, their father, had left some months ago, hoping to trade in their old horse for a slightly younger one, they'd had no way of moving it. Instead they had been forced to remain on a piece of common on the outskirts of Nottingham. When Django had left, the gold hoop in his ear glittering in the sunshine and a gaudy neckerchief tied beneath his chin, he had promised to return as soon as he could, but there had been no sign of him and Constance feared for his safety. There was no way he would have left them otherwise.

Added to her worry about her beloved man, Constance now also feared what was to become of her children when she passed. Her cough had worsened as the winter had progressed until she had been forced to take to her bed. Now she could barely raise her head from the pillow and she sensed that her end was near. At first, she had managed to hide the blood she coughed up from the children, but it had become impossible to do so, and her heart broke at the fear she could see in their eyes.

'D-don't be frightened, my loves,' she said breathlessly. 'We shall be fine.'

Esmeralda blinked back tears. She was nearly fourteen years old, but she was dainty and petite with big blue eyes and hair the colour of spun silver, much like her mother's, and looked younger, while Gabriel, at fifteen, looked like his gypsy father, with hair as black as coal and grey eyes.

'B-but how can we be all right, Mammy?' Esmeralda, affectionately known as Esme, whimpered. 'We've only a few pennies left in the jug an' there's barely any coal for the stove.'

'Don't get worrying about that,' Gabriel said with a confidence he was far from feeling. 'I'm bound to find some odd jobs soon, an' I can go an' collect some logs for the stove from the woods, so we won't freeze. An' I can go an' snare some rabbits, so we won't starve either, I promise you.'

Since his father had left, he had proudly taken on the role of the man of the house but now he felt that he was letting his sister and his mother down dismally.

Even so, Esme brightened instantly. She idolised her big brother and believed every word he said. Unlike her, he was tall for his age so he looked older than his years, but it broke Constance's heart to see him have to shoulder the responsibility for them when he was still just a boy

Gabriel turned and passed the small tin bowl of water to Esme, telling her, 'Come on, lass, you come an' sponge Mammy's head an' I'll go an' get those logs now. Then tonight we can warm up that bit o' stew that's left from yesterday, an' wi' the stove goin' we'll be as snug as a bug in a rug.'

The vardo was a lovely place to live in the summer months when Esme and Gabriel would often sleep outside beneath it, but they all knew that should they ever not be able to feed the stove, they would all freeze to death in the winter.

'But I reckon it's startin' to snow,' Esme told him anxiously as she glanced towards the tiny window.

Gabriel laughed as he shrugged into his warm jersey. 'So what? A bit o' snow never hurt anyone.' He grinned at her then disappeared out of the door as Esme turned her attention back to her mother.

Very soon Constance slipped into an uneasy doze and Esme climbed onto the bed and joined her. When Constance woke some minutes later, Esme was fast asleep and gently snoring. Snuggling into the warm little body, Constance let her mind slip back in time to when she had first met Django, the love of her life.

Her first sight of him had come one evening as she walked home from church with her father, who was the vicar of St Thomas's Church on the east coast. The vardo had been parked close to the rectory where she lived with her father and his housekeeper, and as they passed, Django had smiled and given her a cheeky wink. Her heart was instantly lost to him and she had blushed prettily. Unfortunately, the smile was not missed by her strict father and it earned her a severe beating when they got home. But that was nothing new – she was used to it and it did nothing to erase the thought of the handsome stranger's sunny smile.

During the following weeks, Constance had slipped out to meet Django every chance she got until one evening she had arrived home to find her father waiting for her with his belt in his hand and a murderous expression on his face.

'You *devil's spawn*,' he'd growled. 'Do you deny that you have been to see that . . . that gypsy *scum*?'

For the first time in her life Constance had stared back at him rebelliously. 'Yes, I have as it happens, Father. Though he is far from scum. Django works hard every chance he gets!'

With a roar her father had set about her and by the time the housekeeper came running after hearing her screams, Constance's back was livid with angry bloody wheals.

'Stop it, sir! You'll kill her!'

Breathless, he'd stood back to stare down at his daughter then he'd thrown down the bloodied belt and stormed from the room leaving the old housekeeper to kneel beside the girl.

'I-I'm going . . . this very night, Nellie,' Constance had whispered through swollen lips. 'If I don't, he'll kill me.'

The woman had nodded in understanding, tears sliding down her cheeks.

A few hours later, when her father was in bed and she was able to stand again, Constance had packed her bag and left to begin her new life with Django, and she had never returned. Despite the fact that they had little in the way of material things they had been deliriously happy. Wherever they were Django could turn his hand to any job that needed doing and when the children came along, he had been devoted to his family, and Constance knew that he would never have deserted them voluntarily. Something must have happened to him. But now her most pressing concerns were for her children. What would happen to them when she passed over? Where would they go?

Sometime later, Gabriel returned with a full sack of logs and as he fed them into the stove and the temperature in the little vardo rose, Esme warmed up the stew and divided it into three dishes.

'My loves . . .' Constance gasped as fear gripped her. 'I-if anything should happen to me you must look in my special tin . . . Inside you will find the address of someone who will help you – your grandfather.' The children would never know what it cost her to tell them to go to him, but she was terrified at the thought of what might become of them. She could only pray that the passage of time might have softened the man who had made her life a living hell. Because what other option did she have? It was either send them to him or the workhouse and she couldn't bear the thought of them being incarcerated in that godforsaken place.

'Don't talk like that, Mammy,' Gabriel answered with a catch in his voice. 'You'll be well again soon. You'll see, when we get the winter over with, you'll feel better.'

Constance wished with all her heart that what he was saying could be true but deep down she knew it wouldn't be and looking towards them she gasped, 'I love you . . .'

4

'We love you too,' the children answered in unison as she fell into a deep sleep.

Esme and Gabriel exchanged a worried glance then Esme placed her mother's stew on the top of the stove to keep warm while she and her brother ate theirs.

It was over an hour later when the two children became concerned about how quiet she was. Usually, even when she was asleep, they could hear her laboured breathing but now there was nothing but silence. Suddenly the sound of an owl twit-twooing in the treetops outside reached them and a cold finger traced its way up Esme's spine as she looked fearfully at her brother. Her father had always told them that an owl's cry was the harbinger of death.

'Mammy!' Esme nervously approached her mother and tentatively shook her arm. When there was no response she stared at her brother in panic. 'I-I can't wake her, Gabe!'

He hurried to her side and he too gently called out to her and squeezed her hand. When there was still no response, he stood up and said fearfully, 'Fetch me a mirror, Esme.'

She was back in seconds and she watched in horror as he held the mirror in front of his mother's lips before saying brokenly, 'I-I'm afraid she's gone, Esme.'

'*No, no* she can't have!' Esme shook her head in denial, and yet deep down, as young as she was, she knew that he was telling the truth. The gentle, affectionate mother they had both loved was dead, and in her place was an empty shell.

The next hour passed in a blur as they clung together seeking comfort from each other, but eventually Esme asked, 'What shall we do now, Gabriel?'

Gabriel took a deep breath and noisily blew his nose, then sitting up he took control. 'First of all, we must open the door to set her spirit free.'

Esme silently opened the little door and they shivered as the cold air rushed in until Gabriel nodded at her to close it again.

'Now fetch Mammy's private tin,' he said quietly. 'She told me that our grandfather's address was in there, and he would help us.'

Constance's precious biscuit tin was the only possession she had owned that they had never been allowed access to, but now they had her permission to look inside it. Gabriel gently removed the lid to find a number of letters tied with a red ribbon addressed to their father.

'These must be what Mammy wrote to Dadda before they were married,' Esme whispered reverently. 'Though why she bothered I don't know. Dadda could neither read nor write.'

'I suppose she would have read them to him,' Gabriel answered as he delved beneath them. And there he found another two letters, but this time they were addressed to Reverend Septimus Silver, The Rectory, Crook Bank, Theddlethorpe, Lincolnshire. Gabriel knew that this was a long way away, at least eighty miles, he assumed.

'This must be our grandfather,' Gabriel said. The only thing their mother had ever told them about him was that he was a vicar, but she had always refused to speak of him or of her childhood if questioned. 'I wonder why she never posted them? And I wonder if we have a grandmother?' Gabriel mused. He could never remember one being mentioned.

Esme was still silently sobbing and Gabriel placed his arm about her. It was up to him now to care for his sister and his mind was working overtime. Beneath the letters were a few precious pennies that Constance had always kept as an emergency fund, but they wouldn't get them far.

'Is there enough there to pay for a funeral?' Esme asked in a small voice.

Gabriel shook his head. 'We'll set fire to the vardo with Mammy inside it and do it the way our dadda would have wanted us to,' he said decisively. 'And then we're going to set off to find our grandfather. He won't turn us away in the dead of winter, surely? But tonight, we'll try to get some rest, eh?' He gently pulled the thin blanket across his mammy's beloved face and he and Esme cuddled together for the last night in their home, such as it was.

Early the next morning they stood and gazed about their little dwelling. Gip, the small mongrel who had been their constant companion and who was older than either of them, pressed into Gabriel's side as his young master absently stroked his long silky ears. The children took in the pretty flowered curtains that their mother had stitched to hang at the tiny window, and the horse brasses that were polished to a mirror-like shine. Constance had always taken such pride in them and it hurt them both to know they would never hear her singing gaily as she cleaned them again.

'Come on, lass.' Gabriel's voice was choked as they each placed a final kiss on their mother's face. 'There's no sense in delayin'; it's time we was on our way.'

Esme stepped out into the biting cold as Gabriel sprinkled the last of the paraffin they used to light the lamps about the gaily painted vardo. He then joined his sister outside and struck a match and watched, tears pouring down their cheeks, as their childhood home went up in smoke.

'Goodbye, Mammy,' Esme whispered as the flames licked into the leaden sky. And then she saw it: a white shape floating from the roof and disappearing up into the grey clouds.

From as far back as she could remember Esme had been able to see spirits. Her mother had called it a gift. Her grandmother Griselda had had it too, although she had died when Esme was still quite young.

Then Gabriel took her hand and, squeezing it gently, they turned and, with Gip at their heels, began their long journey to find the grandfather they had never met.

Chapter Two

'Is it far to Grandfather's house?' Esme asked tearfully. They seemed to have been walking forever. It was now mid-afternoon and her legs had started to ache. Gip looked rather tired too and was waddling along at the side of them with his tail between his legs.

'About seventy or eighty miles or so, I reckon.' Gabriel trudged on keeping a tight hold of his little sister's hand. 'I think we head for Newark first then Lincoln an' we won't be that far away by then.'

It sounded a terribly long way away to Esme and, catching sight of her tear-stained face, he said encouragingly, 'It ain't so bad, really. An' we'll probably be able to hitch a lift for some of the way.' He was glad now that he had listened to his mother when she was teaching geography. Although neither of the children had ever attended a school, Constance had made sure that she educated them, so they were both able to read and write – unlike their father. Constance had offered to teach him, but he had never been interested. Gabriel was more like his father in that; he hadn't enjoyed his mother's lessons, unlike Esme, who loved to learn.

Very soon they found themselves in open countryside with Nottingham behind them and, after what seemed like a very long time, Esme told him in a small voice, 'Me belly hurts, Gabriel. Can we stop to get something to eat soon?'

He jangled the few pennies he had in his pocket and gave her an encouraging smile. 'Of course we can. There's a village up ahead, look, and there's bound to be a bakery there where we can buy some bread.'

The words had barely left his lips when the first flakes of snow began to fall and Gabriel cursed silently. That was all they needed on top of everything else. But then they heard the sound of cart wheels behind them, and stepping to the side of the lane, they turned to see a farm cart driving towards them, a ruddy-faced farmer geeing the horse along. As it pulled alongside them the farmer drew the horse to a halt and smiled down at them.

'What's to do then, kids?' he asked genially. 'What's two little 'uns like you doin' out in such bad weather, eh? You ain't run away from 'ome 'ave you?'

Gabriel blinked the snowflakes from his long black lashes and shook his head. 'No, sir, we haven't run away. Our mother has died and we're on our way to our grandfather in Lincolnshire.'

'Hmm, you 'ave a ways to go then, lad.' The farmer frowned. The pair of them looked frozen through and he couldn't help but feel sorry for them. Making a hasty decision, he patted the seat at the side of him. 'So why don't you both hop up here wi' me? I'm sure my missus could find somethin' for you to eat when we get home an' you can sleep in my barn for tonight, if you've a mind to. It'd be better than bein' out in this weather.'

Gabriel glanced at Esme whose teeth were chattering and without hesitation he replied, 'That's very kind of you, sir. We'd be very grateful to accept your offer.'

Well, there was no doubt about it, they were nice, polite children, the farmer thought as Gabriel helped Esme up onto the hard wooden bench seat before joining her. Seconds later they were jogging along and after passing through the small village the farmer turned onto a long drive leading to a large farmhouse.

'This is Yew Tree Farm,' the man informed them as he guided the horse across a big yard to a small stable block. There were chickens pecking amongst the fast-disappearing cobbles as the snow began to settle, and once the horse drew to a halt they climbed down.

'I'll take you into me missus, then I 'ave to get the old 'orse settled,' he told them as he led them inside, the warmth wrapping itself around them like a blanket.

'May! Where are you, woman?' he shouted jovially.

The two children gazed about them in amazement. After living in the confined space of the vardo, the room looked enormous. Brightly coloured peg rugs were scattered across the stone floor and there was a large, black-leaded range against one wall with a pan of something that smelled delicious bubbling away on the top of it. It made their stomachs rumble. On another wall was a big inglenook fireplace above which copper pans hung from a beam, and to either side of it were two wing chairs with comfortable-looking cushions on them. An enormous oak dresser, on which stood the farmer's wife's china, took up most of another wall, and there was a large settle covered in more cushions. Just then, a plump woman with greying hair and clad in a voluminous hucka-back apron appeared through another door.

'I'll give you woman, Bert Miller,' she scolded with a twinkle in her eye. Then she stopped in her tracks at the sorry sight of the two children and their dog, who was leaning protectively into Esme's side. 'And who have we 'ere then?'

'These two 'ave hit 'ard times, lass.' He turned to smile kindly at the children. 'They've just lost their ma an' they're on their way to stay with their granda' in Lincolnshire. But seein' as the weather 'as took a turn for the worse I thought per'aps you wouldn't mind feedin' 'em an' lettin' 'em stop in the barn for the night.'

Taking in their red swollen eyes and their bedraggled state, May's face softened as she ushered them towards a large pine table that took up most of the space in the centre of the room. It had been scrubbed until it was almost white. 'I reckon we could manage that. How does a nice steamin' bowl o' rabbit stew and dumplin's sound, eh? Sit yourselves down an' I'll get it for you. An' you, Bert, go an' see to the old 'orse an' then I'll feed you an' all if you're lucky!'

Despite the harsh words it was evident that the two had a close, loving relationship. They reminded the children of the way their own mother and father had been, and it brought fresh tears stinging into Esme's eyes.

10

'Shush now, pet.' The woman stroked Esme's silver-blonde hair back from her forehead thinking how bonny the child was. 'Let's get somethin' 'ot inside you an' 'appen you'll feel a bit better.'

She bustled away and returned with two steaming bowls of stew. Next she cut some chunks from a fresh loaf of bread and spread them with thick, creamy butter before disappearing again, only to return with a large bone for Gip whose tail started to wag at such an unexpected treat.

As they were eating Esme became aware of a small girl standing in the corner sucking her thumb and she smiled at her.

The farmer's wife frowned as she followed her gaze but all she saw was an empty space. 'Who are you smilin' at, pet?' she asked curiously.

'The little girl standing over there.'

The colour drained out of the woman's face like water from a dam, and her hand rose to her throat as she asked shakily, 'An' what does this little girl look like?'

Esme sniffed as she looked back at the child and realised that she was from the spirit world. Only she could see her. 'Well, she's not very old, about five or six, I reckon, and she's got red hair tied back in a blue ribbon.' She took another mouthful of stew. 'Oh, and she says her name is Elsie.'

'Dear God.' The farmer's wife sat down on the nearest chair with a thud just as her husband reappeared at the kitchen door, stamping the snow from his boots. 'Bert . . .' The woman waved a shaking finger towards the corner. 'This little 'un says there's a little girl called Elsie standin' in that there corner.'

'Oh, May, how many times do I 'ave to tell you? Our Elsie 'as been dead and buried for this past six years,' he said wearily as he removed his cap.

'That's as maybe, but 'aven't I told you I've sensed 'er close to me from time to time? An' now this little girl 'as confirmed that she's still 'ere.'

Farmer Miller chewed on his bottom lip as he wondered how he should answer. He had two strapping grown sons who worked on the farm with him and his only daughter had come unexpectedly when he and his wife had thought her childbearing days were long past. Even so, little Elsie had been the apple of their eye and when they had lost her to a fever at the tender age of six Bert had feared that his wife would go mad with grief. Now hoping to distract her he said gently, 'Get me some dinner, woman. A working man needs to keep up his strength. The lads will be in an' all soon an' no doubt they'll be ravenous too.'

May went to do as she was bid with a sniff and a tear in her eye as the farmer joined the children at the table. Already their dishes were almost empty, which only went to show him how hungry they must have been, the poor little souls.

'So where's your daddy then?' he questioned gently and Gabriel shrugged.

'We've no idea. He left some time ago to go an' trade our old horse in for a younger one, but he didn't come back, an' while he was gone our mammy got really poorly.'

'I see.' The farmer steepled his fingers and frowned. 'And where did you live?'

'Here and there. We travelled in our vardo, but when our mammy died we had to . . .'

'It's all right, lad, I know what the gypsies do when one of theirs pass,' the farmer told him, although he had to admit they didn't talk like gypsy children. They were well mannered and polite. Not that he personally had anything against gypsies. They had a reputation for being thieves but every year he employed them at harvesting time and he had never had a problem. In fact, on the whole, he had found them to be very hard-working people.

'And your grandaddy in Lincolnshire – is he a gypsy too?'

'Oh no, sir. He's a vicar.'

Bert Miller looked confused and scratched his head. 'But I thought you said you lived in a vardo?'

'We did and our dad was a gypsy but our mother wasn't,' Gabriel explained.

'Ah, I see.' Bert smiled up at his wife who had just placed his meal in front of him.

With a twinkle in her eye she asked the children, 'Have either of you got room for some jam roly-poly and custard?'

Their eager eyes were her answer and within minutes she had returned with two dishes, which the children instantly tucked into.

Outside the snow was falling faster than ever and glancing towards the window the woman told them, 'It's too cold for you to sleep out in the barn tonight. I'll put a mattress down in here and you can sleep in front of the fire. But first let's get those wet clothes off you afore you catch your deaths. You can borrow some shirts from one of the lads to sleep in and happen your clothes will be dry come mornin' if I put 'em across the clothes horse.'

She disappeared through a door and was soon back bearing two thick, woollen checked shirts.

'You can pop into the parlour through that door there to get changed.' She pointed towards it and after thanking her the two youngsters scampered through it.

Everything was as neat as a new pin in the parlour and they guessed that this room would probably only be used on high days and holidays. There was no fire in the grate, however, and their teeth chattered with cold as they peeled their wet clothes off and slipped into the warm shirts. They were much too big for them but even so it was nice to feel warm again.

Back in the kitchen they handed their clothes to May just as the back door opened, letting in a blast of icy air and two strapping young men appeared.

'By 'eck, it's enough to freeze the hairs off a brass monkey out there.' The tallest of the two stopped talking abruptly as his gaze settled on the visitors and the farmer quickly explained how he had found them.

'Happen it were lucky as Da did find you,' he said jovially when the farmer had finished. 'T'ain't fit weather for neither man nor beast to be out in tonight.'

His younger brother nodded in agreement as he smiled at the sight of the two youngsters wearing his shirts. Esme's buried her and reached almost to the floor but at least she was warm and dry.

'Enough talkin',' his mother scolded. 'Get your hands washed, get yerselves to the table an' get somethin' warm inside you.'

The two young men, who introduced themselves as Tom and Harry, were only too happy to do as they were told and soon they were tucking into their dinner. Once they were finished, the farmer's wife cleared the table and the three men settled down for a game of cards while she went off to fetch a straw-filled mattress and some blankets, which she put down in front of the fire.

'There you go,' she said amiably as Gip instantly leapt onto it and snuggled down. She had given him a bowl of leftovers and he was comfortably full and drowsy. 'You'll be as snug as bugs in a rug on there.'

The children smiled weakly and joined their dog, sure that they wouldn't sleep a wink in a strange place, but the upset of losing their mother and the hard day had taken its toll and within minutes they had both slipped into an exhausted sleep.

A cockerel crowing woke them early the next morning and they started up to see May Miller, still in her dressing robe and slippers with her hair wound in a long plait, filling the kettle from the pump over the sink.

'Good morning,' she said brightly. 'Did you get a good sleep?'

'Yes . . . yes we did, thank you.' Gabriel knuckled the sleep from his eyes as Esme looked to the side of the fire. The little girl, Elsie, was there again but after seeing how upset Mrs Miller had become when she mentioned her before, she didn't say anything.

'Right, the kettle is on so while it comes to the boil, I'm going up to get dressed. Your clothes are over there, look – and they're dry now so perhaps you two want to do the same while I'm gone. The men will be down shortly.' And with that she bustled away as the children clambered out of bed and made for their clothes.

When Mrs Miller reappeared fully dressed, she began busily frying eggs and bacon. The men appeared next and ushered the children to the table to join them. The meal was delicious and filling and within minutes of finishing it and draining the teapot the men donned their heavy boots and, after wishing the children goodbye, disappeared outside to begin their daily chores.

'Shall I help you with the washing-up, Mrs Miller?' Esme offered quietly.

The kindly woman shook her head. 'Lordy no, child, there's no need for you to do that. You just sit by the fire and let your breakfast go down. Luckily the snow has stopped but it's still bitterly cold out there.' She glanced anxiously out into the sparkling white world. She hated the thought of these two children having to find their way to the coast all on their own, but what could she do about it?

'Right, er . . . I think we should be on our way now,' Gabriel said half an hour later. 'Thank you so much for givin' us shelter an' for all your kindness.'

She waved her hand airily. 'It were nothin', lad. But are you sure you know which way you're headin'? You need to make for Newark next and from there you head towards Lincoln.'

'Aye, I know.' Gabriel lifted their bags but May Miller wasn't quite done with them yet.

'Here, take these,' she said. 'Happen there's enough there to keep you both goin' for a bit.' She proceeded to pile bread, cheese, a bottle of cold tea and some scones into his bag and Esme's eyes filled with tears at the kindness of a stranger.

'Just one more thing afore you go,' Mrs Miller said as she looked hesitantly at Esme. 'Did you *really* see a little girl in here last night?'

Esme nodded solemnly.

'B-but how?'

'I've always been able to see people that have passed,' Esme told her as if it was the most natural thing in the world. 'My Granny Griselda had the gift too so I suppose I got it from her.'

'And . . .' May Miller licked her lips. 'Did my Elsie look happy?'

'Oh yes,' Esme answered without hesitation. 'She's very happy where she is now but she told me she still likes to come back and see you from time to time.'

Tears started to roll down May's plump cheeks, and she swiped them away with the back of her hand, before bending to give Esme a warm hug.

'You just take care o' yourself now, pet, and thank you. What you've told me has given me some comfort.'

She walked with the two children to the door and with Gip plodding along beside them, they set off on their long journey.

Chapter Three

Thanks to getting two lifts on farm carts, they passed through Newark shortly after dark late that afternoon, but by then Esme was freezing and tired and her hands and feet were blue with cold – the only saving grace being that she had lost all feeling in them hours ago.

Gabriel glanced at her with concern as she trudged along with her head down clutching his hand. Earlier in the afternoon, after finding a barn to shelter in while they ate some of the food Mrs Miller had given them, they had unpacked their bags and put on the rest of the few clothes they possessed – not that the extra layers had done much good. Now Gabriel was aware that he must find somewhere for them to shelter for the night. Thankfully the snow had held off but the grass was already stiff with hoar frost and he knew that they wouldn't survive in the bitter conditions outside.

'Come on, lass,' he urged encouragingly. 'We'll find us somewhere to sleep soon.'

Even old Gip was exhausted and Gabriel began to feel desperate. The lights of Newark were behind them now and they were passing the odd lane leading to farms and little cottages scattered here and there. Then, just as he was beginning to fear they would never find anywhere suitable, he saw what looked like a large barn to one side of the road ahead and beyond it the lights of a farmhouse. He could hear cattle inside but that didn't trouble him, the beasts would be warm to cosy up to if he could just get in there.

'Come on, pet, we can rest there, look.'

Esme raised her head and nodded gratefully. After their life in the vardo on the open road, they were used to the great outdoors but today had been a trial for her and she was sure she could have slept on a clothesline. Even Gip seemed to perk up as Gabriel opened the large five-barred gate just wide enough for them to slip through. Up ahead a black and white sheepdog appeared from its kennel and growled, but after a soothing word from Gabriel it slunk back inside again.

Gabriel tackled the barn door next and within seconds they were in the comparative warmth of what turned out to be a cowshed rather than a barn. The cows were housed in stalls all along one side and it was pitch dark but as Gabriel pointed out, at least it was dry and nowhere near as cold as outside. Leaving Esme and Gip standing together, he moved along the stalls pulling a small amount of hay from each one and eventually he had made a pile they could all snuggle down into.

Esme dropped onto it, and as the feeling gradually came back into her hands and feet she winced with pain. Gip, meanwhile, fell asleep instantly. He was very old now and Gabriel was painfully aware that this was a mammoth journey for the old boy. After a while they ate a little more of the bread and cheese that Mrs Miller had kindly provided, making sure to keep enough back for breakfast, but the bottle of tea was long finished and they were both thirsty.

'I'm going to see if I can't coax a couple of the cows to give us some fresh milk.'

He went off again, leaving Esme to rub her sore feet. Soon after he returned with the bottle half full, and they took it in turns to drink the warm frothy milk, which was delicious and Esme was sure nothing had ever tasted so good. She didn't remember much after that as she was asleep in seconds.

The next thing she knew, Gabriel was waking her at dawn and offering her two eggs he had taken from the hen coop.

'You'll have to crack the shells and eat them raw,' he apologised.

Esme frowned. 'That's milk and eggs we've had here. Isn't that stealing?' Her mother had always drummed into them that they should never take anything they couldn't pay for.

'I suppose it is,' Gabriel admitted as he cracked the shell of his own egg and began to suck on it. 'But we haven't taken much;

I doubt the farmer will even miss it. So eat up, we need to get on our way before we're caught in here.'

They quickly divided what food they had left from Mrs Miller between themselves and Gip, and soon after they set off again. It was still gloomy and bitterly cold but thankfully they hadn't gone far when a farm cart approached and they were offered another lift.

'So where you 'eading, young 'uns?' The ruddy-faced farmer enquired.

'Lincoln, sir.' Gabriel pulled his cap off respectfully.

'Then yer in luck. I'm headin' about ten miles that way so 'op aboard. I'm goin' to collect some geese but you'll 'ave to manage best you can in the back.'

Esme scrambled into the back while Gabriel lifted Gip to join her and they instantly snuggled down beneath the sacks to ward off the cold.

It was mid-morning when the farmer dropped them off in Bassingham and they made for the baker's shop in the high street where Gabriel purchased two loaves that had been baked the day before. They were slightly cheaper than the fresh ones but still delicious. They found an empty shop doorway and sat down to eat, breaking off some wedges which they shared with Gip before setting off again.

They walked for days and at night they slept in derelict cottages and barns, desperately huddling together to try to keep warm. On the journey they would talk about what their grandfather might be like and wonder what life held in store for them until eventually one evening they found themselves on the outskirts of Louth, thanks to a friendly farmer who had given them a lift for part of the way.

'I reckon we've only got about another twelve to fourteen miles to go now,' Gabriel told her as they began to search for somewhere to rest. 'We might even get there tomorrow if we're lucky enough to get another lift.'

Soon after they found shelter in yet another barn where chickens roamed and squawked indignantly at being disturbed. Once again they dined on raw eggs and the rest of the bread they had bought in Bassingham, and when they set off as dawn broke the next day there was more of a spring in their step because they knew they were on the final leg of their journey. In the distance they could see the spire of St James's Church in Louth, which was said to have the third tallest spire in the United Kingdom, and as they were admiring it a farmer drew up beside them on a cart loaded with winter vegetables that he was taking to market in Mablethorpe.

'Want a lift?' he offered, wondering what two youngsters were doing out and about in the middle of nowhere at that time in the morning. His own children were back at home still tucked up in their warm beds. 'I's headin' for Mablethorpe.'

'Is that anywhere near Theddlethorpe?' Esme asked sweetly.

The farmer stared at her mop of silver-blonde curls and deep-blue eyes and thought he had never seen such a pretty child. 'It certainly is, me sweet.' He smiled broadly at her. 'In fact, I'm passin' through it. Hop on if you want droppin' there.'

Gabriel hastily lifted Gip into the back and he and Esme clambered onto the hard wooden bench seat beside the farmer, hardly able to believe their luck. He was going to take them right there, which meant that hopefully there would be no more nights spent sleeping in draughty barns and derelict cottages.

Esme slept fitfully as they trundled along, leaning against Gabriel while her brother kept his arm protectively about her.

'So what takes you to Theddlethorpe?' the farmer asked after a time.

'We're going to find our grandfather. Our mother just died,' Gabriel told him in a shaky voice.

'Eeh, I'm sorry to hear that, lad.' The farmer shook his head. 'An' who is your grandad? Is he a farmer? I know most folk from here to Wragby.'

'No, actually he's the vicar of St Thomas's Church.'

'You mean the Reverend Septimus Silver?' The farmer kept his eyes straight ahead. He'd heard that Septimus Silver was a hard man, more feared than revered by his parishioners.

'Yes, that's him.' He had Gabriel's full attention now. 'Do you know him?'

'Can't say as I do personally, lad,' the farmer replied cautiously. 'It's more the farmin' community I know. Had a lot to do with him, have you?'

'We haven't ever actually met him,' Gabriel admitted. 'But Mammy told us to go to him if anything happened to her so we're hoping he'll take us in. If not . . .'

When his voice trailed off the farmer's big heart went out to him. Poor kids, but what could he do to help? he asked himself. His wife would go mad if he turned up with another couple of mouths to feed. Times were hard enough trying to keep their own brood fed. 'Well, let's hope things take a turn for the better for you both, eh?' The farmer tried to inject some cheer into his voice but feared he had failed dismally.

The snow was coming down quicker than ever now and beginning to settle and he urged the horse to a faster pace, keen to get his business done and get home while he still could. The lanes leading from Wragby to Mablethorpe were bordered by deep ditches which could be treacherous, especially when it snowed.

The rest of the journey was made in silence until finally late that morning they arrived in Theddlethorpe.

'Here we are then,' the man told them as he drew the horse to a halt. 'You'll find the rectory down that lane there. It's only a hop, skip and a jump from the beach so happen you'll enjoy living there. Good luck to you, kids.'

'Thank you, sir.' Gabriel skipped down from the bench, helping Esme after him before lifting Gip from the back. 'You saved us a very long walk.'

'My pleasure, lad. Ta-ra.' And with that the farmer set off again and was soon swallowed up by the fast-falling snow.

'So, here we are at last,' Gabriel said, as Esme clung nervously to his hand. 'Best go and meet our grandfather, eh?'

She nodded, scrubbing the snow from her eyes as they set off down Crook Bank past the pretty church of St Thomas's. Just beyond it they came to a picket fence surrounding a large house with a sign on the gate which read, 'The Rectory'.

They stood surveying it for a moment until Gabriel took a deep breath and pushed the gate open before tentatively walking towards the front door, each of them wondering what sort of a reception they were going to get and where they might go from here if their grandfather turned them away.

Chapter Four

A winding path led to a huge oak door, either side of which were large windows covered with white lace curtains. Their stomachs were churning but it was too late to turn back now, even if they had had anywhere else to go, so after taking a deep breath Gabriel pulled the rope to the side of the door and listened anxiously for any sound of movement on the other side. Soon they heard footsteps approaching and the door inched open to reveal a tiny woman who was not much taller than Esme Her steel-grey hair was confined in a bun at the nape of her neck and her plain grey gown was covered by a voluminous apron that was white as the snow outside.

'Good morning . . .' Gabriel said, faltering, remembering his manners. 'May we see the reverend, please?'

'I'm afraid he's out at present. Is it somethin' important you wanted to see him about?'

Gabriel gulped. 'I, er . . . yes it is actually. Our mammy sent us, see? She passed away and the reverend was her father.'

The woman's hand flew to her mouth and shock registered on her face. 'You mean, you are Miss Constance's children?' she gasped. She looked from one to the other and knew they were telling the truth when she saw Esme, who was leaning against her brother. She was the double of her mother.

Gabriel nodded. 'Yes, we are.'

Pulling herself together with what was obviously a great effort the woman surveyed them solemnly for a moment as though wondering what she should do, but then holding the door wider she urged, 'You'd better come in. The reverend should be home for his lunch soon.'

They entered a large hallway from which a staircase curved up to a galleried landing and they were shocked to find that it was almost as cold in there as it was outside. There were no pictures or mirrors adorning the plain walls and no carpets on the highly polished tiled floor, although everywhere smelled of beeswax polish and appeared to be spotlessly clean, if somewhat austere.

'Come through to the kitchen, it's warmer in there. You look frozen through and I dare say a warm drink wouldn't go amiss? Oh, and by the way, I'm Mrs Sparrow, your grandfather's house-keeper.'

'That would be very nice, thank you.' Gabriel tried not to notice the way she was eyeing Gip who was leaving snowy paw prints across the floor as they followed her down a long hallway with a number of closed doors leading off it. Soon they found themselves in an enormous kitchen where a large fire was blazing in the fireplace, and as the warmth met them their wet clothes started to steam.

'Sit yourselves down,' she told them, motioning to a wooden settle to one side of the fire. They both meekly did as they were told as she bustled away to place the kettle on a large range. There were delicious smells issuing from the oven and both their stomachs began to rumble. But it was hardly surprising, they had existed on bread and water for days and felt weak with hunger. Gip sank down onto his belly in front of the fire and was asleep instantly. Again the woman eyed him cautiously as she carried two steaming mugs of hot sweet tea back to them. They took them gratefully and began to drink it, even though it was so hot that it burned their tongues.

'So, you say your mother has passed away?'

When Gabriel nodded solemnly, he thought he detected a tear in her eye and asked, 'Did you know our mother?'

'Aye . . . I did,' she answered quietly.

'And do we have a grandmother?'

She shook her head. 'No, lad. Your mother was just a babe when she and the reverend came here and took over this parish. Your grandmother had passed away. I had been recently widowed and both my lads had grown and flown the nest so I took on the role of housekeeper here an' I've been here ever since. I watched your mother grow up . . . She was a grand girl.'

A tear spilled down Esme's cheek as the pain of loss struck her afresh. They had been so busy trying to get here that she hadn't had time to properly grieve as yet.

'And your daddy? What happened to him?'

'We don't know,' Gabriel admitted. 'He left us in the vardo some months ago to go and get a younger horse but he never came back.'

'You mean he left you?'

'*No!*' Gabriel said heatedly. 'He would *never* have done that. He and our mammy were very happy together and he would never have left us . . . We think something must have happened to him.'

'I see.' She glanced anxiously at the tin clock that was ticking away on the mantelpiece. The reverend would be back any time now and she shuddered to think what he would make of the arrivals.

'D-do you think our grandfather will let us stay?' Gabriel asked anxiously, but she had no time to answer for at that moment they heard the front door open and they all looked towards it.

Seconds later the door into the kitchen opened and a large man stood framed there. He was nothing like they had tried to imagine and certainly looked nothing at all like their mother. Well over six foot tall, he was stockily built with piercing blue-grey eyes, wiry grey hair that stood about his head like a halo and a long grey beard above thick lips. He was dressed in a black frock coat, black waistcoat and trousers and a starched white dog collar. A thick gold Albert chain, which led to a solid gold Hunter watch in the pocket of his waistcoat, hung across his chest.

He glared at the children, his lips tight, before saying to the woman, 'And who are these waifs? I hope you haven't taken it upon yourself to fetch them in and feed them, woman?'

'No. I haven't,' she mumbled nervously. 'These are . . .' She gulped. 'These are your grandchildren. Miss Constance sent them to you . . . she . . . she's passed away, God rest her soul.'

Colour flooded into his face as his lips clenched even tighter and his hands formed into fists. 'And why would she send them to *me*?' he growled.

'Cos they had nowhere else to go,' the woman said coaxingly. 'And surely, you'll not see them out in the cold, sir?'

'Why not?' he snapped. 'Constance chose her path when she ran away with *that* . . . that no good *scum*. She was no better than a *whore*! Why should I now have to take on the burden of her flyblows?'

'But just think what it would look like to your parishioners if you didn't?' The woman spread her hands. 'You, a man of the cloth. Someone they all look up to. Imagine what they would say if they knew you had turned away your own flesh and blood, and in this weather too!'

The reverend stood for some moments saying nothing as he eyed the two children before asking, 'And what are your names?'

Esme was so terrified that she couldn't even speak and had shrunk into her brother's side as he answered, 'I'm Gabriel and this is Esmeralda, my sister, sir.'

'Pah! I might have known she would give you *gypsy* names,' he spat in disgust. His eyes settled on Gip and his colour rose even more, if that was possible. 'And what is that . . . that rabid *cur* doing in my kitchen?'

'He's our dog,' Gabriel said defensively. 'We couldn't leave him behind. He's old now and no trouble, I promise you.'

Joining his hands behind his back the reverend began to march up and down the kitchen as his mind whirled. The last thing he wanted was to take responsibility for these brats but then what Mrs Sparrow had said was weighing heavily on his mind. It was true that should word leak out of their arrival, which it inevitably would in such a small community, it would not bode well for him if the parishioners learned he had turned them out onto the street.

'Very well, you can stay . . . at least until after Christmas while I try to decide what to do with you. But *that* . . . *that* thing goes!' He jabbed a wavering finger at Gip.

Gabriel jumped out of his seat and faced him bravely. 'I'm sorry, sir,' he said with his head held high. 'But where we go, he goes. Gip is older than either of us and if we abandon him now, he would die, especially in this weather.'

'He's right,' Mrs Sparrow butted in, hoping to calm the situation. 'The old chap won't be much trouble and he'll cost nothing to keep. He can eat any leftovers and I'll keep him here in the kitchen wi' me so he won't trouble you.'

Their grandfather was so red in the face now that Gabriel feared he was going to burst a blood vessel. 'Very well,' he growled eventually. 'He can stay, but he can sleep in the stables,' he compromised, confident that he would soon think of a way to get rid of the smelly old mutt. 'That is my offer, take it or leave it!'

Gabriel wasn't at all happy with that idea but one glance at Esme confirmed that he had to accept it for her sake. She looked worn out.

'Thank you.' He sat back down as the man turned his attention back to the housekeeper.

'I will have my lunch now in the dining room, these two' – he waved his hand towards the children – 'can eat in here with you, and make sure that you don't spoil them. I'm not made of money.'

'As you wish, sir.' Mrs Sparrow nodded as Septimus Silver slammed out of the room and that was when Esme started to sob, great gulping sobs that shook her small frame.

'I . . . I don't think I want to stay here, Gabriel,' she whimpered. 'He frightens me and he clearly doesn't want us.'

'Shush now.' It was Mrs Sparrow who comforted her and the children both felt that in her they had at least found one ally. 'He'll come round to the idea. And where would you go if you didn't stay?' She gestured towards the window, outside which the snow was still fast falling. 'It ain't fit for anyone to be out in this. So come to the table now. I'll serve him, then we can have what's left with some nice crusty fresh-baked bread between us, eh? I've got a tray of scones in the range oven an' all, how does that sound?'

Seeing the sense in what she said Esme dried her tears on the sleeve of her old coat and they went to sit at the table while Mrs Sparrow fetched a large steak and kidney pie from the oven. The sight of it made their mouths water and they watched as she served the main of it onto their grandfather's plate. To go with it was a pan of potatoes and another of peas, along with a big jug of thick gravy. Once she had carried their grandfather's food through to him, she divided what was left equally between the three of them.

Seeing Gabriel glance worriedly at Gip, Mrs Sparrow told him, 'Don't get fretting about the old boy. I have some sausages left over from yesterday that I was going to put in the pig bin. I bet they'll go down a treat, so eat up.'

The children needed no second bidding and had cleared their plates in no time. The meal was followed by Mrs Sparrow's delicious scones and for the first time in a long while the children felt full, although still desperately tired after their journey.

'Have you any clothes you can change into?' the woman asked as she cleared the dirty pots from the table.

They shook their heads. 'We only brought what we could carry and then when it was so cold, we piled everything on,' Gabriel explained. All that was left in their bags now was a change of underwear.

'Hmm, in that case I'd best have a word to your grandfather about getting you some new ones.' She wiped her hands on her apron and bustled away to find the reverend who always retired to his study after a meal to enjoy a cigar and a glass of port in front of the fire.

'Come in,' he ordered when she tapped on the door.

She entered the room to find him sitting behind a large polished rosewood desk in his comfy leather chair. The reverend liked his home comforts.

'I've come to talk to you about getting some new clothes for the children,' she told him without preamble. Mrs Sparrow had long since stopped being afraid of him, unlike most of his parishioners.

'The poor souls only have what they are standing up in and they're almost in rags.'

He snorted with disgust. 'I'm not surprised, with Constance as their mother. But what do you want me to do about it? Isn't it enough that I shall have to feed and house the brats for the foreseeable future? If they need more clothes, I suggest you look in the poor box. There should be something in there to fit them.'

'As you wish.' She bristled as she stared disapprovingly at his own smart outfit, then turned and left, knowing that while he was in this mood, she would get no joy from him. It wasn't altogether a bad idea, however, because she knew that some of the local ladies had been collecting clothes for the poor from the bigger houses in the area.

Once back in the kitchen she went to a cupboard and with Gabriel's help dragged out a large box that was piled high with second-hand clothes, shoes and boots.

'Your grandfather pointed out that there might be something in here to fit you, just until we can get you some new things,' she said in a falsely jolly voice as she began to sort through them. 'And if there isn't, there's bound to be some things I can alter for you.'

In no time she had a small pile of clothes put to one side and then she began to look through the footwear.

'What size shoe do you take?' she asked Esme and when the child stared back at her blankly she encouraged, 'Why don't you take one of yours off for me and I can measure it?'

Esme bent to do as she was told but winced as she withdrew the boots. They had stuck to the blisters at the back of her heels, which instantly began to bleed.

Mrs Sparrow frowned as she saw the state of them. 'Goodness me, Esmeralda, you must have been in agony,' she declared as she went off to fetch a bowl of warm water. 'Now soak your feet in there, there's some salt in it,' she ordered when she came back and Esme tentatively did as she was told, catching her breath as the salt stung the open blisters.

Mrs Sparrow, meanwhile, bustled away with one of Esme's old boots and after measuring it she continued to rifle through the box until she came across a pair that she thought might fit. They were still in remarkably good condition and had clearly been expensive.

'You can try these on when I've bandaged your feet,' she told the little girl. 'And I've found a couple of gowns here that might fit you wi' a little bit of altering.' She had also come across a voluminous lace linen nightgown that would cut down to make two for the child, and at least three shirts and two pairs of trousers that she hoped could be made to fit Gabriel. Further rummaging disclosed a pretty red coat that she thought would look wonderful with the child's silver-blonde hair and another pair of boots that would suit Gabriel.

Half an hour later, with Esme's blisters dressed and bandaged, she thrust some of the clothes at the children, telling them, 'I'm going to find out where you are to sleep, and when I have you can change into some of these. Happen they'll need altering but at least they'll be warm and dry.' Off she went again to see the reverend.

'So where are the children to sleep?' she enquired after she had knocked on the study door again, causing the reverend to let out another sigh. He usually took a nap in the large wing chair to the side of the fire after lunch and was getting increasingly annoyed at being disturbed.

'Bah!' he growled. 'Put the girl in her mother's old room and the boy in the smallest bedroom. Oh, and make sure that they both bathe – cleanliness is next to godliness, and goodness knows what diseases the little heathens have!' He fished in a drawer in his desk and handed a key to her. It was the key to the children's mother's room. The room that had never been opened since the day she left it.

'As you wish.' She turned abruptly and mounted the stairs to unlock the door to Constance's old room, then sighed with dismay when she saw the state of it. Every stick of furniture was buried beneath layers of thick dust, and the moths had feasted on the bedding and curtains. It was bitterly cold, too, but she knew it would be useless to ask him if she could light a fire in there. Still, she supposed it was better than having to sleep outdoors, so off she went to fetch her mop and bucket and some polish.

Two hours later the room was unrecognisable. There were fresh sheets and blankets on the bed, the curtains had been changed and there was not a speck of dust in sight. She rubbed her hands together to try and get them warm then went off to start all over again in the bedroom that was to be Gabriel's. It was late afternoon by the time she had finished and she found the children huddled together and fast asleep on the settle when she entered the kitchen. There was a small joint of beef cooking in the oven and some roast potatoes for the reverend's dinner that evening and she hoped there would be enough left when she had served him to make some beef sandwiches for the children. Poor little things! They both looked as if a good gust of wind would blow them away and she was looking forward to feeding them up.

It was dark by that time so she hastily lit the oil lamp in the middle of the kitchen table before dragging in the tin bath that hung on the wall outside. Soon she had it full of warm water from the copper and gently shaking Esme awake she encouraged, 'Come and have a nice bath before dinner, pet. You probably haven't even had chance to wash since leaving home and you'll feel so much better when you're clean again. We can wash your hair too.'

Esme stared at the water in horror. In the summer she and Gabriel had always bathed in rivers and in the winter, they had made do with a wash in the old tin bowl.

Seeing her reluctance, Mrs Sparrow chuckled. 'Come on now, it won't be as bad as you think, I promise.'

And so, while Gabriel turned his back, she stripped off her clothes and climbed into the tub, and for the first time in her life found herself submerged up to the neck in warm water. She soaped herself all over with the rag and carbolic soap that Mrs Sparrow had provided her with, while the kindly woman washed her hair and rinsed it until it was squeaky clean. Her cheeks were pink and flushed when she climbed out and Mrs Sparrow wrapped her in a big towel and told her to go and sit by the fire again. It was Gabriel's turn next and while he was as reluctant as his sister had been, he bathed all the same and found that it was actually quite pleasant.

Perhaps it won't be as bad here as I thought, he mused to himself. It was just as well that he couldn't see into the future.

Chapter Five

'Right, I'll show you to your rooms,' Mrs Sparrow said later that night. Their grandfather had gone out earlier in the evening, which Mrs Sparrow had told them was a regular occurrence. 'He'll be off to one of his prayer meetings, or visiting one of his parishioners who is ill,' she'd informed them. She'd also told them that he wished to see them early the next morning in his study, although as yet they had no idea what he wanted them for.

Lighting a candle to show them the way, she led them upstairs and on the second floor they noticed a staircase that led up to a third floor. It really was an enormous house. She continued on along the second-floor landing, stopping first at their mother's old bedroom door. 'This is where you'll sleep, pet,' she told Esme as she took a key from her pocket to unlock it. 'No one's ventured in here since she left till I came up earlier to put fresh bedding on, but I've given it a good clean. I've no doubt the drawers will still be full of things your mother left behind when she ran away, but if that bothers you, I can empty them.

Esme shook her head. 'Oh no, it will be nice to have her things about me.' Becoming fretful she asked, 'But can't Gabriel sleep in here with me? We've always slept together with Gip.'

Mrs Sparrow hesitated before shaking her head. She had already risked the reverend's wrath by allowing Gip to stay asleep in front of the fire. She just prayed the dog wouldn't bark if he heard Septimus come in. 'I'm afraid not, pet. I don't think your grandfather would like it and he's not a man to cross. But don't worry, he'll only be two doors away along the corridor and you'll see him again in the morning. Oh, and by the way, please don't get going up to the third floor. That is your grandfather's private domain and he won't allow anyone except himself and me up there.'

Then trying her best to ignore the tears on the child's cheeks, she closed the door, and after showing Gabriel to his room she went to retire herself. It had been a very long day.

Once alone, Esme stood in the dark with tears streaming down her cheeks, missing her mammy and dadda and wishing she could turn the clock back to happier times. But she didn't stand there for long; it was so cold that soon her teeth were chattering and she hopped into the bed and pulled the cold sheets and blankets up to her chin to stifle her sobs.

Minutes later she heard the door creak open and her heart leapt into her mouth as someone lifted the blankets from her, but then Gabriel's voice came to her from the darkness as he put a protective arm about her. 'It's all right, it's only me. Stop crying now, things will seem much better in the morning.' Deep down he wasn't at all sure that they would. After all, they had hardly received a rapturous welcome from their grandfather, although Mrs Sparrow was kind. Still, he supposed they should be grateful that he had let them stay. At least their bellies were full and they had a fairly comfortable bed. Esme snuggled into him and soon her gentle snores echoed around the room, and finally he slept too.

Gabriel had no idea how long they had been lying there when someone suddenly yanked the bedclothes off them and a strong hand grasped his arm and dragged him out of the bed to land with a thud on the floor.

'What . . . what . . .'

'How *dare* you behave like this under my roof?' his grandfather's voice boomed as Esme started awake and began to cry.

'L-like what?' Gabriel didn't know what he had done wrong.

'How *dare* you practise incest under my very nose!' The reverend's voice was trembling with rage as he shook Gabriel until his teeth rattled.

Unsure what incest was, Gabriel stammered, 'But, sir . . . Esme is my little sister; I was just giving her comfort and—'

A blow to the side of the head sent him sprawling and now Esme's sobs turned to screams.

His ear throbbing, Gabriel crawled away.

'You are wicked . . . *evil* and you must be taught a lesson,' Septimus growled as he undid his belt and advanced on him threateningly. Suddenly pain shot up Gabriel's leg as the belt landed on his lower leg. He howled with pain and shock just as Mrs Sparrow appeared in the doorway.

'Good Lord, *whatever* is goin' on in here?' she shouted, holding the oil lamp high so that it shone on the child cowering on the floor. 'Sept— sir . . . *whatever* are you doing?' She almost stumbled over her long dressing robe as she raced to Gabriel and dropped to her knees beside him. Her grey hair hung in a long plait across one shoulder and on her head was a night cap.

'He . . . he *dared* to share a bed with his sister in *my* house!' Septimus's voice was quivering with rage. 'They are *bad – evil –* just as their mother was, and they must have the badness knocked out of them.'

'That's quite *enough!*' Mrs Sparrow glared at him. 'Leave the room at once. I will deal with this now and we'll talk in the morning.'

For a moment the children thought that their grandfather was going to ignore her, but then with a grunt of disgust he turned on his heel and stamped from the room.

'Shush now, lad,' Mrs Sparrow soothed. 'It ain't as bad as it feels. The skin isn't broken, so happen you'll just have a bruise there come morning. I'll go and fetch a cold cloth to stop the swelling.' She hurried away, leaving the oil lamp in the middle of the floor.

'I . . . I don't like it here, Gabriel,' Esme whimpered.

He managed a brave smile although his leg felt as if it was on fire. His ear was still ringing too. 'It's all right, I'm just glad Mrs Sparrow turned up when she did. I can't believe how she stood up to him. She's only knee-high to a grasshopper – he could down her with one swipe.'

Mrs Sparrow reappeared with a bowl of cool water and a clean rag, which she placed on his leg, talking softly to him the whole time. 'He don't mean to be so brutal,' she said as if she were making excuses for him. 'I suppose it's just the shock of you both turnin' up that's shaken him. But he'll settle down never you fear.'

'He'd better,' Gabriel winced. 'If he'd hit Esme like that, he could have killed her. She's only little. If this is the way he treated our mother I can understand why she ran away.'

'Aye, well, that were a long time ago now. Let's just live for the here and now, eh? There's no sense in dwellin' on the past. What's done is done.'

Gabriel clamped his mouth shut. There was a lot more he would like to have said but he didn't dare, and so he sat quietly as Mrs Sparrow tended to his leg. When she was content that she had done all she could, she nodded towards the door.

'You'd best get off to your own room now, lad. We don't want a repeat performance of what just happened, do we?'

'B-but I don't want to be alone,' Esme said in a choky voice.

'You'll not be.' Mrs Sparrow smiled at her tiredly. 'I'll sleep in the chair in here with you tonight. But it'll be just for tonight mind!'

Gabriel rose and gave Esme a faltering smile before limping to the door, and once he was gone Mrs Sparrow went to the bed and tucked the blankets up to the little girl's chin. 'You're quite safe,' she promised as she plonked wearily down into the chair. 'Now turn over and try to get some rest.'

Too afraid to disobey, Esme did as she was told but it was a long time before she could sleep and when she finally did the tears dried on her cheeks.

The next morning the subdued children arrived down in the kitchen clad in the clothes that Mrs Sparrow had sorted for them the day before. They were a little large but ten times better than the ones they had arrived in and she smiled as she ushered them to the table.

'Now then, I've made you some porridge,' she said chirpily, trying her hardest to ignore the bruise blossoming on Gabriel's cheek where his grandfather had struck him. 'After breakfast your grandfather wants to see you both in his study.'

Esme's eyes instantly grew round with fear but Mrs Sparrow quickly assured her, 'Don't worry, I've no doubt he just wants to run through the house rules with you.' But despite her cheerful smile she was quaking inside. If he was half as strict with these two as he had been with their mother, she feared that history would repeat itself.

It was at that moment that Esme saw the shadow of a young, fair-haired woman in the corner. Looking away, she saw yet another woman, this one even younger and with dark hair, standing close to her. She quickly turned her attention to the porridge and tried to ignore them. She had enough worries of her own at the moment, without visits from her spirit friends. Normally she would have spoken to them but today she was too nervous to think of anything but what her grandfather was going to say to them.

The meal was a quiet affair, despite Mrs Sparrow's best efforts to draw them out of themselves, and she was surprised to see that they merely picked at the meal. *I shouldn't have told them that their grandfather wished to see them until after they'd eaten*, she thought. But the damage was done now and they were clearly both afraid of him already, so once they'd finished, she brandished a hairbrush and told Esme, 'Come here, pet, and I'll tidy your hair up for you.'

Esme did as she was told and as Mrs Sparrow ran the bristles through the silver-blonde locks she had to swallow her tears. Esme's hair was so like her mother's – the same colour and texture – that she could almost imagine Constance was here with her again. But she couldn't think about that now so hastily tying the springy curls into a blue ribbon at the nape of the child's neck, she told them, 'Off you go then – the study is the second on the right in the hallway. Your grandfather will be expecting you and we don't want to rile him by being late, do we now?'

The two children obediently turned and made their way into the hallway, their hands tight gripped and their faces as pale as lint.

Once they arrived at the study door Gabriel tapped at it and their grandfather's voice boomed, 'Come in!'

Esme shuddered as they entered. Septimus was sitting at a large desk and looked every bit as forbidding as he had the night before as he eyed them both up and down. Esme immediately noticed the two young women she had seen in the kitchen the night before, with a third one now standing behind him.

'Hmm, well at least you look a little more respectable than you did last night.' He propped his elbows on the desk and leaned forward, glaring at them. 'I have asked you here to lay down some house rules,' he went on without preamble. 'First of all, I hope you don't expect to live here and be waited on! While you are under my roof you will work to earn your keep. You' – he pointed at Gabriel – 'will bring in the coal, chop the wood, run errands and do any other job that Mrs Sparrow asks of you.' He turned his attention to Esme, who was positively quaking in her second-hand boots. 'And you will help with the household chores: changing beds, washing up, cleaning floors, etc. Each night after dinner you will both do an hour's Bible study. I will set you each a passage from the Bible to learn by heart and should you not it will result in the cane. Three evenings a week you will attend church with me, as well as the morning and evening services on Sunday. You will speak when you are spoken to and mind your manners at all times. You will both be in bed – your *own* beds – by eight o'clock in the evening, and you will both rise early to light the fires and help Mrs Sparrow. And never – *never* – venture up to the third floor. It is strictly out of bounds. Is that *quite* clear?'

'Yes, sir, perfectly,' Gabriel replied.

Their grandfather steepled his fingers and stared at them for a moment before going on, 'I have decided that should I allow you to stay, you' – he pointed at Esme – 'will attend the local village school after Christmas. And you . . .' He paused to give an evil grin as he looked at Gabriel. '*You* will attend a boarding school in Skegness.'

Gabriel gulped. Neither he nor Esme had ever attended a school before. All the learning they had had come from their mother and the thought of being sent away to live amongst strangers was terrifying. Worse still, he had never shown much of an interest in education, unlike Esme who was as bright as a button and soaked up knowledge like a sponge.

'B-but, sir . . . me and Esme have never lived apart before and—'

'*SILENCE!* Didn't I tell you that you should only speak when you are spoken to,' Septimus growled. 'Now *get out* and don't let me see or hear you again until I have to! Children should be seen and not heard!'

Only too happy to oblige, the two youngsters made a hasty retreat and once out in the hallway Esme began to whimper. 'But, Gabriel, isn't a boarding school one of those places where you live in and don't come home of an evening?'

He nodded miserably but seeing her downcast face he tried to put on a brave face for her. 'I think it is but don't worry, I shall still be able to come home for holidays so it's not as if you won't see me at all. And you'll still have Mrs Sparrow and Gip to look out for you, so it won't be so bad.'

Tears began to trickle down her cheeks, so he took her hand and headed back to the kitchen where Mrs Sparrow was washing dishes at the sink.

She had let Gip out into the yard in case their grandfather chose to make an appearance in the kitchen and now seeing their glum faces she suggested, 'Why don't you get yourselves wrapped up and go and have a look at the beach? It's only a stone's throw from here and happen it'll cheer you up a bit. Put those coats I found for you on; it's bitter out there.'

'But Grandfather said we were to help you . . .' Esme said miserably.

She waved her hand airily. 'Eeh, don't worry about him. I'll find you plenty to do after lunch. Now get off with you but don't stay out too long, mind. Just turn left out of here and walk on till you come to Sea Lane. Straight down there and you'll reach the beach.'

The two children hastily put on the coats she had sorted for them and calling Gip to heel they set off. As Mrs Sparrow had said, it was a bitterly cold day with a harsh wind blowing in off the sea and in no time their cheeks were rosy and their noses red. Gip lolloped along in front of them as they followed at a more sedate pace.

'I don't think I'm going to like living here,' Esme said quietly.

Gabriel glanced at her. He didn't think he was going to like it either but seeing how sad she was he didn't say it, it could only make her feel worse. Strangely, he had thought he would enjoy having a big house to roam about in and yet, after being used to the confined space in their cosy little vardo, he'd felt weirdly out of place.

'I think it's because everything is new.' He forced a note of cheerfulness into his voice. 'Happen we've got to give it time to get used to it.'

They turned in to Sea Lane at that point and started along it, passing small cottages nestled either side on the way. After some time, they reached a sand dune and, climbing to the top of it, Esme's face suddenly broke into a smile as they saw the deserted beach and the sea laid out in front of them. It was even colder and windier here but she laughed with delight as she bounded onto the sand like a small puppy. It was coated with frost and crunched beneath her feet as she raced towards the sea with her brother in hot pursuit. The waves were crashing onto the shore and just for a time the two children forgot how miserable they felt as they played. It was far too cold to venture into the water but they skimmed along the edge, dodging the waves and laughing aloud. Esme stopped occasionally to collect a shell that had caught her eye and soon her coat pockets were full of them.

'Look, look there's a crab,' she squeaked as they gazed down into a rock pool left behind by the outgoing tide. 'Ooh, I wish we could just stay here forever,' Esme muttered.

Gabriel chuckled. 'You wouldn't be saying that come bed time,' he pointed out sensibly. 'We'd freeze to death down here.

Speaking o' which, old Gip is looking a little tired. I reckon we ought to be making our way back now. We don't want to upset the old man any more than we already have, do we?'

'I suppose not.' Resignedly they turned and started to retrace their steps. They had gone some way when she suddenly said, 'It's funny how Mrs Sparrow doesn't seem afraid of Grandfather isn't it?'

Gabriel shrugged. 'I suppose it is, but then she's known him a lot longer than we have. Perhaps his bark is worse than his bite?'

'Huh! I doubt it, otherwise why would Mammy have run away from home.' All she had ever told them was that her father had not approved of their father and so they had eloped to be together. Esme had always thought how romantic it was but now, after meeting their grandfather, she could understand it, particularly if he had been as strict with her as he was being with them. Still, perhaps time would soften him as he got to know them a little better. She could only hope so, because if it didn't, she wasn't sure how she was going to bear it.

Chapter Six

There were just two weeks until Christmas but there was no cheer in the rectory and both Esme and Gabriel were miserable as the first Christmas without their parents loomed. Gabriel in particular was struggling with his new lifestyle. After being used to the outdoor life he felt like a bird in a cage and he and his grandfather had clashed on more than one occasion, as Gabriel's sore palms could bear witness. His grandfather seemed to find pleasure in using the cane and did so at every opportunity – not that it tamed the boy. If anything, he just grew more morose and defiant.

'Did you hear them noises in your room again last night?' he asked as he and Esme cleaned in the hallway one day. Esme had been appointed to mop the tiled floor while Gabriel polished the carved wooden bannisters. She nodded and paused as she chewed on her lip. 'Yes, it sounds like someone walking about in the room above me,' she admitted. 'Though it's probably just my spirit friends.'

She had been barely out of bindings when her grandmother Griselda had first realised that Esme had what she had termed 'the gift', just as Griselda herself did. She'd used her gift to earn money by giving people messages from their loved ones on the other side, but Esme had never wanted to call the spirits to her. She'd grown used to them popping up every now and then over the years, but here, where suddenly she seemed to see spirits everywhere, they were beginning to frighten her.

Mrs Sparrow appeared at that moment and the two youngsters turned their attention back to their tasks as the woman mounted the stairs to change the linen on their beds.

'I'll tell you something else that happened last night,' Esme whispered conspiratorially when she was gone. 'I found a diary belonging to our mother in one of the drawers in her bedroom.'

'Really?' Gabriel scratched his head. 'What does it say in it?'

'I haven't had chance to read any of it yet. My candle had almost burned down, but I shall try to start it this evening.'

Mrs Sparrow appeared again with her arms full of dirty sheets and as she passed them in the hall she told Esme, 'You can come and give a hand with these when you've finished the floor. But make a good job of it, mind, you know your grandfather will inspect it when he gets back, and you also know what will happen if it isn't done to his liking.'

Yes, Esme thought, *I know all too well.* Already she had felt the length of the cane when a task hadn't been done to his satisfaction. As if thoughts of him had conjured him up from thin air, the outer door suddenly barged open and he entered on a gust of wind, bringing a sprinkling of snow to the part of the floor she had already done.

'Don't forget you're to go shopping with Mrs Sparrow this afternoon for new clothes,' he hissed and they both nodded.

Following a heated row with Mrs Sparrow, the reverend had finally agreed to buy them a brand-new outfit each to wear to church.

'What will your parishioners think of you if they keep turning up there looking like scarecrows?' she had railed at him. 'At the moment they think how generous you are to take them in after how their mother ran away, but will they think the same if they don't see them being properly turned out and cared for? And then there's the bishop. Isn't he due to visit soon? Happen that day you should let them eat in the dining room with you. He'll find it strange if he sees your own flesh and blood has been confined to the kitchen.'

'I dare say you're right,' Septimus had growled reluctantly.

And so this afternoon Mrs Sparrow was taking them into Skegness, where the bigger shops were, to be measured for new outfits. For both children it would be a welcome break from chores, for as they'd soon discovered, their grandfather had meant every word when he'd told them they must earn their keep. Their day now began early in the morning when they rose to fetch the coal in and get the fires lit in the dining room, the kitchen and their grandfather's study. Each day he would leave a rota of what he wanted them to do that day and it would be woe betide them if the jobs weren't done to his satisfaction. Some nights when they retired to their own separate beds, they were so tired that they were asleep almost before their heads had touched the pillow.

Strangely enough, Esme didn't mind that. While she was busy, she didn't have time to think of how much she was missing her parents. It was harder for Gabriel who was used to being able to come and go as he pleased. Both he and his father had been excellent at catching rabbits and pheasants, which their mother would make into delicious stews and pies, but now a butcher delivered the meat and for the most part Gabriel was confined to the house, which he hated.

Now, glancing at Esme, he told her miserably, 'I don't know how much more of this I can take, Esme. I almost wish we'd stayed on the road.'

'What, in this weather?' Esme shivered at the thought of it. 'We would have frozen to death. At least here we get fed and we have a warm bed to go to.'

'It ain't just that.' He sank down onto the bottom step placing the beeswax polish and the duster on Esme's clean tiles. 'There's things here that ain't right.'

Esme raised an eyebrow. 'Such as what?'

'Well . . .' He frowned. 'I reckon Grandfather and Mrs Sparrow are closer than they make out. Have you noticed how she sometimes starts to call him by his first name an' then quickly changes it to Reverend or Mr Silver? An' where does he go most nights? Surely there can't be that many parishioners that need a visit or that many prayer meetings to attend. And those noises from upstairs? I hear them sometimes too, even further down the corridor. I reckon we have rats in the attic.'

'Oh, I shouldn't worry about that,' Esme answered calmly. 'As I told you before, it's probably just my spirit friends making themselves known.'

Gabriel shuddered. He'd always found it strange the way Esme reckoned she could see and hear dead people. His father had always told the girl that it was a gift and that she should be grateful for it, but Gabriel was just glad he hadn't got it. It was spooky as far as he was concerned. Still, it didn't seem to overly concern Esme anymore, although she didn't encourage it.

'And have you noticed the way Mrs Sparrow always gets upset if we mention hearing the footsteps upstairs?' he went on. 'I asked her why a few days ago and she got all of a fluster and said we both had overactive imaginations and never to mention it to Grandfather. Huh! As if we'd dare! Even his parishioners seem to be afraid of him, and it's no wonder. All his sermons are full of hell and brimstone for anyone who might stray from the path of righteousness, yet Mammy taught us that God is all forgiving. I don't mind telling you, I hate going to church and the Bible lessons are even worse.'

He ran a hand through his thick mop of curly black hair and Esme gently squeezed his arm. Gabriel had never been keen on learning and she could see how miserable he was but if they didn't stay here the workhouse was their only option and she didn't think she could bear it if they were to be locked away in that place. Poor Gabriel's palms were always red raw from the number of times their grandfather had caned him, but he didn't make things any easier for himself, for never once had he cried or even flinched when the punishments were being administered, which only seemed to incense their grandfather even more.

'You are Satan's *spawn*!' the man would cry, but Gabriel would just stare calmly back at him as the strokes grew harsher. On more than one occasion Mrs Sparrow had had to rush into the room to intervene and then she would whisk Gabriel away to the kitchen and smear ointment onto the wounds. Only then, in front of her, would Gabriel allow his tears to flow, but never in front of his grandfather.

'Come on,' Esme said, hoping to cheer him up. 'Just think, this afternoon we'll be going into Skegness with Mrs Sparrow, so let's get our jobs done, eh?'

He gave her a half-hearted smile and they went their separate ways to finish their jobs.

As arranged, they set off to catch the coach into Skegness with Mrs Sparrow shortly after lunch. It took the coastal road and the two youngsters enjoyed the ride, as well as the fact that they had a whole afternoon with no chores to do.

'I suppose we should think of clearing your mother's things out of your bedroom now that you're using it,' Mrs Sparrow said musingly as they rattled along.

Esme frowned. 'I actually quite like having her things about me,' she replied. 'It sort of makes me feel . . . like she's still close to me.' As yet she hadn't disturbed a single thing of her mother's; the drawers were still full of her clothes and underwear, and her books and personal treasures were still on the shelves. She had brought so few of her own things with her that she hadn't needed the space.

Mrs Sparrow stared at her for a moment before asking tentatively, 'Tell me . . . was she happy with your father?'

'Oh yes,' both Esme and Gabriel said in unison and the old woman nodded.

'Good. I was worried that she'd find life on the road hard. But if that's the case why did your father go off and leave you all?'

It was Gabriel who informed her firmly, 'He didn't, he would *never* have left us.' He went on to explain where his father had gone, ending, 'We can only imagine that something happened to him, otherwise he would have come home.'

'So, he could still be alive somewhere?'

That had never occurred to Esme and Gabriel, and now they stared at each other as a flicker of hope sprang to life in their stomachs.

'I suppose he could be,' Esme answered, silently praying that this might be the case. She felt sure she would have felt it if he had passed on. But now they were away from the house, she

46

decided to ask a few questions of her own. 'Did you ever know our grandmother?'

A closed look came to Mrs Sparrow's face as she stared through the carriage window and shook her head. 'No, I told you, she had already died when I went to look after Mr Silver and your mother.'

'I see.' Esme looked disappointed as the carriage passed through Chapel St Leonard's.

As if hoping to change the subject, Mrs Sparrow told them, 'Shouldn't be long now and we'll be in Skegness.' The two children nodded and fell silent.

They alighted the carriage on the seafront where the bitterly cold wind and the thick mist floating in from the sea almost took their breath away and they had to lean forward to battle the wind until they turned into a side street. They had no doubt that in the summer the front and the beaches would be thronged with holidaymakers but today the waves were crashing on the sand and the place was deserted.

'The shop we want is just up here,' Mrs Sparrow told them breathlessly, and with their heads bent they followed her, keen to get out of the biting cold.

The bell above the door tinkled as they entered, and in seconds a small woman, who was almost as far round as she was high, with grey hair pulled into a bun at the nape of her neck, appeared from a door behind the counter.

'Ah, Mrs Sparrow, Reverend Silver called in yesterday to tell me to expect you.' Her smile was kindly and the children smiled back as Mrs Sparrow crossed to some bolts of material that were rolled onto a long shelf along one side of the shop.

Esme felt quite excited at the prospect of having a brand-new outfit, Gabriel less so; clothes and fashion meant little to him. Just then Mrs Sparrow dropped a bombshell when she told the dressmaker quietly, 'I need you to measure Gabriel for a school uniform. He'll be attending the Lincolnshire School for Boys. I have the list here of what he'll need.'

Since their first day at the rectory, their grandfather hadn't mentioned about Gabriel going to a boarding school again, so the boy had hoped he'd changed his mind. But now his stomach churned as he said shakily, 'So he still intends to send me away?'

Mrs Sparrow avoided his eyes as she nodded, looking guilty. 'Yes, you'll be starting immediately after New Year. Can you have the uniform ready for then, Mrs Golding?'

The woman tapped her lip thoughtfully as she stared at the list Mrs Sparrow had given her before finally nodding. 'Yes, I should think so if my seamstress and I both get working on everything.'

Gabriel stood so still that he might have been turned to stone, but Esme turned to Mrs Sparrow in dismay. 'But he *can't* be sent away! We've never been apart.' It had been bad enough when they had been forced to sleep in separate beds but this was a million times worse and she couldn't imagine how she would cope without him. He was all she had left now that their parents were gone.

'I'm afraid your grandfather has made up his mind,' Mrs Sparrow told her in a hushed voice, afraid that Esme would have a tantrum in the shop. But she needn't have worried. Somehow Esme managed to control her feelings, although her face was as pale as a piece of lint. Suddenly all the joy had gone from the outing – from her life, in fact – and she stood helplessly as Mrs Golding began to take Gabriel's measurements.

There were strict rules on what the children who attended the school should wear so Gabriel had no say in the matter, but when it came to Esme's turn, she found she no longer cared and left the choosing of the material to Mrs Sparrow.

It was a silent, subdued group who eventually left the shop and despite Mrs Sparrow's best attempts to lighten the mood in the carriage on the way home it was a silent journey too.

It wasn't until later that evening when Mrs Sparrow carried their grandfather's meal through to the dining room that Esme and Gabriel had a chance to speak alone. Throwing her arms about him she began to sob. 'How will I cope here without you? Perhaps we should run away?'

He shook his head as he gently stroked her hair. He had thought about doing just that himself but common sense had kicked in. How would they survive in this weather? He had no doubt that he could have, one way or another, but he couldn't stand the thought of Esme having to sleep rough again.

'Perhaps if we'd been a bit older we could have managed, but what chance would we have at this time of year? We'd probably end up in the workhouse and then we'd be parted anyway. At least if I do as he says I'll get to come home and see you from time to time, and you'll still have Gip. It isn't as if the school is on the other side of the world, is it?'

'I . . . I suppose not,' she whimpered. In some ways, she realised, it might even be better for Gabriel. Their grandfather clearly hated him because he looked so like their father and if Gabriel was away at school, he'd escape the harsh beatings their grandfather was so fond of administering. She knew how much Gabriel would hate being cooped up in a school but she needed to be brave for him now. The last thing she wanted was to make things worse for him. And so they huddled together, fearing the future and drawing what comfort they could from each other.

Chapter Seven

It was the week before Christmas and the rectory was as bleak and cold as ever. Their grandfather didn't believe in wasting money on what he termed 'fripperies', although Esme and Gabriel noted that he always seemed to have enough money for the expensive cigars he favoured, and for the bottles of vintage port he drank like water.

Even in their tiny vardo their mother had always made an effort to make it look festive, but here there was no Christmas tree and the only festive reminder were the vases full of shiny green holly leaves, heavy with bright red berries, which they had picked from the garden and dotted about the house.

'Will we be having goose for Christmas dinner?' Esme innocently asked Mrs Sparrow one day, and the woman had looked slightly embarrassed.

'Your grandfather will, but we'll have a nice plump chicken and I'll do us some lovely sage and onion stuffing to go with it. There'll be a brandy fruit pudding to follow as well. That will be nice, won't it?'

The children glanced at each other. They'd noticed that they and Mrs Sparrow always had the cheaper cuts of meat, although their grandfather insisted on having the best. Strangely, they didn't mind that. They were fed, after all, but the longer they were there the more they realised how selfish their grandfather was. His bedroom, study and the dining room were always kept warm while the rest of them shivered. Most nights when they went to bed the rooms were so cold that their breath floated on the air like lace in front of them, making the nights they had spent with their parents in their cosy little vardo seem a million miles away.

They had grown adept at avoiding their grandfather as much as they possibly could but it hadn't softened his attitude towards them. If anything, Gabriel now took a daily beating for the slightest thing, sometimes Esme too, and they'd come to the conclusion that he took pleasure from hurting them.

'I *must* banish the sins of the father from you both,' Septimus would cry as the cane swished up and down on their tender flesh. They bore it bravely, aware that had they screamed and cried and begged for mercy he might have been slightly more lenient with them, but their pride forbade it and they both saved their tears for bedtime. The danger time was always after he had had his dinner and they handed in the Bible passages he had set them to learn the night before. It was rare for Gabriel not to make a mistake and now his palms and the backs of his legs were raw.

'I shall almost be glad when I go to school,' he groaned one evening when his grandfather had been particularly brutal. 'In fact, if it wasn't for you, I'd be off now like a shot.'

Esme chewed her lip anxiously as she bathed the open wheals on the backs of his legs with cool water. Mrs Sparrow was out decorating the church with greenery for a wedding that would be held there in a few days' time and their grandfather was off on one of his regular jaunts into Skegness. When she had finished cleaning the wounds she smeared ointment onto them and went to throw the bloody water into the yard, while Gabriel settled next to Gip and fondled his ears. Thankfully, since they'd been there, they had managed to sneak him into the kitchen each night to sleep without their grandfather knowing. Had it been up to him the poor thing would have been left outside and they both knew that at his age he wouldn't have survived for long in the bitter cold.

When they took him for a walk now, he merely plodded along at the side of them rather than running as he had used to, and when they got back, he would collapse in front of the fire and instantly fall asleep. Neither of them was quite sure how old he was as he had always been there but they knew that he must be very old now.

'I suppose we ought to go up before Grandfather gets back,' Esme said after a time. 'We have a Bible passage to memorise before tomorrow.'

Gabriel groaned. No doubt that would mean yet another beating, because try as he might he never seemed to get it right, even if he stayed awake half the night reading it by the light of a guttering candle. Tonight, he was feeling particularly sorry for himself and he asked unexpectedly, 'Have you heard any more noises from the rooms up in the attic?'

Esme nodded as she dried the bowl. 'Yes, but not all the time. When I do hear it, I swear it sounds just like someone moving about up there. But like I told you, I think it's just a spirit.'

A thought occurred to him and he suggested, 'Why don't we creep up there while no one else is in and have a look around?'

'I-I'm not sure that I'd dare.' Esme paled at the thought. 'What if there *is* someone up there and they catch us? Worse still, what if Grandfather were to come back early and find us up there?'

Gabriel snorted. 'Huh! What could he do to us that he hasn't already done?' His nostrils flared with hatred but he didn't push the idea. He'd taken enough of a beating for one night. And so after making sure that Gip was settled they climbed the stairs and each made for their own rooms.

Once inside Esme shivered as she hastily undressed and shrugged into her nightgown. Beyond the glass she could see big feathery snowflakes drifting down and she turned to the bed only to stop abruptly as she saw four dark forms in the shadows in the corner of the room. Lifting the candle high she peered towards them and gradually she made out the outlines of four young women. There had only ever been three before and since being there she had seen them frequently but now there were definitely four.

'Wh-who are you?' she whispered. 'And what do you want of me?' But even as she spoke the images faded and the tears flowed down her waxen cheeks. Why were these poor lost souls following her about, and where had the fourth one come from? Her father had once told her that most of the people she saw were people who had recently passed and not yet gone into the light, but these poor girls had been here ever since she had arrived.

Plonking heavily down on the side of the bed, her eyes were drawn to the large chest of drawers to one side of the room. Inside them her mother's clothes were still folded. As yet she hadn't wanted to move them, but now she suddenly had a longing to touch something that had once belonged to her and she opened the top drawer and fingered the underwear inside. Everything was washed and neatly folded, until she came to the bottom drawer, and then she frowned as she saw some undergarments screwed into balls and pushed into a corner. Tentatively she drew out a pair of drawers and stared at the dark stain on them. It looked like dried blood, although it was a dirty brown colour now. Perhaps this had been caused when her mother had her monthly courses and she had left home before she'd had time to wash them? Constance had explained all about the courses that Esme would have one day, telling her that this would be the first sign that she was growing into a woman and that when it happened, she need have no fear.

Delving a little deeper she found yet more stained garments and pushing them back into the drawer she slammed it shut in dismay. Her mother had always been such a clean and tidy person. It seemed strange that she should have put them there, almost as if she was hiding them. Esme shook her head; her imagination was beginning to run away with her. She turned her attention to the rows of books on the shelves. The first book was *The Tenant of Wildfell Hall* by an author called Acton Bell and Esme smiled through her tears as she imagined her mother curled up in bed every night in this very room reading it by the light of a candle. She had always loved reading, although her father had drummed into her that it was a sin to read anything other than the Bible.

Gently Esme began to turn the pages and it was as she was doing so that something caught her eye and she carried the book over the room to be closer to the candle. There was something written in the margin and she recognised her mother's handwriting immediately.

He came to my room again tonight . . .

Esme frowned. Who had her mother been writing about? Curious now, she continued to flick through the pages and sure enough soon she found yet more writing.

I don't know how much longer I can bear this . . .

It was then that she heard footsteps on the stairs and hurriedly placing the book back on the shelf she raced over to her bed, lifted the Bible that she should have been reading, and held her breath.

'I'm back, Esme, have you everything you need? And is Gabriel in bed, dear?'

Esme sighed with relief when Mrs Sparrow's voice drifted through the door. She must have finished dressing the church.

'Yes, thank you, and yes, Gabriel is in bed.'

'Very well, I'll wish you goodnight.'

Esme listened to the footsteps recede and forced herself to start learning her Bible passage again. There would be time enough to look more closely at her mother's things another day. She still had her diary to read but hadn't found time as yet.

Meanwhile, in his own room, Gabriel was standing at his bedroom window staring gloomily out at the snowy landscape. This could have been such a lovely place to live had he and Esme received a warm welcome but as it was, he hated the house and he hated his grandfather even more. Every time he thought of starting the school his grandfather had insisted he should attend, his stomach tied itself into knots and he felt sick. How would he bear being cooped up? he wondered. If it weren't for Esme he would have left and tried to make his own way in the world but he was painfully aware that if he did that, he might never see her again, and he felt responsible for her. With a sigh he crossed to the bed and climbed in, shivering as the cold cotton sheets settled around him.

It was only Mrs Sparrow who made living there bearable but sometimes even she seemed fearful of his grandfather and he wondered why she stayed. Surely she could have got a post elsewhere with someone who treated her with a little more respect and kindness? It was then that he heard the front door slam. It would be his grandfather returning home, no doubt, so he quickly blew his candle out and pretended to be asleep. He knew that he should be trying to memorise the Bible passage his grandfather had set him as there would be no chance tomorrow, which would mean yet another caning. But he was used to it by now, and on this dreary thought he eventually fell asleep.

In no time at all there were just a couple of days until Christmas, but what used to be a happy time for the two youngsters turned out to be days just like any other. They still had their rota of jobs to do and were expected to attend their grandfather's service at church in the evening. Neither of them were looking forward to it.

'Must we go?' Gabriel asked Mrs Sparrow as they sat having their evening meal.

She raised her eyebrow as she placed a plateful of mince pies straight from the oven in front of them.

'But of course you must go,' she chided gently. 'We're nearing the anniversary of the birth of our Lord. There's no way your grandfather would let you miss the services this week.'

The children stared glumly at the mince pies. Even they couldn't make up for what they knew was ahead. Their grandfather's services were always full of fire and brimstone and it wasn't unknown for the odd parishioner to fall asleep in the church.

'Think about it,' Mrs Sparrow said encouragingly. 'You'll get to wear your new outfits. That will be nice, won't it?'

Their two heads bobbed in unison because they didn't want to hurt her feelings. She had gone into Skegness to collect their new clothes the day before and they were now hanging in their rooms, ready to be worn. She had also collected Gabriel's school uniform and just the sight of it filled him with dread.

Mrs Sparrow frowned and, eyeing Gabriel, she said tentatively, 'Actually, your grandfather asked me to, er . . .' She paused, as though choosing her words carefully. 'Well, he asked me if I'd trim your hair before we set off tonight.'

Gabriel looked horrified as his hand rose to touch the jet-black curls tumbling over his shoulders. Just like his father before him, he had always worn his hair long. In the summer he would tie it back but he had never worn it shorter than shoulder-length in his life.

'How short are we talking?' he asked bluntly.

'Quite a bit shorter if we're to pacify him.' Mrs Sparrow went to the drawer and came back yielding a pair of sharp scissors. 'Come on, let's get it done and out of the way. There's no sense putting it off. You'd have to have it cut considerably shorter before you started school anyway.' For a moment she thought he was going to refuse as his mouth set in a grim line. But then, knowing what would happen if he didn't do as he was told, he reluctantly crossed to the chair she had pulled out for him and frowned as she placed a towel about his neck. 'Right, here goes. I'll try to make it as neat as I can for you.'

Tears stung Esme's eyes as she saw her brother's beautiful hair falling to the floor but she forced a brave smile for him and squeezed his hand encouragingly. At last it was done and Gabriel cautiously raised his hand to feel his shorn head. Mrs Sparrow had cut the sides to above his ears and the back into the nape of his neck and it was sticking out in clumps; it was clear she would never make a barber, and he felt almost naked.

'There you are, that should be short enough to satisfy him. It wasn't so bad, was it?' she said guiltily.

Gabriel rose, causing yet another few locks of his glorious hair to tumble to the ground. He crossed to the mirror and stared at his reflection, and although he had never been particularly vain, he could hardly recognise himself. All of the gypsy men had worn their hair long and now he felt yet another part of who he was fall away.

'I've done it as neatly as I could,' she told him in a small voice, avoiding his eyes as she hurried away to fetch a brush to sweep up the hair. 'But I believe they'll cut it again for you when you get to school and tidy it up even more.'

Gabriel merely nodded numbly. His neck felt cold but he was determined not to show how bereft he felt; Esme was on the verge of tears already and he didn't want to upset her any more than she already was.

'It'll soon grow again,' she whispered sadly and he nodded before hurrying outside to fetch some more logs for the fire.

Oh Dadda, if you're still alive somewhere please come and find us soon and get us away from this hellhole, he silently prayed, but his only answer was the sound of the wind blowing through the snow-laden branches in the trees by the rectory.

Chapter Eight

The Christmas Eve service was every bit as awful as Esme and Gabriel had thought it would be, and as they sat in the cold church, they couldn't hold back the tears as they both thought back to Christmas Eves past in their colourful little vardo, where they'd sung carols and listened to their mother telling them of the birth of the baby Jesus. They had never been rich financially but they had always known love, and thanks to their father's hunting skills they had never gone hungry.

When the service finally finished, they were forced to stand by the church door next to their grandfather. 'These are the grandchildren I have taken in out of the goodness of my heart,' Septimus introduced them to those who didn't already know, and the children squirmed as everyone praised him for his kind heart. Then he would rattle the donations bowl at whoever was standing before him, waiting until they'd dropped in the coins they could obviously ill afford, before wishing them a merry Christmas.

Gabriel suspected that it was these donations that funded his grandfather's love for expensive cigars and fine port, because it was well known that men of the cloth didn't receive a big salary. But then, Septimus Silver was nothing at all like Gabriel or Esme had imagined a reverend to be.

Last to leave the church was a family who had their own private pews right at the front of the church to one side of the large stone altar. They were clearly gentry if the way they were dressed was anything to go by and Esme's mouth gaped as she stared at the beautiful clothes they were wearing. The lady was clad in a red velvet costume trimmed with white fur. The jacket was fitted tight into the waist with a little peplum and the skirt beneath it was so wide that Esme wondered if it would fit through the door. Her hands were ensconced in a little velvet muff, and on her head she wore a matching bonnet trimmed with white feathers that danced when she moved. The gentleman was dressed in a smart overcoat and a top hat and behind them trailed three children, two girls and a slightly older boy.

'Ah, Esme, Gabriel,' their grandfather said jovially. 'I would like to introduce you to Lord and Lady Fitzroy. They are great benefactors of the church and it is thanks to their generosity that we managed to repair the roof.' He was practically fawning over them and Esme and Gabriel were shocked to see the change in him. 'And these,' Septimus went on, 'are their children and their young relation. Like me, they took him in when he was orphaned, God bless their generous souls.'

One of the girls looked to be about Esme's age, the other one slightly younger. Esme gave them a shy smile while the boy, who appeared to be a couple of years older than Gabriel, inclined his head. Like their mother, both girls were impeccably dressed with fair hair and blue eyes, while the boy was dark-haired with eyes the colour of warm treacle.

'We heard you had taken them in,' Lady Fitzroy answered in a melodious voice. 'How wonderful of you, Reverend.' She bestowed a smile on the children and, apart from their mother, they were both sure they had never seen a more beautiful woman. She seemed kindly too. At this point Lord Fitzroy extracted his wallet and placed a small bundle of pound notes in the bowl as Septimus bowed to him.

'Thank you kindly, my lord,' he simpered, almost grovelling at his feet. 'May I wish you and your *beautiful* family a very merry Christmas. I trust we shall see you here again in the new year?'

'Of course,' Lord Fitzroy replied as he shepherded his wife, the children and their nanny ahead of him. 'And a very merry Christmas to you and yours too.' He doffed his hat and the family hurried through the snow towards the lychgate where the most splendid carriage Esme and Gabriel had ever seen was waiting for them.

'Are they really a *real* lord and lady?' Esme was speechless with wonder, but already their grandfather had resorted to his former grumpy self.

'Yes, they are, and you would do well to remember it when you are in their presence. They are our greatest benefactors. I would die of shame should they ever discover that you are gypsy trash. Now, where is Mrs Sparrow? Get back to the house with her, I have things to attend to here before my sermon tomorrow.'

'Does that mean that we won't be having our Bible lesson this evening?' Esme tried hard not to sound hopeful, and when he nodded, she had to stop herself from doing a little jig of joy. At least that would mean one less caning for Gabriel so it wasn't turning out to be so bad a Christmas Eve after all.

'Lady Fitzroy is very beautiful, isn't she?' Esme sighed to Mrs Sparrow as they made the short walk back to the rectory. 'Whereabouts do they live?'

'On the edge of the village in Fitzroy Hall.' Mrs Sparrow was concentrating on not going her length on the slippery snow. 'Lord Fitzroy owns most of the fishing fleets in Hull and Grimsby and employs a lot of people. Most of the men hereabouts work on his trawlers and many of the local women are employed up at the hall as maids and such like.'

'They must be very rich,' Esme commented dreamily. 'Just imagine having servants to wait on you.'

They had reached the rectory by then and once they entered by the kitchen door Gip raised his head from his place on the hearth-rug and wagged his tail before settling back down and dropping back to sleep. He seemed to spend most of his life resting now and thankfully they had managed to keep him out of the way of their grandfather.

Mrs Sparrow made them all some cocoa and mince pies for their supper and the children went to bed.

'I don't think Mammy was very happy here,' she whispered to Gabriel on the landing and she quickly went on to tell him about the words she had found written in the margin of the book.

He shook his head. 'I'm not surprised if Grandfather treated her like he treats us. It's no wonder she ran away with Dadda.' He wanted to wish her a merry Christmas but somehow the words stuck in his throat. They both knew that it wasn't going to be happy so there hardly seemed any point, and after pecking her on the cheek he went on to his own room.

As soon as she entered her room, Esme saw the figures of the four young women standing in the corner, almost as if they were waiting for her, and before she could stop herself, she asked, 'What do you want of me? Why are you always here?' Their eyes seemed to be pleading with her, but even as she stared at them, they slowly faded away.

With a sigh she hastily got out of her new clothes and after hanging them neatly away she shrugged her nightdress on, snatched the book she had been looking at the night before, and hopped into bed. It was so cold in the room that soon her teeth were chattering but turning to the page she had reached the night before she continued to glance through it. Sure enough she soon came to yet more little comments, all of them pointing to the fact that her mother had indeed been very unhappy living there. As she read them, tears smarted in her eyes. She spoke of beatings, of being locked in her room for the slightest misdemeanour and of how lonely she often felt. Esme felt as if her heart was breaking.

'Oh Mammy, I miss you so much,' she sobbed. Then to her joy yet another shape began to form at the end of the bed and she hoped that it was her mother come to offer comfort.

But it wasn't her mammy, it was Granny Griselda. Esme had few memories of her when she was alive, but her spirit had visited her frequently over the years so she recognised her immediately. 'Stay strong, my pet,' the vision whispered with a beatific smile, and then she was gone as quickly as she had appeared and Esme felt bereft.

'Granny, *please* come back,' she said past the huge lump in her throat. It was the first time that Esme had seen her since they had arrived at the rectory, but now there was only silence, so after blowing out her candle she snuggled down beneath the blankets and cried herself to sleep, clutching the book her mother had written in. It truly was the worst Christmas Eve she had ever spent.

When Gabriel appeared in the kitchen the following morning, his hair was already springing into curls about his head and it didn't look quite so sharp.

'It suits you,' Esme told him, hoping to cheer him up.

He shrugged and coloured as he self-consciously fingered his shorn locks.

'I have a few bits for you,' Mrs Sparrow said as she delved into a drawer and produced two paper bags. She handed them one each with a broad smile. 'Merry Christmas!'

Inside Esme's bag she found an orange, some sweetmeats, a pretty handkerchief embroidered with her initial and a pair of knitted mittens. Inside Gabriel's he found an orange, some toffee and a warm scarf.

Slightly embarrassed they stared up at her, 'I, er . . . I'm ever so sorry but we didn't have any money to get you anything,' Esme faltered but the woman waved the apology aside.

'Oh, don't you be worrying about that. It's only a few bits and bobs. I hope you like them.'

'We do!' the children said in unison, touched that she had thought of them.

'Good, well let's get cracking and get the Christmas dinner sorted, shall we?' And with that Mrs Sparrow pottered away to fetch the goose and the chicken from the slab in the pantry.

Shortly after, Gabriel was instructed to light a fire in the dining room. Their grandfather had decided he would have his meal in there today, although he would be dining alone. It didn't seem to trouble him but the children thought he was mean for not inviting Mrs Sparrow to join him. She did wait on him hand and foot all year round after all.

Esme went in next to set the table with the best linen and crystal and when she was done, she stood back to admire her efforts. She had placed a bowl of holly in the centre of the table, and with the fire roaring up the chimney and the silver cutlery and crystal gleaming it looked festive and cheerful.

They were in the kitchen later that morning when their grandfather suddenly entered and Esme's heart sank. It was rare for him to come in there and Gip was, as usual, fast asleep on the hearthrug. She silently prayed that her grandfather wouldn't notice him.

'Why aren't you all ready for church?' he barked in his usual short way.

'Keep your hair on, we've been getting the dinner on the go but never fear we'll be there for the start of the service,' Mrs Sparrow informed him.

Septimus grunted and turned to leave but as he did his eyes settled on Gip and he scowled. 'What is that filthy *mongrel* doing in my kitchen?' he growled. 'Didn't I say he was to stay in the stables or the yard?'

'We just thought we'd let him in for a warm,' Mrs Sparrow said quickly, hoping to placate him. 'It is Christmas Day after all.'

'Christmas Day or not I'll not have that scabby mangy mutt in my house spreading its fleas about the place. Now *get* him out or I'll take my gun to him, d'you hear me?'

Esme was quaking in her boots but Gabriel stared at him mutinously, his hands clenched into fists.

'I thought it was the season of goodwill,' he said shortly.

Septimus's eyes bulged as he stared at him astounded. 'How *dare* you speak to me like that,' he spat, and before anyone could say or do anything his hand shot out and he slapped Gabriel's face so hard that his head snapped back on his shoulders.

Gabriel went down like a ton of bricks, taking a kitchen chair crashing to the ground with him, but before anyone could respond he bounced back up again, his fists held out bravely in front of him. Already a bruise in the shape of a handprint was standing out on his cheek but he was so incensed that for now he felt nothing but rage. 'You're nothing but a *bully* an' if my dadda were here he'd put you down,' he shouted.

'If your father were here I'd delight in doing the same to him! He was nothing but thieving gypsy scum!'

Gabriel made to attack him again but Mrs Sparrow hastily stepped between them, her eyes flashing. 'That's enough now.' She glared from one to the other of them. 'I'll not have this sort of behaviour in my kitchen, d'you hear me. And today of all days!' Then pointing her finger at Septimus she told him, 'I suggest you leave the room.'

Septimus hesitated, but then throwing his shoulders back he stormed into the hallway, slamming the door so hard behind him that for a moment it appeared to be dancing on its hinges.

Mrs Sparrow let out a long breath and turning to Gabriel, she told him, 'Sit yourself down while I get a cold cloth to put on that cheek.'

Tears were pricking the boy's eyes now but he held them back, too proud to show how much his grandfather had hurt him.

Esme, however, was openly crying and she crossed to him and tenderly took his hand. 'A-are you all right, Gabriel?'

He nodded. 'Aye, I am. It'll take more than a wallop from that great bully to hurt me.'

Mrs Sparrow clucked disapprovingly as she returned with a piece of huckaback and a bowl of cold water. 'That's enough of that talk now. He shouldn't have done that but then again you shouldn't have cheeked him as you did. I reckon you're going to have a right shiner!'

'I was only telling the truth,' Gabriel mumbled, wincing as she pressed the cloth to his sore eye and cheek. 'My dadda *isn't* scum and Gip isn't doing any harm lying there, is he? Saying he's supposed to be a man o' the cloth, I don't reckon he's got an ounce o' compassion in him for anyone!'

Mrs Sparrow chewed on her lip as she continued to bathe his face but it was clear that the incident had upset her. 'I reckon we should go and get changed now else we'll be late for the service.'

'Huh! And how will we explain this away?' Gabriel gestured to his cheek.

Mrs Sparrow frowned. 'Hmm, perhaps you're right. You stay here with Gip and if anyone asks, I'll say that you're not well.'

'I'm not going either,' Esme said. 'I'll stay here too to look after Gabriel.'

The woman looked at the two rebellious faces and after a moment she shrugged. 'Very well.' Then she hurried away to change her skirt and blouse. She reappeared minutes later in her coat and hat and her Sunday best gown and told Esme, 'Keep an eye on the dinner for me, would you, dear? I'll be back as soon as I can.'

'Some Christmas Day this is turning out to be,' Gabriel said glumly after Mrs Sparrow had left. He tentatively touched his sore face, which was beginning to throb and swell. 'Still, at least we got out of sitting through another of his boring sermons. It's no wonder that some of the older people nod off sometimes.'

Esme sat beside him and stared into the fire. 'I think this is a bad house, Gabriel,' she said eventually.

'What do you mean by *a bad house*?'

'Just what I say.' Esme stared around with frightened eyes and lowering her voice, she whispered, 'There are sad spirits here.'

He scowled. 'But you often see spirits. What's so different about the ones you see here?'

'The ones I usually see are peaceful souls. I think they are either people who have just passed and have not yet gone into the light, or they've come back to pay a visit to their loved ones. But the ones I see here . . .' She shuddered and glanced around, almost as if she was expecting them to materialise at any second. 'They are trapped here; I don't know why yet. Perhaps they are trying to tell me something?'

Gabriel shivered, glad that their grandmother hadn't passed this so-called 'gift' on to him. 'I'm sure you're just being fanciful,' he told her, hoping to cheer her up but she shook her head.

'No, I'm telling you, *bad* things have happened here.'

Gabriel wasn't sure how to reply to this, so they snuggled up together on the settle and sat in silence, the only sound that of the logs spitting on the fire, as they each lost themselves in memories of Christmases past.

Chapter Nine

The next week passed in a blur of visits to the church and hours spent each night learning the psalms and Bible passages their grandfather set them.

Gabriel was in a rebellious mood as the time approached for him to leave for school and he didn't even try very hard, which meant almost daily canings. But he was used to them now and joked to Esme, 'I think my palms are hardening up.' There was no way he would show Septimus how much they hurt or say anything to upset his little sister more than she already was.

'I don't reckon the old man came home last night,' Gabriel whispered to Esme on the day before New Year's Eve.

'Oh, what makes you think that?'

They were sitting at the kitchen table eating their breakfast while Mrs Sparrow pottered about.

Glancing over his shoulder to make sure they weren't being overheard, he hissed, 'I didn't hear him and his shoes weren't in the hall when I got up this morning. I haven't seen Mrs Sparrow making him any breakfast either.'

'Perhaps he went out early this morning?' Esme suggested, but Gabriel shook his head.

'No, I would have heard him on the landing. His room is quite close to mine. I reckon he's up to something.'

'Such as what? It could be that one of his parishioners was ill and he's stayed with them.'

'Huh! I don't think he's that charitable,' Gabriel snorted.

Mrs Sparrow joined them at the table to pour herself a cup of tea then, so the conversation came to a halt.

It was almost an hour later, when Gabriel was out in the yard chopping logs for the fire, that Septimus arrived. His clothes were crumpled and he looked tired, which confirmed Gabriel's suspicions. He went straight into the kitchen and Gabriel heard raised voices.

'And where have you been again?'

Gabriel found it strange that the housekeeper should question her employer but as he and Esme had discovered, this was no normal household. He went to stand by the door so he could hear the conversation better.

'I, er . . . had to attend someone who was about to pass?'

'Oh, and who would that be?' Mrs Sparrow knew every one of the parishioners by name and as far as she knew none of them were that ill.

'Oh, it wasn't anyone from our village,' Septimus grunted, then in a sterner voice. 'Now stop questioning me, woman! I'm going for a wash and when I come down, I shall expect my breakfast to be ready.'

Gabriel heard the kitchen door slam and hurried back to finish chopping the wood.

Later that day, as Esme was cleaning the parlour, she lifted the used newspapers her grandfather had left there and took them into the kitchen. But as she placed them in the box to the side of the fireplace, a headline caught her eye.

Another young woman goes missing!
Amy Boss, a nineteen-year-old woman, has been reported missing from her home in Skegness. She is the fourth young woman to go missing in as many months and so far the police have been unable to find any trace of her. Like the previous three women, Miss Boss was a well-known prostitute in the town centre.

Esme wasn't quite sure what a prostitute was. She glanced at the date on the newspaper and saw that it was dated early in December, but she had no chance to read any more because Mrs Sparrow entered the room, so she stuffed the paper into the box kept for that purpose and hurried on with what she had been

67

doing – Mrs Sparrow had been in a funny mood all morning so Esme didn't want to do anything that might upset her more.

It wasn't until later that evening that she and Gabriel had a chance to talk alone. Their grandfather was in the vestry at the church preparing yet another service for the following day and Mrs Sparrow had gone to see a neighbour, who had just given birth to a baby girl.

Esme fetched the newspaper she had seen earlier and showed it to Gabriel who read it and shrugged.

'So what's this to do with us? I mean, it's a shame she's gone missing.'

'What is a prostitute, Gabriel?'

Gabriel blushed to the roots of his hair. He was well aware of what it meant, but how could he explain it to Esme, who in his eyes was little more than a baby?

'Well, it means, er . . .' He scratched his head. 'She's sort of a woman who goes with men . . . for money.'

'Goes where with men?' Esme asked innocently.

Feeling out of his depth, Gabriel bounced out of his seat, wishing his mammy was there to explain in terms that Esme could understand. 'Come on, let's take Gip out for a quick walk while the old man is out of the way,' he suggested, keen to change the subject.

Happy to get out of the house for a while Esme rushed off to put her coat and boots on and he sighed with relief.

As always, they headed for the beach with Gip plodding along at the side of them. Thankfully the snow had stopped falling a few days before and was now melting, although it was still treacherously slippery underfoot and bitterly cold.

'I can't believe you'll be gone in three days' time,' Esme muttered miserably.

Gabriel's face hardened. 'You'll be all right,' he told her, although he hated the thought of leaving her to their grandfather's tender mercies. He was a bullying tyrant and Gabriel hated him with a vengeance. 'And it won't be too long till I'm home for the school holidays. I don't know why Grandfather wouldn't let me come home at weekends. It's not as if the school is a million miles away.'

As they neared the beach they stopped and eyed the grey waves glumly. Every hour that passed brought them closer to being parted and it would have been hard to say who was dreading it the most. Esme knew how much her brother loved the great outdoors and feared he would find the school like a prison. Had it been her that was being sent away she could have borne it; she loved learning, but Gabriel had always struggled with it. Still, there was nothing to be done now but go along with their grandfather's wishes. They walked down to the hard-packed sand and wandered along deep in thought, until it became so uncomfortably cold that they turned back.

The next few days passed in the blink of an eye and all too soon the small case Mrs Sparrow had packed for Gabriel was standing ready in the hallway. His grandfather would be taking him to the school immediately after breakfast and Gabriel was sitting at the kitchen table looking uncomfortable in his new uniform.

'This collar is choking me,' he complained and Mrs Sparrow clucked at him disapprovingly.

'Nonsense, it's because you're not used to wearing one,' she told him as she placed his breakfast in front of him. Today she had cooked him bacon and eggs as a special treat but he found he couldn't eat it. The food seemed to lodge in his throat and he was ghastly pale with dread of what lay ahead. Even so, he knew that Mrs Sparrow had gone to a lot of trouble for him so he craftily fed it to the dog beneath the table rather than hurt her feelings and old Gip was only too happy to accept it.

'That's good,' she commented when his plate was cleared. 'There's nothing like a good breakfast to set you up for the day. Now, stand up and let's have a look at you. We want you looking your best, don't we?'

Gabriel reluctantly rose and allowed her to fuss with his tie and the lapels on his blazer.

'There then, you'll do,' Mrs Sparrow said quietly. 'I'll leave you to say goodbye to your sister while I go and see if your grandfather is ready. We don't want you missing the coach.'

She tactfully left the room and instantly big fat tears began to roll down Esme's cheeks as she clung to her brother like a limpet.

'Hey, come on now,' Gabriel soothed as he put aside his own feelings of dread and stroked her shining hair. 'It's not as if we're never going to see each other again, is it?'

They stood like that, taking comfort from each other, until Mrs Sparrow reappeared to tell him, 'He's ready, lad. Off you go and the best of luck. Make sure you write to us and let us know how you're getting on.'

Too full of emotion to speak, he merely inclined his head and as he disappeared through the door that led to the hallway, Esme began to sob.

'He'll be fine,' Mrs Sparrow told her, but she didn't sound very convinced and Esme sobbed harder than ever.

Gabriel found his grandfather standing impatiently by the front door. 'You ready?'

When Gabriel nodded, Septimus pointed to his case with the silver-topped walking stick he used. The top was in the shape of a horse's head and Gabriel guessed that it must be worth quite a lot of money.

'Good, let's be off. Time and tide wait for no man.'

Much later that morning, after taking the coach into Skegness, Gabriel followed his grandfather on a brisk walk through a labyrinth of back streets until he stopped in front of some tall wrought-iron gates, set well back from the road, beyond which stood a large, imposing building.

'This is it.' He shook the bars and instantly a hunchbacked man appeared from a small cottage at the side of the gates to allow them entry. They walked down a short tree-lined drive until they came to the house and Gabriel realised that it was much bigger than he had initially thought. The front door was in the centre, with huge mullioned windows to either side of it, and it looked bleak and unwelcoming.

Septimus rang the brass bell and it wasn't long before the door was opened by a middle-aged woman who had a face that reminded Gabriel of a pet ferret he had once owned. She was dressed from head to toe in a black bombazine gown with a heavy chatelaine about her waist, from which many keys dangled. Her dark hair, which was kissed with grey, was pulled back into a severe bun on the back of her head and everything about her looked sharp, as was her voice when she abruptly said, 'Yes?'

'I am the Reverend Silver.' Septimus removed his top hat and gave a little bow. 'I have brought my grandson who is due to begin here today.'

She removed a small notebook from the pocket of her voluminous skirt and after flicking through it for a moment, she nodded. 'Ah, yes, Gabriel Loveridge?'

'That is correct.'

She stood aside, allowing them to enter an enormous hallway and Gabriel saw at a glance that the inside of the place was almost as bleak as the outside. The only furniture was a large desk and chair standing to one side of the door but the walls were bare of pictures or mirrors of any kind.

'I am Mrs Ingles, the housemother,' she introduced herself. 'The headmaster will be expecting you, so come with me.'

They followed her obediently, until she stopped and tapped on a door, waiting until a booming voice called, 'Enter!' before opening it.

'Mr Gibbon, the Reverend Silver is here with his grandson,' she said, ushering them in.

Inside Gabriel saw a great bear of a man sitting at a desk and he couldn't help but think that with his thick mane of wiry salt-and-pepper hair, the man's name suited him. He looked like one of the gorillas he had seen pictures of in books.

71

He rose from his seat. 'Ah, Reverend. Good to see you again, and this must be Gabriel.' He motioned Septimus to a seat in front of his desk. Then he narrowed his eyes and steepled his fingers as he stared at the boy.

Gabriel felt himself shrink inside as his eyes fell on a lethal-looking split cane on the side of his desk. He looked suspiciously like another bully so Gabriel wondered if this was going to be a case of 'out of the frying pan and into the fire'.

'So, what lessons do you enjoy, my boy?' the man asked.

When Gabriel shrugged and remained mute the headmaster frowned. He was going to have a rebel on his hands with this one if he wasn't careful, he thought. He would have to show him who was the boss from the start.

'Come on, boy, speak up! Has the cat got your tongue? There must be something you're good at. What is it? English, maths?'

'Don't like either,' Gabriel muttered mutinously, crossing his arms.

The headmaster's nostrils flared as he took a deep breath. 'I see, then we'll just have to find out what you do best and concentrate on that. And stand straight while you're talking to me, boy!' He turned to Septimus. 'Right, Reverend, I believe you can safely leave the boy in our care now. We did all the paperwork and sorted the fees on your last visit so perhaps you would like to say your goodbyes?'

'Yes, of course, sir.' Septimus rose and nodded towards Gabriel and without another word left the room with a wide smile on his face. On discovering that he was a reverend, who had taken in his orphaned grandchildren, the headmaster, feeling it was his Christian duty, had vastly reduced the fees for Gabriel's schooling, so getting rid of the boy had cost Septimus very little indeed.

The second the door had closed behind him the headmaster rang a large brass bell and within seconds Mrs Ingles appeared.

'Ah, Mrs Ingles. Show this boy to his dorm and read the rules to him, would you?' Then ignoring Gabriel, he returned to the pile of paperwork on his desk.

Gabriel snatched up his case and followed the woman from the room. As they walked back along the hallway towards the grand, sweeping staircase that led up to a galleried landing, Gabriel spotted his grandfather striding away down the drive and just for an instant, he had to stifle the urge to run after him and beg him not to leave him here. But then his pride came to the fore and he straightened his back. After all, he reasoned, this place couldn't be any worse than the rectory surely? Could it?

Chapter Ten

The hallway was lined with half-glass doors and as they walked along it, Gabriel could see boys bent over papers on the desks in front of them, all dressed in the same uniform as the one he was wearing, and somehow it heartened him. He wouldn't feel so bad, surely, once he'd made a few friends. They climbed a steep staircase and at the top Mrs Ingles turned left and led him to a door almost at the end of the long passage.

'This is the dormitory where you will sleep,' she told him coldly as they entered.

Gabriel looked around in amazement. It was a very large room with a high vaulted ceiling, and along either side of it were rows of six beds with a small locker between each one. It was bitterly cold and the only light came from a skylight high in the ceiling. Each bed had a pillow and a plain grey blanket across it, apart from the one she led him to at the far end on the right of the room.

'This will be your bed and this is your locker. Make sure that your things are neatly folded away in it. There is a room inspection each morning at six thirty and if your locker is untidy or your bed isn't neatly made it will be the worse for you. You will rise at six, use the bathroom and dress before room inspection. Breakfast is downstairs in the dining room at seven o'clock prompt and if you are late, even by one minute, you will go without food until lunchtime. Bad manners to teachers and staff will not be tolerated and will result in a stay in the punishment room.' She paused here to glance at him but Gabriel's head was already spinning. It sounded as if the place was more like a prison than a school.

'Lessons will commence at eight a.m. each morning with a ten-minute break at ten thirty for refreshments. You will then return to lessons until twelve thirty when you will have half an hour for lunch before going back to lessons in the afternoon.'

'But how will I know where I have to be?' Gabriel asked, wondering how he would ever find his way about the place. It was like a maze from what he had seen of it.

'I shall supply you with a timetable telling you which room you must go to and one of the students will show you about. Now, do you have any more questions?'

He shook his head. 'I don't think so.'

'I don't think so, *Mrs Ingles*,' she snapped, making her look more like a ferret than ever. Her nose was so sharp he was sure he could have used it as a knife. 'Remember what I said, Loveridge. Respect when speaking to members of staff at all times or it will be the worse for you. Your grandfather informed us that you were an illegitimate bastard but we've dealt with your sort before. We will knock the cockiness out of you and turn you into a gentleman if it's the last thing we do! Now, get that case unpacked and sit quietly until I come back with your timetable.' She turned in a rustle of stiff bombazine skirts and slammed out of the room, leaving Gabriel to stare around resentfully.

She returned half an hour later during which time Gabriel had done as he was told and sat on the side of the bed getting colder by the minute. She had another boy of about his own age with her and after handing him a timetable she told him, 'This is William Martin. You will be sharing this room with him and for the time being I've asked him to show you around.'

The boy was tall and thin and didn't look any happier with the idea than Gabriel did but they nodded to each other all the same.

'Right, I think if you look at your timetable, you'll find you are due to go into a mathematics lesson. Make sure he knows where the classroom is, Martin.'

After she'd left, Martin sneered, 'So, you're the gyppo we have to have in here with us, are you?'

'You *what*?' Gabriel's eyes flashed with anger as his hands balled into fists, but William Martin just grinned spitefully.

'Word of who you are has gone round the school like wildfire,' he chuckled. 'And don't get thinking of getting tough with me. My father is on the board of governors and he'd have you out of here in a flash,' he taunted.

Gabriel took a deep breath. There was no point blotting his copy book on the first day, although the way he felt at that moment he would have been happy to be expelled. And to think that the boys' parents actually paid for their offspring to attend this godforsaken place!

'Just show me where I'm supposed to go,' he rasped and with an insolent grin Martin turned on his heel and led the way back downstairs.

'It's that classroom there,' he said, pointing towards a door in the long hallway, then he turned and went on to his own class.

Through the glass in the door Gabriel could see the pupils already taking their seats so he stepped inside and looked for an empty desk.

'Loveridge?' a tall, grey-haired teacher asked.

When Gabriel nodded, painfully aware that every eye in the room was trained on him, the teacher pointed to a desk. 'I'm Mr Jenkins, your maths teacher. Sit there.' He pointed to a desk quite close to his at the front of the room and Gabriel self-consciously made his way trying to ignore the titters from the other chaps. They looked to be around his age and he thought what a waste of time it was for them all to be there. Most boys his age had already left school and were working, but that was the thing with toffs, they thought they were a cut above everyone else and their parents wanted the best education for them, even though it had to be paid for. He had no doubt that this wasn't the case with his grandfather. Septimus would merely be doing it to show his congregation what a wonderful grandfather he was.

As the teacher turned to the blackboard and began to write sums on it, Gabriel cringed. It looked like a foreign language to him; he only knew the basics and this was far beyond anything he had ever been taught. At a sign from the teacher everyone bowed their heads and started to work out the answers while Gabriel stared at the blank page in front of him. It was still blank at the end of the lesson and as the teacher walked amongst the desks collecting the papers he stared down at Gabriel's and frowned.

'What's this?' he barked, and once again the rest of the class began to titter as colour flamed into Gabriel's cheeks.

'P-please, sir, I, er . . . haven't done these sort of sums before.'

The teacher's lip curled. 'What you mean is, you couldn't be bothered to try. It's only simple multiplication,' he growled, grabbing Gabriel by the back of his collar and hauling him to the front of the class. 'I was told I might have trouble with you so perhaps you should learn that I expect you to make an effort. Hold out your hand.'

Wishing the ground would open up and swallow him, Gabriel held out his hand and grit his teeth as the first stroke of the cane slammed down onto his palm. He received six of the best but not once did he murmur and despite the fact that the rest of the boys had been told he was a heathen they couldn't help but be impressed. Mr Jenkins was known for being heavy-handed when it came to the cane and had managed to produce at least a tear in most of their eyes.

'Now get out and make sure you try harder in your next lesson!'

Gabriel quietly filed out of the classroom, following the rest of the boys and feeling as if his palm was on fire. The English lesson didn't go quite so badly but he found himself with lengthy homework to do in his free time. And so, the morning progressed until, at last, Martin appeared to show him the way to the dining room.

It was a narrow, high-ceilinged room with rows of long tables and benches down either side of it. The pupils were queuing at a table at one end where a number of women were serving the dinner and he quietly joined them, feeling like a fish out of water.

Once they had all been served one of the teachers motioned for them to rise and they stood to say grace. 'For what we are about to receive may the Lord make us truly thankful, Amen.' Only then were they were allowed to eat.

The meal turned out to be just as dreary as the school. There was a spoonful of lumpy mashed potatoes, a dollop of soggy, over-cooked cabbage and some sort of indistinguishable stringy meat. Even so Gabriel had a healthy appetite and he was hungry so he forced it down and helped himself to a wedge of the grey-looking bread that was placed along the middle of the table. The pudding, a stodgy rice affair, was little better but at least he felt stronger with something in his stomach. He had almost finished when he became aware of the boy sitting opposite him, smiling at him. He was the only person in the whole place who had done anything to make him feel welcome and he smiled back.

'I'm Jeremy Mitchell,' the boy told him. 'I think we're going to be in the same dorm.'

Gabriel inclined his head. 'Good to meet you.' He noticed that some of the other boys were sniggering again but he chose to ignore them.

'Funny how retards recognise one another, ain't it?' one chap said and Gabriel had to stifle the urge to thump him.

When they rose to return to lessons he noticed that Jeremy, who was tall and thin, had a slight limp, and he realised that must be why he was teased. The boys here were nasty, he realised, but at least he seemed to have made one friend.

The rest of the afternoon passed painfully slowly but at last the lessons were over and he followed Jeremy to the day room, where there were books, a chess set on a table and various pastimes for the boys to do in their free time.

'We get an hour in here before dinner,' Jeremy informed him as they took two hard-backed seats by the window. 'Although if we have any homework we have to use this time to do it.'

Gabriel groaned. He had a stack of the stuff to get through with no idea how to do it. 'It looks like I'll be due another caning tomor-row then because I haven't a clue how to do these multiplications.'

'Let me help you,' Jeremy offered.

Doing his best to ignore the sneers of the other boys who were watching them, Gabriel made a valiant effort and, with Jeremy's help, managed to get some of it done, although he doubted it would be right. Still, he reasoned, it would be better than handing in a blank page.

'So, word has it that you are a gypsy,' Jeremy said when Gabriel had done what he could.

'My father was,' Gabriel said proudly.

'How come you ended up here?' Jeremy was curious.

Jeremy listened sympathetically as Gabriel explained his past as best he could.

'And how about you? How come you're here?' he asked when he'd finished.

Jeremy shrugged. 'I'm afraid I'm rather a disappointment to my family because I'm a bit lame. My older brother is the golden child in our house. He can do no wrong and the worst of it is he's good at everything.' He sighed. 'My father is a politician, quite well known, and we live in London.'

'Does your brother go to a boarding school as well?' Gabriel felt sorry for him.

Jeremy shook his head. 'No, he attends a private day school. I think they just shoved me here to get me out of the way. They want me to go to university when I've done here and train to become a lawyer.'

As Gabriel listened to him, he realised that Jeremy was quite a nice-looking boy. He had blue eyes and thick, dark hair that had a tendency to curl like his own.

'And is that what *you'd* like to do?'

Jeremy shook his head. 'No, actually I'd like to be a vet. I love animals but my parents won't hear of it. They want me to go into a profession they can brag about.'

A bell rang and instantly everyone made for the door. 'That's the bell for dinner,' Jeremy explained. 'Let's just hope it's a bit tastier than the slop they served us at lunchtime, eh? Although I wouldn't bank on it.'

The dinner wasn't any tastier than the lunch and by the time they were ordered to their rooms to get ready for bed, Gabriel's spirits were at their lowest ebb and he was thoroughly miserable. The school was even worse than he'd imagined it would be and he felt as if he was in the grip of a nightmare.

'Lights out is at nine o'clock,' Jeremy told him as he limped up the stairs beside him.

Gabriel groaned. 'Nine o'clock? Christ, do they think we're babies?'

Jeremy shrugged; he was used to it by now. 'Oh, and by the way, watch out for Thomas Broadhurst,' he warned. 'He's the ringleader of any bullying that goes on here and unfortunately, he's in our dorm. He's also the blue-eyed boy of most of the teachers because his father is a benefactor of the school.'

As they entered the dormitory the chatter stopped instantly and the boys all looked towards Gabriel.

'Well, well, if it isn't our own resident gyppo!' Thomas guffawed. He was a tall, well-made lad with red hair and a very cocky attitude.

'Don't let him goad you else it will be you who gets into trouble,' Jeremy hissed.

So, against his better judgement and mustering every ounce of self-control he had, Gabriel pointedly ignored Thomas and made for his bed where he began to pull his clothes off. He showed no embarrassment at having to change in front of them – he was used to stripping off and swimming in lakes and streams. Following Jeremy's advice, he folded his clothes and placed them in his locker, wondering why they were all suddenly watching him so closely. He found out as soon as he drew back the blanket and hopped into bed. The bottom sheet was soaking wet and he leapt out again as if something had bitten him, his self-control out of the window.

'Which of you bastards did this?' he growled just as a teacher walked into the room.

'Please, sir, I think the new chap has had an accident in bed,' Thomas said convincingly.

Gabriel glared at him. 'I've done no such thing. Some lousy sod has tipped something into my bed!'

'That's *enough*, Loveridge,' the teacher snapped as he crossed to the bed and looked down at the sodden sheet with disgust. 'I suggest you go to the washroom and get yourself cleaned up then get some clean bedding from the linen cupboard and get this bed made back up. *Shame* on you at your age.'

Gabriel flushed to the roots of his hair at the injustice of it all but quickly realised that it would do no good to argue so he flung himself from the room with his spare pyjamas under his arm, his face as dark as thunder.

Once he'd changed, he took clean sheets and a blanket from the linen cupboard and made for the dorm, but his humiliation wasn't over yet when he found Mrs Ingles standing at the side of his bed.

'Bed-wetting at your age,' she tutted. 'How disgraceful. If this happens again, you'll be punished severely. You're a young man not a baby!'

Gabriel gritted his teeth and got on with it, aware of Thomas's eyes boring into his back. He had to stop himself from going over to him and pummelling him to a pulp, but if what Jeremy had said was true it would only have got him into more trouble.

The minute the job was done, Mrs Ingles lifted the wet bedding and crossed to the one oil lamp in the room; she blew it out leaving them all in darkness.

'Now get to sleep all of you,' she told them sternly and the door slammed behind her.

Gabriel was actually grateful of the darkness because now, for one of the very few times in his life, he allowed himself to cry as he wondered how he was going to bear this new way of life. He missed his parents, and Esme and Gip, and the lovely life they had led, wandering from place to place free as birds. But that was all gone now and somehow he was going to have to try to adjust to this hell he found himself in.

Chapter Eleven

Back at the rectory Esme was feeling no happier as she huddled beneath the blankets in her own little bed. It had been bad enough when she and Gabriel had first arrived there and been ordered to sleep in separate rooms but at least he had only been a few rooms away. Now that he was no longer there, she felt utterly bereft. And to make things worse, she could hear the noises upstairs again. She lay listening to them for some time, then suddenly making a decision, she swung her feet onto the cold floorboards and padded towards the door.

She had heard Mrs Sparrow retire some time ago, and as her grandfather was staying in Skegness for the night, she decided that now was the time to investigate the mysterious noises. Esme was painfully aware that as miserable as she was now, her grandfather would find a way to make her life even more torturous if she was caught up there. She wasn't sure how much more she could take but she couldn't bear not knowing who or what was upstairs any longer. She held her breath as the door squeaked open, and once she was out on the landing, she crept along it as quiet as a mouse and headed for the steep, narrow staircase that led up to the attic rooms, her heart in her mouth.

At the top she found yet another landing with a number of doors leading off it on either side. She supposed that these must have been the servants' rooms in days gone by but of course they were all empty now – or were they?

There was no light on the long landing and Esme cautiously felt her way along the wall until she came to the first door. Tentatively she tried the handle and it opened immediately, squeaking so loudly that she held her breath. Would Mrs Sparrow hear it? She waited for a few moments but all was quiet so she slipped inside.

In the dim light that shone through the skylight window she could vaguely make out the shapes of boxes and old pieces of furniture that had been stored there over the years, so she continued to the next one. That contained an old bed and a chest of drawers, all covered in a thick coating of dust indicating that no one had entered it for years. She worked her way down the corridor, finding each room the same, until she came to the final door, which was securely locked. Esme pressed her ear against it but there was only silence.

'Hello . . . is anyone in there?' she hissed. Again, there was nothing, so after a time she scurried back to her bedroom as quietly as she could. Once there she sat on her bed and drew her knees up to her chin. Something wasn't right; she could sense it. She had felt a presence up there so strongly that she was sure something was wrong, but how could she get in there to see?

And then it came to her. Mrs Sparrow kept all the keys to the different rooms on hooks hanging on the back of the door in the kitchen. Could it be that the key to that room was there too? Deciding that there would never be a better time to find out she slipped noiselessly from her room once more. As she passed Mrs Sparrow's room she could hear gentle snores, and this gave her the courage to go on. Once in the kitchen she closed the door gently behind her and groping her way to the table she lit the oil lamp. Gip raised his head from his bed in front of the damped down fire and wagged his tail then settled down again as Esme headed to the pantry.

She worked her way through the keys, choosing the ones that she thought might fit before flitting back up to the attic rooms where she tried each of them in the lock. But none of them fit. She went back downstairs, feeling frustrated. Where could it be? A sudden thought came to her. Her grandfather's study! She quaked at the thought of entering it without permission, and hesitated. But then common sense took over: he was away for the whole night and provided she left everything as she found it, he need never even know she had been in there. An opportunity like this might not come again. Before she could change her mind, she set off.

Moments later she crept into his study, wrinkling her nose at the smell of stale cigars that lingered in the air. Mrs Sparrow had kept the fire alight and though it was damped down now it still threw out enough light to see so she crept towards his desk, which was covered in half-written sermons and paperwork. Cautiously she went around it and opened the first drawer. It was full of papers so she quickly went on to the next one and the next until only one drawer remained. This contained what looked like a cash box and various odds and ends, and very gently so as not to disturb anything, she put her hand in and began to feel around it. She was about to give up when her fingers stroked something metal and grasping it, she withdrew it and gasped when she saw that it was a key. Could this be the one to unlock the attic door?

Deciding that there was only one way to find out she set off again and soon she was once more outside the door. She inserted the key and turned it and to her delight she heard a click as the door unlocked. This time she had brought a candle and holding it in front of her she very slowly ventured inside. The feeling of a lost soul was stronger here, so strong that Esme could feel it almost like a physical pain.

A large brass bed stood against one wall with bedclothes crumpled on top of it. As in the other rooms, everything was coated in a thick layer of dust but it was obvious that at some stage a woman had occupied it. A discarded gown, many years out of date, was strewn across a hard-backed chair, and bottles of perfume and a silver hairbrush and comb sat on a dressing table. Lifting the brush Esme saw that it contained hairs the exact colour of her own and she wondered if perhaps this had been her mother's room at one time?

She began to move about and explore. A pile of books stood on a chest of drawers and a small escritoire and chair stood in front of a pair of curtains. As she lifted the curtain aside a cloud of dust erupted into the air and she had to pinch her nose to stop herself from sneezing. This, it seemed, was the only room on this floor that had a proper window and peeping out she realised that it overlooked the extensive gardens at the back of the rectory. Something on the escritoire caught her eye. It was a dainty white handkerchief with the initial M embroidered in the corner of it. So it hadn't been her mother's room. She wasn't sure if she was disappointed or happy about that. Slowly she carried on her search. The hairs on the back of her neck were standing on end now and as she looked towards the bed the shape of a woman with long, flowing fair hair holding her hands beseechingly out to her began to materialise. Esme gasped and nearly dropped the candle. She was used to seeing spirits but this one had clearly been very unhappy here. Perhaps that was why it couldn't move on. But what did it want of her? she wondered.

'Wh-who are you?' she whispered, but even before the words had left her mouth the vision began to fade and Esme felt weighed down with sorrow.

Keen to get out of there she backed towards the door, stopping only once she was out on the landing to relock the door. Then she fled down the stairs so quickly that the guttering candle went out and she banged against the walls of the narrow staircase, bruising herself in her haste to be away from the place. Even so she knew that she must return the key before she went to her room so she quickly made for the study and once it was returned to the drawer she charged back upstairs as if the hounds of hell were snapping at her heels, terrified that at any second Mrs Sparrow might appear. Thankfully all was quiet, but her nightmare wasn't over yet, for as she clambered into bed, shivering with cold, she saw the four young women standing in the corner staring at her balefully.

'L-leave me alone,' she implored them, tears streaming down her cheeks. She was now certain that bad things had happened in this house and she wished herself a million miles away from it. Snuggling down in the bed, she curled herself into a ball and drew the blankets over her head – it was the only way she could rid herself of the apparitions. Yet even then she could sense their presence and she lay shivering with fear until finally, as a frosty dawn broke, she fell into an exhausted sleep.

On waking, as the events of the night before rushed back, the first thing she thought of was her mother's diary. Perhaps that would hold some clue as to who had been kept in the upstairs room. She hadn't found time to read it yet but she decided that now might be a good time to begin. She crossed the room to where she had left it only to find that it was gone. She began to search, thinking that perhaps she had moved it but her search proved fruitless, and in the end, she gave up. Gabriel would have told her if he had it, so it could only have been Mrs Sparrow or her grandfather who had taken it, and without it, she wondered if she would ever find out who the sad, lonely spirit upstairs was.

Esme dressed quickly and went down to start her chores, the first being to get the fires lit. Mrs Sparrow noticed her swollen eyes and pale face when she went in to breakfast. 'Are you not feeling so well, pet?' she questioned as she placed a bowl of porridge in front of her. 'Or are you just missing Gabriel?' She had seen how close the brother and sister were and could only imagine how Esme must be feeling without him.

'A bit of both, I think.' Esme pushed the food about her dish. Suddenly curiosity got the better of her and she asked, 'Why is no one allowed on the top floor, Mrs Sparrow?'

Just for a second, she saw the woman flinch but her voice was calm when she replied, 'Because there's nothing but empty rooms up there. There's no reason to.'

Esme didn't believe her for a second. Every instinct she had was telling her that something was wrong but before she could ask any more questions the sound of the front door slamming reached them, and quick as a flash Mrs Sparrow ushered an indignant Gip outside into the yard. It was just as well because a moment later Septimus entered looking dishevelled and tired.

'Is the fire lit in my study?' he barked. When Esme nodded, he told Mrs Sparrow, 'I'll have my meal in there.' And with that he left as quickly as he had arrived.

The woman instantly fetched a large frying pan and soon the sound and smell of sizzling bacon and eggs filled the kitchen, while Esme went to fetch some dusters and beeswax polish and set off to begin her next household chores.

It was sometime later, as she was polishing the ornately carved wooden bannisters, that her grandfather appeared out of his study to ask her, 'Have you revised the psalm I gave you?'

Esme gulped. Normally she had no qualms about doing as he told her but she had been so upset about Gabriel's departure that this time she wasn't sure that she could remember it all.

'Er . . . I think so . . . or at least most of it, sir.'

His thick eyebrows beetled as he beckoned her to enter his study and her stomach sank. She'd thought she would have the rest of the day to learn it properly as he usually held their Bible studies in the evenings when they didn't attend church, but it didn't look like that was going to be the case today.

Laying her polish and cleaning rag down she followed him into his den.

'Right, let's hear it then!'

Esme took a deep breath as she tried to clear her mind of everything else apart from what he was asking. He had told her to learn Psalm 37, 'Prayer of an Afflicted Sinner', and so she cautiously began to recite.

'Oh Lord in your anger punish me not, in your wrath chastise me not.

For your arrows have sunk deep in me, and your hand has come down upon me.

There is no health in my flesh because of your indignation; there is no wholeness in my bones because of my sin.

For my iniquities have overwhelmed me; they are like a heavy burden; beyond my strength.'

Here she paused and after taking a deep breath she began on verse two.

'Noisome and festering are my sores because of my folly.
  I am stooped and bowed down profoundly; all the days I go in mourning.
  For my loins are filled with burning pains; there is no health in my flesh.
  I am numbed and severely crushed . . .'

Here her voice trailed away and to her horror she couldn't remember another word.

'*Well?* Continue!'

'Sir, I . . . sorry but I can't remember any more.'

Her eyes were great pools of fear and sorrow as she stared at his quivering moustache but he merely reached for the cane and smiled at her mockingly.

'I suppose you think that now your brother isn't here you can do as you like and disobey me!'

'Oh no, sir!' She shook her head. 'It's just that I've been busy and—'

'*Enough!*' His voice was so loud that she started. 'Hold your hand out and see what happens to children who disobey me!'

Tentatively Esme raised her small hand and seconds later the cane whistled through the air and sliced into her tender palm. She cried out in pain but he wasn't done with her yet. 'And again – and *keep* it there until I tell you to lower it, or else I shall double the punishment!'

Again and again, the cane rose and fell until Esme was sobbing with fear and pain, but then thankfully the study door opened and Mrs Sparrow stood there. She saw at a glance what was happening and frowned.

'That's quite *enough*, Septimus!'

Esme sagged as he lowered the cane to his side and Mrs Sparrow rushed to hold her up. The man's face was beetroot red with exertion and Esme's palm was criss-crossed with bleeding wounds.

'She is a *sinner*!' Septimus raged. 'I have to knock the devil out of her!'

Mrs Sparrow glared at him and tutted as she looked at Esme's poor hand. 'Don't talk such rubbish! And just how do you expect the girl to carry out the chores you set her with her hand in this state?' With a final glare at him she led Esme from the room.

Once in the kitchen she plonked the child down on a chair and hurried away to fetch a bowl of clean water and some rags. Esme sobbed all the harder and winced as the woman cleaned her hand as gently as she could and by the time she had finished and bandaged it there were tears in Mrs Sparrow's eyes too. 'I just wish . . .' she began, but quickly clamped her mouth shut. She had clearly had second thoughts about whatever it was she had been about to say.

'I *hate* it here!' Esme said suddenly and Mrs Sparrow started although she could quite understand why the child felt as she did. If only Esme could have known it, she would have liked Esme to get away from there but she had no idea how to help her.

'Now don't take on so,' she soothed as Esme continued to sob, but her words fell on deaf ears, because without another word the girl stood and fled to her room where she lay on her bed longing for her brother and the carefree life they had once known.

Before they knew it, they were nearing the end of January and Esme was eagerly looking forward to seeing Gabriel at Easter. Then one morning she woke to find blood on her nightgown. She was well aware what this meant; she and her parents had lived in such close proximity that she knew all about the courses women had each month so it held no fear for her, but it would mean she would have to ask Mrs Sparrow for some cloths that she could use.

'Oh, you're growing up, me little maid,' Mrs Sparrow muttered when she told her. She had grown fond of Esme and enjoyed her company, especially since Septimus had taken to staying out more of late. She went to fetch Esme some suitable rags and the girl took them to her room and shoved them into a drawer.

As yet she still hadn't removed any of the things her mother had left behind when she ran away with her father. It comforted her to have them about her and now more than ever Esme could understand why she had left and what a miserable childhood she must have had.

Thankfully there had been no more canings as bad as the one after which her palm had taken days to heal and Esme had an idea that she had Mrs Sparrow to thank for that. Even so, she was thoroughly miserable. All she had to look forward to were the letters she received from Gabriel each week, which came as regularly as clockwork. He was always careful not to let his little sister know how hard he was finding it at school for fear of upsetting her, but because she knew him so well, she could read between the lines. Gabriel had always been a free spirit and she knew that he must be feeling like a bird trapped in a cage, but there was nothing she could do to help him.

In truth things weren't a lot better for her. Each day passed in monotonous activity. Chores in the morning, learning a piece from the Bible during the afternoon, then visits to the church or Bible study with her grandfather each evening. The only bright spots were when she saw the Fitzroy family at church and then she would examine the girls' clothes enviously. They looked like princesses in their velvets and satins but the older of the two, who Esme had discovered was called Olivia and who seemed to be the same age as her, always had a smile for her. The younger girl's name was Amelia and the older boy, who looked to be about seventeen was Luke. He was very handsome and friendly too and Esme felt sad for him when she heard Mrs Sparrow and her grandfather saying one morning that, like Gabriel, he was about to be sent away to a university somewhere.

To her delight, they attended the church that evening and so for most of the boring sermon Esme was able to admire their outfits. As always, her grandfather caught the Fitzroys at the church doors as they were leaving and while the two men were speaking, she smiled at Olivia who smiled back.

'How are you settling in here?' Olivia asked pleasantly.

'Oh . . . quite well, thank you.' Esme felt that she couldn't tell her the truth for fear of it getting back to her grandfather.

'Good, and have you started to attend the village school yet?'

Esme shook her head. It was something her grandfather kept promising he would arrange but as yet he hadn't bothered to, although Esme would have welcomed the time she could spend away from the rectory.

'That's a pity.' Olivia gave her a dazzling smile. 'It's a shame you can't come and have your lessons with me at the hall.' She pulled a face. 'Amelia and I are schooled at home so we don't get to see many young people our own age. I shall have to have a word with Mama.'

She inclined her head and moved on to stand with her parents as Esme stared after her open-mouthed. She doubted her grandfather or Olivia's parents would allow such a thing, but imagine being able to have lessons in such a place! She sighed before hurrying outside to catch up with Mrs Sparrow, who was already on her way back to the rectory.

Chapter Twelve

'Loveridge, get here *now*!'

Gabriel sighed as the English teacher stared at him across the heads of the other boys in the class. The man was looking through the homework they had handed in that morning and as usual Gabriel guessed that the teacher had found his unacceptable.

He stood up reluctantly and began to walk through the desks. A titter went up around the room and his face flamed, but he kept his eyes firmly fixed on the teacher's desk. Mr Perkins seemed to take pleasure in belittling him, but then so did most of the other teachers and he was getting used to it now.

He was so intent on looking ahead that he didn't notice someone stick their foot out and suddenly he went flying and sprawled in an undignified heap on the floor, cracking his arm painfully on the way down. Glancing to the side he saw Thomas Broadhurst grinning and it was all he could do to stop himself from punching him in the face there and then. But he knew that if he did, he would be in even more trouble, so gathering what little dignity he still had, he leapt to his feet and continued.

'Clumsy *as well* as stupid!' the teacher roared, adding to Gabriel's humiliation. 'What do you call this? A two-year-old could do better!' He slammed Gabriel's homework down in front of him. 'You will return here after lessons this afternoon and miss dinner while you do the whole lot again.'

'Yes ... *sir*!' Gabriel ground out through gritted teeth. How could he tell the man that most of the homework he set him was like looking at a foreign language and he had no idea how to do it? Lifting the book he made his way back to his seat, aware that every pair of eyes in the room was on him. But at least he had avoided a caning ... for now. It seemed that the teachers here were as keen on the cane as his grandfather had been. Only the night before he had lain in bed listening to the snores of the other lads and considered running away. It would have been so easy to sneak off and make his own way in the world. The only thing that stopped him was Esme. Were he to go she would feel totally abandoned and he felt responsible for her. After all, he reasoned, he would be sixteen years old in a few weeks and they couldn't keep him at the school forever. He'd be old enough to find a job then. Most of the lads there would leave school at eighteen to begin work in their father's businesses. Others would go to university, but as he was well aware, he would never be academically capable of getting a place so he could return to the rectory where at least he could ensure that Esme was all right. He'd get a job and once he had saved enough, they could run away and find a little place to rent. But that was still a long way off – or at least it felt that way – so for now he would just have to put up with the jibes and the bullying for her sake.

When they left the room to attend the next lesson, he turned on Thomas Broadhurst in the corridor and hissed, 'I know that it was you who legged me up in there, Broadhurst, and you're going to be sorry!'

'*Ooh!* Hark at the gyppo playing the big man,' Thomas taunted as he poked him viciously in the chest. His little gang of followers giggled. 'It's a shame his brain isn't as big as his mouth, ain't it, lads?'

Gabriel roared and lunged at him, landing a resounding thump on his nose just as Mr Perkins exploded from the classroom at the sound of the disturbance.

'Just what *the hell* is going on out here?' He took in the situation at a glance, noting Thomas's bloody nose and Gabriel towering over him. He pointed a wavering finger towards the headmaster's office. 'You, get to Mr Gibbon's office right now. It'll be six of the best for you, my lad. We don't want this sort of heathen behaviour in this school.'

'P-please, sir, I reckon he's broken my nose,' Thomas whined pathetically.

'But he started it,' Gabriel objected.

The teacher nodded towards the two boys standing closest to Broadhurst. 'Get him up and take him to the sick room. The nurse will see to him. And *you*, come with me!'

Minutes later Gabriel was facing the headmaster over his desk. 'How *dare* you fight in my school?' the headmaster said ominously quietly as he lifted the lethal-looking split cane. 'Your grandfather will hear of this make no mistake. Now hold out your hand!'

Gabriel's palms hadn't healed from the last caning he'd endured and by the time he left the office they felt as if they were on fire and tears were pricking at the back of his eyes. He was a strong, well-made lad and knew that he could have downed the headmaster with one blow, but he also knew that this would only have got him into yet more trouble so he'd taken his punishment without a word, although he felt sick at the injustice of it all. It appeared that because the majority of the boys had wealthy parents who paid a high fee to keep them there, they could do no wrong, whereas he was worthless.

The day continued to get worse when he arrived late at his next class and was given a hundred lines to do, and by the time lessons finished he was at his lowest ebb. His hands stung so badly that he could barely hold his pen but he still had to report back to Mr Perkins to redo the homework.

'I'll look at it tonight,' the man told him shortly when Gabriel had laid his second attempt on his desk. 'Now get yourself to the bathroom, and when you've bathed you can go straight to bed – there'll be no meal for you this evening. Just think yourself lucky you haven't ended up in the punishment room, boy!'

Gabriel made his way upstairs and along the landing that led to the bathroom. This consisted of a number of baths in a row, with a pipe leading into each one that connected to a large copper in the kitchen that supplied them with hot water. When the boys had bathed, they could pull the plug and the water would drain through a pipe in the bottom of the bath to the yards at the back of the school. His stomach was rumbling by that time but trying not to think of it he quickly half-filled the bath with warm water and stripped off. His hand stung as he lowered himself in but he tried to think of other things as he quickly began to soap himself and wash his hair, which had grown considerably since Mrs Sparrow had cut it.

Suddenly the door opened and Thomas Broadhurst, along with half a dozen of his gang, appeared. His nose was swollen and already both of his eyes were dark with bruises. 'Here he is, lads.' Thomas grinned. 'Shall we help him get clean?'

Gabriel gripped the sides of the bath to haul himself out but before he could they were on him like a pack of wolves, and although he was strong, he was no match for six of them. Rough hands pushed him beneath the water and he began to choke as he thrashed about wildly. Just when he thought he was going to drown they hauled him up again and dragged him out, sending a cascade of water onto the floor. Broadhurst came towards him, wielding a pair of sharp scissors and he knew immediately what they were planning.

'I think his unruly mop of curls needs a little tidy up, what do you think, lads?' Thomas asked spitefully and they all laughed.

With five of them holding him down Gabriel was powerless to help himself as he lay naked while Thomas snatched at a handful of Gabriel's hair and began to hack at it until hair was floating all around him in the pools of water on the floor.

'There, that's better, isn't it?' Thomas chuckled breathlessly and at a sign from him the boys released Gabriel who scrambled to his knees and tentatively raised a hand to touch his shorn locks. Chunks of hair stood untidily across his scalp but the boys weren't finished with him yet and they began to kick and thump him. Gabriel lashed out, trying to defend himself, but it was useless. Then one of the boy's boots caught him squarely in the mouth and he tasted blood before spitting a back tooth out.

'All right, I reckon he's had enough for now,' Thomas told them with an evil grin. The boys dispersed, laughing amongst themselves, leaving Gabriel curled in a ball on the wet floor clutching his ribs.

After a time, he pulled himself up and grabbing his clothes he got dressed. He was aching in every limb but rage pumped through him. One day they'd pay for what they'd done, especially Broadhurst, he promised himself as the bathroom door squeaked open once more. Clenching his hands into fists he turned, thinking they were coming back to give him another beating but it was Jeremy Mitchell who quietly entered.

'Good Lord, what have they done to you, man?' He looked horrified as he saw the blood on Gabriel's chin and the hair all over the floor.

'I'm all right,' Gabriel told him as he leaned heavily against the wall. Right now, he was so weary that he couldn't have fought them anyway.

'Come on, let's get you down to the sick bay. They should be punished for what they've done to you. They're nothing but a bunch of bloody bullies!' Jeremy stepped forward to help him but Gabriel held his hand out to stop him.

'No, no, I'm all right. I just want to go to bed.'

Jeremy fished in his pocket and self-consciously withdrew a hunk of bread and cheese. 'I know Perkins wouldn't let you have anything to eat so I brought you these. It's not much but it should keep the wolf at bay till the morning,' he told him quietly.

That one little act of kindness was Gabriel's undoing and he started to cry. 'I *hate* those bastards,' he cursed as tears rolled down his cheeks, and at that moment, he wondered how much longer he could bear being there, even for Esme's sake. Surely even prison couldn't be worse than this, he reasoned.

Side by side they made their way back to the dormitory and Jeremy stood silently as Gabriel painfully undressed and got into his pyjamas. That was another thing he hated about the place. At home in the vardo, and even at his grandfather's, he had always slept in nothing more than his underpants and he hated the restriction of clothes in bed.

'Here, have a drink, it'll take the taste of the blood away.' Jeremy handed him a glass of water and Gabriel drank it thirstily before turning over and trying to lose himself in sleep. His only consolation was that he knew in Jeremy he had at least one friend.

The next morning when he woke to the sound of the bell one eye was black and blue and completely closed and his face and body were covered in cuts and bruises. He suspected that he had at least one cracked rib because it was painful to breathe and he was limping, but even so he still refused to go to the sick bay. If any of the teachers noticed the state he was in while in the dining room or during lessons not one of them commented on it. And so another long day began.

Chapter Thirteen

On a cold night late in January as Esme was getting ready for bed, the door creaked open and, startled, she whirled about holding the gown she had just taken off in front of her to protect her modesty. To her horror she saw her grandfather standing there with a simpering smile on his face and she blushed.

'Hello, my dear. I thought I'd just come in and wish you goodnight.'

Esme gulped. This room was the only place she had ever felt safe from him and now he was invading that too. What could he want? And why was he being nice to her?

She watched him warily as he crossed to the dressing table and lifted the silver hairbrush that had belonged to her mother.

'Constance liked pretty things, as did her mother before her. Do you like pretty things, Esme?'

'I, er . . . I don't know,' she faltered.

'Hmm, I thought perhaps you'd like a pretty gown?' He laid the brush down and advanced towards her.

Esme began to shake, holding the gown tighter across her developing breasts.

'You look very much like your mother did at your age,' he said softly as he began to stroke the soft skin on her bare shoulder.

It took all her control not to flinch away as one of his fat fingers traced its way down to her breast. And then he shocked her when he asked, 'Did your father ever teach you how to please a man?'

'*NO!*' She stepped back, clutching the gown even more tightly to her. He was frightening her.

'Hmm, well he should have. You'll have a husband one day and it will be your job to keep him happy. Have you started your courses yet, girl?'

Esme blushed to the roots of her hair. 'Y-yes, just recently,' she answered in a small voice.

'Good, good, that's the first sign that you are becoming a woman. The lessons can begin very soon now,' he told her. He turned and quietly crossed to the door where he paused to tell her, 'I shall ask Mrs Sparrow to take you into Skegness with her the next time she goes, so you can choose the material for a pretty gown from the dressmaker's. All I ask in return is that when the time is right you be nice to me.'

As the door closed softly behind him, Esme's mouth dropped open. What did he mean, be nice to him? She was always respectful and nice. She wouldn't have dared be any other way. Her grandfather put the fear of God into her, could he have known it. Dropping onto the bed she shook her head, loneliness coursing through her. She missed her parents and Gabriel desperately and at that moment she would willingly have sold her soul to the devil if she could have gone back to how things had been when they were all together.

As she sat there the four girls appeared in the corner of the room and with a little cry Esme flung her gown aside and slid into bed to hide beneath the blankets. Tomorrow night, she promised herself, she would put a chair beneath the door handle to try and stop her grandfather from entering her room again. She lay tensely, listening to the sound of an owl hooting in the tree outside and shivered as she thought back to what her father had told her: 'The hoot of an owl is a premonition of a death.' She shuddered from top to toe, perhaps soon there would be another lost soul to haunt her, but who would it be?

'You're looking a bit peaky this morning, pet,' Mrs Sparrow observed when she appeared in the kitchen the next morning. 'You're not sickening for something, are you?' She crossed the room to feel Esme's forehead but the girl didn't appear to have a temperature.

'No . . . I just didn't sleep too well,' Esme muttered. She had been up before the larks and had already lit the fires in the kitchen and her grandfather's study, and she was exhausted.

'Hmm, still missing your brother, are you?' the woman said sympathetically. 'Never mind, not too long till Easter now and then he'll be home for a few days.'

Esme nodded as she called Gip to come outside with her while she fetched some wood for the fire. It was another of the jobs that Gabriel had done that now fell to her.

For the rest of the morning, she did her chores then after lunch she sat down to write Gabriel a letter and read the psalm her grandfather had given her to revise. She was still feeling disturbed about him coming to her room the night before and had felt tempted to tell Mrs Sparrow. But then she thought better of it; after all, he hadn't actually done anything wrong apart from touch her in what she felt was a rather inappropriate way, and hopefully he wouldn't do it again, so there seemed no point in causing a ruckus over it. There was enough of that in this house as it was.

She was sweeping the landing later that afternoon when suddenly she sensed a presence. The best of the light had already gone from the afternoon and as she whipped around and stared fearfully towards the attic stairs, she saw the same woman she had glimpsed in the attic room standing on the bottom step. She was clad in a long voluminous nightgown trimmed with lace at the neck and the sleeves, and as Esme watched her, she held her hands out beseechingly towards her.

'Wh-what can I do for you?' Esme whispered as goosebumps stood to attention on her arms. The poor woman looked distraught but already the image was fading, leaving Esme feeling frightened. Something very bad must have happened up in that room. Perhaps the woman had worked here in the past and died up there? But that seemed unlikely when she thought of the laced-trimmed nightgown the woman had been wearing. It was unlikely a servant could have afforded that. So who was she? If she had been a former lady of the house, surely she would have had a room on the first floor.

Suddenly making a decision, she laid down her brush and went downstairs to the kitchen where she found Mrs Sparrow rolling pastry for the meat and potato pie they would be having for their evening meal.

'Mrs Sparrow . . .' Esme chose her words carefully. 'I think Gabriel told you that I am able to see spirits.'

Mrs Sparrow shuddered and looked concerned. She didn't like anything supernatural – it gave her the collywobbles.

'Well, since I've been here, I have twice seen a woman on the stairs leading to the attic.' She decided not to admit that the first time she had seen her was up in one of the rooms because she had been forbidden to go there.

The colour drained out of the older woman's face and she leaned heavily on the edge of the table leaving floury handprints. 'Oh yes . . .' Mrs Sparrow said cautiously. 'And what did this woman look like?'

Esme chewed on her lip as she thought how best to describe her. 'She was probably a little taller than you, and slim, and she had lovely long blonde hair. Oh, and she was wearing a pretty white nightgown. But I have a feeling she was very unhappy when she died. That would be why she hasn't passed over. Sometimes if people don't have a peaceful death, they find themselves trapped here. And that's not all, there are four other younger women here too. There were only two when I first arrived and then another two joined them. I feel that they're all trying to tell me something but I don't know what it is. I just know that something very bad must have happened here. This isn't a happy house.'

'I've never heard such a load of rubbish in me whole life.' Mrs Sparrow snatched up the rolling pin and waved it angrily at Esme, although she was clearly very upset. 'And I'd rather you didn't talk about such things. It isn't holy and there's no such things as spirits and ghosts. Now go and get on with your work, I don't want to hear another word about it, do you hear me?' She turned back to the job in hand and began to roll the pastry as if her life depended on it.

Esme opened her mouth to say something else but thinking better of it she turned slowly and went to finish cleaning the landing.

She hadn't managed to revise all of the psalm her grandfather had set her but when she stumbled over the words that evening, to her surprise he merely smiled. 'Don't worry about it, my dear,' he said as he twiddled his grey moustache. 'Perhaps you'll be able to remember more of it tomorrow. But now I really must go. I shan't be home tonight; I have an appointment with someone.'

Esme was only too happy to escape his company while the going was good and she shot away. Minutes later she heard her grandfather leave. It was eight o'clock at night and pitch black as she slipped out of the front door and hurried around to the back of the house where she could stare up at the attic window. Sure enough, there was the fair-haired woman staring down at her. Esme gulped as the woman began to point beyond her to the orchard. Turning slowly, she walked towards it and was soon beneath the shelter of the leafless apple and pear trees. She had the strangest feeling that the woman had been trying to show her something – but what? It was so dark that she could scarcely see a hand in front of her but she stumbled on until she came to a stream that ran through the centre of the orchard. There, something told her to stop and closing her eyes she suddenly saw in her mind a vision of a dark shape digging. Her eyes snapped open but there was nothing to see. It had started to drizzle and was bitterly cold so pulling her shawl more tightly about her, she headed back, determined to come back the next day in the daylight.

She had just crept back into the house when her grandfather suddenly appeared like yet another apparition from his study and she almost jumped out of her skin.

'Oh . . . sir, I thought you'd gone out,' she said with a catch in her voice.

'So I had, but then I realised that I'd forgotten my keys and I had to come back for them,' he told her, his eyes as hard as flint. 'What were you doing wandering about outside at night in the dark? Meeting someone, were you? A boy, perhaps?'

'No, of course not.' She shook her head. 'I just thought I'd get a bit of fresh air before I retired to bed so I went for a stroll in the orchard.'

'And why there?' he barked, glaring at her suspiciously.

'Well, I . . . I don't know really,' she said lamely.

'I suggest in future you do not leave the house without my permission. Especially in the dark. Is that quite clear?'

Esme was quaking in her boots – he could always have that effect on her. She nodded and he pointed towards the stairs. 'Now go to bed and I don't want to hear another peep out of you until the morning.'

'Yes, sir.' Esme bobbed her knee and without even waiting to take her boots off she shot off to do as she was told.

Her dreams were troubled yet again that night. In them she could see the figure of a man furiously digging a deep hole but he had his back to her and she couldn't see his face. And then the woman in the window appeared standing behind him, and she was crying. Esme woke abruptly in a tangle of blankets with sweat on her brow and her heart thumping. It was still pitch black outside but she crossed to the window and stared down over the orchard. It was clear to her now that the woman, whoever she was, was trying to tell her something and one way or another Esme was determined to find out what it was.

The next morning her spirits lifted slightly when the postman delivered her weekly letter from Gabriel.

'Another one from your brother, is it?' Mrs Sparrow asked as she carried it back into the kitchen.

'Yes. There's one here for Grandfather and this looks like one from the school too.' Esme could hardly wait to open it but there were jobs to be done first so she stuffed it into the pocket of her apron for later. At least it would give her something to look forward to, to break the monotony.

Esme didn't get a chance to read her letter until after lunch when Mrs Sparrow left to arrange the greenery for the church service that evening.

Dear Esme,

As always I ope this letter finds yu well. It's still bitterly cold ain't it, but at least the snow as gone now. How is our Gip? Poor old chap must be feeling the cold at is age but I know you'll be taking gud care of im.

I'm afraid I got into a bit of bother this week. Me an another chap were caught fightin and I got sent to the punishment room overnight with no dinner an no breakfast. To be onest it weren't much of a loss, the food ere is terrible, but I don't suppose I shuld complain. I allus eat it anyway cos its better than going hungry. As always the other lad Thomas Broadhurst got off wiout even a tellin off. Talk about teacher's blue eyed boy. It's probably cos is dad is rich an on the school board of governors.

I'm afraid I'm still struglin with me lessons an fear our grandfather is wasting is money keepin me ere. As our mammy allus said 'you can't make a silk purse out of a sow's ear!' It's funny that you'd probably enjoy all the learnin, you allus were cleverer than me. I suppose alf of the battle is wantin to learn but I don't. I'd much rather be out in the fresh air.

Anyway, not too long till easter now an then I'll be ome for a few days. I can't wait to see you again an hope that mean old sod of a granfather of ours is bein kind to you.

I miss you but keep yur chin up, this won't be forever,
Yur luving brother
Gabriel xx

Esme folded the letter and put it in her pocket, sniffing back a tear. For the first time in his letters Gabriel had sounded really unhappy and she wondered what the punishment room he had spoken of was? It certainly didn't sound very nice and, try as she might, she couldn't imagine him stuck in a classroom from dawn till dusk. Gabriel had always taken after their father in as much as he was never happier than when he was outside. Still, as he had said, it wouldn't be forever and she could start counting down the weeks now until he was home.

The nightmare she had had about the man digging in the orchard was still haunting her but Mrs Sparrow had kept her so busy all morning that there had been no chance to go and explore to see if she could discover anything. Looking at the list of jobs the woman had left her to do in the afternoon there would be no chance to go later either, so with a sigh she set about them.

That evening Esme attended the service at the church with Mrs Sparrow and she was disappointed that there was no sign of the Fitzroys. Luke had recently celebrated his eighteenth birthday and gone to start at university, which meant that only the girls and their parents attended now but she still looked forward to seeing them, especially Olivia who always had a cheery smile for her.

The sermon was as boring as always and Esme was surprised to see that there were very few people attending it. But then Mrs Sparrow had told her that there was an influenza type illness sweeping through the village and almost half the villagers were down with it. Her grandfather seemed to be constantly out of the house at present, visiting the sick and the elderly who were dying.

On the short walk back to the rectory Mrs Sparrow didn't say a word – she was still annoyed with Esme for saying that she had felt a bad presence in the house. Once back, Esme quickly stoked the fire in the kitchen, then fetched some more logs to do the same in the reverend's study. He was sitting at his desk going through his correspondence when she entered, and had just picked up the letter that had come from the school. 'This appears to be from your brother's school. I wonder what they could be writing to me about?'

As Esme piled the logs onto the fire, he slit the envelope open and began to read.

'It appears that your brother is behaving like a heathen,' he ground out, his face red with anger. 'Not that I should have expected any better from him. What can you expect when he's come from gypsy scum! It says he's been fighting. I'll give him fighting, showing me up like that.'

'He is *not* gypsy scum,' Esme said loudly before she could stop herself.

Quick as a flash he was beside her and before she knew what was happening he'd boxed her ear so soundly that she almost flew across the room. She landed heavily against the wall sending a chair flying across the floor and for a moment her ear rang and she felt sick.

Suddenly he came over and helped her up. 'I'm so sorry, my dear. I shouldn't have done that. It's only natural that you should defend your brother. But you must see it from my point of view. I sent him there to learn his lessons and good manners but it seems that he's doing neither.'

The door banged open and Mrs Sparrow appeared. She had heard the commotion all the way from the kitchen. She looked from one to the other of them and took in the situation at a glance. Septimus had obviously lost his temper and hit the girl – there was no surprise there. But what did surprise her was that he was now trying to help her up and apologise, and for some reason that worried her more than the blow he had dealt her. Why was he suddenly trying to stay on the right side of the girl when he had only ever treated her with contempt before?

'Come away out of here,' she ordered Esme, and turning her attention to the reverend she nodded to the pile of logs that had rolled across the floor. 'You'd best get those picked up and stacked on the hearth,' she told him shortly. 'Afore you trip over one and hurt yourself.' Then she took Esme's elbow and led her back to the kitchen.

Esme was still a little wobbly on her feet and she was shaking from the blow but after a cold drink of water and sitting down for a moment she started to feel better.

'All right?' Mrs Sparrow looked concerned.

'I'm fine. I think I'll just take Gip out for his last walk now and then get myself off to bed.'

She fetched her shawl from the hook on the back of the door, then calling Gip to heel, she set off into the dark night. She knew that she would be in trouble with her grandfather for leaving the house without his permission should he find out, but at that moment she didn't care.

As always when she had the chance she made for the beach and once there, she settled down in front of the sand dunes and burying her face in her hands she began to cry. Clearly worried to see her so upset, Gip began to lick her face and placing her arms about his neck she hugged him to her.

'If only we could turn the clock back to happier times, eh, boy? It's just you and me now till Gabriel comes home at Easter.'

He wagged his tail as if he understood what she was saying and they sat huddled together for some time, each drawing comfort from the other, until the cold set in and she rose to lead them back to the rectory. She took the back way and as they walked through the orchard she glanced up and sure enough there was the face at the window again staring down at her. Esme quickly lowered her eyes, every hair on her body standing to attention. Now it happened every time she ventured through the orchard and she had a terrible feeling that something bad had happened here too.

Half an hour later she went to her room, thankful that she seemed to be alone this evening, with no sign of the poor girls who had been haunting her. Her ear was still smarting from the blow she had taken earlier so she hastily changed and hopped between the chill white sheets.

Once again, her sleep was riddled with bad dreams. The fair-haired woman kept appearing to her and each time she did she tried to lead her towards the orchard. Eventually Esme started awake to find herself drenched in sweat with tears on her cheeks.

'Oh, Mammy, where are you?' she whispered to the empty room. 'I need you.' But there was nothing to be heard but the sound of the wind rattling the old wooden window frames and eventually she fell asleep again.

This time her dreams took her back to happier times. She was in the vardo with her parents and Gabriel and they were all smiling, their stomachs comfortably full of the delicious rabbit stew her mother had cooked for them. The sound of pans rattling in the kitchen woke her, and she groaned, reluctant to leave her dream behind. It had been so real that for a moment she was disorientated as she stared around her mother's old room. But then everything rushed back and her heart sank as the happy feeling dissipated.

Wearily she dragged her legs to the edge of the bed and put her feet onto the cold floorboards. It sounded like Mrs Sparrow was already up and about, which meant she must have overslept, so no doubt she would get into trouble for that now too. Sighing she quickly dressed and set off down the stairs to begin another lonely day.

Chapter Fourteen

'I'm sorry to tell you this, Reverend Silver, but if your grandson's behaviour doesn't improve soon, I shall have no choice but to expel him. He is very disruptive and seems to be making no headway in his lessons whatsoever.'

Septimus stared back at the headmaster across the desk, his face red with anger. The report he had just been given was appalling and had Gabriel been there at that moment he would have felt like throttling him. He had come to the school the day after he had received the headmaster's letter and now he wasn't sure what to do. The last thing he wanted was to have Gabriel back living under his roof full-time, so he supposed he had no choice but to try and pour oil on troubled waters.

'I cannot apologise enough, sir,' he said sadly. 'But perhaps it's just taking him a while to settle down because of all he has gone through. I think I explained when I enrolled him here that he had recently lost his mother. Unfortunately, my daughter and I were estranged when she eloped with the boy's father. A most unsuitable man, I can assure you, so he wasn't the best role model for the child. Of course, even then when Gabriel and his sister arrived orphaned and homeless on my doorstep, I took them in out of the goodness of my heart. I had hoped that your wonderful school would teach him how to behave. I know what strict standards you work to here and that is why I chose this school, sir.'

The headmaster preened. 'Hmm, well in view of what you've told me, I am prepared to overlook his behaviour up to now,' he agreed. 'We have the children of many influential people at this school and they expect their offspring to mix with similar boys. But perhaps it would be worth you speaking to him before you leave to try and explain to him how important it is that our pupils are responsible for their own actions at all times.'

'Of course. I will be only too happy to do just that,' Septimus simpered.

The headmaster lifted the small bell on his desk and rang it. Soon there was a tap on the door and the housemother entered the room.

'Ah, Mrs Ingles. Could you show the reverend to the day room and take Gabriel Loveridge in to see him?'

'Yes, sir, of course.'

Septimus rose and after inclining his head to the headmaster followed Mrs Ingles to the day room where she left him while she went to fetch Gabriel.

The boy found him with his hands clasped behind his back staring out of the window. As his grandfather turned, one look at his face told him that he was in for a roasting.

Once Mrs Ingles had left, Septimus glared at Gabriel wondering who in the world had given the boy such a terrible haircut. It stood up in chunks all over his head and his eye was now yellow with faded bruises.

'What have you got to say for yourself, boy?' he snapped.

Gabriel merely shrugged, his face set in a defiant mask. He hoped that his grandfather was going to tell him that he had been expelled. Even having to go back to the rectory would be preferable to having to stay there.

'I believe you have been fighting?'

Gabriel shook his head. 'You could hardly call it that,' he snapped back. 'I was set on by a bunch of chaps in the bathroom. They've made my life hell ever since I've been here and they beat me up and did this to me!' He stabbed a finger towards his hair, angry again at the injustice of it all. They had started the ruckus but he was supposed to take all the blame.

'You must have done *something* to them to bring it about,' Septimus ground out.

'No, I did *not*!' Gabriel hotly denied.

His grandfather merely stared back at him unsympathetically. 'Well, you'd better make your mind up to do better in future else you'll have me to deal with.' Septimus leaned aggressively towards him, his lips curled back from his teeth in a growl. 'And believe me, if this happens again, I will make what you say the boys did to you look like nothing! I have better things to do than keep running back and forth because you don't know how to behave. If I hear one more bad word about you, I shall request that you stay here for extra tutoring during the Easter holidays. Is that quite clear? Now get out of my sight and pray that your next report is better than the one I just received.'

Gabriel's shoulders sagged. So, he wasn't being expelled and if he didn't take what the other boys were dishing out to him, he wouldn't even get to see his sister at Easter. His heart sank, it was so unfair. His grandfather had got him over a barrel and he knew it.

Septimus made for the door without another word and Gabriel had no choice but to slowly make his way back to his history class.

It was that evening in the dining hall that he decided it was time to seek revenge, starting with Broadhurst. They had all poured themselves cups of stewed tea from the large brown teapot and then gone off to fetch their meal. He waited till he was alone and then quickly emptied half a pot of pepper into Broadhurst's mug and gave it a quick stir before joining the end of the queue. Word had gone round that Gabriel's grandfather had visited him and given him a roasting and Broadhurst had been sniggering and sneering at him all day, and Gabriel had had enough.

By the time Gabriel was served, most of the boys were back at the table and there wasn't a lot of choice of food left, but it was a small price to pay if he could bring Broadhurst even a moment of discomfort. Once they were all seated and had said grace, they began their meal. Broadhurst was in fine spirits and grinned at the poor selection of food on Gabriel's plate but Gabriel ignored him and sure enough, soon after Broadhurst took a long swig from his cup. The next second his face looked as if it was on fire as he clutched at his throat and began to choke.

'What's wrong along there?' Mr Tames, one of the teachers, shouted, hurrying over to him.

Broadhurst was struggling to get his breath and could only point at his cup.

The teacher sniffed it. 'Hmm, you must have tipped pepper instead of sugar into it.'

Eyes streaming, Broadhurst shook his head, still gasping for breath, and it was all Gabriel could do to stop himself from laughing aloud.

'You'd best leave the room, boy,' Mr Tames told him, none too pleased. 'You're disrupting the meal. Go and get yourself a drink of water.'

Broadhurst staggered away, still clutching his throat, which felt as if it was on fire and as Gabriel glanced up, he caught Jeremy's eye. He had guessed that it was Gabriel who was responsible and they grinned at each other.

After the meal, while the other boys went to the day room, Gabriel slipped away to their dormitory. He was back in minutes and luckily it seemed that no one had missed him.

'Well done,' Jeremy whispered. 'Serves the vicious blighter right.' Broadhurst had ended up in the sick bay, still struggling to breathe, and Gabriel was just sad that he hadn't choked to death.

His next act of revenge came at bedtime.

'Ugh!' one of the boys shrieked, leaping out of his bed. 'My bed is sopping wet!' It was the boy who had wielded the scissors and hacked at Gabriel's hair.

'So is mine,' another shout went up from Thomas.

'And mine.' This was from the boy who had dislodged Gabriel's tooth when he had viciously kicked him in the mouth.

The door was suddenly flung open and Mrs Ingles appeared. When she saw what was going on she was incensed. Her eyes went straight to Gabriel and Jeremy and she glared at them suspiciously.

'Who is responsible for this?' When no one answered she shook her head. 'Right . . . you will all strip the beds down to the mattress and remake them with fresh sheets from the linen room. And don't think this is the end of it. I will *not* tolerate this sort of tomfoolery and I shall be reporting you all to the headmaster first thing in the morning.'

Grim-faced, the boys filed out of the room after her, casting filthy looks towards Gabriel. They all guessed that he was responsible but they had no proof so could do nothing about it.

'I bet you any money it was him that put the pepper in Broadhurst's tea as well,' one of them grumbled as they trailed off to the linen room. 'Poor bugger's having to stay in the sick room tonight!'

'We'll have to keep an eye on him in future,' another agreed.

Miserably they collected their dry linen while Gabriel and Jeremy lay in bed chuckling. Revenge was sweet, but Gabriel wasn't done with them yet, not by a long shot. This was war! But he would play it their way and make sure that this time none of the blame could be attached to him!

Chapter Fifteen

It was early in February, just as Esme was dropping off to sleep one night, that she heard her bedroom door creaking open. Instantly she was wide awake and gazed towards it. Just as she had feared she saw her grandfather standing there holding a candle but before she could say a word, he had entered the room with a sickly smile on his face and closed the door softly behind him. He had not tried to enter the room since that first time and so she had been lulled into a false sense of security but now she fervently wished that she'd continued to put the chair beneath the door handle. But it was too late for regrets now, and as he moved towards her, she shrank back in the bed.

'Good evening, my dear. I trust you have had a good day?'

She opened her mouth to reply but the words seemed to stick in her throat so she merely nodded numbly as she drew her knees and the blankets up to her chin.

He sat down heavily on the mattress, placing the candle on the table to the side of her and after a moment he said, 'I have been thinking. You have started your courses, which means that you will be a woman soon.'

Esme's cheeks started to burn. It didn't seem right to be discussing things like this with him.

'I am hoping that when you reach a suitable age, I will be able to find a suitable husband for you,' he went on. 'I would not like you to follow in your mother's footsteps. She had her head turned by a heathen and I have no doubt she lived to regret it.'

'No, she didn't!' Esme retorted hotly before she could stop herself. 'She and Dadda were happy . . . *always*!'

'Hmm, so happy that he cleared off and left you all,' he answered smugly.

114

Esme bit her tongue, afraid of what she might say.

'Women must learn to be obedient to their husbands,' her grandfather went on. 'They must learn to please them and bear their children. That is what marriage is all about. Mrs Sparrow is teaching you how to keep house but as I am the man of the house it will be up to me to teach you how to keep your husband happy in other ways.'

Esme gulped, not happy with the way this conversation was going at all. He smiled again and to her horror she saw his hand drop to a bulge in his trousers which he gently began to rub. 'Women were put on this earth to please men.' A strange look had come into his eyes and now she was really afraid and opened her mouth to shout but almost instantly he managed to silence her when he said sternly, 'I have done the best I can for your brother by sending him away to school to get a decent education. One day he will thank me for it when he acquires a good job and marries. That is the role of the man, to be the breadwinner, but you ...' His hand suddenly snaked out and yanked the blanket away and before she could stop him his other hand latched on to her small breast through her nightgown and he began to tweak it painfully.

'P-please stop,' she whimpered in a small voice but almost before the words had left her mouth, he suddenly shivered and gasped and his hand dropped way.

'Ah ...' He lifted his other hand from his lap and smiled at her. 'That was your first lesson,' he told her as he stood up. 'And it must be our secret. Remember that I have the power to make or break your brother, so we will keep this between ourselves and you will tell no one that I have been to your room. Is that clear?'

His eyes were like flints and all she could do was nod.

'Good, then I shall wish you goodnight, my dear.' He lifted the candle and left the room without a backward glance.

Trembling, Esme listened to his footsteps recede, and once she could no longer hear them, she managed to take a breath. What could he have meant? she wondered. Her dadda had never said anything about the man of the house having to teach her anything

115

like that. But perhaps she hadn't been old enough then? It was all very confusing and she wondered if this was the way for all girls. Even if it wasn't, she knew that she had no choice but to do as he said. He had already warned her that he could harm Gabriel if she didn't comply and nothing was worth risking that.

Once she was sure that he wasn't coming back, she slid beneath the bedclothes again, shivering uncontrollably as tears poured down her cheeks. If only she and Gabriel had never come to this awful place. But it was too late for if onlys now. It was a long time before she was able to sleep and when she did her dreams were troubled.

She was walking through the orchard with the fair-haired woman she had seen upstairs and the woman was trying to show her something. Esme was frustrated because she couldn't understand what it was.

She woke in a lather, her eyes wide and her heart beating nineteen to the dozen and there were the young women staring mournfully at her from the corner of the room. Without stopping to think Esme shot out of bed and raced down to the kitchen and there she stayed, hugging Gip tightly to her, until the first light of dawn pricked the sky. Only then did she dare to make her way back to her bedroom where she hastily dressed before going back down to light the fires.

The following morning when she met her grandfather in the hall as she carried his breakfast to him on a tray, he behaved as if nothing had happened. 'Ah, put it on my desk. And did you revise the psalm I gave you to read?'

'Almost, sir.' Her voice came out as a croak but he didn't seem to notice.

'Good, then present yourself to me in my study this evening after we have eaten and I shall listen to you recite it.'

Once she had left the room, Esme's erratic heartbeat slowed to a steadier rhythm and as soon as all the chores were done, she took out the psalm he had set her to learn. But though she tried, she found she couldn't concentrate. The more she read it the more the words seemed to jumble together and she knew that she was going to be in trouble.

'So begin,' he ordered her that evening as she stood quaking before him. 'I believe I gave you Psalm 111 to learn.'

Esme licked her dry lips and shut her eyes, desperately trying to remember the words she had read at least a dozen times. 'Happy the man who fears the Lord, who greatly delights in his commands. His posterity shall be mighty upon the earth . . .' Here she faltered to a stop as her mind went blank.

'And? Come along, that isn't even the first verse,' he barked.

But it was no good, the words had gone and she could only stand there, a solitary tear rolling down her face.

Her grandfather's face set. *'Is that it?'*

'Y-yes, sir.'

'This is not good enough. I fear I have been far too lax with your Bible lessons and your discipline,' he told her in an ominously quiet voice. He lifted the cane and advanced towards her. She waited for him to tell her to hold her hand out but instead he said, 'Lift your skirts and bend over that chair.'

'What?' She was so horrified that her mouth gaped open.

'You heard me. Now do as you are told or I shall do it for you.'

Esme felt as if she was caught in the grip of a nightmare but she was too afraid to disobey him. Shame coursing through her, she leaned over the chair and hoiked up her skirts until they were in a bundle about her waist.

She could sense him come to stand behind her and steeled herself for the first blow but her humiliation was not quite complete yet, for next she felt him tug on her bloomers to expose her bare bottom. He started to breathe heavily, as though he had run a long way, and then she felt his large hand caress her tender skin and she flinched. This went on for a few minutes until suddenly he moaned and withdrew his hand, much as he had done the night before. Seconds later she heard the cane whistle through the air before coming into contact with her bare bottom and she yelped in pain. Five more blows followed by which time she was sobbing uncontrollably.

'Let that be a lesson to you, girl,' he said sharply. 'Women are the weaker sex, so don't think you can control men with your feminine wiles. You are the spawn of the devil! Now make yourself decent. And tomorrow night, make sure you've done as I asked or you'll get the same again. *Now get out!*'

Esme needed no second telling and she dragged her bloomers up and dropped her skirt so quickly that she almost tripped in her dash to the door. She fled to her bedroom where she groaned in pain as she gingerly felt the cheeks of her backside. She felt as if they were burning and, in that moment, she seriously thought of taking Gip and running away from this evil house. But soon common sense took over. If she did that Gabriel wouldn't know where to find her and her grandfather would take his wrath out on him. She couldn't let that happen – Gabriel was all she had left now and she would have walked through fire to keep him safe. Which meant she was virtually a prisoner. Once more she cried herself to sleep.

The following morning her backside wasn't quite so painful, apart from when she knelt down, so she went about her business as best she could – after all, she really didn't feel as if she had much choice.

She was quiet and confused and more than once she saw Mrs Sparrow look at her questioningly, but she said nothing. It would have been too embarrassing for her to tell the woman what her grandfather had done to her. She desperately wished that she could have someone, another girl her own age preferably, to speak to, but she reasoned she would probably have been too embarrassed to tell them what had happened even if she had, so she was just going to have to get on with it.

Thankfully her grandfather had left the house shortly after breakfast and Mrs Sparrow had informed her that he wouldn't be returning that night as he was going to a conference in Lincoln. After lunch she called Gip to heel and set off for the beach. It was a wild windy day but it was nice to get out in the fresh air and she started to feel slightly better once she got away from the house. Gip plodded along at the side of her as usual, his days of running were long behind him now but she still enjoyed their strolls together. Once she reached the beach she set off across the sand in the direction of Hull. She had only gone a short way when she spotted a woman and two girls on the beach ahead of her, and as she drew closer, she was delighted to see that it was Amelia and Olivia Fitzroy with Amelia's nanny.

Amelia was collecting shells but when Olivia noticed her, she smiled a welcome and hurried to meet her.

'Esme, how lovely to see you.' As always, she was dressed in a very pretty gown and matching bonnet with a warm, fur-lined cloak across her shoulders and Esme suddenly felt very shabby and dull in her old skirt and shawl. Olivia cocked her head towards the nanny and told her delightedly, 'We've just come out to get a breath of fresh air. Now that I'm fourteen I don't have to have a nanny anymore. She will just be in charge of Amelia from now on and Mama and Papa have got me a new tutor. He's starting immediately after Easter. Amelia will continue to have our old tutor, who is more suited to teaching younger children. I've already put the idea to them that I'd like you to join me in the lessons so that I have someone my own age to speak to and they've said they will consider it. I've been quite lonely since Luke left for university. Amelia is delightful but I'm afraid the age gap between us means that we have nothing in common. She still likes playing with her dollies and I've grown out of that stage now. But of course, even if my parents do agree to you joining me, they'll have to speak to your grandfather and see how he feels about it. But wouldn't it be nice if they all allowed it?'

'It would be wonderful!' Esme's eyes sparkled as she imagined it. Just the thought of being able to get away from the rectory every day and learn things other than psalms filled her with excitement.

But she knew she shouldn't raise her hopes too much. Olivia's parents might decide that she wouldn't make a suitable companion for their daughter and her grandfather could refuse to let her go. They were from completely different classes, after all. She was aware that most working-class girls her age would already have finished school and started work anyway. But all the same, the day didn't feel quite so gloomy.

They continued on their way speaking of books they had both read and chatting away as if they had known each other forever, and for the first time since coming there Esme felt that she might have found a friend. All she could do now was pray that she might be allowed to share her lessons with Olivia.

Chapter Sixteen

That evening Mrs Sparrow went to visit a lady in the village who had just given birth to her eighth child. She'd told Esme that she'd be gone for a couple of hours, and with her grandfather away too, Esme couldn't resist fetching the key to the attic room and venturing up there. Her heart pounded as she stood by the door, the candle flame guttering in the draught. She really didn't want to be there but she was drawn to the room as if by a magnet. Eventually she plucked up her courage and unlocked the door.

The room was just as she had left it, but the second she set foot inside, the oppressive atmosphere wrapped around her like a cloak. The feeling of unhappiness was so tangible that she could almost touch it. Placing the candle on the small desk, she began to look around. The silver hairbrush was exactly where she had left it on the dressing table and lifting it, she saw strands of fine silver-blonde hair caught in the bristles. She began to open drawers and look in the wardrobe, although she had no idea what she was looking for. Glancing towards the unmade bed, something caught her eye. It was barely visible, but it looked like the corner of a sheet of paper was sticking out from beneath the feather mattress. When she lifted it to see what it was, she discovered a number of sheets, which she quickly stuffed into the pocket of her pinafore. She would look at them later when she was in the privacy of her room.

She half expected the lady she had seen before to appear again but there was nothing, so soon after, she left and quickly relocked the door. Her teeth were chattering for the room had been ice cold, far colder than the rest of the house, and suddenly she wanted to be as far away from it as she could. On the ground floor she hurried into her grandfather's study and replaced the key exactly as she had found it. But when she turned to leave she stopped dead in her tracks when she saw her grandfather standing in the doorway, his face set in an angry mask.

'Just *what* do you think you are doing prying amongst my things, girl!' His voice exploded across the room like a pistol shot and terror pulsed through her as she saw the rage in his eyes.

'I . . . I thought I'd come in and tidy up for you,' she whispered in a small voice. It was the only thing she could think of, but he clearly didn't believe her.

'At this time of night? Pah! Haven't I always told you that this room is completely out of bounds to you?'

'I . . . I'm sorry,' she croaked.

'Believe me, you will be!' he said threateningly and standing to one side he pointed to the door. 'Now get out and don't say I didn't warn you. You'll *regret* disobeying me.'

Esme fled on legs that felt as if they had turned to jelly and she didn't stop running till she reached her room where she hastily placed the chair beneath the door handle and collapsed onto her bed, sobbing noisily. And there she sat trembling as she wondered what her punishment was going to be and heartily wishing both she and her brother were a million miles away.

Early the next morning Esme made her way down to the kitchen to light the fires. She lit the oil lamp in the centre of the table and as a warm glow spread about the room, she looked towards the hearth rug expecting to see Gip welcoming her with his tail wagging. But there was no sign of him and she frowned. He always slept there.

'Gip!' she called softly, staring around the room, but all was quiet and the first stirrings of unease coursed through her. Once she had checked under the table and everywhere he could be she made for the back door just as Mrs Sparrow appeared yawning in the doorway.

'Where are you off to?' she asked, seeing the worry on the girl's face

'Do you know where Gip is?'

'Gip? Why, he was fast asleep on the hearthrug when I went up to bed last night.'

Feeling really worried now, Esme let herself out into the yard. It was a cold foggy morning and she could barely see a hand in front of her as she began to call him. 'Gip . . . Gip, where are you, boy?' But all was quiet. She widened her search and soon she was in the orchard where again she began to call his name once more. The thick fog meant she could see no more than a few feet in front of her, but she did her best. Next she went to the front of the house and looked as far up and down the lane as she could, although she had never known him to wander off before. But still there was no sign of him and aware that she would be in even more trouble than she already was if she didn't get the fires going, she made her way back inside.

'Did you find him?' Mrs Sparrow enquired as she filled the kettle from the pump over the sink. When Esme shook her head miserably the woman frowned. 'That's very strange. He was definitely settled down by the fire last night when I last saw him. How could he have got out?' And then she suddenly tutted. 'Ah, your grandfather pushed a note under my bedroom door last night to say that the conference he had been about to attend had been postponed until today and that he'd had to come back home, but he was going to leave early this morning. I wonder if he threw Gip out last night? If he did, we'll both be in trouble when he gets back because he thought Gip had been sleeping in the stables all this time.'

Esme's breath caught in her throat. Could it be that her grand-father had turned him out to spend a cold night outside to punish her for going into his study? It was just the sort of thing he would do, but if he had put him outside, where was he now? Gip was very old and liked his home comforts so it was unlikely he would have wandered far. But she was behind with her chores now so she set about lighting the fires and helping to prepare breakfast, although her eyes kept straying to the window as she fretted about Gip.

By mid-morning Mrs Sparrow had had enough of Esme's jumpiness. 'For goodness sake, you're as jumpy as a cat on hot bricks. Get yourself wrapped up and go and look for Gip. You'll clearly not settle until you've found him!'

'Thank you, Mrs Sparrow.' Esme snatched up her shawl and ran outside. Thankfully the fog had cleared but it was a damp, dismal day. A drizzly rain was falling and soon her hair was plastered to her head as she made for the stables. But despite searching every inch of them, there was no sign that Gip had ever been there, so she headed for the orchard again.

'Gip! Gip! Come on, boy!' She wandered amongst the leafless trees looking this way and that and then suddenly her heart missed a beat as she saw something lying on the ground ahead of her.

Tentatively she walked towards it and sure enough, she saw Gip's tail sticking out from behind the trunk of a tree.

'Oh Gip, what are you doing lying there?' she scolded softly as she quickened her pace, a smile of relief lighting her face. But as she drew closer his head came into view and the smile slipped away and she gasped in dismay and disbelief. He was lying very still and his head seemed to be at an unnatural angle.

Heedless of the muddy ground she dropped to her knees and threw her arms about him. He was very cold and his eyes were glazed and staring. 'Gip, Gip, wake up *please!*' she sobbed as she lifted his head and lay it on her lap. But it dropped to the side and she knew in that moment that his neck had been broken, just like the rabbits that her brother and dadda used to catch for their stew.

'*No, no,*' she wailed pitifully, not wanting to believe what she was seeing. '*Please* don't you leave me too, Gip. I need you!' Now Gabriel had been sent away to school, the faithful old dog was her last link to their parents and the happy life they used to lead and she couldn't envisage her life without him. He had always been there for as long as she could remember, faithful and loving, and now he was gone.

In her mind she could hear the stories her mammy used to tell her about what Gip had been like when she was born. '*He used to lie at the side of your crib and guard you, and woe betide anyone who tried to come near you who he didn't know. And then when you learned to crawl you used to crawl beneath his legs and he would lick you so hard you'd fall over giggling. You took your first faltering steps clutching Gip's tail and he never once complained, you could have done anything with him.'*

Esme had never tired of hearing these stories. She could remember riding piggy back on Gip's back when she was a toddler, and lying beneath the vardo with Gabriel on warm summer nights, Gip curled up close to them.

Who could have done such a wicked thing? she asked herself.

But she knew the answer: *her grandfather.*

Hadn't he told her only last night that she would regret entering his study and disobeying him? This must have been his way of punishing her, and it was a far worse punishment than any caning or fondling he could have inflicted on her. She sat for a long time talking of happy times to him and kissing him, until finally she rose and made her way back to the shed to fetch a spade. There was nothing she could do to bring him back but she could at least make sure that he was properly buried.

Mrs Sparrow was just emptying potato peelings into the pig bin when Esme walked back into the yard. 'Ah, here you are, I was beginning to think you'd got lost and—' She stopped abruptly as she saw the state Esme was in. Her skirt was covered in mud and she was as pale as a ghost. 'So . . . did you find him?' She was dreading the answer.

'Oh yes, I found him all right!' Esme's eyes were as cold as ice and her voice was laden with hatred. 'But he won't be coming home. Someone killed him. They broke his neck and I think we both know who it was.'

'*What?*' Mrs Sparrow looked shocked. She had grown quite fond of the dear old mutt in the time he had been there. 'Who—' She clapped her hand to her mouth as she realised who Esme was talking about. 'But *surely* you can't believe it was your grandfather?'

'Who *else* do you know who has a cruel streak?' Esme spat. She had always shown nothing but respect to the woman, but at that moment she would tell the truth and shame the devil. 'He made no secret of the fact that he didn't like Gip! He didn't even want him in the house. And last night I upset him and he threatened me and told me that I'd regret it! He's wicked, evil, and I hope he *dies* and burns in hell as he's always threatening everyone else.'

'Oh, my goodness!' Mrs Sparrow leaned heavily on the edge of the sink.

'I want a blanket to wrap him in,' Esme said shortly and Mrs Sparrow heaved herself away from the sink and went to fetch one, which she passed to Esme.

'Would you like me to come and help you bury him, pet?' she asked tentatively. She knew how much the old dog had meant to both Esme and Gabriel.

Manners forgotten for now, Esme snatched the blanket from her and shook her head vehemently. '*No!* I want to do it myself. It's the last thing I'll ever be able to do for him!' Then she turned abruptly and slammed out of the kitchen, leaving the door swinging open behind her.

After collecting the spade from the shed, she made her way through the fruit trees with a heavy heart. Once she got back to Gip she tenderly rolled him into the warm blanket and sat cuddling him to her for a long time. Eventually she laid him aside and set about digging his grave. The ground was solid and it was hard going but she kept on, blinded by the tears that were rolling down her cheeks.

At last when it was deep enough, she pulled him into her arms for the last time, raining kisses down onto his dear face before covering him completely with the blanket and manoeuvring him as gently as she could into his final resting place. Shovelling the cold, wet earth over him was the hardest thing she had ever had to do and it took a long time but at last she was done. Breathless, she stood back to examine her efforts.

'Rest in peace, my sweet boy,' she whispered, and as she walked away, she felt as if her heart was breaking. With Gabriel away at school she was truly alone now and she had never felt as lonely in her life.

Back at the house she walked past Mrs Sparrow and went to her room where she lay on her bed staring numbly at the window. Throughout the day Mrs Sparrow appeared regularly, silently bringing her hot drinks and food to try and tempt her to eat but Esme just turned her face away and Mrs Sparrow was forced to take everything back to the kitchen untouched.

The next day was exactly the same and the woman began to get gravely concerned. It was as if Esme had locked herself away in a world of her own and she had no idea how to get through to her. *I'll fetch the doctor in to have a look at her tomorrow if she's no better*, she promised herself. But as it happened, she didn't have to, for late the following afternoon Septimus returned from his conference and when Esme heard him speaking to Mrs Sparrow in the hallway she appeared on the stairs and stared down at him.

As he looked up at her it was not the face of the timid little girl who had appeared on his doorstep but a face that was filled with hatred.

'Call yourself a man of the cloth,' she ground out through clenched teeth. '*Shame* on you. I hope you *rot* in hell where you belong. Did you enjoy killing an old harmless creature?'

'I . . . I really don't know what you're talking about,' he blustered.

'Oh, I think you *do*, but don't forget, as you are so fond of telling your parishioners, God is all-seeing and one day he will punish you for what you did!'

Septimus opened and shut his mouth, reminding her of a gold-fish she had seen at Appleby Horse Fair one year when she had visited with her family.

Recovering himself quickly, he frowned at her. 'How *dare* you speak to me like that, young lady? Would you like another taste of the cane?'

'Oh, I dare,' she shot back without hesitation. 'And your punishments hold no fear for me anymore, because *nothing* you could do now could ever hurt me as much as what you did to Gip, not even if you flay the skin from my back.' And with that she turned and went back to her room.

'I hope it *wasn't* you who killed that poor old dog?'

Fists clenched in anger, Septimus looked at Mrs Sparrow with contempt. 'Of course it wasn't,' he said a little too quickly for her liking. Then he stormed into his study, leaving her to stare thoughtfully after him.

Chapter Seventeen

'It's good of you to use your free time to help me to do this, Jeremy,' Gabriel said as he gathered the papers containing his maths homework into a neat pile.

'It's no problem, mate,' Jeremy assured him. 'I don't know how the teachers expect you to know how to do the work if they've never taken the time to show you.'

Gabriel shrugged. 'In fairness, I've never been one for learning,' he admitted. 'Not like my little sister. She can't get enough of it – soaks it up like a sponge. I always thought I'd follow in me dadda's footsteps. You know, working with me hands out in the open air. There's nothing like it.'

'Hmm, I suppose it could be nice in the summer,' Jeremy agreed, although he didn't much fancy it in the winter.

'Let's hope I've got at least some of these right this time. Now how about we go and see if we're still in time to get a last hot drink, eh? The bell will be going for bed soon.'

Gabriel had been putting a lot more effort into his work since his grandfather's visit, but only because he desperately wanted to get back to see Esme at Easter. It was only weeks away now and he could hardly wait. He'd been devastated to receive a letter from her a couple of weeks before telling him that Gip had died and he could only imagine how upset she must be. They had both adored their old pet. He just hoped that the old boy had died peacefully in his sleep, but Esme hadn't told him how he had passed.

As he and Jeremy entered the day room, as usual the boys sneered and made rude comments. Things with the other students were no better but now Gabriel tried to ignore them as best he could. It wasn't always easy. He had a quick temper and some of the things they called him and the cruel stunts they played on him made his blood boil. But he was doing his best to turn the other cheek, so he pretended not to notice as he walked towards the table where the teapot was always left out for them.

There wasn't a lot left and what there was was stewed, but as his dadda used to say, '*It's wet and warm an' it'll wet yer whistle.*' Placing his work in a neat pile on the table he poured himself and Jeremy a mugful each.

'Ooh, looks like our gyppo has been tryin' to get in the teacher's good books,' Thomas Broadhurst said mockingly as he looked at Gabriel's homework. 'Ain't he a good little boy!' And before Gabriel could respond he reached across and knocked the tea Gabriel had poured for Jeremy all over it.

'Why, you *lousy* bastard!' Gabriel snatched up the papers, but the damage had been done. The paper was sodden and just tore into shreds when he tried to wipe it dry. All that time and effort had been in vain. At that moment Mrs Ingles appeared and frowning she asked, 'Is something wrong in here?'

She could see Gabriel and Thomas squaring up to each other like two pugilists in a boxing ring but Thomas was instantly all wide-eyed and innocent.

'There's been an accident, Mrs Ingles,' he simpered. 'I knocked some tea over by accident and it's gone all over Loveridge's homework.'

'Well, that's most unfortunate but accidents will happen,' she replied with a glare at Gabriel.

'But—' Gabriel began to object, but before he could utter another word she held her hand up to silence him.

'That's quite enough, Loveridge. Hasn't Broadhurst just told you it was an accident? I'm sure he'll apologise.'

'Of course I will, Mrs Ingles,' Thomas said sweetly and turning to Gabriel with a grin on his face that she couldn't see he told him, 'Sorry about that, old chap.'

'There we are,' she said. 'Now let that be an end to it. I'm sure the teacher will understand when you tell him what's happened, Loveridge. Come along, boys. It's time for bed.'

One by one the boys filed past her and, clutching what was left of his sodden papers, Gabriel had no choice but to follow them.

'That was a lousy thing for Broadhurst to do,' Jeremy muttered as they climbed the stairs to the dormitory. 'But not to worry. I'll help you again tomorrow after classes.'

'Thanks,' Gabriel muttered, feeling thoroughly wretched. It seemed that even when he tried, he was doomed to failure and once again he wondered how long he could bear to be there.

'Where's your homework, Loveridge?' the teacher roared the next morning as everyone else handed theirs in.

'There was an accident last evening and it got tea poured all over it,' Gabriel muttered as a chuckle rippled round the class.

'Did it now? And do you have anyone to vouch for that?'

'I do as it happens . . . sir!' Gabriel answered moodily. 'Mrs Ingles was present just after it happened.'

'Right, in that case I'll let you off this time . . . *if* you're telling the truth. But make no bones about it, I shall check with Mrs Ingles and if she doesn't substantiate your story, you'll be owed six of the best, boy! Meanwhile, I'll give you this evening to do it again, do you understand?'

Gabriel flushed to the roots of his hair as he saw Broadhurst's gloating expression, and it was all he could do not to punch him on the nose, but he managed to answer, 'Yes, sir.'

Things went from bad to worse when Gabriel tried to get into his pyjamas that evening only to find someone had crudely sewed the bottom of the legs up.

'Oh dear, Loveridge, someone stitched you up, have they?' Broadhurst sneered. It seemed there was no end to his spite.

Gabriel grit his teeth as he roughly yanked the stitches out and rammed his legs into the pyjamas. He hated wearing the damn things but knew he would be in trouble if he didn't. Despite his anger, he managed not to rise to Broadhurst's taunting and merely said quietly, 'Looks like they tried to. Makes you wonder what sort of an idiot would do such a thing, don't it? There must be someone with the brain of a two-year-old about.' Then he climbed into bed and lay fuming as he stared at the wall, silently vowing to himself, *I'll have my day with that nasty little bleeder if it's the last thing I do!*

Life didn't improve, but Gabriel was counting down the days now until he could see Esme, so he took it all and tried to keep himself to himself, speaking only to Jeremy, who had turned out to be a true friend. Gabriel had never had a friend his own age before. The lifestyle he'd had with his parents travelling from place to place had meant he'd never had a chance to make one, but he was glad of Jeremy's support.

'What are you doing for Easter?' he asked Jeremy one day as he sat struggling with yet another pile of homework. He was always careful now to keep it well out of reach of Broadhurst.

'Staying here by the looks of it,' Jeremy answered glumly. 'I had a letter from my parents telling me that they'll be in the south of France for the holidays and they'll be leaving before school breaks up so I won't be able to go with them.'

Gabriel frowned, feeling sorry for him. It was bad enough having to be in this place during term time let alone in the holidays. And then a thought occurred to him and he grinned. There was no way he could ask his grandfather if Jeremy could come and stay with them but there might be another way to give him a break.

'How are you fixed for money?'

'Oh, there's never a shortage of that. My parents always send me a more than generous allowance every month. I think it makes them feel less guilty for never having time for me. Do you know, when I was little, I rarely saw them? I had a nanny who took care of me, then when I was considered old enough, they sent me here at the earliest opportunity.'

'Hmm, so you could afford to have a few nights in a hotel then?'

'Well, yes, I could easily. Why, what did you have in mind?'

'I thought perhaps you could come and stay in one close to where I live with my grandfather and Esme. It would be better than staying here with the other chaps who can't go home and we could meet up,' Gabriel suggested.

Thomas thought about it and grinned. 'That sounds like a great idea. But are you sure there'd be somewhere with vacancies?'

Gabriel nodded. 'The next village to ours is Mablethorpe and it's really popular with holidaymakers, apparently. There's sure to be somewhere you could stay. I could write and ask my sister to book you into one if you like.'

Thomas nodded eagerly. 'I'd like that. I was dreading staying here, to be honest.'

And so it was decided and Gabriel wrote to Esme to ask her to arrange it that very evening.

Then at last term was over. Some of the parents arrived to take their sons home, others sent carriages for them, and those left, like Jeremy and Gabriel, made their own way home. They were both in high spirits as they set off for the front at Skegness to board a coach that would take them into Mablethorpe.

'It's only a hop, skip and a jump from Theddlethorpe where my grandfather lives, so we'll see as much of you as we can,' Gabriel assured him. Jeremy had gathered from things Gabriel had said that he wasn't on the best of terms with his grandfather and so he could understand why his friend never referred to the rectory as 'home'.

The coach took the coastal route and the boys enjoyed gazing out of the window at the sea, feeling as if they had been released from a jail.

'I've never been this way,' Jeremy told him.

'I think you'll like it.'

Jeremy smiled at him. His hair had grown considerably and the short tufts that Broadhurst and his bullies had inflicted on him were once more a halo of shiny curls that shone like wet coal.

'Here we are,' Gabriel told him eventually as the coach rattled into Mablethorpe. 'Esme should be here to meet us. I told her what time the coach would be arriving.'

Sure enough, as he hung precariously out of the window he saw her standing on the pavement, waving so hard that it was a wonder her hand didn't fly off.

The second they alighted the coach, Esme threw herself into her brother's arms and started to cry.

'Oh, I've missed you *so* much.' She sniffed, before suddenly becoming aware of Jeremy who was standing staring at her. She gave him a shy smile.

Jeremy swallowed and smiled back, a blush stealing up his cheeks as a million emotions coursed through him. He would never have guessed she was Gabriel's sister, for they were as different as chalk from cheese. Gabriel was well set and dark while Esme was fair and dainty and easily the most beautiful girl he had ever seen.

'It's nice to meet you, Mr Mitchell,' she told him politely, holding her small hand out. 'Gabriel talks about you all the time in his letters. I'm so glad that he's made a friend at the school.'

Jeremy was so tongue-tied that he merely smiled.

Turning to her brother again, Esme told him, 'I found a very nice little hotel in Seaholme Road. It's right close to the beach so I hope Mr Mitchell will like it.'

'Oh, please . . .' Jeremy croaked. 'Call me Jeremy. And . . . I . . . I'm sure I shall, thank you.'

She gave him a dazzling smile and Jeremy's heart began to beat faster.

The boys lifted their bags and the three of them walked to Seaholme Road to get Jeremy settled in before going back to the rectory. The landlady was a plump, kindly little woman who ushered them inside with a friendly smile.

'So, which one of you is it who's going to be staying?' she asked as she looked at the register in the hallway.

'I am.' Jeremy returned the smile and laughing now she waggled her pencil at him as she booked him in and handed him a key to his room.

'Right, young man, we expect our guests to be in for ten each evening and we won't have any hanky-panky. What I mean is, no smuggling young ladies up to your room, do you understand?'

'Er, yes Mrs, er . . .' Jeremy flushed a dull brick red and she chuckled.

'It's Mrs Foster and don't worry, lad. I'm only teasing. Your room is up on the first landing, number four, third door on the right. Dinner is at six o'clock prompt and if you need anything don't hesitate to ask.'

After she'd left them, Gabriel said, 'Right, we'd best get back to the rectory while you settle in. But how about we meet tonight up on the front, say about seven thirty?'

'Sounds great.' Jeremy was really smiling now and getting into the holiday mood so Gabriel and Esme left him to it and began the short walk back to Theddlethorpe.

It was only a couple of miles away and Gabriel basked in the sun shining down on them. Esme, meanwhile, was studying him carefully from the corner of her eye and was surprised at the change she saw in him. His hair was even shorter than when Mrs Sparrow had cut it and he'd lost a considerable amount of weight. Mind you, if what he had told her about the school meals was anything to go by, she supposed she shouldn't have been surprised. But more worryingly, his face was pale and drawn. She could never remember a time when Gabriel hadn't been tanned from the many hours he spent outside, but she supposed his pallor was due to being confined to classrooms. Poor thing, she knew how much he hated to be cooped up and could only imagine how hard being forced to stay in that awful school must be for him. Still, she consoled herself as she slipped her arm through his, he had a whole two weeks with her now, and she intended to make the most of every single minute of it.

Chapter Eighteen

Mrs Sparrow was delighted to see him when they arrived back at the rectory and she gave him a big sloppy kiss on the cheek that made his face burn.

'I'm afraid you won't see your grandfather until next week,' she informed him. 'He went off to a Bible conference this morning, so it will be just us three.'

Both Gabriel and Esme were delighted to hear it and although they couldn't say as much their smiles said it all. To add to Gabriel's joy, Mrs Sparrow had spent the whole morning baking all Gabriel's favourites. There was a deep apple pie covered in golden brown pastry, scones fresh from the oven and oozing with currants, and a sponge cake filled with jam and cream.

'And because I know you love it, I've cooked you a rabbit pie for your evening meal,' Mrs Sparrow told him.

Gabriel beamed. To have such a warm welcome and then to learn that his grandfather wasn't going to be there for days made his homecoming so much better than he had thought it would be.

'And young Esme tells me that you have a friend staying in Mablethorpe,' Mrs Sparrow went on as she began to cut thick slices of bread from a freshly baked loaf. She slathered it in rich creamy butter and plonked it down in front of him, and Gabriel's mouth watered at the sight of it. 'I thought perhaps you'd both like it if he spent a bit of time here with you,' Mrs Sparrow went on. 'At least, just until your grandfather gets back next week. He could perhaps come for lunch tomorrow and you could take him down to the beach?'

'He'd love that.' Gabriel bit into the bread and sighed with pleasure. This was nothing at all like the horrid grey stuff they served them at the school. To go with it were thick wedges of cheese and some pickles, and by the time Gabriel had finished he felt as if he might burst.

Mrs Sparrow laughed. 'I see you haven't lost your appetite, lad. That's good. But now if you're done why don't you both get out and get a bit of fresh air? It might put a bit of colour back into your cheeks.' Like Esme she had noticed how pale Gabriel was and it didn't please her.

Esme looked surprised. 'But aren't there jobs I should be doing?'

'While the cat's away the mouse will play.' Mrs Sparrow grinned, tapping the side of her nose. 'Go on, get off the pair of you, but make sure you're back for dinner.'

And so, the two young people went into the yard where Gabriel asked for the first time, 'Where was it you said you had buried Gip?'

Solemn-faced now, Esme led him through the orchard until they came to the little mound of earth that covered their beloved pet. She'd made him a little wooden cross bound with string.

'Poor old chap,' he muttered thickly, tears springing to his eyes. 'And I wasn't even here to say goodbye. What do you suppose he died of?'

Esme didn't dare tell him the true cause for fear of what he might do to their grandfather. 'He was just old, I suppose,' she whispered, her voice full of tears as she crossed her fingers behind her back.

'At least he was here with you.' Gabriel leaned down to touch the soil that covered their old friend, then they turned and started to walk towards the beach, but somehow it wasn't the same without Gip pottering along beside them.

When they reached the sand, they strolled along in silence for a time, but eventually, making an effort, Esme smiled. 'Look, we only have a few short weeks together so let's try and make the best of it, eh?'

Gabriel nodded in agreement and slowly their moods lightened as they walked along the tideline.

They returned to the rectory feeling more relaxed and Gabriel went to his room to change out of the hated school uniform. He felt better wearing his old clothes and after a delicious meal that evening, they walked into Mablethorpe to meet Jeremy. He was sitting on the sea wall along the front waiting for them, and once again his heart began to race as his eyes settled on Esme, and he wondered what was wrong with him. No girl had ever affected him this way before.

'Why don't we go and get ourselves an ice cream? My treat!' he suggested after a few minutes and Esme's face lit up. She and Gabriel never had the money for such delights.

They took them down onto the beach to eat and then strolled along collecting shells, which the boys gave to Esme. Suddenly Gabriel remembered what Mrs Sparrow had said and asked his friend, 'Fancy coming to the rectory for dinner tomorrow?' Seeing the look of surprise on Jeremy's face, he hurried on, 'Don't worry our grandfather isn't there. He's away at a conference for a whole week so we can enjoy ourselves.'

As the sky began to darken, they saw Jeremy back to his digs, promising to pick him up the next morning, before heading back to the rectory. Both felt more content than they had in a long time and Esme wished more than ever that her brother didn't have to go back to school.

That night, knowing that Gabriel was close by, Esme slept like a baby and woke the next morning feeling refreshed. She and Jeremy had got on like a house on fire the previous evening once they had got over their initial shyness, and she was looking forward to seeing him again almost as much as Gabriel was.

'I know things haven't been so great for us since we lost Mammy and Dadda,' Gabriel said over breakfast. 'But meeting Jeremy has shown me how lucky we were to have them for the time we did. That poor chap's parents have never had time for him. In fact, I wonder why they ever bothered having a kid.'

Esme nodded sadly. 'I suppose we were,' she agreed. 'I just wish we could have had them for longer. Anyway, let's try to make sure Jeremy has a lovely time, despite his horrible parents.'

As soon as breakfast was over, Gabriel went out to chop some logs for the fire, which had to be kept lit even in the better weather for boiling the kettles and cooking. Esme washed up the breakfast pots and tidied the kitchen and then Mrs Sparrow told them, 'Go on, you pair. Be off with you. You may treat this week as a little holiday and go and meet your friend. There's nothing as needs doing here that can't wait.'

'Are you sure?' Esme felt a little guilty at leaving all the house-work to her but the woman shooed them away. She even gave them a few precious pennies to spend on treats.

'Be sure to be back in time for lunch,' she warned them as they left. 'And bring Jeremy with you. It will only be salad stuff and cold ham today but he's welcome to join us.'

The rest of the week passed blissfully for them. They spent the days mooching along the small high street in Mablethorpe looking in the shop windows, or playing on the beach. They sat on the sea wall and ate prawns from the shellfish stall and in the afternoons, they treated themselves to toffee apples and ice cream. But even though they enjoyed themselves immensely, both Gabriel and Esme could see a great change in each other. Esme noted that Gabriel was quieter, as if he had lost his sparkle, and he in turn thought that she seemed to have suddenly grown up. Could he have known it, he was quite right, for Esme had buried her childhood along with Gip.

On Monday morning, though, Mrs Sparrow announced, 'I'm afraid you might have to stay closer to home after today. Your grandfather is due back in the morning, so it might be as well if Jeremy doesn't visit here anymore. That's not to say you won't be able to sneak away now and again to meet him till it's time for you to go back to school.'

The children were instantly subdued but they had no choice but to agree to what she said.

'I'm afraid the old man is due back tomorrow,' Gabriel told Jeremy regretfully when they met him later that day. 'So we might not be able to see quite so much of you next week.' The holiday had clearly done Jeremy a power of good; freckles had sprouted across his nose and thanks to the nice weather and the fresh air he didn't look so pasty.

'Oh, should I head off back to the school?' Jeremy asked.

'Not at all,' Gabriel assured him. 'But the old devil will expect his pound of flesh from us for our keep. What I mean is, he'll expect all the chores to be done before we're allowed out.'

'I have to say he doesn't sound much like a man of the cloth. I thought vicars were supposed to be kind and giving.'

'So did we till we came to live here,' Gabriel agreed and for the rest of the day they were all a little subdued.

It was late that night, just as Esme was dropping off to sleep, when she heard the sound of the front door slamming and she was instantly wide awake, her heart sinking as she heard the sound of heavy footsteps on the stairs. Her grandfather had returned early and she stared at the door fearfully. Thankfully he hadn't tried to enter her room since the night she had buried Gip but she still wasn't confident that it would remain that way. However, on this occasion she heard him pass her door without slowing and once she heard his own door closing, she breathed a sigh of relief. She was safe for now, at least, so eventually she dropped off to sleep again.

The next morning, when Mrs Sparrow carried her grandfather's breakfast through to his study, Gabriel frowned. 'He's back already? I thought he wasn't coming till this morning?' he said through a mouthful of toast, spraying crumbs everywhere. He was making the most of the nice food before having to go back to school.

Esme nodded glumly. 'So did I, but I heard him come in late last night.'

'He goes to quite a lot of these conferences, doesn't he?' Gabriel said, looking thoughtful.

'I suppose he does.' Esme hadn't really given it much thought until he mentioned it.

'And where are they?'

Again, she shrugged. 'I'm not sure. I think Mrs Sparrow mentioned that a couple of them were in Skegness somewhere but I don't know if they all are.'

The conversation was stopped from going any further when Mrs Sparrow came back into the room wiping her hands on her apron. The two held their breath, expecting her to give them a summons to their grandfather's study, but instead she told them, 'The reverend isn't too well today so there'll be no Bible classes this evening. He came home a little sooner than expected and got back last night, but unfortunately, he had a nasty fall in the dark after getting off the coach. He's got a right old lump on his head and his face is scratched from when it hit the floor, so I've suggested he have a nice easy day, resting in bed today.'

It was music to their ears, especially when she told them, 'Get a few of your jobs done and slip off to meet Jeremy while you've got the chance. I'll make sure he doesn't know you've gone. And I'll do you a carry out so as you needn't rush back.'

They needed no persuading and just before midday they set off with a small hamper that Mrs Sparrow had packed for their lunch.

They found Jeremy somewhat at a loose end staring morosely from the window of the hotel's small lounge, and when he saw them his face lit up and he rushed outside to meet them.

'This is a nice surprise. I wasn't sure you'd be able to get away now your grandfather is home,' he greeted them.

'Apparently he took a tumble on his way back last night, so he's having a day of rest and that's let us off the hook,' Esme told him delightedly. 'But only for today, mind. He might be feeling better and be back to his usual self tomorrow so we'd best make the most of it.'

They walked up to the front and settled themselves on the sand beneath a row of brightly painted beach huts that overlooked the sea while Esme opened the hamper to see what treats Mrs Sparrow had packed for them.

The sun was shining down on them from a cloudless blue sky as they all peeped inside the hamper. There were thickly sliced ham sandwiches wrapped in greaseproof paper and some pickled onions in a small jar. Large wedges of cheese, and sausage rolls wrapped in Mrs Sparrow's delicious pastry, and for dessert there were slices of fruit cake as well as a bottle of ginger beer.

'Crikey, there's enough to feed an army there,' Jeremy commented as he eyed the food greedily. It was certainly a long way away from the tasteless stuff they were served at school. It was no wonder none of the chaps had any weight on them, he thought.

Somehow, they managed to clear the whole lot between them, then they lay back, contentedly full, with the sun on their faces and the sound of the waves breaking on the beach. There were children playing with buckets and spades a little further along and Esme smiled as she watched their antics. She could remember a time when she had been as carefree as they were but that seemed a long way away now. Everything had changed since they'd come to live with their grandfather, and sometimes she wondered if she and Gabriel wouldn't have been better off trying to survive on their own. Just then she saw a shape emerge from the waves and as it drew closer, she saw the form of a little boy. No doubt he had drowned there at some stage and his spirit was tied to the place. She looked away quickly. She had enough spirits to deal with back at the rectory and didn't want to spoil the day. Thankfully when she looked back, the child had vanished.

'Right, what shall we do now?' Jeremy asked.

'Let's go for a walk along the front to Chapel St Leonard's,' Gabriel suggested.

They set off in a happy frame of mind and once there, they explored the little village. Time was going on, however, and after a while, Gabriel said reluctantly, 'I suppose we'd better head back now. We had a reprieve today but if the old man discovers we're playing truant he'll make us do twice as much tomorrow if I know him.'

Slowly they made their way back along the beach and once they arrived at Mablethorpe, Jeremy set off back to his digs while they walked on to Theddlethorpe.

'The time is going so quickly,' Esme said sadly as they headed for the sand dunes that would take them back to Sea Lane and the rectory. 'It's been so lovely to have you back; I've enjoyed every minute. I just wish you didn't have to go back to that awful school!'

'I know.' Gabriel squeezed her hand. 'We'll just have to make the most of every second.'

The minute they entered the house the cold atmosphere wrapped itself around Esme like a shroud and she shuddered. The rectory never seemed to be warm, even today with the sun shining outside and the fires lit, but it was particularly frosty now.

'Ah, here you are. Had a nice day, have you?' Mrs Sparrow greeted them when they entered the kitchen. Before they could reply she rushed on, 'Your grandfather is up and in his study, so try and keep out of his way.'

Despite the lovely food she had packed them that day, Gabriel's stomach rumbled with anticipation as he smelled the steak and kidney pie that was cooking in the oven for their dinner. 'I suggest you both go and wash your hands and faces,' Mrs Sparrow told them. 'The meal won't be long.'

They trooped away to their rooms to do as they were asked but just as they were about to climb the stairs their grandfather appeared from his study and glowered at them, although thankfully he didn't say anything.

'Crikey, he looks as if he's done ten rounds in a boxing ring,' Gabriel whispered when they reached the top.

Esme grinned. 'Hmm, he's got a right shiner, hasn't he? And all those scratches! I don't know about a boxing ring; he looks like he's been in a fight with a cat.'

They hurried on to their rooms where they tidied themselves up for dinner and once back downstairs Esme helped Mrs Sparrow to set the table while Gabriel went out to chop more logs for the fire.

They were tired but happy when they retired to bed, or at least Gabriel was. Esme's happy mood evaporated immediately upon entering her bedroom when she sensed that she was not alone and, sure enough, as she glanced into the shadows in the corner of the room there were the restless souls who had been haunting her.

The next day they had no chance to meet Jeremy as their grandfather kept them busy with chores and running errands all day, but the following day he had put aside for visiting his parishioners so they were able to sneak away for a couple of hours and spend a little time with him.

That evening the dreaded Bible studies were resumed and the following evening found Gabriel suffering yet another caning for not being able to remember the whole of the psalm his grandfather had set him to memorise.

'I wonder if you have a brain, you simpleton!' their grandfather roared as he stood intimidatingly over him, wielding the cane. But Gabriel didn't flinch, even when it ripped into his palm.

Esme was deeply upset and as soon as they were dismissed, tears rolled down her cheeks as she followed him to the kitchen to bathe his wounds.

'It's nothin',' Gabriel assured her bravely, although his hand felt as if it was going to drop off. And in truth, it wasn't, not compared to the bullying he had to put up with at school. 'An' don't worry, it won't be forever. Very soon now I shall run away from that school an' when I've saved enough for us to rent a room somewhere I shall come back for you and we'll never have to see that sadist's ugly face again!'

They sat miserably with their arms about each other in the kitchen; what Gabriel was promising seemed a very long way away.

Chapter Nineteen

It was the day before Gabriel was due to return to school and both his and Esme's spirits were low.

'How long is it until your next holiday?' she asked miserably.

He shrugged. 'It'll be in the summer, I should imagine.'

A rap on the front door interrupted their conversation and Esme hurried away to answer it to find the postman standing on the step.

'Mornin', miss.' He handed her an envelope and after thanking him she turned to see her grandfather just coming out of his study in his outdoor clothes, a dark coat, and his crisp white dog collar.

'Is that for me?'

Esme nodded and handed it over and without a word of thanks he slit it open as she scuttled back to the kitchen. She never stayed in his company a moment longer than she had to.

Seconds later he followed her and nodding towards Mrs Sparrow he told her, 'I need to speak to you in my study . . . *now*!'

'All right, keep your hair on!' she retorted as she wiped her hands on her apron and followed him.

'I wonder what that was all about?' Esme mused.

'I don't know, but whatever it was he don't look none too pleased about it.'

'Huh! When does he ever look pleased?' Esme quipped.

They approached the door to the hall and peeping through it they could just see the back of Mrs Sparrow's skirt through the open door of the study. More importantly, they could also just about hear what was being said, although they were both very aware of what the consequences would be if they were caught.

'Read this!' The reverend thrust something into Mrs Sparrow's hand and all was quiet for a moment as she did as she was told.

'Well . . . how wonderful and what a great opportunity for her,' they heard her say shortly after.

'Are you stark staring *mad*, woman? Why, this will give her ideas above her station if I agree to it,' he roared as he began to pace up and down, his hands clasped tightly behind his back.

'Rubbish!' Mrs Sparrow snorted. 'And anyway, I don't see how you can refuse. You wouldn't want to upset them, would you? Think of how much they donate to the church. It's not as if they're asking her to go and live with them, is it? She'd be back here each evening and every weekend as normal.'

'Hmm, I suppose you're right; I can't afford to get on the wrong side of them,' he agreed reluctantly.

'That's better, you're talking sense now. Let me go and fetch her so you can put the offer to her. She might say she doesn't want to go, but I very much doubt it. What sane girl would give up a chance like this?'

When they heard the tap-tap of Mrs Sparrow's heels on the hall's tiled floor they flew to the table so they wouldn't be caught eavesdropping.

'Esme, could you go into your grandfather for a moment, pet?' Mrs Sparrow asked as she entered the kitchen. 'He has something he wants to ask you.'

'Er . . . yes, of course.' Esme cast a worried glance towards Gabriel before doing as she was told, and by the time she got to the study door her heart was pounding so loudly she was afraid her grandfather would hear it.

'Esmeralda,' he said as she entered. 'I have received a letter from Lord and Lady Fitzroy in which they say that you would be welcome to join their daughter in her private lessons up at Fitzroy Hall. How would you feel about that?'

'What! *Me?* Have lessons with Olivia? Why, I'd love it,' she answered instantly, her face lighting up. But when she noticed her grandfather's stern expression the smile faded and she stood

146

silent with her hands folded demurely in front of her and her eyes lowered.

'Personally, I think this is a terrible idea,' he told her scathingly. 'And I shall have to give it some serious thought. I'm shocked that the Fitzroys would even *consider* letting their well-bred daughter mix with gypsy trash.'

Angry colour flooded into Esme's cheeks but again she said nothing. Thankfully he waved his hand dismissively and she scooted back to the kitchen while the going was good.

Mrs Sparrow had obviously told Gabriel why her grandfather wanted to see her and he was smiling.

'This will be wonderful for you,' he said.

'Hmm, it will be if he allows me to go. He doesn't seem too happy with the idea.'

'Don't you get worrying about that.' Mrs Sparrow smiled at her. 'You just leave him to me. Opportunities like this don't come about every day an' it would be criminal if he made you miss it. But now, Gabriel, you'd best go and get your things packed. You need to be up bright and early in the morning to get the coach into Mablethorpe and we don't want you missing it.'

'May I go and help him?'

Mrs Sparrow nodded. 'Of course.' And so the two young people hurried away to Gabriel's room where Esme plonked herself down on the side of his bed.

'I hope he *does* let you go to the hall.' Gabriel took his small bag from the bottom of the wardrobe. 'I wouldn't have to worry about you quite so much if I knew you were out of this place for most of the day.'

'It would be wonderful,' Esme agreed dreamily. 'I just wish you didn't have to go back to school. I don't think Jeremy is any too keen on the idea either.'

'Oh, don't get worrying about us, we'll be all right,' Gabriel assured her cheerily, although his stomach was churning at the thought of it.

Once his bag was packed, Mrs Sparrow allowed them to take a walk to the beach and they made the most of every second they had left together as they strolled along the sand. But all too soon it was evening and time for bed.

'Don't bother getting up to see me off tomorrow,' Gabriel urged his sister as they climbed the stairs together. 'I shall have to be up with the lark, so you might as well have a bit of a lie-in. Let's say goodbye now, eh?' Secretly he couldn't bear the thought of the parting and just wanted to get it over with. And so they stood awkwardly facing each other outside Esme's bedroom door as tears formed in her eyes.

'Be sure to write every week and let me know how it's going up at the hall if the old man allows you to go,' Gabriel said quietly.

Esme's throat was too tight to speak, so she nodded as he leaned forward and gave her a self-conscious peck on the cheek.

'Right, I'll be off to bed then.' His own eyes were full but he managed a smile. 'Just don't forget it won't be that long before I'm home again. Bye, Esme.' And afraid that she might see how upset he was he shot off to his own room.

Despite her brother's request, Esme was up when he left the next morning and she stood on the landing in her nightgown watching him walk away through the window with tears on her cheeks.

'Just *what* the hell do you think you are doing standing there in a state of undress,' a voice suddenly thundered in her ear and Esme whirled about to see her grandfather standing there.

Yet strangely, this time she wasn't afraid of him and she faced him with her chin in the air. 'I was watching my brother leave to go back to the school that he *hates*,' she said bravely and just for a moment, Septimus looked shocked. She had never dared to answer him back like that before apart from the day she had found Gip dead in the orchard.

'He may not like it but he'll thank me for giving him an education when he gets older. Now go and get some clothes on and get about your chores,' he barked.

Esme flounced into her room, leaving Septimus scratching his head as he went down for his breakfast. Esme had changed since she had arrived there. Could he have known it had been on the day she had been forced to bury her beloved Gip. Now the only feeling she felt for her grandfather was hatred.

The day passed miserably for Esme as she was constantly thinking about her brother; she missed him desperately already. She missed Jeremy too; they'd formed a friendship over the two weeks he'd been there and she hoped she would see him again.

That evening as she got ready for bed, she thought of the papers she had stolen from the attic room. She had stuffed them beneath her mattress and left them there. She had avoided reading them because she was slightly afraid of what they might tell her, but now she fished them out and by the light of the guttering candle she began to straighten them out and read them, not that they made any sense.

I'm so unhappy! was written on one. *Will I ever be free?* on another. And so the little messages went on until she had read them all. Her heart ached for the woman who had written them. It appeared that she had been imprisoned up there with no chance of ever being freed, but who could she have been? And who had locked her away and why? She had clearly known there was no chance of any of the messages ever going anywhere so Esme wondered if she had written them purely as a means of passing the time, poor soul. No wonder the eyes of the poor spirit she had seen looked so haunted.

The following evening, she attended her grandfather's sermon at the church and was gratified to see the Fitzroys were present. As soon as the service was over, she hurriedly positioned herself at the church door to collect the hymn books and, as she had hoped, Olivia rushed towards her.

'Did your grandfather receive Mama's letter about you having lessons with me?' she asked immediately and when Esme smiled and nodded, she clapped her hands with delight. 'Oh, that's wonderful. And will he allow you to come?'

'I'm not sure yet but I hope so,' Esme said cautiously. Both girls noticed that Lady Fitzroy was already deep in conversation with the reverend and they fervently hoped that they were discussing the offer.

They watched the two adults with bated breath until, at last, Lady Fitzroy beckoned them to her.

'Good evening, my dear,' she greeted Esme pleasantly. 'I'm delighted to tell you that your dear grandfather has just agreed that as from tomorrow you may visit the hall and have lessons with Olivia.'

Both Esme and Olivia beamed from ear to ear, although they both noted that the smile on the reverend's face looked rather forced.

'Perhaps you could present yourself at the hall at nine thirty tomorrow,' Lady Fitzroy went on. 'Come to the front door and I shall tell the housekeeper to expect you and to show you up to the school room.'

'Thank you, ma'am.' Esme dipped her knee, hardly daring to believe that it was really going to happen.

'But, er . . . what about books and such like? What will my granddaughter need?' Septimus asked, hoping that this wasn't to cost him a great deal of money.

Lady Fitzroy waved her hand airily. 'Oh, nothing at all; all will be provided for her,' she assured him and he looked slightly relieved.

When they eventually left the church, Esme had a spring in her step and momentarily even forgot how much she was missing Gabriel as she looked forward to the day ahead.

'We shall have to get her some more new clothes,' Mrs Sparrow fretted as they walked home. 'The lass has only got the one good outfit she wears for church and you can hardly send her up to the hall each day looking like a foundling. Whatever would her lady-ship think of us?'

Septimus scowled but could see the sense in what she said. To all appearances he was a doting grandfather who did his best for his charges.

If only everyone could know what he's really like! Esme thought.

'I suppose you'd better get the dressmaker to run her up another couple of outfits then. She has her measurements,' Septimus said begrudgingly and Mrs Sparrow winked at Esme.

Esme was so excited at the prospect of visiting the hall that she lay awake all night, unable to sleep. Her grandfather had gone out shortly after the church service and as she was lying there, she heard the sound of the front door opening and shutting and guessed it must be him returning. It was the early hours of the morning by then and she wondered where he had been until so late. Perhaps one of his parishioners was ill?

She blew out the candle and turned on her side, determined to try and get some sleep, but seconds later she heard the door handle turn and flipping over again she saw her grandfather standing there. She could smell alcohol and what she thought might be cheap perfume on him as she stared at him fearfully.

'Eshme.' His voice was slightly slurred. 'I jusht wanted to remind you of the lessons I must teach you about pleashing your hush-band.' He was swaying unsteadily towards the bed and Esme's breath caught in her throat. Without a word he flipped back the blanket and as his large hand settled over her breast, Esme shuddered violently.

'It'sh all right,' he soothed as he saw her terror. 'There'll be no leshons tonight. But shoon . . . very shoon.' And with that he turned and lurched out of the room, leaving the door swinging open behind him.

Esme was out of the bed in a shot, closing the door and wedging the chair tightly under the door handle. With Gabriel home, she had once more been lulled into a false sense of security, but now she vowed to never leave the door or herself unprotected again.

'Are you looking forward to it?' Mrs Sparrow asked the next morning when Esme entered the kitchen. The girl had looked so excited at the prospect the evening before but this morning she seemed a little subdued.

'Yes I am, very much,' Esme told her as she took a seat at the table.

'You could have fooled me. You've got a face as long as a fiddle on you!'

Esme could hardly tell her why so she simply smiled and accepted the dish of porridge Mrs Sparrow had ready for her.

Soon after she set off with a promise to return as soon as lessons were over, and as she walked through the village her spirits rose again. When she came to the enormous iron gates that marked the entrance to the hall, she took a deep breath before slipping through them and walking along the drive that led to two large front doors. Three circular solid marble steps led up to them and to the side was a large bell pull. She tugged it and heard it ring inside and soon a small maid answered the door and gave her a welcoming smile.

'Are you Esmeralda Loveridge?' she asked and when Esme nodded, she held the door wider, allowing her to enter the most enormous hallway she had ever seen. Esme had thought the rectory was large after being used to living in a vardo, but this place was absolutely immense. 'The housekeeper said I was to expect you,' the maid said in a friendly fashion, then lowering her voice she whispered, 'I'm Tilly, by the way.'

She was a short girl who appeared to be little older than Esme, and she had a round face, dark hair and very pretty blue eyes. She was dressed in a plain navy-blue dress, over which she wore a starched white pinafore and a mop cap, both trimmed with broderie anglaise. 'If yer'd like to sit 'ere an' wait, miss, I'll let Miss Olivia know you've arrived,' she told Esme, gesturing to a chair.

Esme had barely sat down when she glanced up to see Olivia charging down a sweeping central staircase that led up to a galleried landing.

'Oh Esme, you've arrived!' Olivia rushed over to greet her with a broad smile on her face. Today she was dressed in a cream satin gown trimmed with lace that shimmered as she moved and Esme instantly felt shabby, even though she was wearing the one smart outfit her grandfather had bought for her.

'We're going to have such fun!' Olivia informed her gleefully. 'Come along and I'll show you my room. Mr Pritchard won't be here for half an hour yet and perhaps you'd like a drink or something to eat?'

'No, no, I've just had my breakfast, thank you,' Esme assured her as Olivia snatched her hand and almost dragged her up the stairs. She found herself on a landing that seemed to go on forever on either side of her, but turning to the left Olivia pulled her along until she came to the door of her bedroom.

'Come on in,' she urged.

As Esme stepped inside, she gasped. It was like something in one of the ladies' magazines her mother used to love when they could afford them. A huge, carved mahogany four-poster bed draped with lace curtains stood against one wall, the mattress covered with a pretty pink silk eiderdown and silk pillows. A deep-pile carpet stretched from wall to wall and rich velvet curtains framed the huge sash windows. A mahogany dressing table with a large ornate mirror took up most of one wall and against the other was a matching armoire and chest of drawers. There was a small escritoire with a little gilt-legged chair in front of it and a marble washstand on which stood a china jug and bowl painted with pink roses. It was the most beautiful, luxurious room Esme had ever been in and she sighed with envy. What must it be like to sleep in a room like this each night?

'I wonder what old pilchard will be like?' Olivia giggled.

Esme raised her eyebrow. 'But I thought the tutor's name was Mr Pritchard?' she said innocently.

'It is.' Olivia gave her a wicked grin. 'But just between us two, pilchard is close enough.'

Esme couldn't help but laugh and for the next few minutes they chatted of this and that until Tilly came to inform them, 'Mr Pritchard is in the school room waitin' fer you both, miss.'

'Thank you, Tilly, we'll be right there.'

Tilly bobbed her knee respectfully and disappeared off the way they had come while Olivia led Esme along the landing to yet another staircase. 'The school rooms and the nursery are up here,' she informed Esme. 'Let's go and see what the old devil is like, eh?'

To their surprise they found a youngish man with a pleasant face waiting for them. He was tall and slim with fair hair and grey eyes that twinkled when he smiled and Esme liked him immediately.

'It's nice to meet you,' he said, holding his hand out to them. As they shook it Esme felt very grown-up. 'I'm very much looking forward to working with you both so shall we begin with English?'

Esme sat down with a happy smile on her face.

Chapter Twenty

The morning passed quickly and at lunchtime Lady Fitzroy appeared in the classroom to see how they were getting on.

'They've both done extremely well,' Mr Pritchard informed her.

'Excellent, then I suggest we all break for lunch now.' Lady Fitzroy gave the girls a warm smile and told Esme, 'Olivia and Amelia dine with me in the dining room and I've arranged to have some lunch brought up for you and Mr Pritchard in here.'

'Oh Mama, can't Esme dine with us?' Olivia pouted and her mother smiled.

'What, and leave poor Mr Pritchard all alone to eat his lunch?' she scolded gently. 'I don't think that would be very nice for him at all.' Although she was more than happy to allow Esme to share her daughter's lessons there were still proprieties to be observed. She was aware that there was already enough gossip down in the servants' quarters about Esme being allowed to be taught with Olivia, without adding to it. 'But first you might like to show Esme where the bathroom is,' she suggested.

The two girls set off along the landing, leaving Lady Fitzroy to have a quiet word with the tutor. Eventually Olivia opened a door and told her new friend, 'You may use this one, this is my bathroom.'

When Esme stepped inside, her breath caught as she gazed about in amazement. She had never seen an inside bathroom before. There was a large roll-top bath with a tap on it and Olivia explained, 'The hot water is pumped up from a boiler in the boiler house and when I've bathed, I pull the plug and the water goes down a pipe into a drain outside. And that there is the toilet. The servants empty it early each morning. I'll wait outside and show you back to the schoolroom just until you get to know

155

your way around. Oh, and I must introduce you to my governess, Miss Trimble, too. She is responsible for teaching some of our lessons – such as embroidery, playing the piano and singing. All well-brought-up young ladies should be able to do all three.'

'Really?' This all sounded like another world to Esme, and she wondered when she would ever use such talents. Even so, she was happy to try anything.

Soon after, Olivia showed her back to the school room. It was just as well she did for the place was so vast Esme was sure she would never have found her way back there on her own.

Mr Pritchard was seated at a table in the window and Tilly was busily loading dishes from a large tray onto it. Whatever was in them smelled delicious and Esme's tummy rumbled in anticipation as she joined him.

'If you need anything else just ring that bell over there,' Tilly told them with a friendly smile. 'I'll be back in a minute with a pot of tea, or would you prefer a cold drink, miss? Lemonade or milk perhaps?'

'Oh no, tea will be fine, thank you, Tilly,' Esme assured her as she took a seat. She wasn't used to being waited on.

'So, what culinary delights have we got here then?' Mr Pritchard said as he lifted the lid of a silver tureen. 'Ah, broccoli and stilton soup, if I'm not very much mistaken, one of my favourites. Will you try some, Esme?'

'Yes please, sir.' Esme soon found that the soup tasted as delicious as it smelled and it was followed by a main course of some white fish cooked in a white wine sauce. Esme had never tasted anything like it and she loved every mouthful. Their dessert was a rice pudding sprinkled with nutmeg, and they were just finishing when Tilly appeared with the promised tray of tea.

'Oh, I don't think I shall be able to eat again for at least a month.' Esme grinned as she rubbed her full stomach and Tilly giggled.

'It's one o' the perks o' workin' here,' she confided. 'We none of us ever go short o' snap.'

Once they had had their tea it was time to resume their lessons. This afternoon they were doing maths and geography and Esme soaked up everything Mr Pritchard told them.

The time passed all too quickly until eventually Mr Pritchard took his silver Hunter watch from his waistcoat pocket and told them, 'That's it for today, young ladies. Well done, and I shall see you both in the morning. Good day to you.'

After he left, Esme rose to do the same but Olivia pleaded, 'Oh *please* don't go yet. I thought we could have a stroll around the rose gardens then I'll walk you to the gates.'

'Er . . . if you're quite sure,' Esme said uncertainly. She wouldn't want Lady Fitzroy to think she was trying to take advantage.

They set off and Esme was enchanted as she walked through the sunken rose garden, which was full of sweet-smelling roses in every hue with honey bees and a wide variety of brightly coloured butterflies fluttering amongst them.

'This is just *so* beautiful,' she breathed and Olivia nodded in agreement.

'Yes, it's one of my mother's favourite places. She likes to come and sit in here and read when she has time.'

Eventually they emerged onto the enormous lawns that surrounded the hall where gardeners were busily scything the grass or deadheading the colourful arrays of flowers in the borders.

'Goodness, I can't believe how many people are employed here just to take care of one house and one family,' Esme said.

Olivia tittered. 'Yes, there are quite a lot.' She began to tick them off on her fingers. 'There's the butler and father's valet, the housekeeper, my governess and Amelia's nanny and mother's lady's maid. Then there is the cook, the kitchen maids, the parlour maids and the housemaids, oh, and the laundry maids. There's the gardeners and the head groom and the stable boys and probably some more that I've forgotten.'

Esme shook her head. This was like another world to the one she was used to but already she knew that she liked it. If only Gabriel could have come here with her it would have been perfect.

She suddenly felt guilty as she realised that this was the first time she had thought of him all day, and she hoped that his first day back at school had been as happy as hers, although she seriously doubted it would have been from the things he had told her.

After a time, she reluctantly told Olivia that she needed to leave and Olivia walked her along the drive to the imposing gates.

'I'll see you tomorrow,' Olivia chirped, planting a peck on Esme's cheek. She had so enjoyed having someone her own age to do her lessons with and she was happy with her mother's choice of tutor too. Mr Pritchard was much younger than her former nanny and she'd taken a shine to him.

Esme set off smiling and the minute she set foot in the kitchen at the rectory she began to tell Mrs Sparrow all about her day and what lessons she and Olivia had had.

'I'm glad to hear that everything went so well,' the woman told her kindly. 'But now I'm afraid you'll have to get changed and pitch in to do a few jobs before your grandfather gets home. He'll expect you to attend the service at the church this evening as well. Oh, and by the way . . .' she added as Esme turned to go and do as she was bid. 'Don't be too effusive about today if he asks you how it went,' she advised. He had made it more than clear that he wasn't happy about Esme having lessons up at the hall already, and she knew him well enough to know that if he thought she had enjoyed it he would be even less pleased.

Esme nodded and skipped away, but even the warning couldn't take the smile from her face that day. By the time her grandfather had arrived home for his evening meal she had polished the drawing room and mopped the floor tiles in the hall before going to get changed ready for church yet again.

'We had the most wonderful lunch,' Esme told Mrs Sparrow enthusiastically as she sat down to her own meal. 'There was a lovely thick soup and then this fish cooked in this lovely sauce and—' She stopped abruptly as she saw the hurt expression on the woman's face and added hastily, 'But it wasn't as tasty as your cottage pie, of course. No one can make those like you do. Gabriel thinks so, too.' She wouldn't have hurt her feelings for the world. She was the only ally she had in the house after all.

'Aye well, it's all down to how the other half live, isn't it?' Mrs Sparrow responded with a sniff. 'They can afford to buy the best cuts of meat and the best of everything, whereas I have to watch what I spend on the housekeeping your grandfather allows me. Not that he goes short, mind! He makes sure that he has the choice cuts and then I do the best I can with what's left for us.'

'And very well you do it too,' Esme told her as she lifted her knife and fork. In truth she was still full from lunch but she cleared her plate rather than offend her.

They did the washing and drying up between them and all too soon it was time to set off to the church for yet another of her grandfather's boring sermons. Only the week before, she and Gabriel had been forced to stifle a fit of the giggles when the old farmer sitting next to them had fallen asleep and snored his way through half the sermon. Thinking of Gabriel made her sad again and after taking her seat on the hard wooden pew, she struggled to concentrate on what her grandfather was saying as she thought of him.

The rest of the week passed as pleasantly as it had begun and by the time Friday rolled around Olivia and Esme were firm friends.

'I'm going to ask Mama if she'll allow you to come and stay over one evening,' Olivia told her as she walked her up the drive after their lessons.

'Oh no . . . don't do that!' Esme blurted out before she could stop herself and seeing the look of hurt on Olivia's face she rushed on. 'Not because I wouldn't want to, of course . . . It's just that I think Grandfather already feels enough in your family's debt for offering me an education.'

'What rubbish!' Olivia snorted, tossing her curls across her shoulder. She still wore her hair loose or tied back in a ribbon as her mother didn't think she was quite old enough to wear it up yet.

'We could have *so* much fun. You could try some of my clothes on and we could go for nice walks.' And then tactfully she said, 'I've noticed that you always wear the same outfit and I have so many clothes. I could sort some out for you.'

'That's very kind of you but actually my grandfather has ordered me some new clothes of my own,' Esme assured her. 'They should be ready very soon and were you to start giving me yours your mama might not like it.'

Olivia shook her head. 'I have so many, I doubt she'd even notice,' she retorted, but she didn't want to make Esme feel inferior so she changed the subject and they walked on talking of the lessons they had had that day.

'I'm afraid on Monday you shall have to join me for lessons in the afternoon with Miss Trimble, my governess.' She sighed. 'Unfortunately they're terribly boring. She's teaching me etiquette and how to behave and run a house when I'm married one day.'

'Etiquette?' Esme raised an eyebrow.

'Yes. You know, how one should always raise their little finger when drinking tea and how one should always leave a little on one's plate.' As Olivia mimicked Miss Trimble, Esme giggled.

'She's awfully old and terribly old-fashioned,' Olivia groaned. 'She was actually my mother's governess when she was a little girl. I keep hoping that she'll retire but she keeps going.'

'Well, I can't really see how I could benefit from learning etiquette,' Esme commented doubtfully. 'After all, you and I come from two very different ways of life. You're rich and you probably will have a big house and servants to supervise one day but it's highly unlikely I ever shall. If anything, I shall probably be one of the servants.'

'Nonsense,' Olivia said crossly. 'With your looks you could marry anyone you chose if you dressed properly and moved in the right circles.'

'Hmm, we'll see.' Esme doubted that very much. After all, who would want to marry her when they discovered that her father had been a gypsy and that she'd spent the first few years of her life

160

travelling the roads in a vardo. Not that she regretted a moment of it. She just wished she could have the chance to do it all again.

In no time they reached the gates and Olivia pouted. 'Oh, it's going to be *so* dreadfully boring not being able to see you all weekend,' she complained.

'You will see me in church on Sunday,' Esme pointed out.

'I know that but it's hardly the same, is it? Still, I suppose it isn't so very long until Monday morning so I'll see you then.' And with that she gave a cheery little wave and set off down the drive again as Esme made her way home.

She was in a mellow mood until she reached the rectory and she smiled at Mrs Sparrow as she entered the kitchen. 'Oh, I've had a wonderful week and I—'

'Ssh!' Mrs Sparrow put a finger to her lips and Esme stopped talking immediately.

'Your grandfather is in a towering rage,' the woman warned her. 'So best keep your voice down.'

'But why? What's happened?' Esme whispered as she undid the ribbons on her bonnet and placed it on the table, letting her glorious silver-blonde hair fall about her shoulders.

'He's had another letter from the school. It seems Gabriel has been in another fight.' Mrs Sparrow shook her head and sighed. 'If only he'd just keep his head down and get on with his work!'

Esme immediately jumped to his defence. 'Actually, from what he's told me, he does. It's the other boys that pick on *him*. It's because they know our father was a gypsy and they don't think he's good enough to be there. And he probably isn't as clever as them either. Gabriel never liked learning as I did. But he's all right, isn't he?'

'As far as I know.' Mrs Sparrow shook her head. 'Go and get changed and try to keep out of your grandfather's way.'

Esme trooped upstairs and suddenly she was sad again. It was funny how this place could have that effect on her, especially when she knew that all was not right with her brother. She had just passed the study door on her way to the staircase when it opened and her grandfather appeared. Esme instantly held her breath. But to her surprise he gave her a pleasant smile before asking, 'How did your lessons go today?'

'Er . . . very well, thank you, Grandfather.'

'Good, good. Then report to me in the drawing room after supper for your Bible lesson.'

He strode away, leaving her to scratch her head in bewilderment. She always worried when he was polite to her. Could it be that he was planning another visit to her room? She shuddered at the thought and promised herself that she would make doubly sure that the chair was placed firmly below the door handle when she went to bed that night.

Chapter Twenty-One

Gabriel sat on the floor in the corner of the punishment room, with his arms around his knees and his head hanging. He'd lost track of how long he'd been there as the room contained no windows and was pitch dark. He thought it must have been at least a day now, and his stomach was rumbling with hunger. In the other corner was a bucket, which he had been forced to use, and now the ripe smell of it was making him feel sick. There was no bed, no chair, no blanket, nothing, so he had napped on and off with his back against the wall as his resentment grew. His left eye was swollen shut and his lip was split after yet another run-in with Broadhurst and his gang. It had started in the dormitory before breakfast when Gabriel had reached into his locker to find the homework he had slogged over, only to find it gone.

'All right, who's had it?' he said angrily.

'Can't think what you're talking about, old chap,' Broadhurst had sneered. 'Lost something, have you?'

The rest of his group had started to snigger and, losing his temper, Gabriel had stormed over to Broadhurst's locker and begun to throw the contents onto the floor.

'I know it was you behind it,' Gabriel had stormed as he looked at them all. 'So come on, own up an' hand it over an' we'll say no more about it, eh?'

Broadhurst shrugged nonchalantly just as Mrs Ingles appeared in the doorway to see what all the ruckus was about. She glanced from one to another of them but then as her eyes settled on Broadhurst's things strewn across the floor, her face set.

'What is going on in here? And what's all this mess? Who is responsible for it?'

'I am, Mrs Ingles,' Gabriel told her immediately. 'But I did it because I was—'

'That's quite enough, Loveridge!' She held her hand up warningly. 'Get it cleared up *immediately*. You can miss breakfast and then report to the headmaster's study. I will not put up with this behaviour!'

'But—'

'*Enough*, I said,' she barked as the rest of the boys began to leave the room.

At the door Broadhurst paused to look back over his shoulder and grin, and Gabriel was so incensed at the unfairness of it all that he had to grit his teeth to stop himself flying at him and giving him the pasting he deserved. He knew if he did, it would only get him into more trouble and that was without having to turn up to his lessons with no homework to hand in yet again.

After warning him that she would be back to check that he had put everything away tidily, Mrs Ingles closed the door firmly behind her. Gabriel sank down onto the side of his bed and dropped his head into his hands as he gazed longingly towards the window. He felt like a bird trapped in a cage and wondered how much longer he could bear it. But as he thought of Esme, he knew that he must. There was no way he could earn enough to rent somewhere for them to live until he was a little older, so he had tried to resign himself to being there a while longer.

Once he had returned everything to Broadhurst's locker, he slowly went down to sit outside the headmaster's office. When the man finally appeared, he gave Gabriel six of the best with his cane on each palm. Gabriel's hands were smarting and wheals appeared across the skin, but not once did he so much as whimper.

'Now get back to your class, boy, and let this be the end of your appalling behaviour,' the headmaster ranted as Gabriel left the room with his head held high. There was no way his pride would allow him to show the bully how much he had hurt him.

The humiliation continued when he entered his first lesson. The rest of the class was already seated and he saw them grin as he crept to his chair.

'Put your homework on the table, boy,' the teacher snapped as he turned from the blackboard and a snigger swept through the class.

'Someone took it from my locker, sir,' Gabriel mumbled, keeping his head down. He felt like a volcano about to erupt but he knew that if he did, he would get into even more trouble.

'Huh! Is that the best excuse you can come up with?' The teacher glared at him. 'See me at the end of class and be sure I'll give you three times what I gave you to do before, and it'll be woe betide you if it isn't done this time.'

Smarting at the injustice of it all, Gabriel sat down, but the day only got progressively worse as each teacher piled yet more work and insults on him, clearly believing that he hadn't bothered to do it.

By the time they went into the dining room that evening, Gabriel was feeling lower than low and Jeremy gave his arm a slight squeeze under the table.

'Don't let the buggers see you're bothered,' he advised quietly, but it was easier said than done and the food, such as it was, seemed to stick in Gabriel's throat.

It was later that evening as Gabriel visited the bathroom before going to bed that things came to a head. Broadhurst and his entourage were in there and they instantly started to mock him.

'Ooh – *poor* little Loveridge,' Broadhurst crowed. 'Did you have a bad day?' He then reached out and poked Gabriel spitefully in the ribs and something snapped in Gabriel as he turned to face him, his face puce with rage.

'Keep your bleedin' hands off me, else I'll knock you into next week, you measly little swine,' he growled and before he could stop himself he swung a punch at Broadhurst's chin and sent him sprawling across the bathroom floor. The next second the whole gang were on to him like a pack of wolves. Jeremy did what he could to help but the two of them were useless against so many and punches and kicks rained down on them.

'What the *hell*!' A voice from the doorway ended the fight, and the boys turned to see Mr Chaplin, the history teacher, standing there.

'You *again*, Loveridge!' He shook his head. 'I might have known you'd be in the thick of it.'

Gabriel opened his mouth to tell him what had happened but promptly clamped it shut again. What would be the point? He knew they were all against him.

'You lot, get back to your dormitory,' the teacher ordered the rest of the boys. 'And *you*, Loveridge, come with me. Perhaps a spell in the punishment room will teach you that we won't tolerate this sort of behaviour here. You're a complete heathen!'

'But, sir,' Jeremy piped up. 'It wasn't his—'

'Shut up, else *you'll* be going with him,' the teacher shouted, and one by one the boys trooped from the room.

Gabriel was led down to the hall and from there down the cold stone cellar steps to where the dreaded punishment room was. He'd heard some of the others say that once you'd been in there you never risked going again, but he didn't flinch as the teacher unlocked a door and shoved him inside. It wasn't until the door had been slammed shut and locked, leaving him in total darkness, that panic set in and he began to feel claustrophobic. He had always had a fear of confined spaces but being locked away and made to feel that he was the last person left on earth made it seem even worse. Despite the fact that his ribs were aching, he spent some time walking back and forth like a caged animal. After that he began to bang on the door and shout, but nothing but silence greeted him and his panic increased. What if they forgot about him and left him there? He knew he wasn't being logical. They'd have to let him out eventually, surely.

After a while he was so exhausted and sore that he was forced to sit down on the floor and there he remained, dozing intermittently and straining his ears for a sound, any sound, that might mean he was about to be freed, but there was nothing apart from the frantic scuttling of little feet across the floor.

And then at last, when he felt as if he had been locked away forever, he heard heavy footsteps on the stone steps and the sound of a key turning in the lock. As the door opened, he blinked in the light.

'Going to behave yourself now, are you?' It was Mr Chaplin's voice and Gabriel dragged himself painfully to his feet, feeling like he'd done ten rounds in a boxing ring with a bare-knuckle fighter.

'Wh-what time is it?' he asked in a weak voice.

'It's nearly supper time. You've been down here for almost a full twenty-four hours. Had enough, have you?'

Gabriel swallowed. He wanted to tell the man to go to hell but what would be the point? 'Yes . . . *sir*!'

'Right, go and get yourself cleaned up and then you can join the rest of the boys for supper. And think yourself lucky that I'm allowing it. if anything like this happens again, you'll be down here for a lot longer. We've tamed far cockier boys than you, I assure you.'

Gabriel didn't reply, merely followed him up the steps. What else could he do?

'Had a nice stay downstairs, did you?' Broadhurst mocked him when they went to their dormitory that night.

'It wasn't all bad, actually. At least it got me away from *you* for a time,' Gabriel retorted. He'd noticed that Jeremy had a black eye and a split lip too, but there was nothing he could do about it. And so, turning his back, he got ready for bed and climbed under the blanket, ignoring the snide remarks that were being directed at him.

Despite his brave words to Broadhurst he had no wish to be returned to the punishment room again!

Chapter Twenty-Two

Back at the rectory, Esme was also preparing for bed and trying to ignore the dark shapes in the corner. She'd hoped that if she ignored them, they would stop appearing but in fact, they were coming more frequently. Once again, she wished that she had never inherited 'the gift'. If anything, Esme considered it to be a curse. After all, who could take pleasure from seeing the spirits of dead people all the time? She had said as much to her father once and he had gently told her that it was an honour to have such a gift and if she developed it, it could earn her a living. Her grandmother Griselda had fed and clothed herself by passing on messages from the spirits to their living relatives, but the thought of that made Esme shudder. She just wanted to be like other girls but she was beginning to realise now that this so-called gift was not something that could be ignored.

After slipping into her nightgown and brushing her hair, she was just getting into bed when a noise made her pause. Glancing towards the door, her heart began to thump when she saw the door handle turning. She had jammed the chair beneath it so there was no way anyone could get in but she knew that if it was her grandfather he would not give in easily and very soon she was proved to be right.

'Esme . . . open this door *immediately*. There seems to be something blocking it!' His voice was no more than a hoarse whisper but she heard every word and she started to shake.

'Wh-what do you want?' Her voice came out as a croak and the spirits in the corner were growing agitated.

'I just want to talk about tomorrow's Bible lesson with you,' his voice came back cajolingly. 'You did *so well* tonight!'

'Can't we talk about it in the morning?' she stammered.

There was silence for a moment and when he spoke again his voice was firmer. 'Open this door *now*. Do you hear me, girl? I will have no door in my own home locked against me.'

She pressed her lips together, praying that he would get tired of trying the door. But then he played his trump card.

'You do *know* that I could make things very uncomfortable for your brother at his school, don't you?'

Esme shuddered. Gabriel was having a bad enough time of it already without her grandfather making things worse for him. And so reluctantly she moved the chair to one side.

'That's *better*.' He gave her an oily smile as he entered, quickly shutting the door behind him. 'Now, why don't we sit down and have a nice little chat. I've brought you something, look.' When he opened his palm she was shocked to see a small gold brooch in the shape of a bird with a tiny sapphire for its eye. 'This was bought for your mother for her fifteenth birthday,' he told her. 'And I think you are old enough to look after it now.'

Esme had never owned a piece of jewellery in her life and it was the prettiest thing she had ever seen, even more precious because it had belonged to her mother. But what price would she have to pay for it? she wondered as she gazed at it solemnly in the fast-fading light.

'I-it looks as if it might have cost a great deal of money,' she said doubtfully and he laughed.

'It certainly did. But your mother didn't even bother taking it with her when she left with . . . Well, I just hope you will value it more than she did. Here . . . take it.'

As he dropped the brooch into her hand she stood quite still and just as she had feared he stepped closer and gently stroked her hair back from her face. 'Such pretty hair,' he said quietly, almost as if he was talking to himself. 'The exact same colour as your mother's and her mother's before her.' Then his hand slid to her shoulder and a faraway look came into his eyes as he began to caress it through her cotton nightgown. She stood so still she might have been turned to stone and after what seemed a lifetime, but was in fact a mere few minutes, his hand began to follow the shape of her back until it slid down far enough to stroke her buttocks.

By that time, she was shaking, although she said not a word. 'Yes,' he said breathily as his other hand dropped to the bulge in his trousers. 'You are developing nicely. You'll soon be a young woman. But don't forget, this is what fathers and grandfathers do to their girls to teach them how to please their husbands when the time comes for them to marry. Not a word to anyone, mind. Now turn around.'

Too terrified to do anything else, she did as she was told, fixing her eyes on the window and praying that he would soon go away. His hand snaked around her and began to fondle her small breasts and she could hear his breathing becoming more rapid. And then suddenly he went rigid and squeezed her nipple so hard that she had to bite her lip to stop herself from crying out. Seconds later his hand dropped away, but still she stood, holding her breath and facing the window until she heard the door open and shut quietly. She stood there until she had plucked up the courage to glance over her shoulder and only then did she sob with relief when she saw that he had gone.

There were no more incidents that weekend, but when Esme reported to Fitzroy Hall the following Monday, Olivia was quick to notice that her friend was unusually quiet and she mentioned it when they were having their lunch – her mother had gone visiting friends that day so she was allowed to have lunch with Esme.

'Is everything all right, Esme?' she asked. 'You've been in a world of your own for most of the morning. I think even Pilchard noticed.'

'What? Oh yes, yes, I'm fine. Really.' But she didn't feel it. Her grandfather's visit to her room was preying heavily on her mind and she desperately wanted to talk to Olivia about it but she didn't dare. What if Olivia told her that what he said was true and that her father did the same things to her? That would mean that the visits would continue and she didn't know how she would be able to bear that.

They sat in silence eating their food for a time until Esme suddenly noticed an old, old woman leaning heavily on an ebony-topped walking stick standing to one side of the door, smiling. She waited for the woman to come forward and say something but then as she watched her, she slowly faded away and Esme caught her breath as she realised that it was a spirit.

'What's wrong?' Olivia looked concerned and suddenly Esme could keep her secret no longer.

'I . . . I just saw an elderly lady standing by the door,' she gulped. 'Or at least I saw her spirit. Her earthly body has passed on.'

'Really?' Olivia was thrilled. 'What, you saw a ghost?'

Esme shrugged. 'Ghost, spirit, whatever you want to call them,' she muttered miserably. 'I see them all the time.'

She had Olivia's full attention now. 'What did the lady look like?'

'Hmm.' Esme spread her hands. 'She was very old and she had rouge on her cheeks and wore lots of jewellery. Oh, and she had a walking stick. A very posh one with an ebony handle in the shape of a dog, I think it was.'

Olivia paled and her hand went to her mouth as she looked towards the door. 'That sounds like my grandmama,' she said quietly. 'She died last year. What colour hair did she have?'

'I think it was fair with quite a bit of grey in it. Oh, and she wore a long string of large pearls about her neck, they reached almost down to her waist.'

'My grandmother had a string of pearls that Grandpapa bought her for Christmas one year. They were her favourite and she wore them all the time. But how come you could see her and I couldn't?'

'I have what my dadda always called "the gift",' Esme told her reluctantly. 'My grandmother Griselda had it before me and she made a living giving people messages from their loved ones who had passed on. The difference is, I don't like having it and wish it would go away.' Strangely now that she had started it was a relief to share it with someone and she went on, 'The rectory is full of spirits. Very unhappy ones, I think.'

'Really, how do you know?' Olivia was fascinated.

'I just sense it,' Esme answered glumly. 'When I first went there, I had two young ladies come to my bedroom regularly but there are four of them now. And there's the spirit of another lady in the room above mine.'

'Do they talk to you?' When Esme shook her head Olivia looked disappointed. 'Why not?'

'Because I always try to ignore them hoping they'll go away. I've never tried to develop the gift and just wish I hadn't got it. I can tell you, though, that your grandmother isn't unhappy. She was smiling.'

Olivia's eyes filled with tears. 'Oh, I wish I could have seen her,' she said regretfully. 'I miss her so much. She had a great sense of humour and we used to spend hours together. Sadly she was bedridden towards the end and I used to go and sit and read to her. Poor soul couldn't walk anymore.'

'Well, she's walking now,' Esme assured her and Olivia gave her a watery smile.

'You really should try to develop this gift you have,' she urged. 'Do the spirits just sort of materialise, you know – float through the walls?'

'Not at all.' Esme couldn't help but smile. 'I see them as clearly as I'm seeing you and then they just sort of fade away if I ignore them.'

'This is amazing!' Olivia declared. 'Could you perhaps teach me how to see them?'

'It doesn't work like that. It just happened that I inherited this gift from my grandmother but my brother didn't.'

After lunch they both reported to Miss Trimble and once again Esme was introduced to a different way of life. 'I shall be teaching you to play the piano, how to be a good hostess and organise dinner parties, and also to embroider and how to dress for different occasions,' the woman told her.

Esme frowned, wondering how any of these things could possibly ever be useful to her. It was highly unlikely that she would lead the life that Olivia would when she grew up. Olivia had already confided that her parents would introduce her to suitable men when she was deemed old enough and that she would marry someone who could keep her in the manner to which she was accustomed, whereas Esme would probably marry a working man, if she ever did marry, that was. She had been tempted to speak to Olivia about the visits her grandfather paid to her room but she was too afraid to, so remained quiet on the subject.

That afternoon began with a piano lesson and Esme admired how good Olivia was. Her own first attempt was appalling. She had no idea how to read music and all the keys looked the same to her so she and Olivia ended up in a fit of giggles, much to Miss Trimble's disgust.

'Tut tut, girls,' she scolded them. 'This will never do; I can see I shall have my work cut out with you, Esme. But never fear, by the time I've done with you, you will be an accomplished pianist.'

Esme thought that was highly unlikely but she smiled politely as Miss Trimble proceeded to teach them how to entertain guests who visited for morning coffee or afternoon tea. It all seemed a terrible lot of palaver to go to just to give someone a cup of tea, she thought, but she listened intently just the same.

As it happened Miss Trimble had an appointment that afternoon and allowed them to finish their lessons an hour early, which was just the opportunity Olivia had been waiting for.

'There's no need for you to go just yet,' she told Esme. 'We'll go to my room and you can try on some gowns that don't fit me anymore.'

Esme was hesitant. It wasn't likely that she would ever have occasion to wear the sort of clothes that Olivia did but she followed her to her room all the same. Anything was better than having to go to the rectory until it was absolutely necessary.

The second they entered the room Esme's eyes fell on a number of gowns that Olivia had spread out on the bed. There were so many and Esme wondered what it must be like to own such beautiful clothes. She could only imagine that just one of them must have cost more than her dadda had been able to earn in a whole year.

'Do try this one on first,' Olivia encouraged excitedly. 'It will complement your hair and eyes, I'm sure.' She lifted a pale-yellow satin gown trimmed with white guipure lace about the sleeves and neckline, and Esme was sure it was the most beautiful gown she had ever seen.

'Oh . . . it's lovely,' she said doubtfully. 'But when would I ever go anywhere to wear it?'

'Well, from now on I shall be inviting you to the parties we have here and as tidy as the clothes you're wearing now are, you could hardly wear them to a party, could you? Go on, just try it, for me! If it needs altering, I can get our seamstress to do it for you.'

And so Esme slowly undressed and stood still as Olivia dropped the gown over her head and began to do up the row of tiny pearl buttons that ran up the back of it.

'That's it,' Olivia said happily when she had done. 'Now let's let your hair loose and then you can look.' She quickly undid the ribbon tying Esme's hair back and arranged it about her shoulders before ordering her to have a look in the cheval mirror.

Esme slowly turned and blinked in amazement as she stared at her reflection. She looked so different that she hardly recognised herself.

'See? Didn't I tell you that it would suit you.' Olivia smiled. 'It looks so much better on you than it ever did on me, and it doesn't need much altering at all. Perhaps a nip in at the waist and a little off the length and it will be perfect.'

'B-but I'm afraid this must have cost a great deal of money,' Esme said, feeling embarrassed. 'And I'm sure your mama wouldn't want you giving it away.'

'Why not?' Olivia wagged a finger at her. 'What else would I do with them? Mama will probably just give them away to charity and I'd much rather you have them.'

For the next hour they tried on the various gowns until Esme's head was spinning.

'There are far too many for me to take them all,' she insisted. Finally she chose two. 'And could you perhaps keep them here for me? I don't think my grandfather would appreciate me wearing clothes like these. He'd say I was getting ideas above my station. Not that I'm not very grateful,' she added hurriedly, not wishing to hurt Olivia's feelings. 'I love them and perhaps if I do ever come to a party here, we could get ready together?'

Olivia nodded enthusiastically. 'I think I can understand what you mean,' she agreed. 'Your grandfather does seem a little strict, and I wouldn't want you getting into any trouble on my account. I'll get them altered for you and keep them here. Mama and Papa are having a ball here in the summer, so perhaps you could persuade your grandfather to let you attend that and you can wear one of them then?'

When Esme set off for home wearing her own clothes and with her hair tied securely back in a ribbon once more, there was a spring in her step and she found that she couldn't stop smiling. In the new gowns she had felt like Cinderella in the story her mammy used to read to her when she was a little girl, and she was determined that, by hook or by crook, when the time was right, she would somehow persuade her grandfather to allow her to attend the ball.

That night as she lay in bed watching the dancing shadows on the ceiling, Esme thought back to Olivia's reaction to finding out about her so-called gift. Rather than be afraid of it, Olivia had found it exciting, and for the first time Esme wondered if perhaps she shouldn't try to develop it after all. She raised herself on one arm and glanced towards the corner, expecting to see the young women – but tonight there was nothing so she lay back down and slept.

Chapter Twenty-Three

August 1876

O ver the next few months her grandfather began to be away from home on a more regular basis for a few days each month, and Esme welcomed the respite.

'Where does he go?' she asked Mrs Sparrow one morning before setting off for the hall.

The older woman merely shrugged and avoided her eyes. 'Oh, there's always some seminar or something going on somewhere that he wants to be involved in,' was all she would say, so Esme didn't question her further.

Thankfully, her grandfather hadn't attempted to enter her room again, which was a relief, but Esme was gravely concerned about Gabriel. He had come back to the rectory during the summer holidays and she had scarcely recognised him. The happy-go-lucky brother that she had known and loved seemed to have vanished and in his place was a mere shadow of the boy he had been. He had lost yet more weight and his once thick, lustrous black hair looked dull and limp. Things had got no better for him at the school, although he never complained to Esme, but he didn't have to. She knew him well enough to know that he was deeply unhappy and it hurt because there wasn't a thing she could do to help him.

Now, it was late in August and up at the hall preparations were beginning for the ball that the Fitzroys would be holding there the following week.

Luckily it would fall at a time when her grandfather would be away and so Mrs Sparrow had given permission for Esme to attend and neither she nor Olivia could wait. A seamstress had altered the lovely lemon gown that Olivia had given her and Mrs Sparrow

176

had also reluctantly agreed to let Esme stay there for the night following the ball.

'It's going to be amazing!' Olivia trilled excitedly when the big day finally dawned. 'Luke's been away visiting friends, but he'll be home from visiting shortly and you'll be able to get to know him a little better.'

They crept downstairs as excited as two little girls to watch the preparations. In the ballroom the members of the orchestra were tuning up their instruments and maids that had been brought in to help were rushing to and fro from the kitchen to the dining room getting the tables ready for the food. Top chefs had been brought in from London to prepare it and the whole place seemed to be organised chaos.

'We shall have the whole afternoon to get ready,' Olivia told Esme with a wide smile. 'And lots of the guests that are coming from far away will be staying overnight so you'll be sleeping in my room with me. Just think what fun it will be. And Papa says we may stay up late! I've always had to go to bed at nine thirty when we've had balls before but Papa says that now I am older I can stay up till whatever time I wish.'

This was like another world to Esme and she just wished that Gabriel had been invited so that he could be there to enjoy it with her.

'My maid will be helping us to get ready and will do our hair for us,' Olivia prattled on. 'Although Papa says I'm still not old enough to wear it up yet.' She pouted prettily then grinned again. 'Still, never mind. I'm sure she will be able to do something with it and with yours too. I do so envy you your hair.' She reached out to pat Esme's curls, and her mood was so infectious that Esme couldn't help but smile too.

They continued to watch the maids scurrying about like ants for a little while longer then Olivia led her out into the garden. Like the house, it was a hive of activity. Some of the gardeners were scything the already pristine grass while others were hanging lanterns in the trees dotted around the extensive lawns and along the driveway leading to the house. They would light the candles inside them that evening when it started to get dark. There were so many of them Esme didn't envy them the job.

They had their lunch in Olivia's bedroom on trays and mid-afternoon the maid arrived to begin running their baths for them.

'If we wash our hair nice and early it will have plenty of time to dry,' Olivia told her, unable to keep the excitement from her voice. Esme was only too happy to oblige. She had never bathed in a proper bathroom before and loved every minute of soaking in the rose-scented water, although she did find it rather embarrassing when the maid entered to wash her hair for her.

Soon they were back in Olivia's room, hanging out of the window to watch what was going on outside, with their damp hair blowing about their shoulders in the gentle breeze. Above them the sun blazed down from a cloudless blue sky and Esme was sure they couldn't have ordered a better day.

At five o'clock the maids began to trail back and forth to the dining room with trays laden with delicacies. There was a whole roasted pig, a huge ham and every sort of meat imaginable on one table, and on another were pies and pasties still warm from the oven. There were enormous bowls of salad grown in the vegetable gardens of the hall and trays of freshly baked bread and dainty rolls. Another table held an assortment of vol-au-vents filled with fresh prawns and shrimps, caught near Grimsby that day, chicken and garlic mushrooms, and so many more. There were pork pies, sausage rolls and every sort of cheese imaginable. Another table was groaning beneath the weight of fancies, cakes and fruit pies. Pastries, trifles and jellies of all the colours of the rainbow were on another.

'It would take an army to eat all this,' Esme breathed in amazement when she and Olivia sneaked down to take a peep later in the afternoon.

'Don't you believe it!' Olivia giggled. 'The guests are like a swarm of locusts after they've had a drink or two.'

A bar had been set up in the drawing room but Olivia had been told in no uncertain terms that although she and Esme would be allowed to stay up, they must not drink alcohol. They were still watching when the maid hurried to answer a knock on the front door and Luke appeared.

Olivia flew over and wrapped her arms about him, delighted. 'You're late! I was getting worried,' she scolded as he picked her up and swung her around.

'Sorry, I got held up.' He looked towards Esme and smiled, and her tummy did a little flip. He was just as handsome as she remembered.

'Do you remember Esme, Luke?' Olivia asked. 'Her grandfather is the vicar at the church.'

'Yes, of course.' He held his hand out and Esme shook it.

'Esme has her lessons with me now and we've become great friends. She's coming to the ball this evening then spending the night here. It'll be fun, won't it? But don't let me hold you up. Mama has been like a cat on hot bricks all day waiting for you to arrive. She's in the dining room overseeing the maids. Do go in and put her out of her misery, won't you?'

As Luke strode away, Olivia grabbed Esme's hand and dragged her upstairs again and once in the bedroom, they found a maid laying their gowns out for them.

'I shall be back shortly to help you both get ready, miss,' the maid told her and with a bob of her knee she hurried away.

'Now, I've found you some nice petticoats to go underneath your dress,' Olivia told her. 'And I also bought you a little present.' She went to her armoire and returned with a box that was prettily wrapped with a ribbon and white paper.

It looked so pretty that Esme was reluctant to open it but when she did, she gasped with delight. Inside was a pair of delicate satin pumps the exact same shade of pale yellow as her gown. They had a small heel and were trimmed with tiny jewels around the front of them that sparkled in the light.

'I'm pretty sure they'll fit because you're about the same size as me,' Olivia told her happily as Esme took them out of the box.

'Oh . . . but you shouldn't have . . . really. They must have cost an awful lot of money,' Esme faltered. She had never had a gift like this in her whole life.

'Well, I was hardly going to let you wear those clod-hopping, heavy black boots under your gown, was I?' Olivia laughed. 'Now try them on, *do*!'

Just as she had hoped they fit Esme like a glove and, lifting her skirt, Esme crossed to admire them in the mirror, turning her feet this way and that so the little jewels caught the light, reflecting the colours onto the walls.

'They're just the prettiest shoes I've *ever* seen,' Esme assured her. 'Thank you so much – although I doubt I'll ever have cause to wear them again after this evening.'

'Nonsense.' Olivia frowned at her. 'Of course you will. Mama and Papa hold at least two balls every year here and you'll be coming to them from now on. But now where has that maid got to?' she fretted. 'The first guests will be starting to arrive at seven o'clock and we should be getting ready.'

An hour later the two girls turned to admire each other. Olivia's mother had bought her a sea-green, full-skirted gown in shot silk that showed off her slim figure to perfection. It was heavily beaded about the neckline and waist and was easily the most grown-up gown she had ever owned. The maid had teased her hair into ringlets, swept it off her face and secured it with jewelled combs on either side of her head. She looked beautiful.

Esme's pale-yellow gown was very plain by comparison and yet it was the simplicity of it that made it look so stunning. Her hair was curling loosely about her shoulders and she wore no jewellery of any kind apart from the gems on her shoes, but she still looked breathtaking.

'Eeh, yer both lovely if yer don't mine me sayin', misses,' the maid said enviously.

The girls smiled at her. 'Thank you, Tilly, and for all your help, but now we really should go down. Mama and Papa will expect us to help to welcome their guests as they arrive.'

'What, *me*?' Esme looked horrified. 'But I'm not family! Perhaps I should stay up here until everyone has arrived before I come down?'

'You most *certainly* will not!' Olivia told her firmly. 'You are my friend and as such I'd like you at my side. All you have to do is smile and bob your knee. After all our lessons with Miss Trimble on etiquette I'm sure you're quite capable of doing that. Mama and Papa are happy for you to be there with me too. I think they've quite taken to you. You're almost one of the family now.'

Esme nodded uncertainly, suddenly feeling totally out of her depth, but she had no wish to offend Olivia so she followed her sedately down the stairs. The crystal chandeliers were ablaze with hundreds of tiny candles and the air was heavy with the scent of the many vases full of flowers that the gardeners had brought in from the hothouses. Esme felt as if she was descending into a magical world – one that she had never known existed.

'Oh, you both look quite charming, my dears,' Lord Fitzroy greeted them when they reached the hall.

He was dressed in a black evening suit with a silk cravat and matching waistcoat and looked very handsome and smart. Luke was beside him, and he too looked very handsome in his suit as he smiled at the girls and added his praise to his uncle's.

'Yes, you do,' he agreed with a wink at his cousin. 'You look quite grown-up, even though you're still just a baby.'

'Oh you!' Olivia playfully slapped his arm before taking her place beside him and pulling Esme in with her.

Esme could hardly take her eyes off Lady Fitzroy, who looked stunning in a pale-blue gown that exactly matched the colour of her eyes. She wore sapphire and diamond earrings and a matching necklace and Esme was sure she had never seen a more beautiful woman – apart from her mammy, of course. And so, they all stood greeting the guests for what seemed an age until the downstairs of the house seemed to be positively heaving with people.

Everyone made their way to the buffet in the dining room where maids were waiting to serve them champagne and tiny hors d'oeuvres from silver trays. The house was alive with the sound of chatter and laughter and just for a second Esme felt sad as she wondered what her parents would have thought if they could have seen her there. But soon she fixed the smile back on her face. This was a special night and she was determined that nothing was going to spoil it.

Eventually the guests made their way through to the ballroom and soon couples were floating around the floor in time to the music from the orchestra, and as Esme watched the couples dancing by, the women all dressed in beautiful gowns with their jewels glittering in the light from the chandelier, she began to enjoy herself.

At one point Luke approached Olivia to ask, 'Fancy a dance, squirt?'

Olivia nodded and Esme stood on the edge of the dance floor admiring how well they danced the polka together. As the dance ended the band began to play a waltz and after leading Olivia back to Esme, he teased, 'How about you having a turn round the floor now?'

Esme bit her lip as she stared uncertainly at the dancers who were taking to the floor. 'I, er . . . haven't ever done this sort of dance before?' she admitted with a blush.

'That's all right, there's nothing to it. Just follow me.' Luke took her hand and before she knew it, they were gliding about the dance floor, and as Esme stared up at him her heart gave a little flutter.

She danced with him twice more that evening and by the time the guests started to depart her eyes were sparkling and she couldn't stop smiling. A whole new world had opened up to her and she had enjoyed every minute – and the night wasn't over yet, because now she would get the chance to stay over in this beautiful house.

'Have you enjoyed yourself, my dear?' Lady Fitzroy asked kindly as she and Olivia made their way towards the stairs.

'Oh yes, my lady, it's been wonderful, thank you so much,' she gushed as she turned and tripped up the stairs after Olivia.

'I think you've made quite a hit there with Esme,' Lady Fitzroy said to Luke with a grin. 'She was quite starry-eyed when you were dancing with her.'

He laughed as he watched the girls climbing the stairs. 'Oh, she's nice enough but she's just a kid. Is it true what I heard the maids saying – that she's a gypsy, I mean? I'd never have guessed it.'

'I do believe that her mother ran away with a gypsy,' Lady Fitzroy answered. 'But as you say, she's quite well spoken and very bright from what Mr Pritchard informs me. She must get that from her mother.'

Upstairs, the maid helped Esme and Olivia get out of their finery while the girls chattered away nineteen to the dozen.

'It was a good evening, wasn't it?' Olivia said and Esme nodded with a dreamy expression on her face.

'It certainly was. I shall never forget it for as long as I live. Thank you so much for inviting me.'

'Let's hope this is just the first of many nights you'll spend here.' Olivia smiled and Esme hoped that it would be.

Chapter Twenty-Four

Septimus Silver arrived back at the rectory three days after the ball, and the instant he stepped in the door Esme sensed that he was not in a good mood. She had just got back from her lessons at the hall and was wearing one of the day dresses that Olivia had finally persuaded her to take, although she wouldn't have worn it that day if she'd known her grandfather would be back. He frowned as he stared at it. The cotton gown was dotted with sprigs of forget-me-nots with a sash belt in a soft lilac colour, pretty puff sleeves and a full skirt. Esme loved it but from the look on her grandfather's face, he certainly didn't.

'*That* isn't one of the outfits I bought you to wear up at the hall,' he said accusingly and Esme flushed.

'No, sir, it isn't. Miss Olivia gave it to me,' she answered as she joined her hands primly at the waist.

'It's the sort of dress a *harlot* would wear. Get upstairs and take it off *immediately*,' he roared as Mrs Sparrow appeared from the kitchen clad in a voluminous apron.

'Now then, what's all this?' She waggled the large spoon she was holding at him. 'You've scarcely had time to put your bag down and you're shouting already. What's the girl done now?'

'It's not what she's *done*, it's what she's wearing,' he raged.

'Oh, and what's wrong with it then?'

'It's . . . it's the sort of thing her mother would have worn. It's too flamboyant!'

'Oh *really*? Let's just hope Lady Fitzroy doesn't hear you say that,' Mrs Sparrow said wryly. 'Her daughter gifted that dress to Esme out of the goodness of her heart and if it was good enough for her daughter, I don't see why Esme shouldn't wear it. It's quite normal for young girls to want to wear pretty clothes. Especially in the warm weather.'

Septimus dropped his bag to the floor and pulled himself together with a great effort. The last thing he wished to do was upset the Fitzroys, as Mrs Sparrow was well aware, so he supposed that he would have to be careful here.

'But what is wrong with the new clothes I bought you?' he asked Esme as calmly as he could.

'Oh, nothing, sir. It's just that they are all made of a far thicker material and because it was unseasonably warm, I thought . . .'

When Esme's voice trailed away Mrs Sparrow quickly stepped in to try and ease the situation. 'Why don't you go up and get changed anyway,' she suggested lightly. 'There are some jobs waiting to be done and you wouldn't want to spoil it, would you?' Turning to Septimus, she said, 'And why don't you come into the kitchen for a drink? You must be thirsty after your journey.'

They both did as she suggested and once in the kitchen she told him sternly, 'I should be very careful if I were you. If you go upsetting the Fitzroys you'll lose your greatest benefactors. And what would your parishioners think if they knew you wanted to deny your granddaughter the chance of such a good education?'

He sniffed and plonked down heavily on a chair as Mrs Sparrow bustled about filling the kettle and setting it on the range to boil.

'That's all very well, but we don't want Esme following in her mother's footsteps, do we? The girl is nothing but a gypsy heathen; she has no right to be prancing around in clothes like that. It's as I feared, since attending the hall I think she's begun to get ideas above her station.'

'Rubbish!' Mrs Sparrow glared at him. 'That girl is as good as gold, though she does have a thirst for knowledge, I'll give you that. But that's no bad thing. What I mean is, I think she could make a good marriage one day because of the education she's getting. She's meeting a good class of people up at the hall and she's pretty into the bargain, so who knows what lies in store for her. Miss Trimble is teaching her etiquette and she's the granddaughter of a reverend, so I've no doubt there'll be many a man willing to marry her when she comes of age. I believe Olivia is going to be presented at court when she goes to London for her coming-out season when she's of age and it wouldn't be a bad idea to let Esme go with her if she's invited.'

Septimus didn't look at all happy with the idea so she changed the subject, but at least he was calmer now; she just hoped that Esme would try to keep out of his way, for the time being at least.

From then on, Esme changed her clothes each day before leaving the hall for the drab serviceable ones her grandfather had bought her.

Almost before they knew it they were racing towards Christmas again, and early in December Esme arrived at the hall one morning to find two enormous Christmas trees being delivered.

'Oh, isn't it exciting?' Olivia greeted her as she clapped her hands with delight. 'The maids are getting the baubles down from the attics and Mr Pritchard has said that we may finish our lessons early today so that we can help to decorate the trees.'

There had never been room for a Christmas tree in the vardo and there certainly hadn't been one at the rectory, so Esme was only too happy to agree.

'I thought we might go out and collect some holly later too,' Olivia gushed. 'The gardeners bring bunches of it in, of course, but I thought we might collect some for the school room. Oh, and there's to be another ball here on New Year's Eve and you're invited. We shall have to find another gown for you to wear.'

'But I've still got the other one you gave me that I haven't worn yet,' Esme pointed out with a smile.

'Oh yes, in that case I'll get the seamstress to alter it for you. It was blue, wasn't it?'

And so the decision was made and once more Esme could hardly wait to dress up again.

'When is your brother coming home for Christmas?' Olivia asked as they strolled about the gardens collecting holly later that afternoon.

'He'll be here the day before Christmas Eve and he goes back the day after New Year's Day,' Esme told her as she stretched to pluck a branch of holly that was particularly loaded with shiny red berries.

'In that case I wonder if we should invite him to the ball too,' Olivia said thoughtfully.

'Hmm, it's a very kind thought but I'm not so sure that he'd want to come,' Esme said doubtfully. 'Gabriel has never been one for dressing up. And anyway, I don't even know if I shall be allowed to attend this time. Don't forget my grandfather was away when you had the summer ball and Mrs Sparrow didn't tell him that I was coming.'

'I can't see why he should object.' Olivia frowned. 'I would have thought that he'd be happy to see you making friends in the village.'

Not for the first time, Esme was tempted to tell her how strict her grandfather was, but decided against it. The front he displayed to Lord and Lady Fitzroy was fawning and charitable and she wondered what Olivia would think if she were to tell her what he was really like – cruel and controlling. But they'd had such a nice day she didn't want to spoil it, and anyway there were still a few weeks to go until the ball so there was no sense in worrying about it just yet, so she quickly moved the conversation on to other things.

The rest of the afternoon was spent dressing the enormous tree that stood in the entrance hall. It was at least twelve feet high and a maid had to stand on the stairs and lean over the bannisters to dress the top of it. One of the gardeners had planted it in a large barrel of soil for them and the girls giggled as they hung the delicate glass baubles around the bottom branches. Esme thought the baubles were quite exquisite – they were made of spun glass in the shape of little animals and she was afraid of breaking them.

'Papa bought them for Mama when they were on their honeymoon in Paris,' Olivia informed her, which made Esme even more nervous. But at last, with the help of the maids and a stepladder, the job was done. Little candle holders holding tiny candles had been added to the ends of the branches and Esme wished that she could stay until it was properly dark to see them all alight, but she knew better than to be late home – it would mean facing her grandfather's wrath – so as the light began to fade from the afternoon, she regretfully told her friend, 'I should be going now. Grandfather has some errands he wants me to run for him this afternoon.'

'Oh, must you?' Olivia pouted, but she hurried off to fetch Esme's warm shawl for her just the same. It had turned bitterly cold over the last few days and Olivia was hoping for snow.

A brisk wind had blown up as Esme set off for the village and she shuddered as she clutched her shawl more tightly about her. She normally enjoyed the walk home in the summer but it wasn't so pleasant in the winter. Lincolnshire was known for being flat, which meant that the wind could whistle across the fields and feel as if it was slicing into you.

Within minutes the straggle of cottages and farms that marked the entrance to the village came into sight and raising her hands to her mouth Esme began to blow on her fingers, which were turning blue. It was then that she spotted a black tail coat disappearing off down the lane towards Molly Malone's cottage, and she frowned. It was a well-known fact that Molly was a woman of low virtue, in fact she had even heard her grandfather say that she was so sinful he was sure the roof would fall in on her if she ever attempted to enter the church. It was whispered that most of the men in the village had visited her at some stage or another, though it would be God help them if their wives ever found out.

'It's common knowledge that she earns her money lyin' on her back, the trollop,' Esme had overheard Mrs Braintree whisper one day in the village shop. 'An' the problem is she don't mind who the man is. I've warned my Bert that if he should ever feel tempted to visit, I'd cut his balls off!'

Now Esme paused. There was something familiar about the way the man approaching Molly's was walking and she was curious to see if she could recognise who it was. His hat was pulled low over his face but suddenly the man turned his head slightly to the side and she caught a brief glimpse of a starched white dog collar and a grey bushy beard, and gasped. It was her grandfather! She lowered her head and hurried on her way. Whatever could he be paying Molly a visit for? she wondered. Perhaps the woman had taken ill? It seemed unlikely. Esme had seen her out and about with her large bosoms almost falling out of a ridiculously low-cut top the day before, and she had looked perfectly fine then.

'Mrs Sparrow, I've just seen Grandfather going in the direction of Molly Malone's cottage,' Esme burst out as she entered the kitchen shortly after. Mrs Sparrow had been in the process of pouring herself a cup of tea and she was so startled that some of it splashed across her clean white tablecloth.

'Now look what you've made me do,' she scolded. 'And you must be mistaken. Your grandfather would *never* go there. He has no time for the wanton. You heard his sermon about the sins of the flesh!'

'It *was* him, I tell you,' Esme insisted indignantly. 'I saw him as clearly as I'm seeing you now!'

'Oh well . . . er . . . happen he had good cause to call on her then. But it's none of our business, is it? So you'd be wise to forget about it and not mention it again. Now, I suggest you go and get changed and start your chores before it gets properly dark!'

She snatched up a piece of rag and began to mop at the spilled tea and Esme was very aware that the subject was closed.

That night she retired to her room early to write a letter to Gabriel. She was becoming increasingly concerned about him. His letters were becoming shorter and shorter and were arriving nowhere near as regularly as they used to, although she still wrote to him religiously every week. Still, she consoled herself, it

189

wouldn't be long until he was home for Christmas now and that would surely cheer him up.

The following evening, when Esme carried her grandfather's meal through to the dining room for him, she instantly sensed that he was in a bad mood. He was sitting in a wing chair in front of the fire and he glowered at her as she entered.

'Put it down and get out,' he barked, and only too happy to do as she was told, Esme plonked the tray down on the table and scuttled away dreading the Bible lesson that was to come shortly after.

As soon as she entered his study, she placed the psalm that he had given her to memorise down in front of him on the desk and began to recite it. But the way he was staring at her over steepled fingers made her so nervous that she had only said a few lines when her mind went a blank and she stumbled to a stop.

'O God, whom I praise, be not silent, for they have opened wicked and treacherous mouths against me.
 They have spoken to me with lying tongues, and with words of hatred they have . . .'

'Yes? Go on then, I don't have all night, girl!'

'I . . . I'm sorry, I seem to have forgotten the rest for now,' she faltered, her legs beginning to shake.

He began to tap his fingers on the desk, before very slowly and deliberately lifting the cane from the edge of his desk and advancing on her. Knowing that it would be no good pleading for mercy she held her hand out but he shook his head.

'Turn around, girl. I think your head is too full of the teachings of Miss Trimble. I feared this would happen when I agreed to you going to the hall. But now I must remind you that the teachings of our Lord should always come first. Bend over the desk.'

'*What?*' She stared at him in disgust

He grasped her arm and swung her about before bending her upper body over the polished surface. And then shame coursed through her as she felt him lift her skirts and yank down her bloomers.

Next, she felt his large hand caressing her buttocks and then suddenly and shockingly the cane sliced into the tender flesh and she gasped with pain.

'N-no *please*,' she implored him as she tried to rise but his free hand was tight on the back of her neck, locking her in position and he was too large to fight. Again and again, the cane sliced into her and between each stroke she felt his hand moving across her flesh. After a dozen strokes, she began to feel strange and the pain lessened as a black hole opened up and thankfully she sank into it.

'You *fool*, she's only a lass, you could have killed her.'

It sounded like Mrs Sparrow's voice but she didn't want to hear it, she wanted to stay in this dark place where there was no pain, no nothing. But it was no good and as her eyes blinked open, she found that she was lying on her bed on her stomach and Mrs Sparrow was bathing the wheals across the tops of her legs and buttocks. The pain was excruciating and a tear slid from the corner of one eye. But worse than the pain was the memory of the feel of his hands crawling across her flesh.

'You've broken the skin in places and she'll be in agony tomor-row.' It was Mrs Sparrow's voice again. 'I doubt she'll be able to walk, and what will you tell them up at the hall when she doesn't arrive for her lessons, eh?'

'I didn't *mean* to be so brutal, but she just made me so angry,' Septimus answered.

'As I've always told you, your anger will be the death of you one of these days.' Mrs Sparrow tutted as she began to smooth a salve onto the wounds, making them sting. 'You'd best think of what you're going to tell Lady Fitzroy,' she told him shortly. 'Cos as sure as eggs are eggs if she finds out the truth your days as the reverend here will be over.'

'We'll tell her that Esme has come down with a cold,' he said urgently as he began to panic. 'Yes, that's what we'll say. It's believable at this time of year.'

'Oh yes, and what if Esme chooses to tell them the truth?'

'She won't,' Septimus said confidently. 'She'll do as I say because she knows if she doesn't, I can make things very difficult for her brother.'

Esme squeezed her eyes shut, wondering when this nightmare would end and silently prayed for time to pass so that she and Gabriel could escape from this place, because now not only was it not a home, it was a prison.

Chapter Twenty-Five

'No homework to hand in again, Loveridge?' the geography teacher said ominously quietly.

Gabriel didn't even bother to answer. He merely held his hand out as the teacher lifted the cane. He'd decided there wasn't even any point in trying anymore. Even when he did the homework it was never good enough so he ended up having the cane anyway. The palms of his hands were now nothing but a mass of callouses but he almost welcomed the hard skin. At least it took away the sting a little. He had spent two more nights in the punishment room over the last two weeks but even that didn't trouble him now. At least while he was locked away in there, he was able to get away from the torment of Broadhurst and his gang. But it wouldn't be for much longer, he'd decided. In a matter of days, he would be going back to the rectory for Christmas and once the holiday was over, he would not be returning here. Esme sounded happy, or at least happier than she had been in her previous letters. She was clearly enjoying the time she spent up at the hall and he hoped that now she had Lady Fitzroy to keep an eye on her, her grandfather would be more lenient with her.

He'd be seventeen come the spring, and if he'd still been living a life on the road he would have been earning his keep by now. And that was exactly what he intended to do, but first he would spend the holiday with Esme and reassure her that he would be all right and that he'd return for her when he had saved enough to keep them both. And then hopefully neither of them would ever have to see their grandfather again.

The only one who knew of his plans was Jeremy, and although he had been saddened to hear that he was going, he was forced to admit that he didn't blame him. Broadhurst and his mob had made his friend's life hell on earth ever since he had arrived and he knew that Gabriel was almost at the end of his tether. He only wished that he had the courage to join him, for his home life wasn't a lot happier than Gabriel's.

Once the punishment was over Gabriel calmly returned to his seat.

'You all right, old chap?' Jeremy whispered as they made their way to the next class a short time later.

Gabriel nodded. 'Aye, I am, matey. The holidays can't come quickly enough for me now. It's just as well I'm going cos I don't know how much longer I can be responsible for me actions. Sometimes I have to stop myself from putting me hands round Broadhurst's neck and throttling the life out of him.'

Finally, when the lessons were over, they moved to the dining hall. Tonight there was lumpy mashed potato and cabbage that had been boiled to within an inch of its life. The meat that was served with it was so full of gristle that it was impossible to tell whether it was beef or pork, but Gabriel and Jeremy ate it just the same. It was either that or lie awake with their stomachs rumbling with hunger so this was the lesser of two evils. Jeremy went off to fetch them a mug of weak tea each and he had just placed Gabriel's in front of him when Broadhurst suddenly stretched across the table and smirked.

'Sugar, Loveridge. Oops, sorry, looks like I mistook the pepper for sugar.' It was swirling about the top of the mug and before Gabriel could stop himself, he snatched it up and flung the whole mugful into Broadhurst's face.

The boy began to cough and splutter as a teacher bore down on them and a silence settled on the room as all eyes rested on him.

'Have you got no manners at all, boy!' the teacher roared.

'Aye, I've got manners,' Gabriel retaliated loudly. He was beyond caring now. 'But this low-life *rat* hasn't!'

'Silence! How *dare* you answer me back!'

Gabriel leapt to his feet, his fists clenched. 'It's always *me*!' he said through gritted teeth. 'The whole lot of you have been against me since the day I started here an' I'm *sick* of it!'

'Yes, and you'll be sicker still after this outburst.' As the teacher advanced menacingly Gabriel swung his fist, catching the man on the chin and sending him crashing into the table behind. Plates of food, crockery and mugs full of tea flew everywhere and suddenly all hell seemed to break loose as two more teachers rushed forward and grasped Gabriel's arms. But he was beyond reason at the injustice of it all and he fought them like a tiger, growling and kicking.

'Get him down to the punishment room,' the headmaster ordered grimly. 'I think this boyo needs a little time to cool off, and once he has, he'll be sorry for what he's done this day. I will not tolerate this sort of behaviour in my school! He's gone too far this time!'

The two teachers began to drag Gabriel towards the door and still he fought them with every bit of strength he had, but he was no match for the two of them and eventually they managed to drag him down the steps to the punishment room and fling him inside.

Gabriel landed heavily on the floor and once the door slammed, the darkness closed around him, and he wrapped his arms about his knees. Slowly the anger faded and despair took its place. He had already decided that he would not be coming back here after the Christmas holidays but now he wished he had left sooner. God knew what punishment the headmaster would come up with for this latest episode. Gabriel had realised long ago that the man was a sadist who took pleasure in inflicting pain. The palms of his hands bore evidence of that. Still, there was nothing he could do about it for now, so curling himself into a ball on the cold floor he tried to sleep. At least when he was asleep, he didn't have to think.

Once more the hours ticked slowly away, each one feeling like a day. Gabriel spent the time sleeping and pacing up and down the confined space. Hunger and thirst soon set in and when the bucket in the corner became almost full, he knew that he had been there for far longer than he had before. Had they left him here to die? he wondered.

At last he heard footsteps on the stone steps and then the sound of the key in the lock. He pulled himself shakily to his feet and blinked in the dim light that poured into the room.

'Follow me, boy.'

Gabriel found himself staring at the teacher he had punched, but he didn't feel sorry. In fact, he knew if he had his time over, he would do the same again. It was about time he stood up to them all.

He lurched unsteadily out of the room and as he went, a rat that was almost as big as a cat ran across his foot, dragging its thick tail behind it before disappearing into a hole in the wall.

'Headmaster's office, *now*!' The teacher ordered when they entered the hallway, and without a murmur Gabriel did as he was told, gratified to see the bruise on the teacher's chin. Served him right, and he'd be damned if he'd apologise if he was asked to.

The headmaster was already flexing the cane when Gabriel entered the office and he held his hand out without being asked – he knew the procedure by now. But this time the headmaster was like a man possessed and by the time he'd finished, the palms of Gabriel's hands were raw and bleeding and the man was out of breath.

'Now *get out* of here and clean yourself up, you *scum*,' he roared, waving the cane towards the door. 'And stay in your dormitory until I tell you otherwise. You're not fit to mix with the other boys here and I shall be sending you home early.' That was music to Gabriel's ears, although he didn't tell him so.

Once upstairs he made for the bathroom to clean his hands up and as he entered, he almost bumped into Broadhurst who was coming out of one of the toilet cubicles. It was hard to say who was the more shocked, but it was Gabriel who recovered first to say, 'Fancy taking a swing at me now, Broadhurst? While you haven't got your cronies to back you up?' He held out his bleeding palms and asked, 'Proud of yourself, are you?'

Broadhurst was clearly uncomfortable. Like all bullies he was not so keen on picking a fight when he hadn't got back-up. Even so, he moved forward and made to pass Gabriel, sneering, 'Get out of my way, gyppo! Otherwise, you might wind up spending your Christmas in the punishment room. Best place for you, I say!'

He made to elbow Gabriel out of the way and jabbed him painfully in the ribs as he passed.

'Why, you little *bastard*!' Once again Gabriel completely lost his temper as he viciously poked him back. Broadhurst clearly hadn't been expecting it and with a cry he fell. As he went down there was a sickening thud as the side of his head hit the porcelain sink and he dropped like a stone to the floor.

'Get up, you *coward*, and fight properly,' Gabriel growled. When there was no movement, he rolled the boy over with the toe of his boot and gasped as he saw the blood flowing from Broadhurst's temple and his cold, staring eyes.

The door banged open then and Jeremy appeared and as he looked at the scene before him the blood drained from his face.

'Christ, I reckon you've killed him, Gabriel.'

Gabriel was standing stock-still, clearly in shock. He hated Broadhurst for the way he had treated him but he had never meant to kill him!

Pulling himself together with an obvious effort, Jeremy hissed, 'You have to get away, man ... *now*! They might think he just slipped and cracked his head and that you'd already done a runner. Go on ... go now before someone comes in; there isn't a second to lose.'

Gabriel still stood wide-eyed as if rooted to the spot, paralysed by the enormity of what had just happened, so Jeremy grabbed his arm and began to drag him towards the door. '*Go on*,' he urged desperately. 'Go out by the garden gate. No one will see you go that way at this time of day. Everyone is in lessons.'

'B-but what about you?' There was a wobble in Gabriel's voice as he tried to come to terms with the fact that he was a murderer.

'Don't worry about me. I'll just go back to class and make out that I saw nothing. But come on, there's not a second to lose! I'll come with you to the door in the boot room that leads into the garden and give you a nod if anyone is about.'

Jeremy stuck his head out of the bathroom door and when he saw that all was clear he and Gabriel headed for the back staircase that led down to the gardens. Once at the bottom, they could hear the clatter of pots and pans from the direction of the kitchen but luckily no one was about.

'Here take this, it'll keep you going for a while at least.' He pressed a wad of crisp pound notes into Gabriel's hand, then smiled. 'I never leave any money my father sends me in the dormitory because I don't trust that thieving lot.'

'But I can't take all this,' Gabriel protested, tears pricking at the back of his eyes.

'Yes, you can. I don't need it for anything.' Jeremy suddenly took Gabriel's bloody hand and shook it up and down and Gabriel was in such a state that he didn't even wince.

'Now get off with you,' Jeremy said bossily. 'And take good care of yourself, I . . . I shall miss you.'

'I shall miss you too,' Gabriel said in a choky voice, but then Jeremy was pushing him through the door and seconds later he heard it close softly behind him.

Keeping within the shadows of the trees that edged the large garden, Gabriel made his way to the gate, heaving a sigh of relief when he found that it was open. He would have liked to have had time to get changed, because he knew he would stick out like a sore thumb in his ridiculous uniform, but he decided he could always dispose of the tie and the blazer when he got a safe distance away and then he could go to a pawn shop to buy himself a cheap jacket with some of the money Jeremy had given him.

He opened the gate as quietly as he could, looking up and down the street. Luckily it was such a bitterly cold day that there were very few people about, and those that were took no notice of him, so he slipped through and set off as fast as his feet would carry him. He had no idea where he was going, he only knew that he needed to put a safe distance between himself and the school.

Every second, he expected to feel a hand on his shoulder as pictures of Broadhurst bleeding on the floor flashed in front of his eyes, but he made it to the seafront and once there he slipped down an alley and abandoned his blazer. The sea was grey and choppy and so, heading into the town, he made for a pawnbroker's. He needed to buy some sort of a jacket otherwise he knew he was likely to freeze to death. He found one in the first pawn shop he came to and parted with a small amount of the money that Jeremy had given him. He wondered if they had found Broadhurst yet, but there was no way of knowing so he set off again in the direction of Theddlethorpe, keeping to the coastal path, as there were likely to be fewer people there. He guessed that the rectory would be the first place they would come looking for him but even so he knew that he couldn't move on until he had said his goodbyes to Esme.

It was a long walk but he daren't risk getting into a coach so, with his head down, he strode purposefully on.

Chapter Twenty-Six

'There then, pet, you rest now,' Mrs Sparrow said kindly as she laid a loose sheet across Esme. She was in too much pain to manage the weight of blankets on her and so she was forced to sleep as best as she could on her stomach. Mrs Sparrow had just bathed her open wounds and gently smoothed more ointment over them and now there was nothing more she could do for her. 'Call me in the night if you need anything,' Mrs Sparrow went on.

Esme frowned. 'I'm sure Olivia will be very worried when I don't turn up for my lessons,' she fretted.

'Don't worry about that.' Mrs Sparrow patted her hand before lifting the bowl of bloodied water. 'I sent a message up to the hall yesterday morning with little Johnny Wainwright to tell them you had a chill and wouldn't be in for a few days. Goodnight.'

Once alone, Esme turned her head to stare at the window and was just in time to see the first flakes of snow falling. It was two days since her grandfather had thrashed her and for the first day she had run a fever. Mrs Sparrow had been worried because she knew that the girl needed a visit from the doctor, but how could she send for him without him realising what had happened? It was more than obvious that Esme had been severely beaten and as she had sternly told the reverend, 'Should the real reason she's in bed come out, that will be the end of your clerical career, have no doubt about it.'

Thankfully, today Esme had been cooler but every time she moved the pain was excruciating and she was worried about what Gabriel might do when he came home if she wasn't fully recovered.

Much later that night she was wide awake and willing herself to sleep. She had heard both Mrs Sparrow and her grandfather retire to their rooms some time before but still sleep evaded her. Suddenly a noise caught her attention and she frowned into the darkness. She lifted her head and stared towards the window, and there it was again, like a gentle pat on the glass. It occurred to her that someone was out there throwing pebbles at her window and with a great effort she shuffled to the edge of the bed wincing with pain at each movement. It took a while to reach the window, by which time she had broken out in a sweat. Peering down into the garden she saw a dark shape and her heart lurched as she recognised who it was. Gabriel. But what could he be doing here at this time of night and why wasn't he at school? As quietly as she could, she lifted the sash cord window just enough to lean out of it.

'Esme, it's me . . . Gabriel,' a voice hissed from the shadows. 'Can you come down and let me in? I need to speak to you urgently. But be careful not to wake anyone. I'll come round to the kitchen door.'

She nodded and quietly closed the window again before painfully crossing to the door. By the time she reached the top of the stairs she could feel blood on her buttocks and legs. Some of the wounds had opened but it couldn't be helped. If Gabriel was here something must be wrong and she needed to get to him.

It seemed an age before she reached the kitchen and once inside she shuffled across the red-tiled floor and quietly slid the bolt on the door. And then Gabriel was inside and she flung herself against his chest and began to cry.

'What's wrong? Why are you here? I didn't think you were due home for a few days.'

'I wasn't but something's happened.' He stamped the snow from his boots and crossed to the fire to warm his hands in front of the glowing embers. 'Is there any chance of a hot drink and something to eat. I can't stay long and then I have to leave.'

Esme was more worried than ever now but without a word she lit the oil lamp on the table with a spill from the fire and swung the kettle across the coals to boil while she hobbled to the pantry to fetch bread and cheese. Soon, with a large mug of tea in front of him, Gabriel was tucking into it as if he hadn't eaten for a month, and when he'd had his fill he hesitantly began to tell her what had happened.

'So . . . you *killed* him then?' Esme could hardly believe what she was hearing. Gabriel had always been a free spirit but he had never been aggressive or violent. If anything, he was just the opposite; when they had lived in the vardo she had lost count of the number of injured animals he had rescued and brought home to nurse back to health. The only time she had known him to kill animals was if they were to eat, and even then, he had always made sure their death was quick and painless.

'Something inside me just snapped,' he told her miserably. 'The chap made my life a living hell from the day I arrived but I didn't mean to kill him, I *swear* on your life I didn't. I was only retaliating.'

'I believe you, but what are you going to do now?' she whispered fearfully. 'You can't stay around here. They'll find you and we can't rely on Grandfather to help you.' She knew the penalty for murder was hanging and just the thought of it made her feel sick.

'I know, so on the way here I came up with an idea. I'm going to go to Hull to see if I can get taken on on one of the fishing boats.'

'But you've never been to sea!'

'I can learn, can't I? And it's got to be better than being stuck back in that hellhole. At least I'll be out in the open air and no one will be able to find me if I'm out at sea.'

She could see the sense in what he said and nodded miserably. The thought of being parted from him yet again was painful but better that than having to see him dangle at the end of a rope. She knew she wouldn't be able to bear that. Gabriel was all she had left now.

'Will I ever see you again?' she asked in a choky voice.

He nodded. 'Of course. And at least now I know you're spending a lot of time up at the hall I won't worry about you so much. But, Esme, you *must* promise me that you'll tell no one you've seen me. When the police come looking you must act surprised, as if you know nothing about what's happened. Can you do that for me?'

'Of course. You should know I would do anything for you.' Then she was in his arms and he planted a tender kiss on her hair; it was time to leave. The police could arrive at any minute and there was no time to delay.

'I'll get word to you of where I am somehow,' he promised as they clung to each other. 'But there's one more thing I want you to do: I want you to try and develop the gift you inherited from our grandmother.'

When Esme raised an eyebrow, he rushed on, 'I know I've never encouraged it before but I somehow feel that if you do it will help to keep you safe until we can be together again.'

Although she had never had any interest in doing this before, she nodded slowly as he gently eased the door open. It was snowing heavily now and he pulled the collar of his jacket up before dropping one last kiss on her cheek and disappearing into the night without looking back. She stood there for a long time until, teeth chattering, she slowly turned and dragged herself back to bed, her heart breaking.

'Someone was down in the kitchen last night,' Mrs Sparrow commented when she took Esme some porridge the next morning. 'There was bread and cheese on the table and an empty mug.'

Thinking quickly, Esme nodded. 'Oh yes, that was me. I felt peckish so I got up to have a bite and a warm drink.'

'Really?' Mrs Sparrow was surprised seeing as she had been trying to tempt her to eat all day. 'And how are you feeling today?'

'A little easier, I think.' Esme painfully turned over and allowed the woman to place a tray on her lap. She still didn't have an appetite but she made a valiant attempt to eat at least a few spoonfuls. It was then that her grandfather appeared in the doorway and instantly Esme froze.

'I think it might be best if you left, sir,' Mrs Sparrow said curtly and without a word he turned and disappeared.

Seconds later there was a loud banging on the front door and after ensuring that Esme had all she needed, Mrs Sparrow hurried away to see who was there. Meanwhile Esme sat there with her heart in her mouth. Could this be the police come looking for Gabriel?

It seemed an age before Mrs Sparrow reappeared and Esme immediately asked, 'Who was at the door?'

Obviously ill at ease, the woman avoided her eyes as she took the tray from her lap. 'Actually, it was one of the teachers from the school. They've come to speak to your grandfather. I should imagine Gabriel has got himself into some sort of trouble again.'

Thankfully she failed to see the colour drain from Esme's cheeks or the way her hands began to tremble.

'Will you let me know what they wanted?'

'Of course, pet. Now you just turn over and rest. I'll be back to make the fire up presently and when the room has warmed up a bit, we can take the sheet off you and let the air get to those wounds.'

The second she had heard her descend the stairs, Esme squirmed to the end of the bed and crossed the room to stare out of the window. Thankfully the falling snow had long since covered up Gabriel's footprints so hopefully no one would ever know he had been here last night. She certainly wasn't going to tell them. It seemed an age before she heard the front door close after the visitor and another age before Mrs Sparrow reappeared to find her sitting on the edge of a chair.

'Is Gabriel all right?' Esme asked the second the woman set foot in the room.

'I'm afraid not.' Mrs Sparrow chewed on her lip. 'It seems there has been another incident at the school and Gabriel has run away. They're trying to find him.'

'Who are?' Esme asked feigning ignorance.

'The police. Unfortunately, it appears a young man was attacked in the washrooms and left for dead and they are assuming the one who attacked him was Gabriel. Why else would he have run away?'

'Did the young man die?' Esme hardly dared ask and held her breath as she waited for a reply.

'Not yet, apparently. He's in hospital, but he's gravely ill and according to the master who came to see your grandfather his condition could go either way. If he should survive, Gabriel could be charged with grievous bodily harm when they catch him. But if he should die . . .' There were no more words needed, they both knew what the sentence for murder was.

'Are you quite sure Gabriel hasn't been in touch?' Mrs Sparrow asked.

Esme shook her head vigorously. 'Of course he hasn't. If what you say is true his only thought would have been of escaping, I imagine. And I'll tell you something else, if the young man who was attacked was Thomas Broadhurst, I'd bet anything that he was the first to start any trouble. He's made Gabriel's life a misery ever since he started at the school. Jeremy will vouch for that!' she said vehemently.

'All right, don't go getting yourself into a lather,' Mrs Sparrow said quickly. 'You're not well yourself and fretting about this won't improve your condition.'

'No, it won't, but we both know who was responsible for it, don't we?' Esme's eyes flashed. 'Grandfather is a *bully*, no better than Thomas Broadhurst! What do you think Lady Fitzroy would think if she were to find out what's really wrong with me?'

'That's enough of that silly talk,' Mrs Sparrow blustered, all of a dither. 'Your grandfather has a temper, I'll give you that, but he's not a bad man at heart.'

'You could have fooled me. He's treated both myself and Gabriel like scum ever since we arrived here.' Esme didn't care what she said now. The worst thing that could have happened to Gabriel already had and she was beyond caring now. 'Furthermore, are you aware that he has been coming to my room? He touched me in private places and touched himself too and told me that he had to teach me what I had to do to please a husband one day. What do you think of *that*? My dadda *never* touched me like that and I've never heard Olivia say that her father does either!'

Mrs Sparrow seemed to shrink before her very eyes. She opened her mouth to speak but then turned abruptly and left the room without another word.

When she had gone Esme began to sob. She felt as if she were caught in the grip of a nightmare but her main concern was for her brother and she could only pray fervently that he would get away to somewhere safe.

Downstairs Mrs Sparrow headed for Septimus's study and barged in without even bothering to knock.

He looked surprised to see her for a moment then said brashly, 'So, the laddo is finally going to get his comeuppance, eh? Didn't I tell you he was evil?'

'If what I'm hearing is true then you're not far behind him,' Mrs Sparrow snapped with tears in her eyes. 'Whatever were you thinking of, touching that child upstairs inappropriately?'

He swallowed, setting his Adam's apple bobbing. 'I . . . I don't know what you mean.' His voice was strangled and sweat stood out on his brow despite the coldness of the day.

'Esme has told me about the visits to her room.' She stood hands on hips glaring at him. 'And if she's told me then what's to stop her telling those up at the hall? You'll lose your position and be sent away in disgrace.'

'But surely you can't believe anything that heathen tells you,' he choked. 'She and her brother are cut from the same cloth. She's just trying to get me into trouble. And after all I've done for them!'

'*Done* for them?' she scoffed. 'And what is that exactly? You only took them in because of what it would look like to your congregation if you didn't. It certainly wasn't out of the kindness of your heart or because they were your grandchildren and homeless orphans. And ever since, you've made both of their lives a misery with your bullying ways. Well, now you may have to pay the price and even I won't be able to save you anymore!' She turned abruptly and left him sitting there staring blindly into space.

Chapter Twenty-Seven

Upstairs Esme made her painful way to the window and as she stood there staring out at the swirling snow her brother's words came back to her. *I want you to try and develop the gift you inherited from our grandmother.*

But how do I do that? she wondered, screwing her eyes tight shut. Images of Granny Griselda flashed into her mind and suddenly she sensed that she was no longer alone. Turning she saw the old woman standing there with a worried frown on her face.

'*Granny!*' She felt no fear, just an overwhelming relief to see someone who had been dear to her. The old lady looked just as her mother had described and vague memories of happy times they had spent together when she was tiny flooded back.

She could remember black velvet nights being rocked to sleep on the steps of the vardo in Granny's arms as she sang lullabies to her. She remembered the treats she would make for her in her little clay oven and the kisses she would plant on her cheek if she stumbled and fell. She was wearing the long, vibrant, heavily patterned skirt that she had always favoured, and her favourite shawl was tucked about her shoulders. Her grey hair was plaited and hung across her shoulder like a silken rope, and her favourite large gold hoop earrings dangled from her ears. 'I've missed you so much,' Esme whispered and her granny smiled, a sad smile that tore at Esme's heart and made her remember again all the dear ones she had loved and lost.

'You must get far away from here, my child,' the woman whispered. 'This is a bad house.'

'I know!' Esme started to cry as Granny looked around.

'There are unhappy spirits trapped here and they need you to free them so they can move on to the light,' she told her.

'But how can I do that?'

'They need revenge.'

'Revenge for what?' Esme was confused and afraid. Granny's image was beginning to fade but she didn't wish to be left alone again. 'Tell me how to do it! And please don't go!' Esme was distraught as the image faded some more.

'You will know when the time is right. And I will never leave you. Remember, I always walk at your side. When you need me, I will be there.' And then there was nothing but silence as Esme sat worrying her bottom lip with her teeth.

What had Granny meant? None of it made any sense to her but one thing she knew, she must get away from here somehow.

Two more days passed, by which time Esme was able to rise from her bed and spend a little time slowly pottering about. Christmas was just days away now and she was missing Olivia dreadfully.

One day, as she was sitting listlessly by the fire in the kitchen, a loud rapping on the front door had Mrs Sparrow hurrying to answer it.

She heard voices in the hallway then Mrs Sparrow appeared in the doorway to tell her, 'Lady Fitzroy and Miss Olivia are here to see you. I've shown them into the parlour.'

Esme's face lit up as she rose painfully from her seat and made her way to join them. The first thing she saw when she entered the drawing room was an enormous hamper on the table and Olivia beaming at her.

'Ah, we thought we would come and see how you were recovering,' Lady Fitzroy told her as she removed her gloves.

'Yes, and we brought you some treats,' Olivia told her, hurrying forward to give her a hug. 'There's fruit and cakes and sweetmeats, I hope you enjoy them. But when will you be coming back to the hall?'

Esme licked her suddenly dry lips, very aware that Mrs Sparrow was standing behind her watching her closely.

'I should think she'll be well enough to come back in the new year,' Mrs Sparrow answered for her, and Esme's face fell, as did Olivia's.

'Oh, but that means you'll miss the ball on New Year's Eve,' Olivia said sadly.

'What has been wrong with you exactly, my dear?' Lady Fitzroy asked with a frown. If she wasn't very much mistaken there was something amiss here. Something didn't feel quite right, although she couldn't put her finger on what it was, and she didn't like the way Mrs Sparrow was almost standing guard over the girl.

'She's had a bad cold,' Mrs Sparrow chipped in again before Esme could open her mouth.

'Oh . . . how awful, but I wonder could we trouble you for a cup of tea, Mrs Sparrow? It's so bitterly cold out there. I think Olivia and I could do with something to warm us up before we set off for home.'

Mrs Sparrow hesitated. She clearly wasn't happy about leaving Esme alone with them but eventually she hurried away to do as she was asked. The second she had gone, Lady Fitzroy asked, 'Is everything all right, dear? You seem to be somewhat on edge.'

Esme stared at her. This was the best opportunity she might ever have to tell them about the thrashing her grandfather had given her, but somehow, she felt as if she would be betraying Mrs Sparrow and the words stuck in her throat.

'Er . . . yes,' was all she could manage and soon after Mrs Sparrow reappeared with a tray of tea and some sponge cake that she had made that morning.

The rest of the visit passed somewhat awkwardly and when the visitors eventually left, Mrs Sparrow breathed a sigh of relief as she showed them out, while Esme stayed in the drawing room, cursing herself for not telling them what had really happened.

Chapter Twenty-Eight

The following day when Mrs Sparrow opened the door to the postman, he handed her a parcel for Septimus and asked, 'Have you heard the news? Molly Malone has been found dead in her cottage.'

From the kitchen, Esme's ears pricked up.

'Yes, poor sod had her throat cut from ear to ear they're sayin', an' she'd been there sometime afore anyone found her, by all accounts.'

Mrs Sparrow tutted. 'Dear me, I know the woman was no better than she ought to be but I'm sorry to hear that. No one deserves to end up that way. Do they have any idea who might have done it?'

The postie shook his head. 'Not as yet. Could 'ave been any one o' the blokes who wore the path to her door out, if truth be told. An' I saw in the paper last night that the reverend's grandson is in trouble an' all, ain't he?'

Mrs Sparrow frowned, not knowing how to answer. She'd known that it would be common knowledge soon enough but had hoped they might get Christmas out of the way first. 'Er . . . yes, I'm afraid he is, although we are not aware of all the facts yet so we're reserving our judgement.'

'They reckon he could 'ave attacked one of his school mates in the washroom at that posh school the vicar sent 'im to an' the police are lookin' fer 'im now,' the postman went on with relish. He was the biggest gossip in the village and seemed to know everyone's business.

'Well, I . . . I really must get on, thank you, George.' Mrs Sparrow took the parcel from him and shut the door firmly in his face, before leaning her back against it and letting out a deep breath. She dreaded to think how Septimus was going to take the news that everyone was now probably aware of what Gabriel had done.

Meanwhile in the kitchen, Esme's mind was working overtime. Molly Malone. That was the woman she'd seen her grandfather furtively creeping off to visit some days ago. And what was it George had said? She'd been dead for some time before anyone found her? A cold finger crept up her spine. Could it be that her grandfather had murdered her? She pushed the thought away immediately, aware that she was letting her imagination run away with her. He might be a bully but he couldn't be a murderer, surely?

'I suppose you heard that, did you?' Mrs Sparrow asked when she returned to the kitchen some minutes later.

Esme nodded solemnly. 'Yes, I did. I suppose we knew there would be something about Gabriel in the local papers eventually. I also suppose that there was no mention of the boy he's supposed to have attacked dying. And that Molly Malone . . .'

'What about her?' Mrs Sparrow asked suspiciously.

'I never actually knew her personally but I knew of her and the strange thing is . . .' She wondered if she should say any more but Mrs Sparrow clearly wasn't going to let it go.

'Go on then, if you've something to say, spit it out,' she ordered frostily.

'If you cast your mind back to some days ago, I mentioned to you that I'd seen Grandfather walking towards Molly's cottage one afternoon as I was on my way back from the hall.'

Mrs Sparrow's colour rose as she began to pluck at her apron. 'Hmm, and as I told you then, I'm sure you must have been mistaken. I reckon nearly every chap in the village has visited Molly Malone at some time or another, but your grandfather certainly wouldn't visit the likes of her.'

'But it *was* Grandfather,' Esme insisted doggedly.

'Don't talk such rubbish,' Mrs Sparrow said sharply. 'Why ever would he visit a woman with a reputation like hers?'

'I saw his face as clearly as I can see yours now and it *was* Grandfather, I tell you.'

'Then, as I told you before, I suggest that's something you should keep to yourself,' the woman replied primly, slamming the dirty pots into the sink and making it perfectly clear that the conversation was at an end.

There was yet another visitor later that day but this one had Esme smiling from ear to ear for the first time in days. It was Jeremy.

'I was on my way home for the holidays and thought I'd call in and see you on the way,' he said awkwardly, standing on the step covered in snow.

'I dare say you'd best come in,' Mrs Sparrow said, although she looked none too happy about his arrival. 'If you take him into the parlour I'll make you both some tea,' she told Esme. 'Though I warn you there's no fire lit in there.'

Esme was only too happy to do as she was told, and once they were inside and she'd closed the door behind them she asked, 'Have there been any more developments?'

'There have, actually,' he answered, thinking it was almost as cold in the parlour as outside. 'But first, did Gabriel manage to see you?'

She nodded. 'Yes, he did but I haven't told anyone. How is Broadhurst?'

'Still unconscious but holding his own, apparently.' He glanced towards the door before lowering his voice and telling her, 'But things aren't as bad as you think.'

Esme frowned. 'What do you mean?'

'A witness came forward and told them that it couldn't have been Gabriel who hurt Broadhurst. They told them that they'd seen Gabriel leave the school much earlier and that Broadhurst must have been on his own in the toilet block when he slipped and cracked his head, because Gabriel would already have left.'

Esme looked confused. 'But Gabriel told me that it *was* him that pushed Broadhurst in retaliation,' she murmured, and then as the truth dawned, her eyes stretched wide. 'It was *you* who lied for him, wasn't it?'

Jeremy shrugged. 'What's a white lie now and then?'

Esme could have kissed him. 'And did they believe you?' she asked anxiously, hope flaring within her.

He frowned. 'I'm not sure, to be honest, but they can't prove otherwise so they've called off the search for Gabriel for now. Of course, if Broadhurst wakes up and tells them otherwise it'll be a different kettle of fish altogether but we'll cross that bridge if and when we come to it. The school won't want a scandal attached to it so I'm hoping they'll prefer to believe that it was an accident rather than an attack.'

Esme let out a big sigh of relief, then her face clouded again. 'But how can we let Gabriel know? He thinks he's on the run for murder.'

'I'm afraid we can't until we can find out where he is.' He shook his head. 'Between you and me, I'm surprised Gabriel held his temper for as long as he did. Broadhurst had it coming to him, and it happened it was him who started it, as usual. I dare say Gabriel told you he pushed him and Gabriel just pushed him back.'

Esme nodded, her mind racing, but they had no time to say more as Mrs Sparrow appeared in the doorway with two mugs of tea, which she plonked down unceremoniously on a small table. 'I think you'd best drink that and be on your way, young man,' she told him. 'Esme's grandfather is due back any time now and he won't like it if he finds her with a young male visitor.'

'But Jeremy is my and Gabriel's friend,' Esme pointed out and with a shrug Mrs Sparrow left the room again.

It was when Esme stood up to take his tea to him that Jeremy noticed how stiffly she was walking and he frowned. 'Are you all right?'

She nodded solemnly as she handed him his drink. 'Yes, I'm afraid Grandfather just got a bit overzealous with his cane.'

'Calls himself a man of the *cloth*,' Jeremy said angrily as he took the mug from her. 'When I think of how he's treated you and Gabriel since you arrived here, I'd like to take a horsewhip to him and give him a bit of his own medicine!'

'Never mind about that for now. How are we going to find Gabriel?' she asked anxiously.

Jeremy flicked a lock of thick dark hair from his forehead. 'I'm afraid we can't. It would be like looking for a needle in a haystack.

But I told him to write to me at my home address when he has somewhere to stay and once he does we can let him know what's happening. Until then we just have to be patient. And I should tell you, I've made a decision. I won't be returning to the school either. I'm going to tell my father when I get home that I'm applying for a position at a veterinary college. I've always wanted to be a vet and whether my parents like it or not that's what I'm going to do.'

'But won't a veterinary college cost money?'

He nodded. 'Yes, it will, but if my parents refuse to pay for it I do have some money of my own that my grandmother left to me. I'll pay the fees with that and leave home if I have to. I'm damned sure if Gabriel is brave enough to make his own way in the world I am too.'

'Then good luck to you ... and thank you for standing by Gabriel,' she said sincerely.

He gave a wry smile. 'He's a good chap ... but I hope you and I can keep in touch. Would you mind if I wrote to you and came to see you now and again?'

'I'd like that, but why don't you send the letters to Fitzroy Hall?' she suggested as he handed her his address, which he had already written down for her. 'I'm afraid if you send them here Grandfather is likely to open them.' As if speaking of him had summoned him up, the door suddenly swung open and Septimus stood there.

'And who is this?' he said disapprovingly.

'This is Jeremy, Gabriel's friend from school,' Esme answered. 'And he came with good news. It appears that Gabriel didn't attack Thomas Broadhurst. They think now it may have been a simple accident.'

'Oh, I find that hard to believe,' her grandfather said sarcastically. 'The boy is wild like his father before him. I thought the school would tame him, but it seems that I was wrong. At any rate, whatever happened I don't want him back here. I've washed my hands of him. From now on he can make his own way in life. He's got bad blood flowing through his veins!'

Realising that this conversation could quickly turn into a row, Jeremy stood up hastily. 'Well, sir, I merely called to give you the news and I dare say the police will also call soon to reinforce what I've said. So now I've come to do what I set out to do, I'll take my leave. Good day, sir, good day, Esme.' And with that he rammed his hat back on and strode to the door.

'Jeremy . . .' Esme called. He paused to glance back at her. 'Thank you,' she said sincerely.

Seconds later Esme heard the front door close behind him.

Now that they were alone her grandfather glared at her and opened his mouth to say something but then, seeming to think better of it, he clamped it shut again and left to go into his study while Esme stood there trying to take everything in.

It was wonderful that Jeremy had defended Gabriel but what if Thomas Broadhurst woke up and told them that it had been her brother who had attacked him. And even if he didn't, how were they to let Gabriel know that there was no need for him to hide anymore? Everything was such a mess and not for the first time she wished with all her heart that they had never thrown themselves on their grandfather's mercy. It was no wonder that their mother had always refused to speak of him; the man was a tyrant and a bully. Slowly she made her way upstairs and curled up on her bed as tears slid down her cheeks, until eventually, she slept.

It was dark when she woke and some instinct told her that she wasn't alone. Fearfully she peered into the darkness, then turned her head towards the door to see a large form lumbering towards her and she cursed beneath her breath; she had forgotten to put the chair under the door handle. She could smell alcohol and stale cigar smoke and she knew instantly that it was her grandfather.

'Wh-what do you want?' she rasped as panic flared in her chest.

'It's time to reshume your lesshons,' he slurred and she knew that he was very drunk. But this time, instead of being afraid of him, she was angry. Dragging herself up in the bed she reached towards the bedside table and grabbed the nearest thing that came to hand. Luckily it was the brass candlestick that saw her to bed each night and she grasped it as he lumbered towards her.

'*Get out*,' she spat with disgust as he drew closer.

He chuckled. 'Now don't be like that.' The moon sailed from behind a cloud at that moment and in the dim light pouring in through the window she saw him undoing the buttons on his trousers and her heart sank. 'Jusht think how difficult I can make it for your brother if you don't do as I shay,' he purred as he exposed his manhood. Esme had seen men's willies many times before. It would have been hard not to, living in such confined quarters in the vardo with her dadda and her brother. In the summer her whole family had regularly gone skinny dipping in lakes and rivers together when they found a secluded spot. But this was different and Esme was prepared to fight for her virtue.

'You can do nothing more to hurt my brother now,' she told him with venom in her voice as she shuffled towards the edge of the bed. 'So get out of my room or I swear I shall scream so loudly I shall waken the dead.'

He laughed as he dropped his trousers to the floor and inched even closer and suddenly he lunged at her knocking her back onto the mattress. For a moment the pain from the broken skin on her buttocks and legs took her breath away as he groped at her tender young breasts and began to drag her nightdress up, but then she lifted her arm and with every ounce of strength she had, she brought the candlestick crashing down towards him. It connected with the top of his arm and he howled with pain and toppled off the bed in an undignified heap. Heedless of the pain it caused, Esme was up and out of the room in a second just as Mrs Sparrow appeared in her robe and nightcap.

'What the—'

'I'm getting out of here,' Esme screamed as she dashed past her, heading for the stairs. She was in a blind panic and only knew that she couldn't stay there a moment longer. And then she was at the front door and once she'd managed to unlock it, she dashed out onto the frozen snow and ran as if her life depended on it.

She'd gone some way into the village when she realised that she hadn't even stopped to put her boots on, but she was too afraid to turn back.

The windows of the cottages she passed were in darkness and everywhere was so quiet that she could almost believe she was the last person left in the world. Soon she was out of breath and the pain in her buttocks and legs and frozen feet was unbearable, but still she plunged on, intent on putting as much distance between herself and her grandfather as she could.

At last, the gates of Fitzroy Hall loomed ahead of her but she knew that she wasn't going to make it and just inside the gates she dropped onto the freezing snow and curled up into a ball. A strange lethargy was creeping over her and suddenly she just wanted to sleep. A little voice in her brain was telling her that if she did she might never wake up, but she didn't care. Death would be preferable to the life she had led since coming to the rectory, so she closed her eyes and knew no more.

Chapter Twenty-Nine

There was a light ahead, a wonderful light that glowed and beckoned to her, and Esme began to move towards it. But then a face appeared in front of her and Granny Griselda stood there wagging her finger at her.

'It's not your time, girl,' she scolded. 'Now open your eyes this instant!'

Esme shook her head. 'I . . . I can't. I'm too tired.'

'No, you're not, now turn around and go back.'

And then there was another voice. It seemed to be coming from a long way away and Esme groaned as the light began to fade and pain kicked in.

'Esme, that's it . . . Come along, my dear. Open your eyes.' The voice was familiar and as her senses slowly began to return, Esme realised that it was Lady Fitzroy. There was another voice too, a man's voice, and was that Olivia she could hear? If it was, she was crying, but why?

Slowly her eyes blinked open and she gasped as pain enveloped her. Every single bone in her body seemed to be stabbing her with little needles and she felt as if she was on fire. Slowly Lady Fitzroy's face swam into focus and Esme opened her mouth to say something but no sound came out.

'It's all right,' the woman soothed, gently stepping aside for the doctor to examine her.

'Wh-where am I?' Esme managed to ask eventually when the doctor stood aside.

'You're at the hall,' Lady Fitzroy told her softly. 'And you've been very poorly. But don't worry, you'll start to get better now.' She gently lifted Esme's head from the pillow and held a glass of water to her lips, which Esme gulped at greedily. 'You gave us quite a scare for a time there,' the woman told her with a smile. 'But, Esme, what happened to you? Who beat you? Your back and your poor legs are covered in wheals, and what were you doing out all alone at night in your nightclothes?'

Olivia stepped forward and clasped her hand, and Esme saw that there were tears in her eyes. 'We thought you were going to die,' Olivia told her with a sob.

Esme heard the sound of the doctor's large bag being snapped shut and then he told Lady Fitzroy, 'There's no more I can do for now, unfortunately. Time must be the healer. Just get plenty of fluids into her and keep bathing her head to bring the fever down. I shall be back to see her tomorrow unless you need me before. In the meantime try to get her to tell you who did this to her. She's had a very lucky escape. If your servant hadn't found her when they did she would not have lasted the night out there in these conditions. Good day, Lady Fitzroy.'

'I'll see you out, Dr Walters,' the woman answered.

After they left, Olivia and Esme were alone in the room and Olivia pulled a chair close to the side of the bed.

'What happened to you?' she asked gently. 'Luckily one of our servants had been out to see their sick mother and arrived back at the hall late. If they hadn't spotted you, goodness knows what would have happened. We couldn't help but notice the state your back and legs were in when we changed you. Who did this to you, Esme? And what were you doing out so late at night in your nightclothes? Something very bad must have happened to make you run away like that!'

Her voice was so full of genuine concern that tears began to trickle down Esme's face. She lay staring up at the ceiling, wondering if she should tell all, but suddenly she was desperately tired and before she could decide her eyes closed and she slept again.

The next time she woke, a weak light was shining through the window and she saw that it was snowing again. There was a fire roaring in the grate and she recognised the room she was lying

219

in as the one next to Olivia's. It was a pretty room decorated in shades of pale grey and lilac and next to her bed a maid sat fast asleep.

When she sensed a movement in the bed, the young maid sprang awake and asked, 'Would you like a drink, miss?' When Esme shook her head she stood up. 'Right, I'll just go and tell the mistress you're awake again. I shan't be long.'

Lady Fitzroy and Olivia soon arrived by her bedside. 'I have just had your grandfather here, Esme,' Lady Fitzroy told her. 'He wanted to know if we had seen you. Of course, I had no choice but to tell him that you were here, but I refused his request to see you until I knew if you wanted to see him or not, so he's left and is going to return later.'

The frightened look that appeared on Esme's face at the mention of him told Lady Fitzroy all she wanted to know and she scowled.

'You must be honest with me, my dear, was it he who beat you and is that why you ran away?'

Esme sighed. It was time to tell the truth. 'He *did* beat me,' she said in a small voice. 'But I ran away because . . . because . . .'

'In your own time,' the woman said soothingly and glancing towards Olivia, she asked, 'Would you rather speak to me alone?'

When Esme nodded Olivia backed towards the door, closing it softly behind her.

And so with her cheeks flaming Esme haltingly began to tell Lady Fitzroy about her grandfather's visits to her room, the beatings he had inflicted on her and Gabriel, and finally what had happened on the night she had taken flight.

The woman listened without interrupting and when Esme was done, she pursed her lips, looking pale and upset. 'I feared it might be something like that,' she said eventually. 'I can tell you now, I have *never* liked that man. But have no fear; you will not be returning to him and he won't be staying there if I have my way. I shall contact the bishop in Lincoln immediately and once I've told him of the reverend's despicable behaviour, I doubt he will be allowed to carry on here, or anywhere else for that matter.

It sounds to me like the man is a sadistic pervert and you have done exactly right in confiding in me. I can only begin to imagine what you must have been through.' The thought of any man, especially a man of the cloth, treating anyone, let alone his own flesh and blood, that way made her feel nauseous. 'So now I shall go and set the wheels in motion to make sure that he is defrocked and removed from the parish as soon as possible,' she told Esme. 'And have no fear, when he comes back, he will go away with a flea in his ear!'

Esme lay there with mixed emotions pouring through her. She was glad that she would not have to go back to the rectory and cared nothing for what happened to her grandfather after the way he had treated her and Gabriel, but she couldn't help but feel sorry for Mrs Sparrow, who had always tried to protect her. She just couldn't understand her loyalty to the man. After all, it wasn't as if he treated her with respect or affection. But then as her dadda had always said, 'There's none so strange as folks!'

Her thoughts moved on and she began to fret. It was all very well Lady Fitzroy fighting her corner and helping her escape from her grandfather but what would become of her when she was recovered? She didn't even have Gabriel to lean on and the thought of being all alone in the world was frightening.

Olivia came back soon after her mother had left the room and seeing Esme in a sombre mood she assured her, 'Don't worry, Mama is making sure that you won't have to go back to that beast. You're quite safe now.'

'For now, yes, but what's to become of me?' Esme asked tearfully.

'I've already spoken to Mama about that and we've come up with a few ideas already, so don't worry,' Olivia told her with a smile as Esme yawned. She seemed to be doing hardly anything but sleeping at present. 'Now you have a nap and rest assured all will be well.'

The following day Lady Fitzroy again visited her to tell her, 'I have Mrs Sparrow downstairs, my dear. She would like to see you. How do you feel about it?'

Esme nodded. 'Yes please.' She owed the woman that much at least, she supposed.

Minutes later Mrs Sparrow was shown into the room by one of the maids and Esme saw that her eyes were red from crying and she was a bag of nerves.

'How are you, pet?' the woman asked as she approached the bed.

'I'm recovering, thank you.' Esme stared at her solemnly and the woman lowered her eyes.

'I . . . I've come to say that I'm sorry . . . for everything.'

'None of what happened was your fault,' Esme told her gently. 'But *why* do you stay with him, Mrs Sparrow?'

'I stay because . . . because . . .' Mrs Sparrow gulped. 'Because Septimus is my nephew. He is my sister's child. She died when he was only ten years old. I promised her I would take him on and love him as my own, although he was a difficult child even then. When he met and married your grandmother and he became a member of the clergy I thought he would change, and he did for a time, but soon the cruel streak started to come out in him again and . . . well, there's no point in going into all that now. I moved back in with him when your mother was just a baby, but they never had a good relationship. He believed that to spare the rod was to spoil the child and he treated your mother much as he's treated you, even though I did my best to protect her. I wasn't surprised when she ran away with your father. But anyway, that's all by the by. Lady Fitzroy has just informed me that she's sent word of his behaviour towards you and Gabriel to the bishop so I've no doubt he'll be defrocked. I was shocked when he became a vicar in the first place. So I've come to say goodbye, but before I do there's something you should know . . . the footsteps you used to hear in the room above your bedroom and the silver-haired woman you saw from time to time . . . she . . . she was your grandmother. Your mother's mother and Septimus's wife.'

Esme frowned in confusion. 'But my mother told me that my grandmother died before you moved to Theddlethorpe?'

Mrs Sparrow sighed as she nervously twisted her hat between her hands. 'Aye, that's what we told everyone but in truth she came with us. You see, your grandfather was brutal to her during their marriage and in the end, she ran away with another man, who showed her a little kindness. It broke her heart to go because she didn't want to leave your mother but she was so afraid of your grandfather that I think she thought that running away was her only option. Anyway, soon after the man left her, and by the time your grandfather tracked her down, she'd had a complete breakdown and was only a shadow of the beautiful woman she had once been. He locked her away in an asylum for a time but I didn't think that was fair so eventually he agreed that we would move to Theddlethorpe and she would come with us. I was to nurse her but your grandfather insisted that she must be kept locked up. He said she was a threat to herself and everyone around her so I had no choice but to allow it. He never forgave her for leaving him. The poor young woman, she was a gentle soul and being kept locked away like a prisoner only made her state of mind worse. I did what I could for her but one day when your mother was still tiny, I took her meal up to her and found her dangling from the curtain rail in the bedroom. She had hanged herself. Your grandfather buried her in the orchard. I'm so sorry.'

Esme felt a lump forming in her throat. So that was what the poor spirit and the bad dreams had been trying to tell her. Poor Gip wasn't the only soul that was buried in the orchard. 'You've done nothing to be sorry for,' she told her in a small voice. 'But where will you go now if Grandfather loses the parish and his home?'

Mrs Sparrow shrugged. 'I've no idea, but I dare say I'll survive. I realise now I can do no more to help him. He's bad through and through, although I've never allowed myself to admit it. When I get back I'm going to tell him that I'm leaving and I want nothing more to do with him. I suppose I should have done it years ago but I kept thinking he'd change. Anyway, you just worry about yourself from now on. Goodbye, pet.'

And with that she left the room with tears in her eyes.

Late the following evening, Lady Fitzroy entered Esme's room with a serious expression on her face and Esme knew instantly that something was wrong.

'What's happened?' Esme pulled herself up onto the pillows with Olivia's help as Lady Fitzroy stood at the end of the bed wringing her hands together. 'Is it Gabriel? Has something happened to him?'

'No, my dear, there has been no word of your brother as yet, as far as I know . . . but I do have bad news. It's Mrs Sparrow. I'm afraid the postman found her dead in the kitchen of the rectory this morning.'

Esme gasped. 'B-but how? She was only here yesterday and apart from being upset about what has happened she seemed all right. She told me that she was going back to tell my grandfather that she was leaving.'

'It appears that she had her throat cut,' Lady Fitzroy told her with a catch in her voice.

'*No!*' Esme shook her head in disbelief. 'But who would do that to her? There was nothing of any great value in the rectory to interest thieves.'

'Your grandfather has gone missing and I'm sorry to tell you that the police are looking for him as they believe it could have been him that did it. They believe her murder might be linked to that of Molly Malone too.'

'She must have told him that the bishop had been informed of what he did to me and that she was going and he must have lost his temper again,' Esme said, feeling somehow to blame.

'I'm so sorry to be the bearer of such sad news,' Lady Fitzroy said quietly. 'It seems that sorrow is following in your footsteps at present, my dear. But never mind, things can only get better, and they will, I assure you.'

Esme plopped back on the bed and stared vacantly at the ceiling, praying that this kind lady was right, because she felt at her lowest ebb and didn't know how much more she could take. Poor Mrs Sparrow, she hadn't deserved to meet such a brutal end.

Chapter Thirty

Gabriel stood on the docks in London and breathed a massive sigh of relief. It had taken him over a week to get here by walking and hitching lifts on carts whenever he could, and he was footsore, weary and very afraid. After running away, he had made for Hull where he had been fortunate enough to be taken on by the captain of a fishing trawler. It had been damned hard work but he had felt safe while he was at sea. It was only when the boat returned to the docks with its load that the fear of being captured had kicked in again.

Thanks to the money Jeremy had given him and what he'd earned on the fishing trips, he had managed to sleep in one of the cheap boarding houses surrounding the docks, but every time he spotted a policeman his heart would begin to thump with fear and he would shrink into the shadows. It was no way to live and eventually he decided that the more miles he could put between him and the school the better, so he had set off for London.

What he hadn't reckoned on was that here many of the ships transported cargo all over the world, and with no experience he wondered if he would find a captain who would be willing to take him on. Esme was another constant worry. He had hated leaving her at his grandfather's mercy knowing what a sadist he was, but what choice had he had? It was hard enough for him to hide and it would have been harder still with two of them. He had deliberately avoided reading any newspapers since he'd fled. He knew that if he had seen his name in the paper, it would only have panicked him more and so now, although he longed to rest after his long journey, he began to approach the ships that were docked there to see if there was any chance of work aboard any of them.

Christmas had come and gone uncelebrated and now he just wanted to get away and find some peace, even if it meant making a home in another country. But it would only be until he had earned enough to be able to keep both himself and Esme and then, he promised himself, he would return to fetch her and hopefully neither of them would ever have to set eyes on their evil grandfather again.

With his purpose renewed, he climbed yet another gangplank and asked for the captain. But it seemed that all the ships ready to sail already had a full crew so, as the daylight faded, he began to lose heart, and realised he had no choice but to try to find some lodgings and hopefully some food, for he hadn't eaten since he had stolen two raw eggs out of a barn that morning and his stomach was growling.

Once he had left the docks behind and entered the busier streets of London he looked around in amazement. The roads were full of traffic: passenger cabs, dray horses and smart carriages full of people dressed in fine clothes. There was an old woman selling posies of dried heather, another selling seed for the tourists to feed to the pigeons that seemed to be everywhere, and then at last a cart selling faggots and peas.

Pulling out some change Gabriel bought some and sat on the edge of a wall to eat, marvelling at the sights. He had never seen so many people in one place at the same time before. Eventually he asked an old lady if she might direct him to a cheap lodging house and she pointed him towards the docks again. 'Take that lane there, dearie,' she told him cheerily. 'Then yer first right and you'll come to Ma Picks place sure enough. T'ain't no palace, mind, but it'll be somewhere to lay yer 'ead.'

He soon found she hadn't been lying when she'd said that the place wasn't posh. Outside women of the night with highly rouged cheeks and painted lips stood flaunting their breasts to attract customers and Gabriel scooted past them. The three-storey house seemed to be packed to the rafters with sailors of every nationality and he discovered that if he wanted a bed he would have to share an attic room with a Chinese man who didn't speak a word of English. Still, that was better than braving a night on the streets so he took the bed and threw his kitbag down beside the lumpy straw mattress gratefully. His heels were so sore from all the walking that when he removed his boots the skin came with them and he winced. The blanket provided was thin and did little to keep out the cold, but his stomach was full and he was exhausted so in no time at all he was fast asleep.

He woke at first light, blinking as he gazed around at the unfamiliar surroundings. But then remembering where he was, he decided that he would go and find something to eat and start his search for a ship early. His hand dropped to the side of the mattress as he felt around for his boots and he noticed that the Chinese man had already gone – no doubt to sail on one of the ships that would be waiting to depart. His hands felt nothing so he slung his feet onto the cold floorboards and stared down, his heart sinking. There was no sign of his boots or the kitbag that contained the change of clothes he had purchased from the pawn shop in Lincoln. Frantically he began to throw things about but soon he had to acknowledge that everything was gone: his boots, his clothes and what was left of the money Jeremy had so kindly given him. All he had left in the world now were the clothes he stood up in and the small amount of change that he had kept in the pocket of his trousers.

Dropping his head into his hands, he allowed despair to wash over him for a time, but soon, with a determined set to his mouth, he counted out the coins he had left. There was less than two shillings, which would hopefully at least buy him some breakfast and a pair of boots if he could find a pawn shop. He was just grateful he had slept in his jacket and his clothes, otherwise he was sure they would have been stolen too.

As he left the boarding house, he shuddered as his stockinged feet sank into the slush left behind by the snow. Within seconds his socks were sodden. He had thought things couldn't get any worse, but how wrong he was. He had never felt so miserable in his life.

There would be no point applying for a job on a ship if he didn't even own a pair of boots so he would make finding them a priority. As he trudged back to the city centre, he passed no pawn shops, but after a time he came to a market with a rag stall that sold clothes and boots, and there he managed to find a pair that at least fit him. He haggled with the old woman on the stall and got the price down to sixpence, then he invested another penny on a pair of thick, very darned socks. The soles of the boots were well worn and the socks smelled as if they had never been washed but at least his feet were warmer, so he set off to find a stall where he could get some food.

The first one he came to was selling jellied eels, but just the smell of them made his stomach revolt, so he quickly moved on until he came to one that sold meat pies. Once he'd eaten he headed off for the docks, feeling slightly better. At the dock, a thousand different smells met him from the cargo that was being loaded and unloaded from the ships. There were large barrels of tea arriving from China, barrels of coffee beans from India and barrels of rum coming in from Jamaica, all mixed in with the smell of wet tar rising from the enormous coils of ropes dotted about. But overriding everything was the stench of the stagnant water slapping the walls of the dock.

His search for a position on one of the outgoing ships was more desperate now for he knew that he had scarcely enough money left to pay for a bed for another night let alone feed himself. The first three boats he approached turned him away and Gabriel began to panic. What would he do if no one would take him on? But then he approached a merchant ship. Burly seamen were busily carrying great bales of cotton aboard and one of them directed him to the person in charge.

'Have you ever done this sort of work or sailed before?' the first mate asked, staring dubiously at Gabriel's thin frame. He had lost a lot of weight while living at the school and looked quite puny.

'No, sir, but I'm a quick learner and I'm stronger than I look,' Gabriel answered.

The first mate stroked his chin. He was two men down and he supposed it would be worth giving him a chance.

'We'll be sailing to Nova Scotia on the tide and will be away for some months. I could take you on as an OS – that's an ordinary seaman to you. It means you'll be responsible for doing any jobs that need doing – scrubbing the decks or helping out where necessary. If you've no experience that's the best I can offer.'

'So sort of an odd-job man?'

When the man nodded, Gabriel smiled with relief. 'That sounds good to me, sir. And thank you, I won't let you down. I'm not afraid of hard work.'

'It's just as well,' the first mate told him wryly. 'Now you'd best start by giving a hand bringing the cargo aboard. I'll get someone to show you where you'll be sleeping shortly.'

And so it was arranged, and Gabriel made his way back to the dock and began to lug the large bales of cotton up the gangplank.

Sometime later a sailor led him down some steep ladders into the very bowels of the ship. They came to a large room where a number of hammocks were suspended between the rafters. 'This is where you'll be sleeping, son. When you get the chance to sleep, that is. The job you're takin' on ain't easy so be warned, an' if yer feel yer won't be up to it now is the time to say cos once we've sailed there's no turning back. There ain't even time fer you to go an' tell yer folks we'll be goin'.'

Looking at Gabriel the sailor wondered if the lad would be up to the job. He wasn't as far through as a rake and looked as if one good puff of wind would blow him away, but then who was he to judge.

'That's all right,' Gabriel assured him, hiding his nerves. 'I've no one to say goodbye to and I'm sure I'll manage.'

'So be it then. Don't say I didn't warn yer. Now come on, there's still lots to do afore we set sail.'

For the next hour Gabriel rushed about like a mad thing doing anything he was asked until at last the gangplank was pulled aboard and it was time to set sail.

He stood for a few brief minutes watching the shores of his homeland fade into the distance and thinking of Esme, praying that she would be all right. He had no idea how long it might be before he came home again, or even if he ever would. Who knew what the future had in store for him? Then he set his shoulders and went to begin his new life at sea.

Chapter Thirty-One

January 1877

The doctor finally declared that Esme was well enough to get up for a few hours each day in the first week of January. The wheals on her back and legs were healing well as were the bruises she had sustained on the night of the attack. The New Year's Eve party had gone ahead as planned and although Esme hadn't been well enough to attend she had insisted that Olivia should go.

There had been no word of her grandfather's whereabouts despite the fact that the police were still searching for him, which worried her considerably. She realised now what a dangerous man he was and knew that she would never feel completely safe until they had him under lock and key.

During the time she had been forced to stay in bed, Olivia had been her constant companion. She had spent hours reading to her, chatting and trying to tempt her with tasty titbits to eat and now the girls were closer than ever, although Esme was still fretting silently about what might become of her once the doctor declared her properly well again. Would Lady Fitzroy feel that she had done her duty by her and turn her out into the cold?

'I'll have the maid drag the chair over to the window for you so you can see what's going on outside,' Olivia volunteered when the doctor had left.

Esme gave her a half-hearted smile. She did feel much better but she was plagued with nightmares of the night her grandfather had attacked her and woke up most mornings feeling as if she hadn't been to sleep. Soon after she was settled in the chair in a warm dressing robe with a thick blanket across her knees.

'I shall have to get off to Mr Pritchard now,' Olivia told her regretfully. 'Else I shall be late for my lessons.' She handed Esme a book to read, ordering, 'Be sure to ring the bell when you're feeling tired and the maid will come and help you back into bed.' A twinkle appeared in her eye then and she giggled. 'I shall be back to see you at lunchtime with Mama. She has something to tell you and I hope it will make you happy.'

Esme raised her eyebrow. She was feeling very sorry for herself at present and couldn't imagine anything making her feel happy. She was missing Gabriel so much that it hurt to think of him, but she was intrigued to hear what Lady Fitzroy had to say to her.

The maid appeared an hour later to help Esme back into bed and she slept until she heard the door open sometime later. She opened her eyes to see Olivia and her mother framed in the doorway.

'Ah, you're awake, my dear, and looking so much more like your old self, thankfully. The doctor is very pleased with your progress.' The woman approached the bed and sat down in the chair next to it as Olivia hovered by her shoulder looking excited. 'I've been giving your future some thought, as I realise that you have no home to go to now. A new reverend has been appointed to take your grandfather's place and is due to move into the rectory later this week. And so Olivia and I have decided that we would like to offer you a position here.'

'As a maid?' Esme asked, but the woman shook her head.

'No, Olivia would like you to continue with your lessons with her, and so although this is rather unorthodox and you are still very young, we thought you might consider the position of becoming her lady's maid cum companion. Olivia is still quite young to have her own lady's maid but I think in the circumstances this could be permitted. You would, of course, receive a salary annually, and it would mean that you would have to move to the servants' quarters. What do you think?'

Esme managed a smile for the first time in days. 'I think that's very generous of you,' she replied as a mixture of emotions flooded through her. She felt relief that she would never have to enter the rectory again, yet guilt because she wouldn't be able to help the poor spirits that would still be there move on.

'You will of course stay here until you are completely recovered,' the kindly woman went on. 'And once you are, you can begin your new duties. But as I said, you will be allowed to continue with your lessons at Olivia's request.'

'Thank you, my lady,' Esme said gratefully. At least she knew she wasn't going to be turfed out onto the streets, and she actually liked the idea of working for this kind family.

'I think it might be as well if we got you measured for some sort of uniform,' Lady Fitzroy said thoughtfully. 'Perhaps something suitable for a lady's maid to wear. But leave that with me. I shall get my seamstress to come and see you.' Lady Fitzroy nodded with satisfaction. It had actually been her daughter's idea and she knew that she would have been given no peace if she had refused to go along with it, but she was slightly concerned about what the rest of the staff might have to say about it. Still, it was decided now so everyone would have to like it or lump it!

She rose and, with a smile, left the two girls to chatter.

'It will be wonderful,' Olivia said happily. 'I'm just sad that Mama wouldn't allow you to stay close to me in this room, but I suppose she does have to think of what the rest of the staff might say.'

'I won't mind living in the servant's quarters at all,' Esme assured her and seeing the worried expression that formed on her friend's face she asked anxiously, 'What's wrong?'

'Nothing . . . well, not exactly. It's just that we've heard that some of the staff have been gossiping – about your grandfather. He is wanted for murder, after all. Not that that is your fault,' she hurried on. 'But that plus the fact that they've heard you came from gypsy stock might make it a bit difficult for you.'

Esme scowled. 'I can handle a bit of gossip,' she assured her. 'I don't care what they say about my grandfather and I'm certainly not ashamed of where I came from. My dadda might have been a gypsy but he was a good, hard-working man.'

234

'I'm sure he was.' The girl frowned at her. 'But you do realise that you'll have to eat with the servants down in the kitchen?'

Esme shrugged and squeezed her hand. 'I shan't mind that,' she promised. 'I'm just grateful to know that I shall have a roof over my head and that I'll still be able to see you.'

'Oh, we'll have such fun!' Olivia clapped her hands. 'And because you will be officially my maid it means that you'll be able to come to our London town house to stay there with me in the summer. We can go sightseeing and shopping ... although I'm not sure that Mama will think it's proper for you to come to the theatre with us.' She gave a pretty pout. 'Still, at least we'll get lots of time to spend together. I can't imagine how I survived without someone my own age to talk to before you came,' she confided. 'So we'll just be glad for what we can do together, shall we?'

Esme nodded, feeling as if a great weight had been lifted from her shoulders. All she needed now was to know that Gabriel was safe, but as yet there had been no word from him and she knew that she would have to be patient.

'There's just one thing I'd like to ask,' Esme said hesitantly. 'I wonder if perhaps your mother would allow me to return to the rectory to collect my things when it's convenient?'

'I'm sure that won't be a problem. In fact, I shall come with you. It wouldn't be very nice for you to have to go back to that place alone after what's happened. But we shall need to go soon before the new reverend takes up residency there. I'll ask Mama if she would allow the carriage to take us.'

They set off three days later and Esme was a bag of nerves as she relived in her mind what had happened on the night she ran away.

'It'll be all right,' Olivia comforted her as the carriage rattled through the village.

When it pulled up outside the rectory, Esme shuddered. She had always felt it was a bad place and now she knew why. Her poor grandmother. What state of mind must she have been in to take her own life as she had?

'Would you mind very much if I went in alone?' Esme asked, and Olivia nodded.

'Of course, if you're sure?' she answered. 'Take as long as you like. We'll be right here waiting for you.'

Esme swallowed before alighting from the carriage and walking round to the back of the rectory. Mrs Sparrow had always kept the spare key in a plant pot beside the door and after fishing it out she let herself in. Someone had been in and cleaned the kitchen and there was nothing to show that poor Mrs Sparrow had been murdered in there. Even so there was a chill in the air and Esme knew it was nothing to do with the fact that no fires had been lit. As she climbed the stairs to her room with her heart in her mouth, she realised that Granny Griselda was beside her.

'I know who the lovely silver-haired lady is,' Esme told her. 'But that doesn't explain who the other four young women who kept appearing to me are?'

'Put two and two together, my dove, and you'll come up with four.'

Esme turned to ask what she meant but Granny had already gone. Once in her bedroom she dragged a valise that Mrs Sparrow had given to her from the bottom of her wardrobe and began to pack her clothes. As she did, the four young women began to materialise but this time she wasn't afraid. Her granny's words came back to her. *Put two and two together, my dove, and you'll come up with four.* What could she have meant?

She stood staring at the women in consternation, and suddenly things became clearer. The girls who had been murdered in Skegness . . . They had all had their throats cut.

'It was *my grandfather* who murdered you, wasn't it?' she said.

But there was no answer from the spirits, as they disappeared as quickly as they had appeared. 'I shall tell the police what I think, have no fear. You can go on now and rest in peace knowing your deaths will be avenged.'

Esme didn't know if they had heard her, but as she returned to her packing, she was sure the room felt more peaceful.

'Are you all right?' Olivia asked anxiously when Esme climbed back into the carriage.

'Yes, I am.' Esme nodded. 'But I just realised something in there. The young women who have been murdered in Skegness over the last year or so . . .'

'What about them?'

'They all had their throats cut, didn't they?'

Olivia stared back at her blankly.

'Well, don't you see? I think my grandfather was responsible for their deaths too. Think of Molly Malone and Mrs Sparrow – and I know he could have killed the last two girls at least because their deaths occurred while he was staying away from the rectory.'

'Oh goodness!' Olivia shivered as her hand flew to her mouth. 'You could be right but what are you going to do about it?'

'I'm going to tell your mother about my suspicions, and then I shall speak to the police,' Esme told her in a small voice.

Olivia frowned as she stared from the window. 'He must be a very wicked man indeed. It makes you wonder how he ever got to be ordained. And they haven't caught him yet, have they? It's frightening. You don't think he would try to come back to harm you, do you?'

'I think he would if he could,' Esme admitted. 'He certainly never appreciated me and Gabriel turning up on his doorstep, and he punished us both brutally at every opportunity.'

'Don't worry, we'll make sure you're safe.' Olivia patted her hand. 'But you must promise me that you won't go out on your own until he's been found. Now, I just want to get home so you can speak to Mama and tell her your suspicions and then I hope you never have to set foot in that dreadful house again!'

'I realise now, it wasn't the house that was dreadful . . . it was him!'

The girls lapsed into silence until they got home.

The minute she had finished telling Lady Fitzroy her suspicions, the woman dispatched a footman to fetch the local bobby and an hour later Esme relayed her fears to him as he sat scribbling notes in his notepad, although she was careful not to mention Granny Griselda or the spirits she had seen. She didn't want him to think that she was as mad as her poor grandmother Silver had been.

'It does sound highly likely that he could have been responsible for all six deaths from what you've told me,' he said cautiously. 'Following one of the deaths I believe a witness got a glimpse of a man running away from the scene. I shall have to check with the police in Skegness to see if the man matched your grandfather's description. Meanwhile, I suggest you don't stray too far away from the house on your own, Miss Loveridge. Thank you for your help.'

He rose and bowed to Lady Fitzroy. Now all Esme could do was wait to see what the outcome would be and pray that her grandfather would be apprehended very soon.

Chapter Thirty-Two

Esme started her new position two weeks later. The seamstress had made her two gowns to wear in the house and Esme was very pleased with them. They were made of a very fine wool, which was soft against her skin, with lace-trimmed necklines and full skirts that swished when she walked, making her feel very grown-up. Although identical in style, one was deep blue, while the other was a soft silver-grey.

On the first morning, Tilly, the young maid, accompanied her to her new room in the servants' quarters. It was very sparsely furnished by comparison with her old room, with a metal-framed bed, a small chest of drawers, a tiny bedside cabinet, a table and chair and a washstand upon which stood a sturdy pottery jug and bowl. There were nails hammered into the back of the door to hang her clothes on, and in place of the plush wall-to-wall carpet she had become accustomed to were bare wooden floorboards. There was no fireplace in this room and it was cuttingly cold. Cheap, faded but spotlessly clean curtains hung at the window, which had a superb view across the grounds. Despite the fact that Esme was just grateful to have a roof over her head and to be able to earn a living, she couldn't help but compare it to the beautiful bedroom she had just left.

'Will that be all . . . er, miss?' Tilly asked. She wasn't quite sure what to call Esme now. After all, she was now a maid the same as she was, but a maid with advantages.

'Oh yes, thank you, Tilly. And please call me Esme.'

Tilly swallowed and scuttled away like a cat with its tail on fire. They were saying below stairs that Esme was a gypsy with the power to see the dead and she was more than a little afraid of her now.

Blissfully unaware of Tilly's fear, Esme put her things away before rushing off to commence her lesson with Olivia and Mr Pritchard.

'Oh, it doesn't seem right that we can't lunch together anymore!' Olivia complained at the end of the morning.

Esme smiled. 'At least I'm still here,' she pointed out. 'But now I must go and fetch your tray up and then I shall have my lunch in the kitchen with the rest of the staff.'

The kitchen was humming with chatter as she entered, but the minute the staff noticed her, they all fell silent and looked pointedly down at their plates. Esme felt her face grow hot; they had obviously been talking about her. But she supposed she couldn't really blame them. After all, both her brother and her grandfather were on the run from the police. Add to that the fact that she came from gypsy stock and it was no wonder that they were gossiping.

'I've come for Oli— Miss Olivia's lunch tray,' Esme said, and without glancing at her the rosy-faced cook nodded towards a small table.

'It's all ready for her on there.'

'Thank you.' Esme took it without another word and as the green baize door that led back into the hallway swung shut behind her, she heard the chattering start up again.

'Here we are. I've no idea what it is but it smells delicious,' she told Olivia with forced brightness as she entered the schoolroom again. Olivia's mother was out visiting so she was dining alone that day. 'But I'd best get off now. The staff are all at lunch already and if I don't hurry there'll be none left for me. See you shortly.'

The second she left the room the smile slid from her face and her shoulders slumped. She dreaded going into the kitchen again. But what choice did she have? If she didn't go down, she wouldn't eat, it was as simple as that, so she squared her shoulders and set off.

Once back in the kitchen she stared at the table uncertainly. Many of the staff had already left and the cook told her shortly, 'You can sit there. Not that there's a lot left, mind. You'll have to make do.'

'I'm sure it will be lovely,' Esme said as she sat down, not wishing to make the cook dislike her any more than she clearly already did. Those that were seated didn't say a word to her as they finished their meals and left the table while Esme helped herself to a small portion of boiled potatoes, the remains of what looked to have been a huge cottage pie and some peas. The strained atmosphere meant that Esme really wasn't that hungry anymore so it was more than enough to appease her appetite.

It was some minutes before anyone spoke to her and then it was the cook who asked shortly, 'Have they caught yer gran'father yet?'

Esme flushed and shook her head. 'No, I don't think so.'

'Huh! The sooner they do the better. Filthy murderer! Hangin' will be too good for 'im.'

Esme didn't know what to say so she said nothing and soon the table was empty but for herself.

'So are yer goin' to eat that or sit there pushin' it about yer plate all day?' the cook grumbled as she carried some of the dirty pots to the sink. 'Got used to better things, 'ave yer, upstairs wi' Miss Olivia?'

'Oh, the food is lovely,' Esme hastened to assure her. 'It's just I'm not . . . er, very hungry.'

'So scrape it in that bin there fer the pigs,' the older woman ordered. 'We ain't 'ere to wait on the likes o' you, yer know!'

With her cheeks flaming Esme did as she was told before scuttling away back upstairs. Already she could see that the current arrangement was going to be difficult for her. She was neither one thing nor the other now. She wasn't part of the family, yet she was still being given privileges that weren't available to the rest of the staff and that clearly irked them.

'Nice lunch?' Olivia asked as Esme lifted her tray to take it back downstairs. It would be part of her duties to wait on Olivia now.

'Yes, very nice, thank you.'

They had another hour with Miss Trimble that afternoon who taught them the right way to lay a table for dinner guests if entertaining. There were so many different sets of cutlery for the different courses that Esme was baffled. 'Just remember, girls, when dining one should always use the cutlery from the outside in,' Miss Trimble said primly. Once again Esme thought it was a skill that she would never need to use but she went along with it. Next, it was how to write and send out invitations for morning coffee and Esme was sure that she could have been putting her time to better use. But at last, it was over and she could spend some time with Olivia.

'Is your room really awful?' Olivia enquired with a worried frown.

'Not at all. Beggars can't be choosers and I'm just grateful to have a room.'

'Oh, please don't say that.' Olivia's lip trembled. 'You're not a beggar.'

'I probably would have been if your mother hadn't kindly given me this post,' Esme pointed out as she started to tidy Olivia's underwear drawers. She really was terribly untidy.

'Luke is coming home the day after tomorrow for a whole month,' Olivia told her, making Esme smile for the first time that day. Olivia sounded pleased about it too. 'He's been given four weeks off from university for study time. It will be lovely to have him back again.'

'You must miss your brother when he's away,' Esme said and Olivia giggled.

'You forget, Luke isn't my brother,' she told her. 'He's a cousin. His parents died in a carriage accident when he was quite young so Mama and Papa took him in. He's very handsome, isn't he?'

'I, er . . . hadn't really noticed,' Esme muttered and Olivia giggled again.

'But you must have! All the maids are secretly in love with him. And he's actually going to be very rich when he reaches twenty-one. His parents left him an enormous amount of money plus an estate in the Midlands somewhere. There are caretakers there looking after it for him until he comes of age and leaves university.' She leaned a little closer and lowering her voice she confided, 'Between you and me I think my parents hope that we will make a match when we're older.'

'What? You mean get married?' Esme was shocked.

Olivia nodded. 'Yes, and I have to say I do quite like the idea as I get a little older. After all, he is a good catch, isn't he?'

'I . . . I wouldn't really know,' Esme mumbled, wondering why she felt so disappointed.

'Anyway, you're supposed to be my companion as well as my maid so why don't you stop tidying up now and come here. I want to teach you to play chess.'

That evening Esme spent another uncomfortable half-hour in the kitchen over supper and once again no one spoke to her. It was as if she was invisible and she could hardly escape quickly enough.

'What's wrong?' Olivia questioned when Esme went to help her prepare for bed. 'And don't say nothing! I can tell by your face that something is troubling you.'

Esme hesitated as she chose her words carefully. 'There's nothing wrong exactly. It's just that I don't think the rest of the staff are very pleased to have me here. I suppose I can't blame them. After all, my grandfather is being hunted for murder and my brother has had to run away too.'

Olivia looked annoyed before offering, 'I can have a word with Mama, if you like? She'll soon sort them out.'

'Oh no, *please* don't,' Esme begged. 'If they think I've gone tittle-tattling about them it could only make things worse. I'm sure things will improve when they get used to me.'

'Very well, I won't say anything . . . for now,' Olivia agreed. 'But you must tell me if things don't get any better.'

Things actually did get a little better when Esme received a letter from Jeremy the following morning. Esme had just taken Olivia's breakfast tray down to the kitchen when it was handed to her by a disgruntled butler. She longed to read it, but first she would have to get through the morning's lessons, so she shoved it into the deep pocket of her gown for later. It would be something to look forward to.

Luke arrived home mid-morning and barged into the schoolroom to give Olivia a hug. They were clearly delighted to see each other and Esme felt a little flame of jealousy burn in her stomach. He was certainly the best-looking young man she had ever seen and she wondered why she had noticed that when she had never taken much notice of boys before.

He smiled at Esme and she felt herself blush.

Mr Pritchard said kindly, 'I can see we're not going to get a lot of work done today with all this excitement. Why don't I give you girls some homework to do and let you have the rest of the day off?'

'Oh, thank you, sir,' Olivia said happily. 'Luke and I can go riding when he's settled in. It's never as much fun when I go alone.' She turned to Esme. 'And you can have a little bit of time to yourself for a change, instead of always running around after me.'

Taking that as a dismissal, Esme discreetly left the room and hurried back to the servants' quarters. At least now she would have time to read Jeremy's letter and she decided that when she had she might go for a walk – but not too far. She wouldn't feel safe straying too far away from the hall until her grandfather had been apprehended.

Once in the privacy of her own little room she sat on the bed and opened the envelope.

Dear Esme,

As you will see from the address at the top of this letter I have now enrolled in a veterinary college in Hull. In future could you send any letters to me there, please?

As it happens, I didn't have to tell my father that I wasn't returning to school but I'll tell you all about it when I see you. If you still get Sunday afternoons off, perhaps I could come and see you this week?

I have so much to tell you and would rather do it face to face. If I don't hear from you, I shall call at the hall at 2.30p.m. Look forward to seeing you then.

Kind regards
Your friend,
Jeremy

Esme scowled. The letter was very short and sweet and she wondered what could possibly be so important that he felt he had to tell her about it face to face? Could it be something to do with Gabriel? Could he have heard from him, or better still discovered where he was? And how had he possibly managed to enrol in a college all of a sudden when his parents had been so against it?

She read the short letter through again and sighed as she returned it to its envelope. Suddenly Sunday seemed a very long way away and she didn't know how she was going to contain her curiosity.

Chapter Thirty-Three

Esme saw very little of Olivia that week apart from when they were in the schoolroom. The rest of the time Olivia and Luke spent mainly together and it was plain to see how close they were.

'I'm so sorry if I'm neglecting you,' Olivia apologised as Esme was helping her get changed for dinner one evening. She was dining with her parents and Luke and they had dinner guests joining them. After lessons that afternoon Olivia and Luke had been riding and now her cheeks were glowing and her eyes shining.

'It's quite all right,' Esme assured her. Since taking on the role of Olivia's maid things had changed dramatically. Lady Fitzroy considered it was no longer acceptable for them to spend quite so much time together apart from when they were studying or Esme was seeing to Olivia's needs. Although they were still firm friends, it had emphasised to Esme the huge gulf between them in class. And now Esme was very much a servant, the rest of the staff went to great pains to point it out to her.

'I really can't think why 'er ladyship allows you to 'ave lessons wi' Miss Olivia,' the cook grumbled one day as she slapped a meal down in front of Esme. 'After all, you ain't no better than the rest of us, in fact, you ain't as good, if truth be told.'

Up until then Esme had taken everything they had thrown at her without a word, but suddenly she knew it was time to stand up for herself. If not, the staff were more than capable of making her life a misery.

'And *why* am I not? As good as you, I mean,' Esme said angrily.

The cook looked slightly taken aback, as did the others who were in the kitchen. This room was very much the cook's domain and everyone did as they were told when she gave an order.

'Well . . . yer a gypsy, ain't yer?'

246

'My father was a gypsy,' Esme said with a proud toss of her head. 'And he was also a very honest, hard-working man!'

'Hmm.' Cook wasn't sure how to reply to that.

'And as for my grandfather . . . I can hardly be blamed for what he did, can I?'

The cook was clearly flustered. 'I, er . . . dare say yer can't,' she admitted.

Esme felt as if she had won a small victory. At least from now on the cook would know that she couldn't keep talking down to her without some sort of retaliation.

Suddenly the strangest sensation swept over Esme and she found herself looking at a small boy standing close to Cook's skirts, smiling at her. 'It's Daniel,' she muttered. She was so intent on watching him that she failed to note the way the cook's head snapped round to stare at her or the way the colour drained from her face.

'*What* did you just say?' the cook asked, staggering towards a chair and leaning unsteadily on the back of it.

Esme shook her head and the child was gone. 'I . . . I'm so sorry. But I just saw a lovely little boy standing close to you. He had the most beautiful smile.'

'What did he look like?'

'He was about five or six years old, I would say, and quite small for his age with deep-blue eyes and wavy brown hair. Oh, and he was leaning to one side as if one of his legs had been paining him, but he said to tell you it's all better now.'

Tears rolled down the cook's face and Esme asked, 'Did that mean anything to you?'

The cook sniffed and nodded as she scrubbed at the tears on her face with a piece of rag. 'It does,' she said in a choky voice. 'Danny was my son. He was born with a lame leg and he died when he was five years old.'

'Well, I think he just wanted you to know that he isn't lame now and he's happy.'

'But how could you have known that?'

'Sometimes I just see people,' Esme told her in a small voice.

'What, you mean . . . ghosts?'

Esme shrugged. 'Call them what you will – spirits, ghosts. My granny Griselda could see them too.'

'And you say he looked happy?' the cook asked, smiling through her tears.

'*Very* happy,' Esme assured her. 'I imagine he just popped by to let you know that and, oh . . .' She closed her eyes tight and when she opened them again, she told her, 'And he wants you to know that he's with Harry and Esther.'

The cook started crying again. 'Harry was me 'usband, God bless 'is soul, an' Esther was me ma.'

The rest of the staff were staring at Esme curiously.

'Can you summon these spirits at will?' the under-footman asked.

Esme shook her head. 'I've never really tried. To be honest, I've never really liked being able to see them, but I suppose now I'm getting older it isn't so scary.'

A bell above the door tinkled, and the cook turned to the parlour maid. 'That'll be Lady Fitzroy in the drawing room. Go an' see what she wants an' look lively about it.'

Suddenly the kitchen was a hive of activity again and Esme felt as if she had just jumped the first hurdle to being accepted. It was the first time the cook had ever spoken civilly to her and she hoped that it would continue.

From then on some of the staff were kinder to her but if anything, the rest kept well away from her, branding her 'a witch'.

At last it was Sunday and after lunch Esme told Olivia, 'I'm going to go and get ready to meet Jeremy now. He should be here in a minute.'

Olivia frowned. 'I worry about you straying too far away from the house. Perhaps Luke and I should come with you?'

'It's a kind offer but it's highly unlikely anything is going to happen to me if I have Jeremy with me, is it?'

'I suppose not,' Olivia agreed. So the two girls parted and at two thirty prompt Esme saw Jeremy striding down the drive towards her. She hurried to meet him and turning about they walked back the way he had come.

Esme noticed that he was solemn-faced and a feeling of dread settled over her as she sensed that she wasn't going to like what he had come to tell her.

'What's happened?' she asked as they turned into the lane beyond the gates.

'I got expelled from the school.' He gave her a wry smile. 'Broadhurst came round and told them that it had been Gabriel who attacked him.' Esme's heart skipped a beat. 'Anyway, the headmaster then decided that I must have lied to cover up for him and he expelled me, simple as that. Could he have known it, he did me a favour, but the thing is . . .' He gulped. 'The thing is, Broadhurst died the following day, so now they're searching for Gabriel again.'

'For murder?' Esme's voice came out as a squeak.

'I'm afraid so.'

'And have you heard from him?'

He shook his head. 'Not as yet but my mother did promise that any mail that arrives for me will be forwarded on to the veterinary college. They were only too happy for me to start there once I got kicked out of school. It keeps me out of their way, doesn't it?' he said bitterly.

Esme felt as if her world had fallen apart yet again. She had prayed that Broadhurst would recover so that Gabriel could come back to her one day, but how could he now? Should he be seen, he would be arrested and who would believe the truth about what had happened?

'I'm so sorry I couldn't bring you better news,' Jeremy said sadly.

She touched his hand gently. 'It's not your fault. You were the only one who ever stuck by him and I'll always be grateful to you for that. I just hope that wherever he is he's all right.'

'Gabriel's a fighter,' Jeremy assured her. 'He'll survive. But we can still keep in touch, can't we?'

'Of course. You're about the only friend I've got outside of the hall,' she told him sadly.

He stared at her intently. She'd grown up over the last few months and although she was still very young, he could see what a beauty she'd be one day.

'Well, I suppose I'd better set off back to Hull,' he told her after they had walked a little further. 'I had quite a job getting here, it being a Sunday. I walked for miles and hitched a ride whenever I could. But I'll come again, I promise. Meanwhile, we can still write to each other.'

She nodded. He had come all this way and they had spent less than half an hour together, but it was still bitterly cold and they had nowhere to go. Even the tea shops in Mablethorpe would be closed today, so he walked her back to the gates of the hall and after saying their goodbyes they parted and Esme made her way back to her room with a heavy heart.

In June the maids started to pack for the family's holiday in their town house in Kensington.

'You'll love London,' Olivia told Esme. 'But I wish you didn't have to come as my maid.'

'I don't mind.' Esme was packing one of the large trunks of clothes that Olivia would be taking with her and wondered how she was ever going to wear so many gowns.

'Oh, I shall need them all,' Olivia had told her. 'Some day ones for when Mama has visitors for morning coffee and afternoon tea. Some for going to the theatre and balls, and some dinner gowns. My parents have a lot of dinner parties when we're in London. And I've no doubt I shall be coming home with many more,' she said happily. 'The shops are just wonderful there. Wait until you see them. Your eyes will pop out of your head. There are none to compare around here so Mama buys most of hers while we're there.'

'It sounds wonderful, although I'm not looking forward to the train journey,' Esme admitted. 'I've never been on a train in my life.'

'Oh, you'll love it. The carriages we travel in are very comfortable.' Olivia was bubbling with excitement and clearly very much looking forward to it. 'And of course, Luke will be joining us at the end of the first week and will spend the rest of the time there with us.'

Esme's heart fluttered when she heard that, although she didn't say anything as she clicked the lid of the first trunk down.

'What do you want me to pack next?' she asked and they were off again. It seemed never ending.

At last the day of their departure dawned and they all piled into the carriages. The Fitzroys had staff at the London house so only Esme, Amelia's nanny, Lady Fitzroy's maid and the master's valet would be accompanying them and they would all travel in a separate carriage. Olivia wasn't too happy about that as she would have liked Esme to travel with her, but her mother had pointed out that it wouldn't be fitting. Esme didn't mind in the least and was happy to travel with the rest of the staff, although Lady Fitzroy's maid was quite snooty.

Her first train journey ended up being quite enjoyable and Esme spent most of it staring from the windows at the fields and towns they passed. Then at last they arrived in London and she felt as if she had entered another world. The family were immediately taken to the town house while Esme and the rest of the staff had to stay at the station to supervise all the luggage being taken from the goods van at the back of the train and then packed into yet more carriages. Eventually it was done and they too set off to join the family, with the luggage following on in another carriage. Once again Esme stared out of the window in awe. So many people, so much traffic, such busy roads and so many different nationalities.

'It's very different to the small neck of the woods where we came from, isn't it?' Lady Fitzroy's maid commented as she saw Esme's wide eyes.

Esme nodded. 'It is . . . I never realised there were so many people in the world.'

251

The woman smiled. She didn't know what to make of Esme, although her mistress seemed quite fond of her. From what she had heard from the other servants, Esme had had a hard time of it, what with losing her parents and then being left at the mercy of her murdering grandfather. What she didn't like was what the servants whispered about Esme being able to see the spirits of dead people! Miss Batten had never believed in all that jiggery pokery, although after spending some time with her she had to admit that the girl was intelligent. She was nicely spoken and polite too, despite coming from a gypsy background, so she supposed she couldn't be all bad.

At last, they drew up in front of a grand town house in Kensington. It was a tall, three-storey building in a terrace, but there was no time to admire it for then began the long job of getting the luggage taken to the right rooms.

'I think we should have something to eat and a nice cup of tea before we begin the unpacking,' Miss Batten told the young maid who opened the door to them.

The girl bobbed her knee. 'I'll see to it right away, ma'am,' she said in a curious accent Esme had never heard before.

They were taken to a servants' hall, a small cosy room at the back of the house that looked over the garden, where they were served tiny cucumber sandwiches, little fancy cakes and a huge pot of tea. It was late afternoon by that time and they were all feeling weary. But once they had eaten, they then had to begin the long job of unpacking the clothes and putting them neatly away.

'Oh, here you are at last,' Olivia greeted Esme when she was shown up to her room. 'I do wish you could have travelled with me.'

'I was quite all right with the others,' Esme assured her. 'Now tell me what gown you want to wear to dinner. I'll get that unpacked first and when we've got you ready, I'll carry on putting everything away while you go and eat.'

Soon after, Esme met the staff who ran the house when she went down to dinner and for a time, she could scarcely understand what they said. Most of them were born and bred Londoners and had a very distinct accent.

'What's your name?' the kitchen maid asked in a friendly fashion when Esme sat down at the long table with her.

'I'm Esme.'

''Ello, Esme. I'm Nell, nice to meet yer, where are you from?'

Esme wasn't quite sure what to answer to that, she had been born in the vardo and she and her family had never stayed in one place for long. Still, she didn't want to go into that so she simply said, 'I've come from Lincolnshire.'

'Ooh, I'm a cockney, born wivvin the sound o' Bow bells,' Nell informed her proudly. ''Ave yer got any bruvvers or sisters?'

'Er . . . one brother but he's working away.' Once again she didn't want to go into lengthy explanations.

'An yer muvver an' favver?'

'Sadly they've both passed away,' Esme told her, keeping her fingers crossed. She was telling the truth about her mother at least, but deep down a little flicker of hope remained that her dadda was still alive somewhere. She was sure she would have sensed it if he wasn't.

The staff seemed a friendly lot and Esme thought that she was going to like it there, even though London was far busier than anywhere she had ever visited before.

'Well, the 'ousekeeper 'as informed me that you'll be sharin' my room,' Nell informed her with a smile. ''Ave you ever been to London afore?'

When Esme shook her head, Nell grinned. 'In that case I shall take you sightseein' when you get an afternoon off, if you'd like?'

'It will all depend on whether or not Miss Olivia needs me,' Esme told her as she helped herself to a juicy lamb chop from a dish on the table. There were mashed potatoes and cabbage and mint sauce to go with the meal and she suddenly realised that she was hungry again.

'So what is your job exactly?' Nell asked next.

'Um, I'm sort of a companion cum lady's maid to Miss Olivia.'

'Crikey!' Nell was impressed. 'You're young to be a lady's maid, ain't you?'

Once again, telling the girl how the job had come about would have meant going into a lengthy explanation so Esme just answered, 'Yes, I suppose I am. Miss Olivia wanted someone her age for the job.'

'Lucky you.' Nell was envious. 'An' 'ere's me up to me elbows in soap suds scrubbin' dishes 'alf the time. Good on you.'

Esme smiled at Nell; she showed no resentment for her position, and looking around at the rest of the staff, she didn't sense any coming from them, either. It was such a relief to feel welcomed and suddenly she was glad she had come.

Chapter Thirty-Four

The great ship was being tossed about like a cork as a storm raged, but thankfully Gabriel managed to sleep through it. It hadn't been like that during the first storm he had encountered not long after he had joined the ship. Back then, he had been so violently sick, he had been sure he was going to die. In fact, he was so ill that the captain had been forced to send the ship's doctor to him. That storm had also shown him why the seamen slept in hammocks: though the swinging motion had made him sick, had he been sleeping in an ordinary bed he would have been tossed out of it. They weren't easy to get in and out of, but he had now mastered the art and these days, by the time he dropped into it, he was so exhausted that he could sleep through anything. The muscles that had wasted away during his time at the school were firm and strong again and his shorn hair reached down to his shoulders once more in thick black curls.

The jobs he was expected to do were tedious: sweeping and scrubbing the deck with a stiff broom and sea water, being at the beck and call of the captain, cleaning and emptying the toilets – which Gabriel considered the worst of all jobs – checking the cargo was dry and secure, and any general maintenance jobs that needed doing. His hands were split and raw from regularly manhandling the thick, tarred coils of rope about the deck and he had started to follow another sailor's advice to soak them in his own urine to harden them up. He regularly worked from six in the morning until ten o'clock at night but he was becoming used to that too. He thought of Esme often and prayed that she was safe and well, and he missed Jeremy who had been the only true friend he had had at the boarding school.

The food he ate was little better than he had been served at the school. His diet consisted mainly of salt pork, which he was allowed four times a week, and ship's biscuits or hard tack, which were biscuits made from flour, water and salt. The seamen were, however, allowed rum and ale each day and Gabriel was developing quite a taste for it and looked forward to his ration each night before he retired to bed. On the three days when they weren't allowed meat, they would be served with a stew consisting of onions, vegetables and water thickened with flour. It was fairly unappetising but at least he never went to bed hungry. He was actually grateful for the fact that most of the time he was so busy he didn't have time to fret about Esme or wonder about what had happened to Broadhurst. And, of course, he was looking forward to receiving his wages once they had done the return journey to England.

The first mate had already told him that if he continued to work as he was doing there was a possibility of a promotion from an ordinary seaman to an able seaman, which would be a big step up for him. He'd also said that he would be offered the opportunity to sail again with the next cargo and Gabriel had already decided that he would take it. The way he saw it, he was safe from the police while he was away from his home country and if he saved every penny he earned, it shouldn't be too long before he'd be in a position to encourage Esme to sail to another land and start a new life with him where nobody knew them. After all, they had nothing to keep them in England now. These were the thoughts that kept him going. He'd already decided that when they reached Nova Scotia he would post a letter to Jeremy. Of course, he wouldn't be able to give a return address but at least Jeremy would be able to let Esme know that he was safe and well and that in itself would give him some peace of mind.

The next morning Gabriel awoke early to a calm sea and, swinging himself out of the hammock, he clambered up the ladder to the deck and went to wash in the great barrels of water placed there for that purpose. Next he made for the dining room, such as it was, which consisted of worn wooden tables and chairs with their legs fixed firmly to the floors – there was no way it could ever be classed as salubrious. While he waited for the meal, he lifted one of the old newspapers that were kept there and began to flick through it. He had got about halfway through when his heart skipped a beat as he read the headline.

Schoolboy sought for the murder of school pal!

Suddenly he felt sick, and as he read on, he felt even more so. He was named in the article and there was a description of him. The only good thing was that he had altered vastly since leaving the school, but there was still the matter of his name. Perhaps he should change his surname? Yes, he decided, when they returned to England, he would do that before signing on for another voyage. Very carefully he ripped the page out and screwing it into a ball he went out on deck and tossed it as far away from the ship as he could, watching with fascination as the waves closed over it and sucked it beneath the boat.

'No work to do, boyo?' A voice at the side of him barked and Gabriel started as he looked at the first mate.

'Yes, sir, plenty, but I woke early so I thought I'd grab a bit of fresh air and a bite to eat afore starting.'

The man nodded. 'See as you do then. There's no room for slackers aboard this ship.' In truth he had been impressed with the way the lad had turned his hand to anything he had been asked to do, but it didn't hurt to keep the young 'uns on their toes. 'Very well, as you were.'

As the man strode away, Gabriel breathed a sigh of relief before heading back to the dining cabin.

They reached Nova Scotia thirty-one days after setting sail, and then began the job of unloading the cargo. It was back-breaking work but at last it was done and the crew were told to report back to the ship in a week's time to begin loading the return cargo.

Gabriel was given a small advance on his salary, which was just as well for otherwise he would have had no money.

'What do you usually do and where do you stay when you're on shore?' Gabriel asked one of leading seamen innocently.

The man threw back his head and guffawed as he slapped Gabriel on the back and winked at him. 'Look down there, me lad.'

Gabriel stared from the deck down to the dock where gaudily dressed women in low-cut gowns and with painted faces were sashaying to and fro. 'First of all, we get usselves a gal, lad. A man has needs an' he can't satisfy 'em aboard a ship full of sailors, can he?'

Gabriel blushed. He knew exactly what the man was intimating but how could he tell the chap he was still a virgin?

'Come on, laddy, you stay along o' me an' I'll see yer right.'

He took Gabriel's arm and started to yank him down the gangplank, although in fairness Gabriel didn't put up much of a fight.

'Don't bother wi' this lot 'ere,' the sailor told him as the women began to walk towards them. 'They're all full o' the pox, no doubt, but I know a nice little 'ouse where you can pick an' choose.'

They made their way through a maze of dark cobbled alleys until at last, the sailor stopped and knocked on a door. It was opened almost instantly by a middle-aged woman wearing nothing but a pair of silky pantaloons, a lace corset top and a floaty dressing robe, which left nothing to the imagination.

'Barney, it's good to see you.' She clearly knew the sailor and stood aside to allow him to enter. 'Not seen you for a while, sweet'eart!'

'No, we've not done this run fer some months,' Barney answered as she led them along a passage and into a room with thick red velvet curtains. It was dimly lit and on the sofas that were scattered about Gabriel saw other women and girls in a similar state of undress lounging about smoking and drinking.

'So, who do yer fancy 'aving some fun wi' tonight, Barney?'

'As if you need to ask, Lil, me angel,' Barney chuckled. 'Yer should know be now that you're the only gel fer me.'

'Ooh, you old charmer,' she teased as she kissed him full on the lips and took his hand.

'But what about the lad 'ere?' Seeing the blush in Gabriel's cheeks, she smiled knowingly. 'Ah, I see, it's like that, is it? Well, as it 'appens I reckon I've got just the right girl fer 'im. Wait 'ere a minute.'

She shot away and soon returned with a girl who looked to be little older than Gabriel. Unlike the other women she wore no paint and powder, although the gown she was wearing was cut provocatively low.

'This is our Serena,' she said proudly as the girl hung her head. 'Pretty as a picture, ain't she? Just joined us she 'as, an' I'm sure she'd suit yer little pal 'ere down to the ground.'

Gabriel's heart did a little flutter. As Lil had said, the girl was very pretty. She was dainty with a heart-shaped face and dimples, cornflower-blue eyes and long, straight dark hair that hung down her back like a silken cloak.

The girl raised her head to give Gabriel a shy smile and, in that moment, he was smitten.

'Go on then, girl,' Lil ordered with a giggle. 'Yer know the ropes be now. Go an' make this young man 'appy, an' don't forget it's money up front.'

When the girl stepped forward and gently took Gabriel's hand he followed her like a puppy as Barney and Lil walked on behind. She led him up a staircase covered in a deep-red carpet and once they reached the landing they passed several closed doors, and from the sounds issuing from behind them, Gabriel was left in no doubt as to what was going on.

'This is my room,' Serena said, opening a door and leading him inside. An oil lamp was burning on a small table to one side of a bed, which was covered in a black silken sheet. Gabriel swallowed so hard that his Adam's apple seemed to dance up and down.

'It's, er . . . a shilling,' she said quietly as she began to fumble with the buttons on her gown.

Without a word Gabriel took it from his pocket and laid it down next to the lamp. Seconds later the gown dropped into a silken pool at her feet and he stared at her naked figure as if he had never seen a woman before, thinking that he had never seen anyone more beautiful.

'Have you ever done this before?' she asked gently and when he hesitated before shaking his head, she smiled. 'Don't worry, I hadn't either until I came here.'

'But why *are* you here?' he asked before he could stop himself. 'You don't seem like the other girls somehow.'

'I didn't have much choice,' she told him. 'My father died last year and I stayed on in our house with my mother but then she died a short time ago too and I was turned out. I had nowhere to go. It was either here or the streets.'

His heart filled with sympathy for her as she advanced on him slowly and placed a gentle kiss on his lips. At that moment all the normal urges of a young man surged through him like fire in his veins and he found his manhood standing to attention as she slowly began to undo his trousers. Tentatively he reached out and gently stroked her naked breast and immediately her nipple hardened under his touch. Within minutes they were lying on the bed naked and what followed came naturally.

It was over all too quickly for Gabriel, but with Serena lying with her head on his chest, he felt as if he had died and gone to heaven. So this was what loving a woman felt like. He wished he had tried it before.

'I . . . I don't usually let the men kiss me,' she told him in a small voice. 'But you seem different.'

He felt a lump swell in his throat as he stroked her silken hair. Gabriel was in love.

'You're very beautiful, Serena,' he told her softly.

Lifting her head she smiled. 'That isn't my real name,' she confided. 'My real name is Emma but Lil likes the girls to have more exotic-sounding names.'

He nodded before asking, 'May I come and see you again before we sail back to England?'

'I'd like that.' She snuggled close to him once more, enjoying the last few moments of their time together.

'So how was it, matey?' Barney asked as they walked away a short time later.

'It was wonderful,' Gabriel told him still tasting her lips on his.

Barney laughed and gave him another sound clout on the shoulder. 'There yer go then. You'll not forget this evenin'.'

'No, I won't,' Gabriel agreed and he meant every word he said. 'I thought perhaps we could come back again before we sail for home?'

Barney frowned as he glanced at him. 'We can do that all right. But, lad . . . don't forget that Serena is a whore. She's there to satisfy men's needs but she ain't wife material, so go steady, eh? Now let's go an' find us a lodgin' house fer the night. I could sleep on a clothes horse I'm that whacked.'

Three days later Barney and Gabriel returned to the whore-house. It would be the last time before they sailed for England for Gabriel's small wage advance wouldn't stretch to any more after paying for food and board.

Emma's face lit up at the sight of him and as Lil watched them trot away together hand in hand, she frowned. 'Looks to me like those two are lovestruck,' she told Barney worriedly.

He grinned. 'Happen they are but don't get frettin' about it. He's a young, healthy man. Happen he'll fall in love wi' a fair few more girls over the next few years afore he finds the one he wants to settle down wi'. Yer first is allus the one you'll remember. Now come on, Lil. What we wastin' us time talkin' about them pair for? It's me you should be payin' attention to.'

Lil giggled and taking his hand she led him away, only too happy to oblige.

Chapter Thirty-Five

'Come along, Esme, we're going shopping,' Olivia told her boss-ily the next morning immediately after breakfast. 'I may not be allowed to take you to the theatre and the parties, but Mama insists I have a chaperone if I wish to go shopping. I'm sure you'll enjoy it. The shops here are nothing at all like they are back at home. They're so much bigger and better and they have such a wonderful selection of anything you can think of. We'll get a hackney cab to take us into the city. And then when we've finished shopping, we can go to lunch. I don't have to be back until late this afternoon so we have the whole day ahead of us to enjoy ourselves.'

Olivia was looking particularly pretty in a dark-green velvet gown with a matching jacket and bonnet and Esme felt quite drab by comparison.

'But don't you want to go shopping with your mother?' she asked.

Olivia chuckled as she pinned her bonnet on. 'Mama is enter-taining some of her London friends for coffee this morning so I think we should make the most of it.'

As they set off, Esme was shocked to find that the streets were shrouded in a thick yellow smog.

'That's quite normal for here,' Olivia told her as she flagged down a passing cab. 'You get used to it. Oxford Street, please,' Olivia told the driver, and they clambered inside and leaned back against the grimy leather squabs.

'London isn't nearly as clean as I thought it would be,' Esme commented and Olivia smiled, enjoying herself already. The London visits were always some of the highlights of her year.

'I suppose it's the same in any city,' she answered as the cab rattled over a bridge across the River Thames. Even this wasn't anything like Esme had expected it to be. The water was brown and sludgy-looking and the smell from it made her hold her nose. However, she soon perked up when the cab dropped them in Oxford Street and she stared in amazement at the rows and rows of shops. The first one they entered was a shoe shop with racks of all sorts of ready-made shoes, from dance slippers to fancy leather boots.

'I'd like some satin slippers in cream, please?' Olivia told the young shop assistant who had hurried forward to serve them. The girl measured her foot, then hurried away, returning a short time later with a selection of the prettiest dance slippers Esme had ever seen. Some were adorned with glass beads that sparkled like jewels, others with lace.

Olivia tried them all on, turning her foot this way and that until she had narrowed the choice down to two pairs.

'Oh, I really can't make my mind up which ones I like best. What do you think?' Before Esme could answer she decided, 'Oh, they would both go well with my new evening gown so I shall take them both. Could you have them delivered to this address, please, and charged to Lady Fitzroy.'

'Of course, miss,' the girl answered reverently as if she was addressing royalty. 'Will there be anything else I can help you with today?'

'Not for now, thank you.' Olivia sat while the girl put her boot back on for her and then she and Esme left the shop.

The next shop they entered was a perfumery and Esme had never smelled anywhere so exotic in her life. After trying a few different scents, Olivia bought an expensive bottle of French perfume which she again charged to her mother before moving on.

The morning passed in a blur for Esme as they entered one store after another. By lunchtime Esme dreaded to think how much Olivia might have spent. It was certainly far more than she could earn in a whole year, although Esme didn't begrudge her anything.

In the last store Esme fell in love with a shawl the like of which she had never seen before. It was in all the colours of autumn, deeply fringed and so fine that it reminded her of cobwebs.

'Do you like that?' Olivia asked when she saw Esme fingering it. Esme grinned. 'Who couldn't like it? It's so delicate.'

'Then you shall have it,' Olivia said decisively as she snapped her fingers for the sales woman. 'I intended to treat you today and you may as well have something that you love.'

'Oh no . . . you mustn't.' Esme was alarmed at the price tag but Olivia was as hard to stop as a runaway train when she had made up her mind to something and very soon that had been ordered too.

'And now we shall go and have some lunch,' Olivia told her as they left the shop. She was smiling from ear to ear and clearly enjoying herself immensely. 'There are some very nice eating houses in this area.'

Soon they were shown to window seats in a very smart establishment and poor Esme felt a little like a fish out of water as Olivia studied the menu.

'Oh, the Dover sole with lemon sauce sounds delicious,' she said. 'Would you like to try it too, Esme, or is there something else you would rather have?'

'Oh, er . . . that will be fine,' Esme answered self-consciously.

The meal was delicious, but as they left Esme asked cautiously, 'Don't you think we should be getting back now? I mean, don't you have a party to go to tonight? You'll want time to get ready.'

As she was fast discovering, Olivia would probably quite happily have shopped till she dropped, but Esme was reeling at the amount of money she must have spent and she didn't want her to get into trouble with her mother.

'Hmm, I suppose we should,' Olivia said regretfully. 'I don't want to be too tired to enjoy myself this evening.' And with a grin she added, 'But we can always come back another day!'

By the time they arrived back in Kensington, many of the things Olivia had bought had already been delivered, including the beautiful shawl she had treated Esme to, so they spent a pleasant hour unpacking everything.

'I think I shall lie down and rest for a little now,' Olivia decided when everything had been put away. 'And you must be tired too, so go and put your feet up and be back here for six o'clock to help me get ready, please.'

Esme was only too happy to oblige and made her way to her own room in the servants' quarters. She had bought a book with her from Fitzroy Hall and contentedly spent an hour on her bed reading it before making her way down to the kitchen for the evening meal. The cook had made a very tasty stew for the staff and despite the large meal she'd had at lunchtime with Olivia, Esme thoroughly enjoyed it. *I shall be as fat as a porky pig at this rate*, she thought to herself as she made her way to Olivia's room to help her get ready.

Olivia looked absolutely stunning in her new cream satin gown, and the satin slippers she had bought to go with it were a perfect match.

'You look absolutely beautiful, very grown-up,' Esme told her when she was ready.

'Thank you, but I wish you were coming,' Olivia answered sincerely. Although she was very spoilt, she had a kind heart and Esme was coming to love her as the sister she had never had.

'Oh, don't worry about me.' Esme smiled. 'I've got more than enough to keep me occupied here.' They both glanced around. The room looked as if a tornado had ripped through it and Olivia felt a little guilty. She had never been the tidiest of creatures. 'You just go off and enjoy yourself – we'll be on the way home before you know it so make the most of every minute.'

Over an hour later when the room was tidy again Esme retired to her own room until the family returned when she would go back to help Olivia get out of her finery. She dreaded to think what Olivia's beautiful gown would look like if she didn't, she thought with a wry smile. Knowing Olivia, she would just yank it off and leave it in a heap on the floor.

Nell was in their room when she got there, staring at the book Esme had been reading that afternoon.

'Can you really read this?' she asked and when Esme nodded, she whistled through her teeth. 'Cor, you must be very clever!

I have to sign fer me wages wi' a cross. Me mam could never afford to send us to school. There were nine of us kids, yer see, and money were allus tight.'

It was then that Esme felt the strange sensation she recognised so well, and before she knew it, she had blurted out, 'You lost three of your siblings not so long ago, didn't you?'

The colour faded from Nell's face. 'Yes, we did in the flu epidemic last year.' Her eyes filled with tears. 'But 'ow come you know that?'

'The three that passed are standing beside you right now. Or what I should say is two of them are standing and the girl is holding a baby, another little girl.'

'That'd be our little Gracie,' Nell told her in a choked voice. 'The other girl were Lucy and the boy were me little bruvver Tommy.' She glanced nervously to the side of her before asking in a shaky voice. 'An' are they aw'right?'

'They're looking really well,' Esme assured her. 'In fact, they're standing with an older couple. The old man has a limp, or at least he did have in this life. It's better now and they're watching over the children.'

'Me granma and granpa,' Nell told her tearfully. 'Me granpa injured 'is leg workin' on the docks an' the infection he got in it carried 'im off, God bless 'is soul. Gran followed not long after. I don't think she were ever the same after she lost Granpa. But 'ow come you can see 'em all an' I can't?'

'I can't answer that. It's just something I've been able to do since I was a toddler. At first my mammy thought I'd made up an imaginary friend when I chuntered away to someone she couldn't see, but it was Granny Griselda who realised that I had "the gift" – meaning I could see spirits, just like she could. I used to wish that I couldn't, but it doesn't really scare me; after all, what is there to fear? The dead can't hurt you – it's the living you have to watch out for.'

'Why don't yer use this gift to your advantage?' Nell questioned. 'What I mean is, there's lots o' folk who would pay good money to get messages from loved ones who've passed over. Yer could make yourself a fortune.'

'I've never tried to summon a spirit,' Esme admitted. 'They just appear when I least expect them to.'

'Perhaps yer should try summonin' 'em then?' Nell suggested.

Esme shook her head. 'No, I've never really liked the idea of doing that. You never know who you might call up!'

Nell frowned. 'So what did me family look like?'

Esme sighed; they had faded away now. 'The baby had blonde curly hair and blue eyes . . . Oh, and she had the sweetest smile. The little girl was blonde too, aged perhaps six or seven and she was dressed in a grey skirt and had a shawl about her shoulders, but the boy had dark hair with dark eyes.'

'That sounds like them all right,' Nell admitted as any slight suspicion that Esme might have been having her on disappeared.

She was still clutching the book and Esme asked her, 'How would you like me to help you with your alphabet? I mean, we won't be here long enough for me to teach you to read and write fluently but I might have enough time to help you to learn to write your name so that you don't have to sign for your wages with a cross anymore.'

'You'd do that for me?'

When Esme nodded, Nell flung her arms about her and gave her a big hug. 'Eeh, I'd love that. Imagine goin' 'ome to me family on me days off an' bein' able to show 'em. They'd be tickled pink.'

And so from that moment on every spare minute they had together was spent with Esme helping Nell to learn the letters of the alphabet. Nell proved to be a very willing and intelligent pupil, and within two weeks could already write her first name.

The time seemed to pass in the blink of an eye. Olivia was constantly attending balls, parties and the theatre with her family, especially after Luke arrived, but she and Esme still managed to do some sightseeing and spend time together. As for Luke, he was as charming as ever and Esme was now completely under his spell, although she knew that nothing could ever come of her feelings for him.

Before she'd left Theddlethorpe, Esme had passed on the London address to Jeremy, and she heard from him regularly. He seemed happy and content at the veterinary college and she was pleased that he was now being allowed to follow the career he had always wanted. She missed him too; he had become a good friend, not least because he was her only link to Gabriel. It had been more than six months since she'd last seen her brother, and she worried about him constantly. Then one day, Jeremy forwarded a letter to her that made the breath catch in her throat. It was from Gabriel! He'd sailed all the way to Canada and it seemed he knew Broadhurst was dead now. Esme had cried as she'd read Gabriel's scribbled note – he never had enjoyed writing! – explaining that he could never come back to England now. But at least he was alive and well, and that was enough for her after all these months of uncertainty.

All too soon for Olivia it was time to start packing up to go home. 'I can't believe we shall soon be into September, the time has passed so quickly,' Olivia said mournfully as Esme carefully began to pack some of her gowns into a trunk. The family would be going home with far more than they had arrived with after the numerous shopping trips they'd had.

'Aw well, look on the bright side. It'll be no time at all before you're back here,' Esme consoled her. Secretly, Esme was delighted to be leaving. To begin with, she'd enjoyed being in London – there was so much to see and do, and the weather had been glorious. But it hadn't been long before she'd started to find the heat stifling in such a built-up area, and she'd begun to yearn for the country-side. It made her realise that as exciting as it was, she wouldn't like to live in the capital.

'Mm, I suppose you're right, but it will be *so boring* back at home.'

Esme merely smiled and carried on with what she was doing. The only thing she herself would really miss about being in London was Nell's company. The two girls had grown close over the time they'd been there.

The staff of the London house all stood on the steps to wave them off on the day they departed and Esme was touched to see that there were tears in Nell's eyes. 'Make sure you carry on with learning your alphabet, I shall expect you to be able to read something to me the next time we visit,' Esme told her.

The girl nodded. 'I will, I promise.'

Then the carriages drew away and Esme waved at Nell until they turned a corner in the road and the long journey back to Lincolnshire began.

Chapter Thirty-Six

As the land mass appeared through the sea mist, Gabriel felt a tingle of excitement. It had been too long since he had been able to board a ship with a cargo bound for Nova Scotia again, but he had never forgotten Emma and still thought of her constantly. And soon, very soon now, he hoped, he would see her again.

'Land ahoy!' A shout went up and suddenly there was furious activity as the crew prepared to sail into the harbour.

Once they had docked, the long job of unloading the cargo began and Gabriel didn't have time to think of anything apart from the job at hand. But at last it was done and the seamen queued for their hard-earned wages.

'If you are doing the return journey, be back here a week from today promptly at nine a.m. to load the next cargo,' the captain ordered.

Touching his cap, Gabriel nodded. 'Aye, aye, Cap'n.'

He had changed immensely from the young boy he had been when he had first sailed and was now an able seaman, tall and well muscled. He had sailed to parts of the world he had only read about in books, but his heart was still in Nova Scotia with Emma, and now he could scarcely wait to see her again.

The minute his feet touched the dock, he headed immediately for Lil's whorehouse. It didn't matter that it was only mid-afternoon, he knew that Lil's girls worked day and night. He just hoped Emma would be available. It drove him mad to think of her being with other men but he didn't hold it against her and it didn't lessen the feelings he had for her. After all, who was he to judge? As far as he knew he was still being hunted on a murder charge, which was why he spent most of his time at sea. Emma had done what she had to do following the death of her parents but hopefully very soon now he would be able to change all that. He had saved almost every penny he had earned since going to sea and now he meant to put it to good use. If Emma was agreeable, he would use it to make a home for them both and then hopefully Esme would join them.

His main fear was that he wouldn't be able to find the whore-house again, but his feet led him straight through the maze of little cobbled alleys and he rapped on the door.

'Looking for company, young sir?' the scantily clad young woman who answered his knock asked with a saucy wink.

'I am, as it happens.' He removed his cap and stepped past her into the hallway. Everything was just as he remembered, right down to the red carpet and the dark, patterned paper on the walls. 'I was hoping to spend some time with Serena.'

Her face fell. She'd been hoping to entertain this one herself. He was a handsome young bugger!

'Can't say as I know anyone 'ere be that name,' she told him surlily.

Luckily Lil sailed through the door of the parlour at that moment. 'Is something amiss?' she asked, seeing her girl's sulky expression.

'This chap 'ere is askin' fer someone called Serena,' the girl told her.

Lil frowned. 'Serena?' She stared at Gabriel blankly for a moment then suddenly smiled. 'Didn't you come 'ere once wi' Barney?'

When Gabriel nodded, she grinned. 'Ah, I think I know the little queen yer on about. Unfortunately, she left some time ago. She were a nice kid but not cut out fer this game, I'm afraid.'

Gabriel's heart sank like a brick. 'But where did she go?'

'She found a job at the Crab and Lobster, an inn in the town. Yer can't miss it. it's in the 'igh street. I were sorry to see her go, though. She could 'ave been set up fer life if she'd stayed 'ere wi' 'er looks, but there yer go, each to their own. I never keep prisoners; my girls can leave anytime they like. Still, now yer 'ere, ain't there anyone else that takes yer fancy?'

He gave her a dazzling smile and shook his head. 'Thanks, Lil, but I reckon I'll go and see if I can find Serena, if it's all the same to you.'

'Suit yersen,' she said shortly, but she was smiling as he hastily turned and made his way back out into the alley.

It took him a matter of minutes to find the Crab and Lobster and with his hopes high he stepped inside. The air was heavy with the smell of beer and stale tobacco and the straw on the floor didn't smell too good either. The place was packed with sailors of all nationalities but no one looked at him twice as he picked his way through the tables to the bar. A dirty-looking middle-aged man with the largest beard he had ever seen and a bald head was drying tankards at the bar. He looked up. 'An' what be yer pleasure then, son? I can recommend the ale or we've some nice rum if you've a fancy for it.'

'I'll have a tankard of ale.' Gabriel fished in his pocket and put the money on the bar and once he'd been served, he asked casually, 'Do you have a young woman called Emma working here?'

The burly barman looked at him suspiciously. 'An' who's askin?'

'A friend,' Gabriel answered. 'I've just docked and thought I'd look her up.'

'Well, Emma works downstairs in the kitchen but she'll be busy at present preparin' the meals fer this evenin'. I don't want her disturbed so per'aps yer should call back later tonight.'

Gabriel had no intention of waiting a second longer than he had to. He finished his ale and with a nod to the barman left. Once outside he walked along the length of the inn until he came to a dark narrow alley that led to some steps. Guessing that these must lead to the kitchen he went down them. The door was open at the bottom and he could feel the heat from the ovens rushing out to meet him.

Very cautiously he peeped inside and at first, he saw no one. But as his eyes adjusted to the heat and the steam, he saw a small figure standing at a deep stone sink and his heart began to race. It was Emma.

'Psst!'

She glanced around with a frown, then as her eyes settled on him her mouth gaped and she dropped the potato she was peeling. Hastily drying her hands on her apron, she hurried across to him. Her eyes were wide as if she could barely believe what she was seeing.

'Gabriel . . . is it you?'

'Of course it's me,' he laughed as he picked her up and swung her around. 'I told you I'd come back, didn't I? Didn't you believe me?'

'I . . . I didn't know what to believe,' she told him in a croaky voice and it was then he noticed the dark shadows under her eyes and how much weight she had lost. She looked exhausted.

'I went to see Lil as soon as we got here,' he explained. 'And she told me where I'd find you. But what are you doing in a place like this?'

'It's better than the last place I was in, isn't it?' she answered with a wry grin. 'Here the only man I have to fight off is the landlord. He's a bit of a slave driver, but at least it gives me somewhere to stay and I can do an honest day's work.'

He gently stood her back on her feet, his face solemn now. 'Well, it's not going to be for much longer if I have my way,' he told her. 'I've saved almost every penny since I met you and if you'll have me, you and me are going to find a little place we can rent and I'll find a job here to keep us.'

She shook her head sadly as she stared up at him. 'That's a lovely kind thought but we hardly know each other,' she pointed out.

'So? I knew you were the girl for me the first moment I set eyes on you. Didn't you feel anything for me?'

'Of course I did. Why do you think I left the whorehouse? You showed me that there are still kind men out there somewhere and it made me more determined to make my own way in the world.' She glanced apprehensively over her shoulder and told him nervously, 'Look, you really should be going. If Will, the landlord, finds you here I'll be in no end of trouble. Why don't we meet tonight after I've finished work and then we can talk some more away from here?'

He nodded and leaning forward planted a kiss smack on her lips. 'All right, what time?'

'Be outside the front for ten o'clock. I can't get away before then.'

'I'll be there,' he promised and after one last kiss he went back the way he had come.

Gabriel was there exactly on time and he paced impatiently up and down outside the inn until Emma appeared some ten minutes later from the alley leading to the kitchen.

'Phew, you had me worried there for a while,' he teased. 'I didn't think you were going to come.'

'Why wouldn't I?' He tucked her small hand into his arm and they began to stroll along in the direction of the harbour with no real idea where they were going; they were just content to be in each other's company.

'You look tired,' he commented and she smiled.

'I work most days from six in the morning till ten at night. But I do get Sundays off, although I usually spend most of that cleaning the kitchen. I haven't anything better to do.'

A little further along was a gate leading into a small public park and although it was dark, he led her inside. At least in there they could sit on the grass and talk.

It was a beautiful evening with a million stars twinkling in a black velvet sky above them and when they came to a small copse, they sat down beneath one of the trees and began to talk.

They told each other all about their childhoods, their parents and then, because Gabriel wanted her to know everything about him, he told her about being wanted for murder and why.

'But surely it couldn't be termed as murder if he started the pushing about and you only retaliated?' she said.

He shrugged. 'I agree, but I don't suppose the police will,' he said glumly. 'I've written to my sister and my friend occasionally to let them know that I'm all right but I've never had a return address to give them. So now you know everything, what do you think of my idea about us finding a place together?'

She sighed into the darkness. 'It sounds like heaven,' she admitted. 'But we're both still so young. And anyway . . .' She was glad of the darkness to hide her blushes. 'I promised my parents I would never live with a man without a ring on my finger. They'd be so ashamed if they knew about the time I spent at Lil's whorehouse, but at the time it was either there or the poor house.'

'I'll marry you then!'

Emma laughed. 'Don't you think we should take it a little more slowly? My mother was a great one for saying, "Marry in haste, repent at leisure!" When I do marry it will be forever.'

'It'll be the same for me,' Gabriel assured her. 'So why don't we continue to see each other when we can, then when and if you're ready you can say the word?'

'That sounds fine,' she agreed, and for the next hour they simply enjoyed each other's company.

On Sunday they spent the whole day together, and every night when Emma had finished work in the kitchen, she sneaked out to meet him. But all too soon it was time for him to board the ship for the return journey to England, and Emma risked her boss's wrath by sneaking out in the morning to see him off. They had only spent part of one week together but Gabriel was more certain than ever that Emma was the girl he wanted to spend the rest of his life with.

'I'll come back just as soon as I can,' he promised as she clung to him with tears glistening on her lashes. 'But first, once I'm back in England I think it's time I went to seek my little sister out. I need to know that she's all right and tell her about you. Will you wait for me and be my girl, Emma?'

She nodded. 'I will wait, and I already am your girl.'

Then the captain called for everyone to come aboard and after a final kiss, Gabriel swung his kitbag onto his shoulder and strode up the gangplank, feeling as if he was leaving part of his heart down on the dock.

When the ship set sail, Emma and Gabriel waved to each other until they were just tiny dots in the distance. Only then did Gabriel leave the rail and go about his duties.

Chapter Thirty-Seven

In October, Olivia celebrated her sixteenth birthday, and as Esme's was just a month later, it was decided that their education with Mr Pritchard was complete.

'I shall miss you both,' Mr Pritchard told them on the last day he was to teach them. Now that they were both sixteen his services would no longer be required. They had proved to be willing pupils, although had he been asked Mr Pritchard would have been forced to say that of the two Esme was by far the brightest.

'We shall miss you too,' the girls said in unison.

'Goodbye, and good luck for the future. I hope you like your finishing school and that your ball goes well,' he told Olivia. As they spoke, there was a hive of activity going on downstairs as maids, an orchestra and caterers brought in especially for the occasion ran about preparing for the evening.

Olivia frowned slightly at the mention of the school, but then smiled. 'I'm sure it will, goodbye and thank you.'

He turned his attention to Esme next. She was the one that concerned him the most. Now it seemed that Olivia was going to be sent away to a finishing school in Switzerland, what was to become of Esme? he wondered. She would no longer hold the job of being Olivia's maid and he considered her to be in a very awkward position, for she was neither a lady nor a servant. Still, he supposed it was none of his business, so he wished her well and left as the two young ladies made their way from the schoolroom to prepare for the ball that evening.

'I *shan't* go to finishing school!' Olivia declared petulantly. She hated the idea, although Esme thought it sounded very exciting.

'Don't think of that for now,' Esme urged. 'Think of this evening; you don't want to spoil it do you?'

'I suppose not,' Olivia agreed grudgingly, although the thought of Switzerland was always on her mind. However, the moment she stepped into her room and saw the sea-green gown she had had made especially for that evening she brightened again. It was a stunning concoction of satin and lace and her parents had presented her with a beautiful emerald necklace and matching earrings to wear with it. Luke had bought her an emerald ring, which had made Esme feel more than a little envious.

Esme had changed during her time at the hall and, surprisingly, was now slightly taller than Olivia, although she still had a boyish figure, whereas Olivia was softer and curvier as was the fashion. Lady Fitzroy had insisted that Esme should also attend the ball and had bought her a gown in a lovely pale silver colour that set off her silver-blonde hair to perfection. Compared to Olivia's gown, Esme's was very simple with no adornments at all apart from a tiny fringe of Nottingham lace about the sweetheart neckline, but it was the stunning simplicity of it that Esme loved and she could hardly wait to wear it.

She had been surprised when Lady Fitzroy had invited her to the ball, insisting that Olivia wouldn't enjoy it half so much if Esme wasn't there, and she had been even more surprised when she had presented her with a single strand of pearls as her birthday gift. Esme knew that the pearls would have nowhere near the value of Olivia's emeralds but she loved them and knew that she would treasure them always. In fact, she loved the family and often wondered what would have happened to her in the dark days following her grandfather's attack if they hadn't taken her under their wing. Admittedly what the future might hold for her now was preying heavily on her mind but she was determined that nothing should spoil this evening, and so for now she pushed all thoughts of the future away.

Lady Fitzroy had agreed that they could both wear their hair up that evening for the first time – after all, they were sixteen years old now and officially young ladies – so they had been practising different styles on each other for weeks.

As they were laying out the underwear that they would wear beneath their new gowns, someone tapped on Olivia's bedroom door, and when Esme hurried to open it, she was shocked to see Luke standing there.

'Ah, just the person I wanted,' he said. As always at the sight of him, Esme's heart did a little flutter. 'I thought I'd give you your present now in case you wanted to wear it this evening.'

Esme's jaw dropped as he handed her a long velvet box and when she flipped the lid her eyes almost started from her head as she stared down at a delicate pearl bracelet.

'Oh . . . i-it's beautiful, but I can't accept this,' she stammered, deeply embarrassed.

'Of course you can,' Olivia, who had come to look over her shoulder, told her with a grin. 'It will match the necklace Mama gave you, so smile and be grateful.'

'Oh . . . oh, I really am,' Esme said, blushing the colour of a beetroot. 'Thank you, Luke.'

'You're welcome.' He gave her a smile that melted her heart, then turned and left.

'Your family have been so very good to me. I don't know how I can ever repay them,' Esme said humbly as she stared down at the bracelet.

'You don't have to. It was you who did them the favour if you did but know it. I was a terrible pain until I had you to keep me company so it's worked out for the best for all of us. Now come along, it's time the maids were drawing our baths. Today you get pampered too. Oh, and what time is Jeremy arriving?'

'I think he said he'd be here for seven.' That was yet another privilege that Lady Fitzroy had bestowed on her when she had told Esme that she was welcome to invite a friend. Seeing as she only had one, Jeremy had been the obvious choice and he had been tickled pink when Esme asked him if he would like to come.

At last, they were ready to go downstairs. The afternoon had passed in a blur of titivating and now they felt ready to greet Olivia's guests.

'You look just amazing,' Esme breathed as she stood behind Olivia, who was admiring herself in the cheval mirror. The emeralds at her throat and neck were twinkling in the light and with her hair piled high into curls on her head she looked very grown-up.

'Thank you, and so do you,' Olivia responded, turning about to view Esme. The silver gown fit her like a glove and the pearl necklace and bracelet gleamed softly. Esme had chosen to wear her hair pulled up into pearl combs above her ears and teased into ringlets and although her gown was so much simpler than Olivia's she looked equally beautiful.

'Ooh, I have a feeling our dance cards are going to be full all evening,' Olivia giggled as she lifted her fan and drew on long silk gloves to match her gown.

'Then let's just hope I can remember all the steps to the different dances,' Esme said with a grin.

The smell of hothouse flowers greeted them as they descended the stairs and the many tiny candles in the crystal chandelier that hung low in the stairwell twinkled like stars.

Luke, and Lord and Lady Fitzroy were waiting for them in the hall and Esme blushed as she noticed Luke staring at her appreciatively. He was only used to seeing her in her uniform dresses and he couldn't believe how beautiful she looked.

He greeted Olivia with a peck on the cheek before taking Esme's hands and saying quietly, 'You look just absolutely stunning.'

'Th-thank you.' Esme was conscious of Olivia watching them closely.

Thankfully the moment passed when the liveried butler announced, 'The first guests are arriving, sir, madam.'

They quickly got into a line to greet them and the next hour passed quickly as the guests streamed in, most of them bearing gaily wrapped gifts for Olivia, which were placed on a long table.

'I shall have such fun opening them all in the morning,' Olivia said excitedly, then taking Esme's hand she dragged her away to mingle and chat to the guests.

Many of them eyed Esme curiously, wondering who the very attractive young lady was and Olivia graciously introduced her as her dear friend. Within no time the champagne was flowing like water and guests stood about with plates loaded with fancy food. Luke seemed to be close to Esme every time she turned around and there was an awkward moment when he asked, 'When the music begins, may I have the first dance?'

Esme was flustered. There was nothing she would have liked more but it was officially Olivia's party and she didn't wish to offend her so she suggested politely, 'Perhaps we could have the second one. I think Olivia was expecting you to have the first one with her.'

'Oh, of course. The second one then. I shall very much look forward to it.' And with a little bow he went off to speak to someone he knew.

It was then that Esme spotted Jeremy looking very handsome in a dark evening suit and she quickly made her way through the assembled people to greet him.

'I was getting worried and didn't think you were going to make it,' she told him.

'Sorry, just as I was about to set off there was an emergency and the vet on call wanted me to assist him as part of my practical training,' Jeremy apologised. He stared at her, mesmerised. He'd always thought Esme was beautiful, but she had been his best friend's little sister. Now, however, he realised she had grown up to be a stunning young woman.

'Am I too late to book the first dance with you?' he asked and she smiled with relief. At least now she needn't be a wallflower while Olivia danced with Luke.

'I'd like that,' she said as she wrote his name in her little book.

For the next minutes, Jeremy told her all about what he had been doing at college – he clearly loved it from the enthusiasm in his voice.

'The college has a veterinary practice attached to it where we can study for our practical exam,' he explained as they helped

281

themselves to a glass of champagne a maid offered to them on a tray. 'And I'm allowed to work with the qualified vet there once a week to get some hands-on experience. You wouldn't believe the animals we treat. Most of them are call-outs to farm animals but we also get people bringing their pets in.'

'That sounds wonderful.' Esme felt a lump form in her throat as she thought of Gip, but this wasn't a night for being sad so she pushed the memory away.

They continued to chat easily as they approached the buffet and helped themselves to food before going to sit side by side on a little gilt-legged chaise longue. And all the time they were sitting there Esme's eyes kept straying towards Luke. How she wished she could have taken him up on his offer of having the first dance with her but she didn't want to upset Olivia.

Slowly the guests began to wander into the ballroom to take their seats around the edges of the dance floor and Esme was just about to follow them when Jeremy placed a gentle hand on her arm.

'Before we go in, I have a little something for you for your birthday,' he said self-consciously as he fished in his pocket. But for a few moments Esme didn't hear him. She was too busy watching a number of ladies and gentlemen who were milling about in strangely old-fashioned costumes. There was something about them that looked vaguely familiar but for a while she couldn't think why. And then it came to her and she smiled. These were Lord Fitzroy's ancestors whose portraits adorned the long landing upstairs. They were all laughing and smiling and she knew that their spirits had returned briefly to relive the sort of balls they must once have held there. They disappeared as fast as they had appeared and she suddenly became aware that Jeremy was talking to her.

'Sorry . . . what were you saying?' She gave him her full attention and he flushed.

'I was saying that I have a gift for your birthday. Sorry it isn't much.' He pushed a small box towards her and, intrigued, she opened it. Inside was a dainty silver chain bracelet and suspended from it was a charm in the shape of a dog that reminded her so much of Gip that she had to blink to stop the tears from falling.

'Oh Jeremy, that's such a thoughtful gift. And it's just beautiful,' she breathed. 'Will you fasten it on for me please.'

Jeremy was all fingers and thumbs as he fastened it next to the expensive pearl bracelet Luke had given her.

'What a night,' she laughed. 'I've never owned a bracelet in my life and suddenly I have two and they're both just beautiful.' She leaned over to give him a quick peck on the cheek and Jeremy felt as if his whole face was on fire. 'Come along, I can see people taking their partners for the first dance in the ballroom and we don't want to miss it.'

From that moment on the night took on a magical quality and Esme felt as if she was caught in a fairy tale. Her dance card was full in minutes and she whirled and twirled about the dance floor as the young men smiled at her admiringly.

'This is what Cinderella must have felt like,' she whispered to Olivia when she finally got a moment alone with her.

'Hmm, you could be right. You've certainly found your Prince Charming?'

Esme raised an eyebrow. 'What do you mean?'

Olivia laughed. 'Why, Jeremy, of course. Can't you see he's totally besotted with you?'

Esme looked shocked. 'B-but Jeremy and I are just friends,' she said haltingly.

'So you say,' Olivia said teasingly. 'I would say you two are made for each other, just as Luke and I are. Anyway, let's get back, shall we? I don't know about you but this champagne is going to my head and I feel quite happy.' With that she made a beeline for Luke and dragged him back onto the dance floor.

Esme glanced around to see Jeremy walking towards her. As he took her in his arms and they joined Luke and Olivia on the floor, she glanced up at him and looked at him as if for the very first time. He was a very handsome young man, she had to admit, but she had never looked at him as anything more than a friend before. But perhaps Olivia was wrong? Jeremy had never even hinted at having more than friendly feelings for her, so she pushed what Olivia had said to the back of her mind, determined to enjoy what was left of the evening.

Chapter Thirty-Eight

'But I don't *want* to go to a finishing school, Mama!' Olivia declared pettishly, stamping her satin-clad foot. It was two weeks after the ball and she stood facing her mother angrily across the drawing room.

'I'm sorry, darling, but it's already been arranged,' her mother told her gently. 'You'll thank me for sending you one day. All the very best-brought-up young ladies attend the place we've selected for you. It's in Switzerland in a beautiful location overlooking Lake Lucerne and I'm sure you'll love it there. They'll teach you to skate and you'll learn Latin, French and German. You will leave at the beginning of next year and return for your eighteenth birthday in time for your coming-out ball in London.'

Tears stood out in Olivia's eyes. 'And what about Luke and Esme?'

'Luke will finish his university course and Esme . . . Well . . . I'm sure we shall be able to find her another position here somewhere.'

'But she'll be miserable without me,' Olivia said sadly. She could see from her mother's face that she had made her mind up and nothing was going to change it, so turning about in a flurry of silken skirts she stormed from the room.

'Whatever's the matter?' Esme asked when Olivia barged into her bedroom.

'It's Mama. She's just informed me that I'll be going to finishing school in the new year!'

'Oh . . . I see.' They'd known this might happen, but until now, Olivia had been hopeful she could change her parents' minds. But now it was clear that she couldn't, they were both uncertain, but for different reasons. Olivia was concerned that Luke might find another young lady he was attracted to during her time away. And Esme couldn't help but wonder what would become of her. But then, she told herself, she had lived a very privileged life since Lady Fitzroy had taken her under her wing and she had always known that it would have to end one day. The dear woman had given her a wonderful education so hopefully that would help her to find a job somewhere, though doing what, she wasn't quite sure yet.

'Mama says she will find you another position in the house,' Olivia said as if she had been able to read Esme's mind, but Esme shook her head.

'I don't want your mother to feel that she has to,' she said quietly. 'She's done so much for me already and I've loved the time I've had here, but perhaps it's time to strike out on my own and find my own way in life. Perhaps I could apply for the post of a governess – or would I be considered too young?'

'Possibly, and you haven't had any experience of working with children, have you?' Olivia pointed out. They stared at each other glumly, painfully aware that the happy time they had spent together was about to come to an end.

'Well let's not fret about it for now; we still have one last Christmas to spend together, don't we?' Esme said, trying to inject some lightness into her voice.

When Jeremy came to see her the following Sunday, they walked out towards the beach and he couldn't help but notice that Esme seemed to be very down in the dumps.

'You seem a bit down,' he said softly as the wind whipped roses into their cheeks. 'But I just might have something to cheer you up.'

Esme looked at him expectantly.

'I received a letter from Gabriel last week and he enclosed this one for you.'

Esme's face lit up and she almost snatched it from his hand. 'Is he all right? Did he say where he was? And did he say when he was coming home?'

'Phew, you're firing questions at me so fast that I can't think which one to answer first.' He smiled.

'Sorry.' She grinned at him sheepishly.

'I'm sure he'll tell you everything in your letter so I won't spoil it for you,' he said as he tucked her hand into the crook of his elbow. 'But I will tell you that he's well.'

'In that case I shall save my letter to read later.' She shoved it into the inside pocket of her warm cloak and they moved on until they came to the sand dunes.

The sight of the sea never failed to cheer her and they strolled down onto the sand and began to wander along the beach.

'This is all very well and good in the summer but it's blessed cold in the winter,' Jeremy complained as he limped along. His limp always seemed more pronounced in the cold weather, although he never complained. 'Let's see if we can find somewhere with a little shelter where we can sit out of the wind.'

Eventually they found a hollow in one of the dunes and they tucked themselves inside it.

'That's better.' Jeremy looked at her solemnly. 'Now, perhaps you'd like to tell me what's wrong? And don't say nothing because I know you better than that.' The wind had whipped a stray silver curl from beneath her bonnet and he had to resist the temptation to reach over and brush it away.

'Oh, it's nothing, really,' she began, but then with a sigh she rushed on. 'It's just that Olivia's mother has informed her that she'll be going to attend a finishing school for young ladies in Switzerland in the new year.'

'I see.' He stared at her intently. 'And where will that leave you?'

Esme shrugged. 'Lady Fitzroy told Olivia that she'll find me another position but I'm not sure that I want her to. I wonder if it isn't time to strike out on my own. The trouble is, I'm not really qualified to do anything. Thanks to Lady Fitzroy I have had a good education but I'm afraid my age will be against me for the jobs I'd like to do.'

'Mm, I can see what you mean.' Jeremy frowned as he rested his elbows on his knees and stared out at the choppy sea. 'But you say you have until the new year to find something?'

She nodded.

'Right, then leave it with me. I'll see what I can do. There might be a suitable job in Hull for you.'

An hour later they returned to the house and Jeremy set off back to the college while Esme scuttled away upstairs to read her letter from Gabriel.

The second she was in the privacy of her room she sank onto the chair and tore the envelope open without even stopping to take off her cloak and bonnet.

Dear Esme,

As always I 'ope that this letter will find you well. It's a constant worry not bein' able to be in touch but on that score I 'ave good news. I shall be returnin' to England shortly and then I shall be callin' to see you at the rectory. I hope Grand-father is treatin' you better? I worry about you so much!

On a 'appier note I 'ave something to share with you. I've met a girl called Emma and I 'ope that sometime in the not too distant future she will consent to bein' my wife. I know I'm young but the moment I met 'er I knew she were the one for me and that won't change. When we do get wed, I'll obviously not be settin' up 'ome in England but I shall make sure that you can come and join us and then we can both start a new life in another country away from Grandfather and the bad things that 'ave 'appened.

I 'ope you will be pleased for me and that this letter I am sendin' to Jeremy reaches you.

Know that I think of you all the time and 'opefully I will see you again soon. Don't worry, I shall make sure Grandfather doesn't know of the visit,

Stay safe,

Your loving brother Gabriel.

Xxxxx

Esme sighed. Gabriel had no way of knowing that she had left the rectory some years ago, or of anything that had happened after he had left and she had no doubt it would all come as a terrible shock to him. She just hoped that when he did try to find her, he would head to Jeremy's parents' home in London first and Jeremy could tell him where she was – that is if she was still at the hall. Should he arrive after Christmas when Olivia had left for Switzerland she could already have moved and that would only make things even more difficult! She could imagine how angry he would be when he found out how wicked their grandfather had truly been.

He was still wanted for murder, although the search for him had slowed. It seemed that not one person had seen him since the night of Mrs Sparrow's murder. It was if he had simply disappeared off the face of the earth. But while he was still at large Esme was nervous of going out alone and she knew she would never feel truly safe until he had been apprehended. And Emma . . . it was strange to think of her brother all grown up and preparing to get married and she wondered what Emma was like; she had clearly stolen her brother's heart and she hoped they would be happy together.

Then there was his suggestion that one day she should join them in their new life in another country and she didn't know what she thought about that. She had never even considered living anywhere but England but, she asked herself, what did she have to keep her here now that her parents were gone? There was Luke, Olivia and Jeremy. But in reality, the likelihood was that once Olivia returned from Switzerland she would have her coming-out ball and marry Luke. Their future had been mapped out for them and it was doubtful she would see them anymore, or if she did, it would be very little. As for Jeremy – she smiled as she thought of him – he had always been so good to her; a true friend and she would certainly miss him.

The future was suddenly uncertain again and lowering her head she sighed.

It was two days later, as she was making her way upstairs with Olivia's clean laundry, that she met Luke in the hallway and after glancing about to see that they were alone he approached her with a broad smile on his face. He had been particularly nice to her since the evening of the ball.

'Working again?' He grinned.

'It's what I'm paid for,' she reminded him, returning his smile. Then he shocked her when he suddenly reached out to stroke her cheek. She had always dreamed of this happening but now it felt wrong and she flinched away.

'Don't worry, I'd never hurt you,' he said softly. 'In fact, I wanted to tell you that I haven't stopped thinking about you since the night of the ball.'

'Oh?' Esme was flustered. 'B-but why? Aren't you and Olivia promised to each other?'

He laughed as he waved his hand airily. 'Oh yes, but that needn't stop you and me having a bit of fun together surely?'

'I . . . I don't know what you mean. How can you want to have anything to do with me when you're almost betrothed to someone else?'

'Oh Esme, you're so naïve and innocent,' he chuckled. 'That's just one of the things I love about you. That's how marriages work in our circles. We marry who is chosen for us and then have our fun on the side.'

Esme was appalled and shocked, and it showed by the look on her face so he rushed on, 'Don't worry. I wouldn't expect anything to happen until Olivia has left for school and then we would be very discreet.'

'You mean I would be your fancy woman?' Her voice was dull.

'Well, I wouldn't put it quite like that. Gentlemen of my class prefer to call our lover our mistress. I would look after you – you can be sure of that. I could even rent us a little cottage or a house somewhere where you could live and I would come to see you whenever I could, if you'd like that. All I would ask in return is that you would be loyal to me. You'd never have to work again and you'd want for nothing.'

Ever since she had met Luke, she had put him on a pedestal. She had considered him to be kind, handsome and generous – the perfect man. But now her stomach churned and she suddenly saw him in a different light. Out of the goodness of their hearts, Lord and Lady Fitzroy had taken him into their home and treated him as one of their own since he was just a small boy and yet he was prepared to break their daughter's heart. Esme knew Olivia well enough to know that her feelings for Luke were genuine, and should she ever find out about the proposition he had just put to her, not only would she be devastated, it would be the end of their friendship.

'Could you move aside and let me pass, please?' Her voice was as cold as ice and Luke looked slightly surprised.

'Look, just think about what I've said before you make your mind up,' he urged but she swept past him with her nose in the air.

More than ever now she knew that it was time to leave, but not until Olivia did – she would never hurt her. Luke had made it more than clear that he looked upon her as a menial, a servant he could use as he wished, and Esme had enough pride to make sure that never happened.

Once upstairs it was hard to keep up a cheerful façade in front of Olivia, but somehow she managed it, although she was grateful when her friend went down to the drawing room to take afternoon tea with her parents.

Only then did she allow the tears to fall as all the feelings she had harboured for Luke crumbled to ashes now that she had seen him for who he truly was: a spoilt little rich boy. All she could do was hope that Jeremy would be true to his word and try to find her a new post somewhere in Hull. Also, God willing, very soon she might be reunited with her brother, even if only for a short time. The thought of that would keep her going in the days ahead until she could see Olivia off to her new school with her dreams of becoming Luke's wife intact.

Chapter Thirty-Nine

They had been at sea for two days and it was not proving to be a good voyage. Ever since setting sail the ship had encountered one horrific storm after another, and added to that was the fact that it was mind-numbingly cold. The wind was as sharp as a blade and seemed to slice through Gabriel every time he set foot on deck, but he was used to it now. He had been on deck since early that morning supervising the ordinary seamen and assisting them when necessary. There were many new seamen aboard as several of those that had sailed to Canada with him had decided to stay where they were until the spring, when the weather would hopefully have improved. Now, though, he left the men to it and made his way unsteadily to the dining cabin for a hot drink.

Once inside it was still cold, although nothing like as bad as it was outside in the wind. Fetching a large mug of tea, he sat down and wrapped his hands about the steaming mug and glanced around. There were a few other sailors in there doing the same as he was but one man hunched in the far corner caught Gabriel's eye. There was something about him that looked vaguely familiar but he could only see the back of his head and his shoulders from where he was sitting. Gabriel continued to stare at him until eventually the man rose and turned to leave the cabin.

Gabriel's eyes almost popped out of his head and his hand started to shake so much that the hot tea sloshed across the table. The man looked old and his once jet-black hair, so like Gabriel's own, was now streaked with grey, but there could be no mistaking him.

'*Dadda!*' The word tore from Gabriel's throat before he could stop it.

The man looked towards him, then stopped, standing as though frozen to the spot. '*Gabriel . . . Son!*'

Suddenly they closed the distance between them and threw themselves into each other's arms, tears running down their faces as they clung together as if they would never let each other go.

'B-but me and Esme thought you were dead,' Gabriel choked eventually as his father held him at arm's length. He could hardly believe the change in him. The memories he had carried of his son all this time were of a boy, but standing before him was a young man. 'Why did you go off and leave us like that?'

'I didn't have a choice,' his father answered bitterly. 'I was arrested and thrown into prison for something I didn't do.' Taking Gabriel's arm he led him to a table. 'Let's sit down and I'll tell you everything.'

For a moment they sat drinking in the sight of each other until haltingly Django began to explain what had happened. 'After I left you, I went to the horse fair and traded the old nag in. Then I bought a lovely horse that was years younger than the old one and I had a marvellous deal with her. She was a dapple grey an' a real beauty and I could hardly believe me luck.' He shook his head as the memories flooded back. 'Anyway, I set off for home immediately. I was so excited to show 'er to you. I knew you'd all love 'er. But I'd only ridden 'er a few miles when the coppers stopped me an' accused me o' stealin' 'er. I told 'em that I'd bought 'er fair an' square off another gypsy at the 'orse fair but o' course I couldn't prove it. We do deals wi' a handshake not written receipts, an' it turns out that this 'orse 'ad been stolen from a farmer near the fair an' were worth a lot o' money. So, the long an' the short of it is, they 'ad me up in front o' the magistrates an' I were found guilty o' theft an' they threw me in jail.' He gulped before going on. 'When they finally let me out, I made straight back fer where I'd left you, out o' me mind wi' worry cos I knew yer mammy were a sick woman. An' then when I got there . . .' He lowered his head as the tears started again. 'All I found were the remains o' the burned-out vardo. I guessed what 'ad 'appened to yer mammy an' I thought me 'eart would break, but worse still I 'ad no idea how to find you or Esme. I asked everyone in the area if they knew where you'd gone but none of 'em 'ad a clue so eventually I made fer Theddlethorpe. It were the only place where I thought yer might head.

'When I got there, I found the rectory empty an' locked up. It were plain no one was livin' there, so next I went to the church. There were a sign on the gate statin' that a new vicar would be startin' the services the followin' week an' I had no idea where to go from there. I didn't even know if you an' Esme had even been there. Eventually I found a woman outside one o' the cottages workin' in her little garden so I stopped to ask her if she knew if you and Esme had ever been stayin' with the Reverend Silver. She scuttled away inside like a scalded cat as if I were the devil 'imself, so that's when I decided to go to sea. I couldn't face life on the road wi'out me family around me an' I never thought I'd see either of you again.'

'Oh, Dadda. We *did* go to Grandfather, we didn't know where else to go,' Gabriel told him and slowly he explained about the terrible time both he and Esme had while living with him. 'He were a sadistic old bugger,' he said bitterly. He then told him of his trouble with Broadhurst and explained that when he had run away Esme had still been living with their grandfather and Mrs Sparrow at the rectory.

'So where is she now? And where is your grandfather and Mrs Sparrow?' Django asked with a worried frown.

'I don't know but as soon as we get ashore, I intend to find out,' Gabriel told him. 'I'm sure my friend Jeremy will know. I've written to him and Esme since coming to sea but of course I was never able to give them a return address to write to.'

Django's mouth set in a grim line. 'If that cold-'earted bastard has 'armed one 'air on me girl's 'ead I'll swing fer 'im,' Django muttered and Gabriel had no doubt that his dadda meant every word.

'I was intending to go and find Esme when we got ashore anyway,' Gabriel told his father, then he went on to tell him about Emma.

'Seems to me you've been bit by the love bug, son,' he said with a smile, noting the way his son's eyes lit up when he talked about her. 'Good on yer. I looked just as you do now when I first clapped eyes on yer mammy. She were the most beautiful girl I'd ever set eyes on an' I knew straight off she were the one fer me. I just wish . . .' As he thought of her dying without him at her side his heart broke afresh, but at least he had found his son now, and soon, very soon he was determined to be reunited with his daughter.

'We should dock within a month,' Gabriel told him. 'And then I was intending to find Esme and bring her to live with Emma and me. You could come too, Dadda. Now that I've found you, I don't want to lose you again. Esme always told me that you were still alive somewhere; she said she would have felt it if you had died. But I'd all but given up hope. Now you could come with us too and we can be a family again.'

His father patted his hand tenderly. 'Let's just concentrate on finding Esme first, son,' he said softly. 'And then we'll go from there, eh?'

Gabriel nodded, disguising his impatience; the ship couldn't arrive back in England quickly enough for him.

Chapter Forty

'I can't believe it's Christmas Eve already,' Olivia said pensively, staring moodily from her bedroom window as Esme put her clean laundry away. Normally it was one of her favourite times of the year, but now she was faced with the prospect of being sent away to school as soon as it was over. On top of her concerns for herself were the ones she had for Esme. As yet her mother hadn't offered the girl an alternative post and Olivia was worried about what would become of her. They had grown close in the time they had spent together at the hall and she was going to miss her. She knew that Esme was fretting too, although she'd done her best to hide it from her. She'd been quieter and somewhat withdrawn for weeks and Olivia had also noticed that she seemed to be avoiding Luke.

'What about this gown for this evening?' Esme asked, pulling a dress from the wardrobe. Olivia's parents were throwing a dinner party that evening so she knew Olivia would want to look her best.

Olivia stared at the gown – a pretty light-blue affair trimmed with lace and beads – and nodded absently, which wasn't like her at all. She was usually very fussy about what she wore. 'That'll do,' she said dully.

Esme went to her and gently shook her hands up and down. 'You must stop worrying about going to Switzerland,' she told her sternly. 'It's not as if it's forever and you might actually find that you enjoy it when you get there.'

'And pigs might fly.' Olivia forced a smile. 'But enough of me being grumpy. Yes, that gown will be fine. Now you go and get yourself ready; Jeremy will be here in an hour or so.' She had kindly given Esme a couple of hours off to see Jeremy and she wanted her friend to enjoy the visit, so with a nod Esme trotted off to do as she was told.

She changed out of her uniform dress into one of the pretty day gowns that Olivia had given her, and after putting on her bonnet and her warm cape, she hurried downstairs and went to wait at the end of the drive for Jeremy. Very soon he came into view and she hurried to meet him. The sky overhead was a curious grey colour and the air had become unnaturally still.

Jeremy gave her a warm smile and tucked her arm into his. 'I reckon we're going to have some snow. The sky's full of it,' he observed.

'I think you could be right.'

Jeremy glanced at her as she trotted along at the side of him and as always thought how beautiful she was, both inside and out. He had known for a very long time that he was in love with her but had never told her so, for he feared that his feelings weren't returned and he wouldn't do anything to risk losing her as a friend. But then, unable to contain his news a moment longer, he tugged her gently to a halt and turned her to face him.

'I've got some news for you. Very good news, I hope.' He grinned down at her.

'You've heard from Gabriel again?' Her eyes were wide with hope, but he shook his head.

'Not that, I'm afraid, but good news all the same. At least I hope you'll think so. You see, as I promised I've been looking around for a new post for you for when Olivia goes off to school, and believe it or not there was one there right under my nose, although I didn't realise it straightaway.'

'Oh?' She stared at him expectantly.

'As you know, there's a veterinary practice attached to the college where we do our practical hands-on training for so many hours a week. Anyway, the college employs a nurse who lives on the premises to look after any animals that have to stay in overnight. I have to be honest and admit that it isn't the most glamorous of jobs and the living quarters are tiny, but the nurse they have at present leaves in the new year to get married. And so, I thought of you and had a word with the vet about you – if it's something you might be interested in, that is?'

Esme frowned. 'I think I'd love working with animals,' she told him. 'But the trouble is, I haven't had any training as a veterinary nurse.'

'Oh, that's not a problem,' he assured her. 'Any necessary training would be given. What we need more than anything is someone who loves animals and wouldn't mind getting up in the night to check on any that are kept there. I should warn you that the wages aren't brilliant, but you do get somewhere to live thrown in and the college would supply your meals. So what do you think?'

'I think it sounds absolutely wonderful!' she told him enthusiastically, her eyes lighting up.

'In that case I shall have a talk to the vet straight after Christmas and we can make the arrangements.'

Esme felt as if a great weight had been lifted from her shoulders. A fresh start somewhere new was just what she needed; somewhere far away from Luke's wandering hands. He hadn't wasted an opportunity of trying to get her alone since putting his proposition to her and she had a horrible feeling that things would only get worse once Olivia was gone if she stayed at the house. She would be eternally grateful to Lady Fitzroy for rescuing her and giving her an education, and she knew that she and Olivia would be friends always, but it was time to move on and start the next chapter of her life.

'Thank you *so* much for going to so much trouble for me,' she told him sincerely and without thinking she stood on tiptoe and planted a big wet kiss on his cheek, which made him blush to the roots of his hair.

It took every ounce of control he had not to grab her close and kiss her mouth. Instead he fumbled in his pocket and withdrew a small package, saying, 'Er . . . seeing as I won't see you tomorrow, I might as well give you this now.'

She hastily unwrapped it and smiled with delight when she saw the delicate silver chain on which was suspended a tiny silver heart locket.

'Oh Jeremy, it's beautiful. Thank you so much. I shall wear it tomorrow.' She fished in the deep inner pocket of her cloak and withdrew his gift. It was a book of sonnets with a fine leather cover tooled in gold that she had found in a little bookshop in Skegness one day when she had been shopping with Olivia.

He handled it reverently, knowing that he would always treasure it because Esme had chosen it.

'I remember you saying once how much you loved poetry,' she told him and he beamed at her.

'I do indeed. It's perfect, thank you.'

Just then, the first gentle flakes of snow began to float down and Esme felt a strange little feeling flutter to life in her stomach as she looked up at Jeremy. It was as though she were seeing him for the very first time. He really was very handsome. She suddenly felt as if they might have been the only two people left in the world and, embarrassed, she turned and started to walk.

They strolled along for some time as Jeremy explained some of the things she would be expected to do in her new job. As he'd said, none of it sounded very glamorous, but then Esme loved animals and was sure that she could handle anything that was thrown at her.

'And of course, the hardest and the worst part about this job will be caring for the ones that don't make it,' he pointed out. 'Unfortunately, we can't save all the animals that come to us.'

Esme nodded. That was a part she would find hard, she was forced to admit, but as Jeremy pointed out, it was important to focus on the many animals they did help.

'Are you still quite sure you want to give it a try?' he asked when he had finished telling her all the pitfalls of the job.

She nodded and gave him a dazzling smile that made his heart beat faster. 'I certainly am. But now I'd best get back to the hall to tell Lady Fitzroy and Olivia the good news. The snow's coming down faster and I don't want you to get caught in it and not be able to get back.'

He walked her back to the gates where she gave him a chaste kiss on the cheek and thanked him again for her beautiful gift. 'When will I see you again?'

'I shall be here before New Year to tell you when you're to start,' he promised. 'And I'll also make arrangements for a carriage to collect you. You'll probably have too much luggage to carry. Merry Christmas, Esme.'

'Merry Christmas,' she said, and turning she lifted her skirts in a most unladylike manner and shot off down the drive like a young colt, eager to share her good news.

As soon as she got inside the hall, she dashed off to her room to take off her cloak and bonnet before seeking Olivia out, but the second she closed the door behind her she sensed that she wasn't alone and whirling about she saw Granny Griselda standing there with the four young women who had haunted her back at the rectory behind her. And joining them was Molly Malone and Mrs Sparrow.

Granny looked troubled as Esme told her, 'I've had some wonderful news, Granny . . .' It was the first time the young women had appeared to her since coming to the hall and Granny's visits had been seldom too, so now the sight of them struck fear into her heart.

The old woman shook her head. 'Take care, my love . . .'

'What do you mean?' Esme frowned. 'Jeremy has found me a wonderful new position . . .'

But already the spirits were fading and a feeling of foreboding crept over her as she wondered what Granny could have meant. Then with a shrug, she tried to dismiss it from her mind as she went to share her news with her friend.

'Oh, we *must* tell Mama,' Olivia exclaimed once Esme had told her about the new job. 'I know she's been trying to think of a new post here that would be suitable for you.' She was sad, but happy for Esme all at the same time; happy because Esme seemed happy and excited about the prospect of her new career, but sad because she would be leaving the hall and it would add finality to the time they had spent together. Yet deep down she knew it was for the best.

They went off side by side to seek out Lady Fitzroy and found her in the drawing room going over the menu for that evening with the cook.

'Then if you are quite sure that this is a job you would be happy doing, I'm pleased for you,' the kindly lady said, once Esme had told her the news. 'Although I have to say we will miss you, dear.'

'I shall miss you too,' Esme told her truthfully. 'And I'll never forget the kindness you've shown me.'

'It was our pleasure,' Lady Fitzroy assured her.

For the rest of the day, Esme went about her duties with mixed feelings. While sad to be leaving the hall, she was excited at the prospect of a new job, and now the decision had been made she just wanted to be gone. She hated goodbyes – there had been far too many of them in her life.

The next day Esme had her Christmas dinner in the kitchen with the rest of the staff. By that time word had spread that she would soon be leaving them and she got mixed responses. Some of them said they would be sorry to see her go while others, who feared her gift, were secretly relieved they would be seeing the back of her.

The week before New Year passed quickly, and suddenly it was New Year's Eve. Jeremy had been to see her the day before to confirm that she would be starting her new job on the second of January, the same day Olivia would be leaving for Switzerland. He had organised a carriage to come and collect her and her possessions, and Esme began to feel nervous. What if she couldn't do the job? And what had Granny meant when she told her to take care? But it was too late to change her mind now, so she decided that she would just have to hope that all went well and she had made the right decision.

As always, the Fitzroys held a ball on New Year's Eve but this time, despite being invited to it, Esme declined, telling Olivia that she had her packing to do. Because of Olivia's generosity she would be leaving with a lot more than she had arrived with, although she realised already that a lot of the beautiful gowns she'd been given would be far too grand for the job she would be embarking on.

Lady Fitzroy had kindly given her a chest to pack her things in and, with the ball in full swing downstairs, Esme was folding some of her belongings into it when a tap came on her bedroom door. Wondering who it might be, she didn't even have time to open it before Luke came into the room, looking very handsome in his evening suit.

'Luke . . . why aren't you downstairs at the ball?' she asked nervously.

He closed the door quickly and strode towards her. 'I had to see you. Have you given any more thought to what I asked you?'

Esme scowled at him. 'I told you quite clearly the answer is no,' she said spiritedly. 'And if Olivia should ever find out about your proposition it would break her heart. You should be ashamed of yourself!'

'Oh, don't be such a little prude,' he responded, his face darkening. He'd been unable to stop thinking of her and the more she had shunned him the more he had wanted her. 'I can't believe you're taking such a menial job,' he ground out. 'When I could have kept you in comfort. You're only gypsy trash after all! You should be grateful that I even looked the side you're on. You would never have had to worry about money or working ever again.'

'Yes, I would have been a kept woman,' she snapped back. 'And gypsy trash or not, I'm worth more than that, so get out of this room right now or I shall show you up for what you really are.'

His hands clenched into fists as colour flooded into his cheeks. Luke had led a charmed life; he had been spoilt shamelessly and had always had everything he wanted. Because of his good looks girls fell at his feet – apart from Esme, and her rejection of him had only served to make her more desirable. But now he saw that his attempts to woo her were falling on deaf ears and with an angry growl he stormed away.

The next morning Esme and Olivia clung together. Lady Fitzroy and her lady's maid, who would be accompanying her to Switzerland, had already said their goodbyes and were waiting in the carriage.

'Promise you'll write to me often,' Olivia pleaded with tears in their eyes.

'Of course I will, and you must write to me too.'

'Come along, darling, we should be on our way,' Lady Fitzroy called through the snowy air.

So with one last hug, Olivia clambered inside the carriage. As they set off, she hung out of the window and waved while Esme stood waving back until they were out of sight, tears rolling down her pale cheeks.

Eventually she turned to go back into the house to finish her own packing, stopping abruptly when she saw Granny Griselda standing in front of her, wringing her hands.

'You *must* take care,' she told Esme.

As she began to fade, a cold hand closed around Esme's heart. What could it be that was troubling Granny so much? she wondered. But there was no more time to fret. The carriage that would be taking her to her new home would be arriving within the hour so she rushed inside and up to her room.

Once she had finished the last of her packing a young footman carried her trunk down into the hall while Esme went to say good-bye to the rest of the staff in the kitchen. Minutes later the carriage was there and she was grateful to see that Jeremy had come to accompany her.

'That's it,' he told her cheerfully once her luggage had been stowed on board. 'Are you all ready?'

'Ready as I'll ever be.' She smiled nervously.

As the carriage drew away from the hall, she wondered if she would ever see it again. Granny's warnings were loud in her ear but she tried to ignore them as Jeremy squeezed her hand and gave her a warm smile. She had made her decision and there could be no going back now. So why, she wondered, did the feeling of dread in the pit of her stomach persist?

Chapter Forty-One

As they drove into Hull past the docks, Esme stared in awe at the enormous ships.

Jeremy smiled. 'Big, aren't they? But then they need to be. Hull is the biggest port in the country now and these ships travel thousands of miles. As far as Iceland, I believe, so they have to be very strong and seaworthy.'

Esme nodded. She hadn't realised what a big place Hull actually was. 'Is the college much further?' she asked.

Jeremy shook his head. 'No, only about another mile or so.'

At that point the carriage turned away from the docks and began to wend its way through the town. It was very busy and there seemed to be people milling about everywhere. It was a different world compared to the sleepy little village of Theddlethorpe and Esme had no doubt it would take some time to get used to living there.

Eventually they pulled up in front of a large building. 'Here we are. And the veterinary practice is just over there, look.' Jeremy pointed towards a much smaller building set slightly away from the larger one. It looked very unprepossessing – a far cry from the grand hall she had become accustomed to living in, but she was determined to make the best of it.

It was snowing heavily again and Jeremy made her stay in the carriage while he and the driver humped her heavy trunk inside. Once that was accomplished, he came back and helped her down before hurrying her inside out of the fast-falling snow.

'It's a good job we came today,' he said practically. 'With the way the snow is coming down the roads could be impassable by tomorrow.'

She nodded in agreement as they entered a small foyer with a desk to one side of it. It didn't look any too clean and was very basic. A door behind the desk opened and a middle-aged man in a white coat appeared. He was a giant of a man with hands like hams and a big grey beard but his smile was kindly.

'Ah, you must be Miss Loveridge.' He came towards her with his hand outstretched and Esme knew instantly that they were going to get along.

'It's Esme,' she told him in a small voice as he looked at her doubtfully. She was stick thin and looked very much like a genteel young lady.

'I'm Mr Carter,' he told her. He was at least willing to give her a chance. 'I'm the person you'll be working with for most of the time. Jeremy here tells me that you haven't done this type of work before but don't worry, you'll learn as you go along and I won't ask you to do anything that you feel you can't. How about I show you where you'll be living? You can have today to settle in. And then I suggest you have a nice hot cup of tea. I dare say you could do with one after your cold journey. You can make tea, can't you?'

When Esme grinned, he laughed. 'Well, there we are then. That's the most important part of the job. On the days the students are in here you'll get fed up with putting the kettle on. Come on through.'

Esme and Jeremy followed him through the door he had appeared from through yet another room that looked like some kind of small operating theatre. Beyond that was another room, this one full from floor to ceiling with cages of various sizes. Inside one was a cat lying on a blanket mewing loudly and when Esme stopped to speak to him gently, Mr Carter gave an approving nod to Jeremy.

'That's Tigs,' Mr Carter told her. 'Unfortunately, he was involved in an accident in the town. A dray cart ran over him and I didn't think he was going to make it when he was first brought in. He was in a terrible mess. I've had to amputate his leg.'

'Ah, poor thing.' Esme put her finger through the cage and gently stroked the poor cat's head. 'Will he survive?'

Mr Carter nodded. 'Oh yes, I'm pretty sure he will. You'd be surprised how well cats and dogs can manage with only three legs when they get used to it. He'll be in for some time yet though, so he'll be your first patient. I've no doubt he'll have you up to him during the night – he's a demanding little chap.'

'I shan't mind that,' Esme answered quickly and Mr Carter glanced at Jeremy and smiled.

'Right, here are your living quarters,' he said almost apologetically and when he threw the next door open, Esme saw why. They entered a small living room with nothing but a tiny sofa, a table and two chairs, and an open fireplace in it. The hearth was full of ashes and the curtains that hung at the small window were dirty; it looked cold and uninviting. Off that was a tiny kitchen and another door from the sitting room led to a bedroom. It contained a metal-framed bed, a chest of drawers and a washstand, and was so small that Esme was sure she couldn't have swung a cat around in there had she felt the need to. Like the rest of the rooms, it was grubby, but as Esme stared around, she could picture it as it could be with some tender loving care. The vardo had been even smaller than this and yet her mother had had it cosy and shining like a new pin before she took ill, and Esme determined that she would do the same here. There was nothing that a little spit and polish and a lot of elbow grease couldn't put right, she was sure.

'It will be fine,' she told Mr Carter with a smile.

'In that case I shall leave you to unpack and settle in,' he told her, relieved. From the way she was dressed she had clearly been used to better, but the state of the place didn't seem to faze her. 'I have a class to take over at the college shortly but I shall be back this evening to tell you what to do with Tigs should he need you in the night. You can start properly tomorrow . . . and, er . . . You might wish to wear something a little plainer. It would be a shame for you to spoil what you're wearing.'

'I shall,' she told him with a grin.

Once Mr Carter had gone Jeremy looked around and asked, 'What can I do? I've got today off and I don't mind mucking in to help you get the place looking a bit more homely.'

'In that case you could start by getting the fire cleaned out and a fresh one lit,' she said, not wanting to make him feel in the way. 'It's nearly as cold in here as it is outside. And while you do that, I'm going to get cracking on cleaning this place up.'

'There's a log store just out the back,' Jeremy told her as he lifted the bucket at the side of the hearth to go and fill it. 'There's a pump on the sink in the kitchen so you won't have to fetch water in from outside and there's a small range in there as well that you can cook on if you want to. I'll get that lit too. The only thing is, you'll have to fill the tin bath hanging in the yard outside when you want to bathe. There's an outside toilet too. I did warn you it wasn't posh.'

'It will be fine,' she assured him, feeling slightly better by the minute. It would be the first little home of her very own she had ever had and she was determined to make it comfortable.

While Jeremy saw to the range and the fire, Esme changed into a plain grey gown, then filling a bucket with water, she began to clean the place from top to bottom. At some stage during the afternoon Jeremy went out to fetch bread, butter and milk from a nearby shop, which they shared between them at teatime.

'You can have your meals over in the college dining hall,' he told her. 'And the food is not bad at all, or if you prefer, they'll bring it over here to you.'

'I think I'll let them do that if they won't mind,' she said; she didn't fancy having to sit in a dining hall full of young men, feeling like a fish out of water.

Before she knew it the first week had passed. By then, the practice's small foyer was spotless and her tiny home as neat as a new pin, and with the fire blazing away it felt warm and cosy. She had taken the sitting room and the bedroom curtains down and washed them before drying them in front of the fire and whenever Jeremy visited her now, he was surprised to see how comfortable she had made it.

She was also very much enjoying the job, although she didn't see quite as many animals as she would have liked to. The majority of the ones that Mr Carter treated were farm animals that he visited on his rounds; only the smaller domestic pets found their way to the surgery but when they did, she cared for them devotedly no matter what their complaint. And when she wasn't looking after the animals, she was kept surprisingly busy taking notes from people who called in requesting a visit from the vet.

'She's a little gem,' Mr Carter told Jeremy one day. 'Nothing is too much trouble for her. I've even got her writing my bills out for me now. She's a very bright girl and she keeps my instruments spotless.'

Esme was just as happy with him as her new boss was with her. He was a very easy-going man and urged her to take time off when they weren't busy, but she never took advantage of that, although she did like to explore the new area she was living in.

She saw Jeremy almost every day in his free time and they were easy in each other's presence. On Sundays he would take her for a walk to the docks or to a park if the weather permitted. Thankfully the snow had stopped falling in mid-January but as they moved into February it was still bitterly cold so they would often return to her home to toast bread in front of the fire on a long toasting fork and drink cups of hot, sweet tea.

Jeremy teased her that half the chaps at the college were smitten with the vet's new nurse, although he was pleased to see that she showed no interest in any of them.

One Sunday as they were returning from the park Esme got the curious sensation that someone was following them. She tensed and looked behind her and was just in time to see a figure step smartly behind a tree.

Seeing the look of unease on her face, Jeremy asked, 'Is anything wrong?'

Forcing a smile to her face she tucked her arm into his and hurried him along. 'No, nothing, I just thought I heard someone behind us that's all.'

He looked back, but seeing nothing apart from a crowd of children running amok, he shrugged and moved on.

For no reason that she could explain, Esme felt nervous and when Jeremy left to return to the college later that afternoon, she locked all the doors and pulled the curtains. Then after dragging in the tin bath and bathing in front of the fire she went to check on the sheepdog she was caring for. The poor thing had become entangled in barbed wire and had been a mass of cuts when his master had brought him in. Thanks to Mr Carter's skill and Esme's tender nursing, he was now well on the road to recovery and would hopefully be well enough to return home in a few days' time. Just then, she heard the door handle rattle and looking towards it she saw that someone was trying to open it.

'Who's there!' she shouted, sounding a lot braver than she felt, and instantly whoever was there stopped. Esme quickly went back into her little sitting room and after lifting the heavy poker she returned and tentatively opened the door. But when she peeped outside there was nothing but the sound of the rain slapping the ground and the wind soughing through the leafless branches of the trees. Unnerved, she quickly relocked the door. When she turned, she saw Granny Griselda standing there, her old face creased in a frown.

'You *must* get away from here, child,' the old woman warned her as she started to fade.

'But *why*?' But it was too late, the vision was gone and Esme suddenly felt very vulnerable as she thought back to the afternoon when she had felt that someone was following her.

That same evening, the four young women, along with Molly and Mrs Sparrow, visited her again and like Granny they looked afraid.

'Why are you all doing this to me?' Esme asked with a catch in her voice. 'What are you trying to tell me?' But they vanished as quickly as they had come and Esme spent the rest of the evening huddled in her nightgown with a shawl about her shoulders beside the fire.

Over the next few days, the feeling of being followed persisted whenever she left the practice and she became nervous and on edge.

'Are you sure there isn't something troubling you?' Jeremy asked one evening. 'You haven't seemed yourself for a few days now.'

'I'm fine,' she told him, but she could tell he didn't believe her. The constant visits from her granny and the poor young women who had been murdered were beginning to affect her and one evening after another visit from them she knew that she must get out into the fresh air. It was quite late and dark as pitch outside but even so she hoped that a brisk walk would clear her head and tire her. She put on her warm cloak and bonnet and set off through the empty streets towards the docks. Jeremy had told her that it wasn't safe to walk the streets of Hull alone at night and Esme knew that he wouldn't be pleased when he found out, but she was so on edge that she was prepared to risk him being annoyed with her.

She hadn't gone very far when once again she had the sensation that someone was behind her and whipping around, she stared back down the narrow alley. The street lights were throwing pools of yellow light across the cobbles but the areas between them were deep in shadow so there was nothing to be seen. It was damp and drizzly and most folk had stayed at their firesides so the streets were deserted. Until the inns closed, that was, and then they would be filled with drunken sailors trying to stumble their way back to their lodgings.

Esme wasn't overly concerned about that. She intended to be safely back in her little home by then so she hurried on. But the feeling of being followed persisted and she grew more and more nervous. In the next street, she passed some of the inns and through the windows she glimpsed an assortment of seamen swilling ale and laughing. Lowering her head, she scurried past them. And then at last the tall masts of the enormous ships came into view and within minutes she was standing on the docks. These, too, were deserted and she picked her way through thick coils of rope and an assortment of barrels that were waiting to be loaded. At the water's edge, she stared down at the flotsam in the dirty water and listened as it slapped against the hulls of the ships. Even the ladies of the night who usually frequented the place were absent tonight and Esme shuddered. Looking up at the sails she thought of Gabriel.

He would no doubt be on a ship just like this somewhere and the ache to see him again was like a physical pain.

Footsteps behind her made the hairs on the back of her neck stand on end and turning about apprehensively her worst nightmare was realised when she found herself staring into the face of Septimus Silver. He had changed drastically but she knew him immediately. He was now stick thin and his long grey beard was matted and filthy. The clothes he was wearing were little more than rags and he could easily have been taken for a tramp, but there could be no mistaking those evil eyes and his malicious grin.

Esme's heart began to thud painfully as panic rose in her and she began to edge sideways along the quay.

'I knew I'd get you alone if I waited long enough, you little *bitch*!' he ground out, taking a menacing step towards her.

It was then that she saw the glint of a knife in his hand and she knew in that instant that he intended to kill her. 'B-but *why*?' Her voice was choked. 'Why have you always hated me so much?'

'You're your mother's daughter! She was a tramp too, just like your grandmother before her.'

With the knife in his hand and the light of madness shining in his eyes, Esme knew she was done for. There was no one to help her and even if she put up a fight, her strength would be no match for his.

'*Please* don't do this,' she whimpered, tears in her eyes. 'You need help. You're ill.'

He shook his head as he took another step closer and she could smell the ripe scent of him. 'No, it's women who are sick. You use men and you *all* deserve to die.'

He was so close now that there was no way to get past him and she felt helpless. Suddenly, just when all hope was fading, the quay began to glow with a strange light and the four young women appeared, with Molly and Mrs Sparrow standing in between them. But they looked nothing like Esme had ever seen them before. Their poor heads lolled to one side, their tongues hanging slackly from their mouths, and beneath the deep gashes in their throats their clothes were soaked in deep-red blood. Septimus gasped with terror as the women slowly surrounded him and Esme realised that he had seen them too. She quickly ran to one side as the apparitions advanced on him.

'*No, no!* You're not real,' Septimus screamed with terror as he raised a hand to try and protect himself but the spirits didn't stop their advance, and Septimus stumbled ever nearer to the water. They stopped right in front of him, their wavering fingers pointing at him. In a bid to get away from them, Septimus teetered on the very edge of the quay. The knife clattered to the ground as he desperately flapped at the air, trying to regain his balance.

'*Esme!*'

She turned to see Jeremy racing towards her and as soon as he reached her, she collapsed into his arms as they both stared in horror at the scene playing out in front of them.

The women seemed to be involved in some ghastly dance as they drew even closer to her grandfather, blood gushing from their horrific wounds, then suddenly he was gone and they heard a loud splash. Racing to the edge of the quay they were just in time to see him flailing helplessly in the filthy water before it sucked him under and he was lost to sight.

'Don't look,' Jeremy urged as he turned Esme's face into his chest, but she didn't hear. She had fainted clean away.

Chapter Forty-Two

'It's all right, you're quite safe,' Jeremy soothed as Esme came out of her faint sometime later.

She shook her head to clear it and was shocked to find that she was lying on her own bed in her own little home. As the events of the night rushed back she gasped with dismay. 'B-but how did I get home and where is Grandfather? Did you manage to get him out of the water?'

Jeremy solemnly shook his head. 'In answer to your first question, I carried you home. And as for the second question . . .' He shrugged. 'Let's just say that your grandfather has gone somewhere he won't be able to hurt anyone else. There was no way I could have got him out, Esme, he was sucked under the ship by the currents.'

'What should we do now?' she asked tearfully.

Jeremy shrugged. 'We do nothing,' he said quietly, tenderly stroking her hand. 'There was only you and me there to witness what happened and what you have to remember is, he was a murderer. If the police had caught him, he would have been hanged anyway. He got what was coming to him.'

Esme pulled herself up onto the pillows. 'Did you see what happened?'

He gulped, his face chalk white as he nodded. 'I saw something strange, although I couldn't quite make out what it was. When I arrived there appeared to be bright lights floating all around him, driving him to the edge of the quay and he was screaming at them to go away.'

'It was Mrs Sparrow, Molly and the young women he murdered,' Esme told him woodenly.

Jeremy believed her. She had confided to him long ago about the spirits that appeared to her but this was the first time he had ever witnessed anything, and he prayed that he never would again. 'You saw them?'

'Yes, they've been trying to warn me that he was about here somewhere for weeks – that's why they kept appearing. I understand now that it was him that was following me.'

'And what will happen to the poor souls now?'

'Hopefully now that their deaths have been avenged, they will move on and find peace,' Esme whispered.

'Amen to that!' Jeremy was clearly shaken.

'But what will happen to Grandfather's body?'

'Once the ships sail tomorrow, he'll get caught in a current and no doubt his body will wash up somewhere.'

Esme shuddered and wrapped her arms around her damp clothes. 'What a horrible way to die. He was absolutely terrified; you could see it in his face.'

'I dare say the poor women he murdered were terrified as well, and the way they died was horrific too,' Jeremy pointed out.

Esme started to sob and Jeremy wrapped her in his arms, holding her close until the crying subsided a little. 'How did you know where to find me?' she asked.

'When I called in and found you were out, I guessed you'd gone for a walk, despite me asking you *not* to go out alone,' he said, but although his words were stern his eyes were gentle. 'Knowing how you love to watch the ships I had an idea you'd head for the docks. I'm just grateful I got there when I did.'

'So am I,' Esme admitted, feeling safe in his arms.

'But now we've got to both put this behind us and get on with our lives. And at least you won't be living under the threat of your grandfather suddenly turning up like a bad penny anymore.' With that he held her so close to him it was all he could do to stop himself from telling her how very much he loved her, but he knew this wasn't the right time, so instead he gently put her away from him and stroked her hair before standing up. 'I'll leave you now, but remember, as far as anyone else is concerned we didn't witness what happened this evening.'

She nodded and once he had gone, she quickly changed out of her wet clothes and got into bed. A part of her felt nothing but relief to know that her grandfather could never harm her again, but the sad thing was that his death had come far too late for Gabriel. Because of her grandfather's treatment of her brother, he was now a fugitive. Had he not been sent away to a school he hated he would never have been bullied and the incident with Thomas Broadhurst would never have happened. She still had no idea where he was or even if she would ever see him again and she knew that until she did she would never be truly happy.

A week later, Jeremy came to see her one evening with a news-paper tucked under his arm. 'They've found your grandfather's body,' he told her solemnly. 'It washed up on the beach four miles down the coast.'

'And they've identified him?' she asked, not even wanting to read it.

'Not definitely,' he told her. 'Although they said they think it could be him because of the description they had of him. Don't forget, his body had been in the sea for some days so it wouldn't have been easy to identify, but there can't be that many bodies floating about round here, can there? I wouldn't mind betting it was.'

'So what will happen to his body now?'

'Huh! He'll be buried in a corner of a churchyard somewhere in a pauper's grave without even being given a proper funeral,' Jeremy growled. 'And serves him right after what he did to those poor women and what he would undoubtedly have done to you. If your spirit friends hadn't appeared when they did, I have no doubt it would have been *your* body they would be fishing out of the sea right now so don't waste any sympathy on him. He was an evil man and he doesn't deserve any!'

He was right, Esme knew, but it didn't stop her feeling a little guilty.

Suddenly, Jeremy's mood brightened. 'But that's an end to that now. I also have some very good news for you.'

'You do?' She paused from her task of folding the clean towels she had washed from the vet's surgery.

'I certainly do!' Jeremy fished an envelope from his pocket. 'This came today from Gabriel. My mother forwarded it on from our house in London so goodness knows how long it's taken to reach me since it was posted. And can you believe? He's coming to see you!'

'*What!*' Esme sat down heavily on the nearest chair with a plop and a look of wonder on her face. '*When?*'

'That I can't tell you,' he answered with a grin. 'I imagine when he gets to England, he'll head for Theddlethorpe thinking you'll still be at the rectory. Then I suppose he'll head for my parents' house, hoping that I'll know where you've gone. I had no way of letting him know that I didn't live there anymore because he never had a forwarding address.'

'But what if he can't find us?' Esme asked in dismay. It would be just too cruel now if Gabriel had come back and couldn't track them down.

Jeremy chuckled. 'Oh, he'll find us all right,' he promised confidently. 'And he could turn up at any time so just prepare yourself.'

Esme beamed, her earlier despondency completely disappearing now it looked like her dearest wish was about to come true: she would finally see Gabriel again!

On a beautiful spring day, Esme was just putting her new bonnet on when she heard the door of the surgery open and she smiled. It was Sunday and she and Jeremy had arranged to spend the day together. First, they would go for a walk in the park then for a treat they were coming back to her little home where she would cook dinner for him. Their friendship had blossomed to the point where she couldn't imagine her life without him in it now.

'Almost ready,' she shouted cheerfully as she slipped into the room next to hers to check on a litter of kittens she had been hand-rearing – one of the townspeople had brought them in two weeks previously, having found them abandoned in a box.

'I can rear them,' Esme had told the vet. 'And then when they're old enough I'll find new homes for them all.'

Mr Carter had chuckled. 'Do you have any idea how much work you'll be taking on?' he'd asked. 'They'll need feeding every couple of hours, day and night, and they're so young there's no saying they'll survive.'

'*Please*, at least let me try,' Esme had begged. Now after all her tender loving care they had doubled their size and were thriving, and she was more than a little fond of them. But as Mr Carter and Jeremy had soon discovered, she was just as loving with any of the small pets that came into the practice.

The kittens all came to the front of the cage as soon as they saw her and after stroking their little pink noses she told them fondly, 'I shan't be gone for too long and when I come back you can have some nice warm milk. Be good now.'

Smiling broadly, she slipped into the foyer and stopped dead in her tracks, the colour draining from her face. For standing next to Jeremy was Gabriel and next to him was her father. She blinked and scrubbed at her eyes with the back of her hand, sure that she was seeing things. But when she looked again, they were still there and with a strangled cry of joy she launched herself at them.

'*Gabriel, Dadda* . . . I thought I was never going to see you again,' she sobbed as they returned her hugs.

'Oh, my sweet girl.' Django was openly crying too. 'Gabriel told me what your gran'father put you through. I'm so sorry, but I promise I'll make it up to you.'

'We've been trying to track you down for weeks,' Gabriel told her as he led them all to the bench to one side of the room. There was so much they had to tell each other that none of them quite knew where to start.

Eventually it was Django who told her of his arrest and all that had followed. He could hardly believe that this lovely young woman in front of him was the same little girl he had held in his heart all this time, and she was just as shocked at the change she saw in him and Gabriel. Her father looked so much older and Gabriel had grown into a handsome young man.

Jeremy went to put the kettle on to make tea – the family had so much catching up to do and he felt in the way.

'Are you back for good now?' Esme asked hopefully when they had briefly told each other all that had happened to them in the time they had been apart.

The smile slid from Gabriel's face as he cradled the mug of steaming tea Jeremy handed him in his two large hands. 'I'd love to be but I'm afraid it won't be possible. Don't forget I'm still a wanted man because of what happened with Broadhurst. No, Esme, my life will be with Emma in Nova Scotia from now on and I hope Dadda and you will come back with me. At least there we can all be together without me having to look over my shoulder all the time.'

Esme supposed what he said made sense, but she wasn't sure whether she wanted to leave England. She didn't notice the way Jeremy's face fell at Gabriel's suggestion and when he quietly left a few moments later to give them some time alone, she hardly noticed him go.

'Where are you staying?' she asked after a time.

'We found a little room down near the docks in Hull.' It was her father who answered. 'But we won't risk staying for long in case the police catch up with your brother. I'll be damned if I see him thrown into prison fer somethin' that wasn't 'is fault. We've been 'ere fer too long already, if truth be told, tryin' to track you down – not that it wasn't worth it,' he added, giving her an affectionate hug. 'An' Jeremy told me what 'ad 'appened wi' your gran'father. Good riddance to bad rubbish, that's what I say. He made yer mammy's life 'ell an' yours an' all, let alone what 'e did to them poor women.'

For the next two hours they scarcely stopped talking and their joy at being together again was plain to see.

'I just thank God Jeremy was here to keep an eye on you,' Gabriel said when he and his father reluctantly left later that night.

'It's as plain as the nose on yer face why he did, ain't it?' Django chuckled.

'What do you mean?' Esme asked with a frown.

'He loves yer, lass, surely yer knew?'

Esme flushed. 'Of course he doesn't, we're just very good friends,' she insisted.

'If you say so.' Her father nodded and he and Gabriel left, promising to return the following night when the surgery had closed, leaving Esme in a pensive mood.

'Somebody's in a good mood today,' Mr Carter commented the next morning after Esme had finished going through the visits he was to make that day with him.

She gave him a smile, but didn't explain as she hurried away to feed her kittens.

Jeremy popped in at lunchtime and asked, 'Have you decided what you're going to do yet? I mean about going to live abroad with your family.'

'I've been so excited about seeing them again that I haven't given it a lot of thought as yet,' she admitted. 'But I dare say I will go with them. They're all I've got left now, aren't they? And it's not as if there's anything to keep me here.'

Could she have known it, her words sliced through him like a knife but he kept his smile in place. 'I've had good news today as it happens. Well . . . sort of?'

'Oh?' She stared at him, curious to know what it was.

'I had a letter from a solicitor telling me that my Aunt Maude has died.' He grinned. 'That's not the good news, of course, the poor old soul, but the good news is she's left me some money in her will.'

'Really?'

'Hmm, quite a lot of money as it happens. Enough to buy my own house and set up my own veterinary practice when I've finished my training.'

'Why, that's wonderful. You so deserve it,' she told him, genuinely pleased for him. 'You're going to make a wonderful vet!'

'Thank you.' *And you'd make a wonderful vet's wife*, he thought, but that was never going to happen now. 'Anyway, I'd best get back. I won't come over this evening because you'll be busy with Gabriel and your father.'

Esme watched him go with a serious expression on her face, suddenly realising how much she was going to miss him when and if she departed to start a new life.

Chapter Forty-Three

The world seemed to be coming alive after a long, cold winter, just as Esme was after the lonely years apart from her family. But she knew that soon they would have to leave and if she wanted the family to stay together, she would have to go with them.

'There's a boat leaving for Nova Scotia in two weeks' time,' Gabriel informed her one sunny afternoon as they sat in the park admiring the spring flowers, which were bursting into life all around them. 'Dadda and I have already signed on for the trip and the captain has told us that you can come along as a passenger if you want to.'

'I see.' Esme stared towards the lake where children were sailing tiny boats, and ducks were swimming.

'So, what do you think?' Gabriel persisted and after a moment Esme nodded. She had felt so alone without them and knew that she didn't really have much choice.

'I shall come with you,' she answered in a small voice.

Gabriel beamed but her father stared at her anxiously. 'Are yer quite sure that's what yer want, pet?'

She nodded, although different emotions were pulsing through her. There was an element of excitement at the prospect of making a brand-new start in another part of the world but also sadness at what she would be leaving behind. She loved her job at the vet's, loved caring for the animals and was very fond of Mr Carter, who had proved to be a remarkably wise and kind man. She even loved the tiny rooms that she now called home. She would miss Olivia who wouldn't be away at school forever – she still wrote to her regularly and they were as close as ever.

And then there was Jeremy, of course. Ever since Gabriel had been forced to flee from the school, Jeremy had been her rock. He had stood by her through her darkest days and looking back she dreaded to think of how she would have coped without him. But he was young and with his gentle ways and warm heart some girl was sure to snap him up soon. The thought caused a tiny pang of jealousy to pierce her heart but she had no idea why and tried to ignore it. It made sense to go with her brother and father. There were so many bad memories here and if she went with them, they could start to make happy ones again.

'In that case I'll ask the captain to prepare a cabin for you, although it won't be posh,' Gabriel warned. 'And it can be choppy at sea when there's a storm.'

'I'll cope,' Esme assured him, but already her mind was racing ahead. She would have to inform Mr Carter that she would be leaving, and Jeremy. She wondered how he would take the news but tried not to think of it.

After pulling his cap down over his face as far as it would go, Gabriel and her father left to return to the room they were renting. Gabriel never felt comfortable being out during the daytime and they normally restricted their visits to the evenings when it was dark and the surgery was closed.

Later that evening as Esme was feeding the kittens, Jeremy arrived with a bunch of spring flowers for her. She smiled at him as she put the kittens back into a large box she had found that gave them room to play in, then went through to her little living quarters to find something to put the flowers in.

'I'm afraid a specimen jar will have to do for now.' She grinned. 'I haven't got around to treating myself to a vase yet.'

'I thought seeing as it's such a lovely evening we might go for a walk,' Jeremy suggested.

Esme nodded, her stomach doing a little flip. She would have to tell him about her decision to leave, and she wasn't looking forward to it one little bit.

As they strolled along, she finally plucked up the courage to say casually, 'Dadda and Gabriel came to see me earlier.'

He smiled. He was pleased that they'd been reunited because he knew how much Esme had missed them both. 'That's nice. What did they have to say? Have they any plans to sail yet?'

Looking straight ahead she swallowed nervously. 'Yes . . . they have actually. There's a ship sailing for Nova Scotia in two weeks' time and they want to be on it.'

'I suppose it makes sense, although I'll miss them.' As usual he had tucked her hand into his arm. 'And have you decided what you are going to do yet?' Jeremy subconsciously held his breath waiting for her answer.

'I have actually,' she said quietly. 'You see, I've thought about what they said and I've decided to go with them so that we can make a new start and be a family again.'

Jeremy stopped walking so abruptly that Esme almost tripped over as she felt every muscle in his body tense.

'*You!* . . . Go with them? You mean to live there for always?' He'd hoped that she would stay here with him.

She forced herself to look into his face and cringed at the pain she saw in his eyes. 'It makes sense,' she answered in a small voice. 'After all, it's not as if I have any other family left here, is it? I know Gabriel will never come back because of what happened to Broadhurst, and for all this time I didn't even know if my dadda was dead or alive. Now that I've found them both again it's natural that I'd want to be with them, isn't it?'

'Yes . . . I suppose it is,' he said dully. 'But . . . I'm going to miss you.'

'And I shall miss you too,' she said, meaning every word of it. 'But it's not as if we'll never see each other again. I mean, I can come here to visit you from time to time and you could come to see us whenever you could spare the time. We'll always keep in touch.'

They started walking again but had only taken a few steps when Jeremy said unexpectedly, 'I, er . . . I've just thought of some revision I've got to do, so could we head back now?'

'Yes, of course, if that's what you want.' Esme was surprised as they'd walked no distance at all but as Jeremy turned to go back, she followed him meekly.

Back at the vet's surgery, instead of coming in for a last drink with her as he usually did, Jeremy smiled and wished her good-night before striding away.

Esme watched him go, her small white teeth gnawing on her bottom lip. He was clearly upset and that upset her, for he had been the only one she had had to rely on for so long and she felt deeply indebted to him.

Once he had disappeared into the college, Esme let herself into her living quarters and went to push the kettle over the flames for her last drink, but her heart was heavy. Suddenly she got the familiar prickly sensation on the back of her neck and turning quickly she saw the glow of a spirit materialising in the corner. And then she gasped with joy as her mother slowly started to take shape.

'Mammy . . .' It was the first time Esme had seen her since the night of her death and a lump formed in her throat. Her mother was still dressed in the nightgown and shawl she had died in but her hair was lustrous again and all the ravages of pain had gone from her face.

'*Choose very carefully, my love,*' Constance said quietly, and as quickly as she had come, she began to evaporate.

'No, Mammy, *please* don't go,' Esme cried, but already the vision was gone and she felt bereft. What had her mother meant – choose carefully? Was she talking about Esme's decision to go and live abroad? She could have no way of knowing and that night she tossed and turned as she tried to figure it out.

The next morning when Mr Carter arrived ready to begin work, he found Esme with a steaming mug of tea ready for him as always, but he also noticed the dark circles beneath her eyes and asked with concern, 'Are you all right, Esme? You look tired.'

'Oh, I just didn't sleep too well,' she admitted as she added sugar to his tea and handed it to him. Then taking a deep breath she plunged on, 'And I'm afraid I have something to tell you . . .'

'Oh?' He raised his eyebrow.

'The thing is . . .' Esme licked her dry lips. 'I'm afraid that I'm going to have to give you two weeks' notice.'

He looked shocked. 'But why? Have you been unhappy here? Is it the wages? If it is, I'm sure we could manage a small rise.'

'No, no it's nothing like that,' she hastily assured him. 'I've loved every minute of working here and the wages are more than adequate for my needs, but I've decided to go abroad and live with my dadda and my brother. They've been visiting me as you know, and I've made up my mind to go with them when they leave. There's nothing else here for me now apart from my job.'

'Really?' He looked shocked. 'But what about Jeremy? I thought that you and he were . . . you know?'

She shook her head. 'Jeremy and I have never been more than just good friends, although I do admit I shall miss him.'

'Hmm, and I'm sure he'll miss you too,' he said darkly. Placing his mug down, he sighed. 'I can't pretend I won't be upset to see you go. You have the makings of an excellent veterinary nurse and all I can say is if you ever want to come back there will be a job here waiting for you. I shall certainly miss you but I understand that you must do what you think best. And now I'd best get out to see that sick cow at Langston's farm.'

After he'd gone, Esme felt miserable. She couldn't understand why though. It wasn't every day she was offered the chance to start a new life in a different country where she could leave all the bad things that had happened firmly behind her. And then her mother's face appeared again in front of her eyes and her words rang in her ears, *Choose very carefully . . .*

Esme shook her head as if to clear it and went off to feed the kittens, feeling annoyed with herself.

That evening Jeremy failed to visit her, which was unusual and she missed him, although she found quite enough to keep herself busy. She wrote a long letter to Olivia telling her of her intentions to start a new life in a new country and promising to write again when she had a forwarding address, before settling the kittens for the night and sitting down to read a book. But she couldn't concentrate and went to bed early, finally falling asleep from sheer exhaustion.

The following week she managed to find loving homes for all the kittens, who were all healthy and strong now, and she shed a little tear each time one of them left, although she knew it was for the best.

Jeremy still popped in most evenings to see her but she noticed that he seemed strained with her, as if he was being careful what he said to her.

Suddenly there was just one week to go until she sailed for Nova Scotia and while Gabriel could hardly wait, she still had mixed feelings about it.

'You and Emma are going to love each other,' he promised every time he spoke of the girl, which was often, and Esme was sure he was right.

The ship was due to sail on the tide in the second week of April and before she knew it, it was the day before and she was busy packing her things.

'I'll hire a carriage to take you and your luggage to the ship,' Jeremy told her, and she was grateful.

The night before she said her tearful goodbyes to Mr Carter and spent her last night in the tiny home she had been so happy in. She even managed to get a few hours restless sleep but soon Jeremy was there with the carriage and it was time to leave.

They made the journey in silence and as the docks came into sight, they saw Gabriel and Django waiting for them at the bottom of the *Ocean Queen*'s gangplank. The sailors were bustling up and down it like busy little ants, loading barrels and cargo onto it and the place was a hive of activity.

'All set are you, pet?' her father asked anxiously as he looked at her pale face. She certainly didn't look excited or happy to be going and Jeremy looked as if he was about to face a firing squad.

Gabriel, meanwhile, was helping Jeremy manhandle her luggage from the carriage with a broad smile on his face. The ship couldn't set sail quickly enough for him, for the sooner it did the sooner Emma would be in his arms again.

'Y-yes, I'm set,' she answered as her eyes followed Jeremy.

'Then if you're sure I suggest yer say yer goodbyes to that young man an' we'll get you an' yer luggage aboard an' get you settled in yer cabin, eh?'

Esme nodded solemnly and turned to Jeremy as Gabriel began to tug her trunk up the gangplank.

As the seagulls dipped and dived in the sky above them, Jeremy took her hands, his eyes sad. 'So . . . this is it, then?' She stared back at him with tears in her eyes and suddenly he made a decision. 'I know it will make no difference,' he said awkwardly, 'but there's something I have to tell you before you leave . . . You see, I think I fell in love with you the first time I set eyes on you and from that day to this I've known you were the only girl in the world for me!'

Shock registered in her eyes as she gasped. 'B-but why didn't you say something before?'

He shrugged. 'Because I knew the feelings weren't returned. I was all you had when Gabriel left and I didn't want you to feel obliged. Anyway, all I could offer you was a small house somewhere as the wife of a poorly paid veterinary surgeon. I can understand why you're going. It's natural that you should want to be with your family and I want you to be happy. But just remember, if things shouldn't work out, I'll always be here . . . waiting.'

'Oh, Jeremy.' Tears were rolling down her cheeks now. 'Thank you for all you've done for me. I shall never forget you and I shall write to you often . . . Goodbye.'

She turned and staggered up the gangplank, gripping tight to the rope rail, and when at the top she stood against the ship rails looking down at him. He looked so bereft that it tore at her heart. Suddenly she sensed that she wasn't alone and glancing to her side she saw her mother standing beside her.

You've felt lost and alone for so long, pet, she said softly. *But just remember, true love comes only once in a lifetime. It's a very precious thing and not to be thrown away lightly.* And then she was gone and Esme felt as if all the air had been sucked out of her as she finally understood what her mother had been trying to tell her. She had thought she was in love with Luke until he had shown his true colours, but now she realised where her heart truly lay and she knew what she had to do. Turning, she found her dadda right behind her with a sad smile on his face.

'Dadda . . . I'm so sorry, but I just realised I can't—'

He reached out and gently stroked her hair, which was glinting silver in the early morning sun. 'You don't have to explain to me,' he told her. 'Now you just get back to where you belong and be happy, and know that you'll always be here in my heart.' He touched his chest. 'I'll get Gabriel to bring your luggage back down to the quay. And tell that young man I said he's to take good care of you otherwise he'll have me to answer to!' She was in his arms then and after a hug she tore herself away and ran down the gangplank again, tripping over her skirts and swaying dangerously from side to side in her haste. She saw the look of astonishment on Jeremy's face as she made her perilous descent and then laughing and crying happy tears, she threw herself into his arms.

'*What?* But I don't understand, what . . .?'

'Neither did I,' she laughed as she took his face in her hands. 'But now I know I love you too with all my heart and I'm not going anywhere. I can't think of anything I'd rather be than the wife of a hard-working vet. That's if you're prepared to make an honest woman of me?'

His face lit up brighter than the sun as he lifted her up and swung her around as if she weighed no more than a feather. 'It's a deal,' he laughed, but there was no more time for talking as his lips came down on hers.

High above them on the ship, Django stood watching, and although it pained him to leave her behind his heart was light.

He knew his little girl was where she was meant to be. He turned away just in time to see his wife smiling at him. *Be happy, my love,* she whispered, and then she was gone. She could rest and be at peace now but he knew she would never be more than a heartbeat away as they all embarked on a brand-new life.

Acknowledgements

As always, I'd like to say a massive thank you to each and every person in the 'Rosie Team' at Bonnier. There are too many of you to mention but I hope you all know how much I appreciate what each and every one of you does to ensure each one of my books is as good as it can be.

Secondly many thanks to my brilliant agent Sheila Crowley for her unfailing support and my lovely copy editor Gillian Holmes.

Thanks also to my long-suffering family and my hubby for the endless cups of tea he supplies, and last but never least my wonderful readers. You are all very special!

Welcome to the world of Rosie Goodwin!

Keep reading for more from Rosie Goodwin, and to find out more about Rosie Goodwin's next book . . .

We'd also like to welcome you to Memory Lane, a place to discuss the very best saga stories from authors you know and love with other readers, plus get recommendations for new books we think you'll enjoy. Read on and join our club!

Here we are again facing another winter and Christmas! Where does the time go? As always, I have been very busy and am pleased to bring you my latest offering 'The Lost Girl'.

After many requests from some of my readers this one has a ghostly theme and I really hope you'll enjoy it. In this book you will meet Esmeralda, affectionately known as Esme, and her big brother Gabriel who find themselves orphaned and at the mercy of their strict grandfather who until the death of their mother they had never met.

Esme has what her mother and father always termed as 'the gift' which she inherited from her grandmother. She has the ability to see spirits who have passed. As a child Esme wished she didn't have it, especially when after moving into her grandfather's rectory she finds herself confronted with troubled spirits who need her help-but for what reason?

I particularly love the cover of this one, it's so snowy and festive and as usual, I think my graphic designer has excelled!

Anyway, I don't want to give too much of the story away and look forward as always to hearing what you all think of it.

The next one after The Lost Girl will be the start of a brand-new series of six books, more news to follow on that!

And now in between writing as I'm sure most of you are, I'm out and about busy doing my Christmas shopping! It just seems never ending as the family continues to grow, my spare bedroom is already beginning to look like a toy shop! And soon, it will be time to turn the house into a Christmas grotto again. I can hardly believe it-it only seems like yesterday when I was packing everything away!

I hope all of you had a wonderful summer. We spent as much time as we could at our place at the coast with our fur babies, but the summer already seems a distant memory with the change in the weather, doesn't it? The warm coat and the boots are out again and my flip flops put away for next year.

Anyway, it only remains for me to wish you all a wonderful Christmas and a very happy and healthy New Year with your families.

Please keep your messages coming. As any author will tell you, we tend to lead very lonely lives locked away for hours with our imaginary characters, and when we hear from you it makes it all worthwhile.

Also, for those of you who haven't yet done so, do join The Memory Lane book club on Facebook where you'll be able to read all about what myself and the other authors are up to. There are some great competitions and prizes to be had on there as well.

Take care all,

Much Love

Rosie xxx

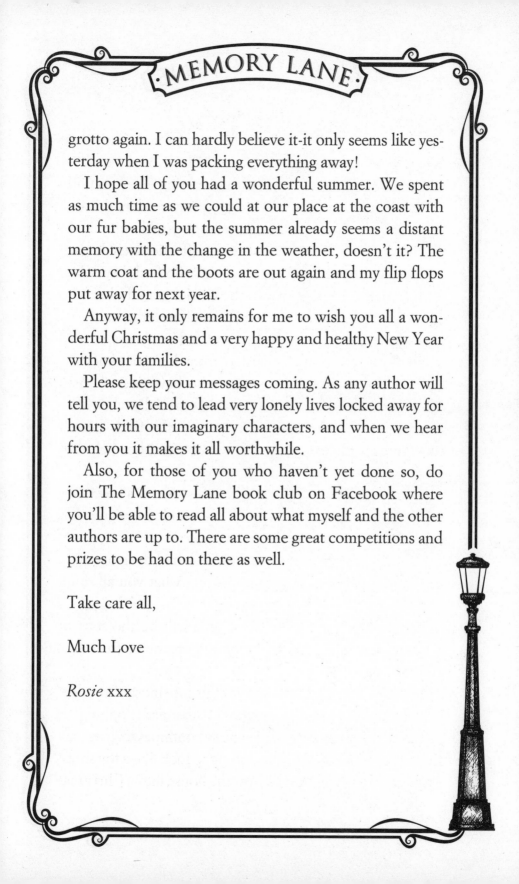

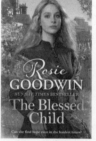

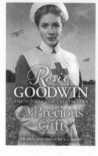

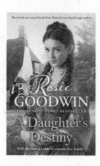

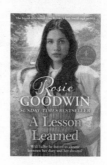
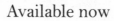

·MEMORY LANE·

Introducing the place for story lovers – a welcoming home for all readers who love heartwarming tales of wartime, family and romance. Join us to discuss your favourite stories with other readers, plus get book recommendations, book giveaways and behind-the-scenes writing moments from your favourite authors.

·MEMORY LANE·